Advance Praise for
The Other Side of Yesterday

"As intriguing as its title, *The Other Side of Yesterday* takes us back in time to solve a mystery of the Civil War that has long puzzled the family of young Carter McGlone. Time-traveling back from 1927, he experiences firsthand the wartime conflicts of his ancestors, falls in love, and is faced with a dire dilemma of his own. For Civil War buffs, this adds another fictional dimension to our never ending fascination with the subject."

—Madge Walls, author of *Paying the Price*

"In 1912 in Harrison County Kentucky, two youngsters hunting mushrooms in a forbidden cemetery find a skeleton with remnants of a blue uniform and a unique medal and chain. Locals believe the man had been a Civil War soldier. *The Other Side of Yesterday* by Kenn Grimes sets up a mystery that promises more intrigue and fascinating history as we follow Carter McGlone and Sara Jane Williams to adulthood."

—Mary Popham, writer, editor, reviewer

"…the authenticity is there, loud and clear."

—Maggie Wise Riley, retired actress

"*The Other Side of Yesterday* is an intriguing story with so many intricate twists and turns, that it is hard to put down. The story of Carter McGlone, his surprising travels and complex relationships, creates a thought-provoking look at life, the time-line of the universe, and the question of who is living among us."

—Allan Sevener, filmmaker and screenwriter

"Take a trip into the past with *The Other Side of Yesterday* by debut novelist Kenn Grimes. A fresh new voice in the world of time/travel fiction, Grimes has proved himself as a master storyteller with this gripping tale of adventure and suspense. *The Other Side of Yesterday*—one part time/travel, one part mystery, and one part romance—will thrill fans of historical fiction and is a must read for Civil War buffs!"

—Kathleen Irene Paterka, author of *Fatty Patty*, *Home Fires*, and *For the Love of a Castle*.

"Ken Grimes has created an unlikely weave of historical novel and science fiction in *The Other Side of Yesterday*. Aficionados of Civil War history as well as those intrigued by the prospect of time travel and exchange of identities will find a satisfying read here."

—Mary O'Dell, poet, president of Green River Writers, Inc.

"This sci-fi Southern Gothic romp, *The Other Side of Yesterday,* the latest book from the author of <u>Camptown</u>, whips through history at the speed of dreams, taking Kentucky boy Carter McGlone from the youthful discovery of a skeleton in 1912 through World War I and to the Civil War and back. You won't want to miss what he discovers among the lovers, enemies, and ancestors he encounters along the way."

—Elaine Palencia. author and poet, four time Push Cart Nominee

"Like the work of Octavia Butler, this novel is an ingeniously crafted tale that almost defies categorization. Compelling characters, a riveting plot, and the authentic rural Kentucky setting combine to make this book so absorbing you'll have trouble putting it down. I highly recommend *The Other Side of Yesterday.*"

—Nancy Gall-Clayton, Playwright

"Kenn Grimes in his latest book, *The Other Side of Yesterday*, has placed his novel in a historically accurate setting. The unexpected twists and turns will keep you turning the pages."

—William Penn author of *Rattling Spurs and Broad-Brimmed Hats: The Civil War in Cynthiana and Harrison County, Kentucky*

THE OTHER SIDE OF
YESTERDAY

A NOVEL

BY

KENN GRIMES

To Cindy.
Hope you enjoy
this trip through
time.

Kenn Grimes

THE OTHER SIDE OF YESTERDAY

The Other Side of Yesterday is a work of fiction. Any resemblance to actual persons, living or dead is purely accidental.

This book is manufactured in the United States of America.

© Copyright 2012 Kenn Grimes
.
Publisher:
Deer Lake Press
PO Box 4593
Louisville, Kentucky 40204
deerlakepress@aol.com

Editions ISBN 978-0-9860020-0-7
Soft cover
First Edition
E-book ISBN 978-0-98600020-1-4

Library of Congress Number 2012954308

Grimes, Kenn
        The Other Side of Yesterday

Interior Layout
Peggy DeKay, peggy@tbowt.com
http://tbowt.com

Contact the author at kenngrimesauthor@aol.com

Orders: deerlakepress@aol.com

Dedication

This book is dedicated to my wonderful wife, Judy, who never doubted that I would finish it, and who gave me the time, space, and encouragement to do so.

Acknowledgments

In the ten years since I began writing this book, I have written (and had published) a collection of short stories (*Camptown . . . one hundred and fifty years of stories from Camptown, Kentucky*); one other novel (unpublished), which I then adapted as a feature-length screenplay; and two other feature-length screenplays. I also adapted this book as a TV mini-series. But I always knew I would one day return to *The Other Side of Yesterday* to see it published.

To do so would not have been possible, however, without the help and inspiration of a number of individuals over that period of time. And so, I wish to express my heartfelt thanks to the following people: my earliest critic, Madge Walls, who was absolutely brutal in her critique of my early drafts, challenging me to write better than I thought I was; my writing instructors over the years, John Pahl, and Elaine Palencia at several Novels In Progress conferences in Louisville, Kentucky; William Penn, whose book, *Rattling Spurs and Broad-Brimmed Hats: The Civil War in Cynthiana and Harrison County, Kentucky* provided a treasure trove of information about the battle that took place there in 1864, and whose help with other details regarding the area around Cynthiana was invaluable; Susan Lindsey, who edited my manuscript and, in the process, helped make me a better writer; Peggy DeKay, my book coach, who helped shepherd this story to its final publication; and Didi Brown, who served as my proof-reader.

I would be remiss if I did not also remember my grandmother, Ethel Weaver McGlone Grimes, a native Kentuckian who crossed the river into Ohio to marry my grandfather, bringing with her her Kentucky roots. And my kin, the McGlones, Cartees, Carters, Kitchens, Hendersons, and Burtons, who have called Kentucky home for the last two centuries, ever since my great-great-great-great-grandfather, Owen McGlone, brought his family from Virginia around 1800 to settle in what later became known as McGlone Creek in Carter County, Kentucky.

And, finally, to everyone who proudly claims Kentucky as their home.

∞

The past is history.
The future is mystery.
This moment is the gift.
That's why it's called the present.

But if one could travel from the present to the future,
would that period of time leaped then become a mystery?

And if one could travel from the present to the past,
then does the past become both the present and the future,
and all of it become a mystery?

Perhaps only time will tell.
Perhaps.

Attributed to several people, but most often to Nigerian
master drummer, Babatunde Olatunji.

Harrison County, Kentucky

1864

The man sat astride the horse, hands tied behind his back. He moved his head, trying in vain to alleviate the discomfort caused by the coarse noose around his neck.

Two other men, also on horseback, slowly circled him, studying him.

The man avoided their eyes, his concentration focused on the initials and the date carved into the tree next to where his horse stood: S.J. + H.J., 1863

A movement in the brush caught the man's attention. He looked and saw a young boy, standing silently, staring at him. Then, suddenly, the boy was gone.

The man turned back to the tree. One of the two men brought his whip down across the horse's rear end.

Thwack!

Chapter One
The Skeleton
1912
Harrison County, Kentucky

Eeeeee................

Sara Jane's scream shattered the air. My whole face, including my eyes, scrunched up, and I threw my hands over my ears in a futile attempt to shut out the screech. It was as bad as the sound Billy Winchester made when he scraped a piece of chalk across the blackboard in Miss Everly's classroom. I dropped the gunny sack filled with the mushrooms I'd been picking.

"Sara Jane, for God's sake, stop that screa . . ."

I never got the rest of the word out, because as I rounded the old sycamore tree I bumped into Sara Jane and knocked her to the ground.

Unfortunately, the screaming only increased in intensity. She quickly jumped up, knocking me backwards against the tree. I grabbed her and clamped my hand over her mouth in an attempt to quiet her. It helped some, but not much.

"What are you . . . ?"

Then I saw what had set her off. Stretched out at our feet, almost hidden by leaves and dirt, was a skeleton. A human skeleton.

Sara Jane was shaking almost as badly as I was. "Be quiet," I said, "and I'll take my hand away."

Sobbing, she nodded, and I removed my hand.

Her pale face was as ashen as the skeleton. She was still trembling, but had calmed down some.

"Who do you suppose it is?" she asked in a whisper.

"How should I know?" *Ten-year-old girls can be pretty stupid sometimes,* I thought. "I know this, though. We're going to be in a heap of trouble when we tell our daddies about this."

Her eyes grew large, huge tears welling up. "Wh . . . why do we have to tell?"

"Why do we have to tell? We have to tell because this here's a dead body—or at least what's left of it—and we found it. We cain't pretend like it never happened. And the reason we're going to get in trouble is because we ain't even s'pose to be here. You know our daddies told us to not *ever* come here to the darkies' cemetery."

"But . . . but there ain't even any grave markers over here in this part. Only this big old sycamore tree."

"Don't make no never mind. You see that stone wall?" I asked, gesturing to the wall some ten yards behind us. "That's for this cemetery. And we're in the cemetery, no two ways about it."

Neither of us said anything for a long time, as the enormity of our offense sank in. The air was still, as still as the skeleton lying there at the base of the old sycamore, the only sound the call of a whippoorwill from the nearby woods, gearing up for his nightly hunt for supper.

Sara Jane placed one of her long braids between her teeth, and began to slowly chew, a nervous habit that I found downright disgusting. I couldn't imagine anyone wanting to put hair in their mouth, not even their own hair.

Usually, I'd tell her to stop. This time I didn't say anything. After a while my curiosity overcame my uneasiness, and I began to examine the skeleton more closely. When I glanced up at Sara Jane, her eyes were glued to the grinning skull staring up at us. Then, abruptly, she turned away.

"Wow!" she cried. "Carter! Look at this!"

"What?" I said, not bothering to turn around. I was too busy brushing leaves and dirt off the skeleton to pay her any mind.

"There's something carved in this old tree: 'S.J. + H.J. 1863.' How long ago is that, Carter?"

"Eighteen sixty-three? Forty-nine years," I said, quickly doing the calculation in my head. I turned to look, then stood up to better see the carving. I ran my forefinger around the letters, tracing the initials.

"You know, if whoever done this carving was about our age, they could still be alive. Forty-nine plus thirteen would be . . . sixty-two. They'd probably only be somewhere in their sixties. Who do we know with the initials S.J. or H.J. who's old?"

"I don't know," replied Sara Jane, turning back to the skeleton. Her interest in the carving had vanished as quickly as it had come. "Look, what's that around its neck?"

I turned back to the skeleton. There *was* something there. Funny, I hadn't noticed it before. Whatever it was, it was partially hidden under what remained of the collar of the jacket the skeleton wore. I knelt down and bent my head closer to the skull to see if I could make out what it was. As I did, I noticed some letters on the jacket collar. But the object around the skeleton's neck grabbed my more immediate attention.

"It's some sort of medal, or something," I said.

I carefully unlatched the hook that held the chain together and lifted the medal from around the neck bones.

"Ugh," exclaimed Sara Jane. "Did you touch it?"

"Touch what?"

"The *bones*. Did you touch the *bones*?"

"No, I didn't touch no *bones*," I said, exasperated. I brushed some dirt from the medal, and held it up. It was about the size of a silver dollar, but heavier. I could see through it, like it was glass, except it wasn't. But I couldn't tell what it was made of, although I was pretty sure it wasn't metal. The rim was gold colored. The chain was gold colored, too, but I couldn't tell if any of it was actually gold or not. In the middle was something else that looked gold.

"What's it say?" asked Sara Jane.

"Don't say nothing. Got a big circle in the middle. Looks more like a chicken egg." I gave the medal a quarter turn, so that the loop and chain were on one side. "This way it looks like a tear drop. Whatever it is, looks like it's on the inside, not out on the outside." I turned the medal over. I saw the gold circle—or whatever it was—from that side, too. A spiral groove ran from the outer edge to the center.

"Looks like it must screw on to something. You know, like that little round picture case your ma's got."

"The little union case."

"Yeah, that's the one."

"You gonna keep it?"

"I reckon so. It sure ain't going to do him no good no more."

I resumed examining the skeleton, this time paying more attention to the letters on the jacket collar.

"You know what!" I exclaimed. "This here's a uniform! He must've been a soldier. He must've been in the war!"

"How can you tell?"

"See here, on the collar? It's got the letters 'USA.' And the other collar—well, I cain't quite make out what it says. Looks like it's torn, maybe. But I think it says '*something . . . C H . . . something*'?

Heck, I cain't tell what the rest of it is. Look here, though, see this? The jacket's kind of blue, too. At least, I think so. That'd mean it's Union. And the 'USA'—that'd be Union, too. If he died in the war why, he must've been laying here for nigh on to fifty years!"

"How come no one ever found him before?"

"'Cause for one thing, it looks like whoever put him here must've covered him over with dirt. But I reckon lots of it's washed away with all the rain we've got lately. And, for another thing, most people don't come around here, like we wasn't *s'pose* to. Speaking of which, we better get on home." I looked sternly at Sara Jane. "Now, don't you say nothing to your daddy 'bout this. I'll tell mine in the morning."

"Don't worry," she answered, shaking her head from side to side. "I sure ain't going to say *nothing* to my daddy about this!"

Sleep didn't come easily that night. I lay in bed, thinking about the skeleton, all the while fingering the medal. Finally, I fell into a restless sleep, tossing and turning. I dreamt of a man, dressed in a uniform, sitting on a big horse, the biggest horse I'd ever seen. The man's hands were tied behind his back, and a noose was cinched around his neck. He didn't say a word, his eyes fixed on the tree by his side. For a brief moment, he turned and looked straight at me. I thought maybe he recognized me. Then he looked back at the tree.

Suddenly, someone slapped the horse's rear end and it took off, leaving the man dangling in the air, feet quivering, eyes still fixed on the tree. He hung there for the longest time. Then—all at once—he disappeared into thin air.

I sure was relieved when morning came.

Chapter Two

The Skeleton Identified

1912

"You found *what*?"

My father was a man of few words. But when he did speak, everyone listened—especially me.

"What do you mean you found a skeleton? And *where*, may I ask, did you find this skeleton? And *when*? Certainly not this morning, since you hain't even been out of the house yet."

I flinched at the force of my father's anger. This wasn't going to be easy.

"You see, Pa," I said, trying my best to keep my voice steady, "Sara Jane and I were hunting mushrooms yesterday, and we happened to end up by the old sycamore tree out there by the corner of the darkies' cemetery, and—"

"You happened to end up *where*?" My father's face was now just inches from my own; I smelled the coffee he'd had for breakfast.

I started to shake. "Pa, I . . . I know we warn't s'pose to be there, but we was following this row of mushrooms, and when we got to the wall and looked over—gosh, you never saw so many mushrooms in your life! It was like—"

"I don't care about no *mushrooms*!" my father exploded. "You were in the *darkies'* cemetery?"

"Yes, sir." My response wasn't much more than a whisper, so soft I wasn't sure if Pa even heard me.

"And how many times have I told you never, ever to go in there?"

"Lots," I answered, bowing my head.

"That's right—lots. Ain't no reason for no thirteen-year-old boy to be anywhere near that cemetery. Believe me, once we get the matter of this skeleton settled, we're going to talk about your punishment."

"Yes, sir."

"Now," said Pa, "do you know if Sara Jane said anything to her daddy about this?"

"I told her not to. I told her I'd tell you, and I figured you'd tell him."

"You're plumb right 'bout that," said Pa. "Get your coat on. We're going over to the Williamses' house right now."

The Williamses' farm lay less than a mile from ours. In twenty minutes we were there.

Unlike my family's home, just a plain old farmhouse, the Williamses lived in what at one time was a mansion, a real plantation house.

Only a few buildings remained from the many I knew used to be there. Often, as Sara Jane and I played in the yard, I'd ask what had been here or what had been there. For the most part she had no idea.

A pair of two-story columns framed both the first floor porch and the second floor porch, all of which spanned the middle third of the front of the house. The third floor, designed in the shape of an octagon, contained windows all the way around. For as long as I remember, the windows had all been boarded up.

The stair hall, some thirty-five feet wide, rose two stories high, with two staircases, one on either side of the room, spiraling their way up to the second floor. I was befuddled by those staircases, as they didn't seem to have anything holding them up. Mr. Williams told me once they were what was called "self-supporting." I called it magic. A third staircase provided access from the second floor to the third floor which was boarded up and not used. Ma said there used to be a ballroom up there that took up the whole floor.

The first floor consisted of four large rooms, two on each side of the stair hall. Sara Jane's bedroom was one of four rooms on the second floor.

As Pa and I walked up the lane toward the house, I glanced up at Sara Jane's window, and saw her peeking out from behind a curtain. I knew she was crying over what was about to take place. It didn't take much to start her crying.

Mrs. Williams greeted us at the door. I'd always thought Athena Williams one of the prettiest women I'd ever seen. Unlike Sara Jane, who got her red hair from her father, Mrs. Williams's hair was coal black, and she always wore it rolled into a double bun on the back of her head. I thought she had nice breasts, too, even though I knew I wasn't supposed to think about those kinds of things.

"Madison. Carter. It's mighty early for you two to be out and about. Come on in. The coffee's hot, and I've got biscuits in the oven."

"Thank you, ma'am," said Pa, removing his hat.

"Thank you, ma'am," I echoed.

"Horace," Mrs. Williams called out to her husband, "Madison McGlone and Carter are here."

I loved Sara Jane's home, especially the big kitchen, which Mr. Williams had converted from what used to be the master bedroom. Originally, the kitchen was in a separate

building, but Mrs. Williams found that to be just too
unhandy. She always seemed to have a fresh supply of
homemade cookies and cold milk on hand. On cold winter
days, a fire blazed in the big stone fireplace Mr. Williams
had built at the same time he put in the kitchen. It made the
room a refuge from the chill of outdoors. Mrs. Williams
would serve Sara Jane and me warm apple pie and heated
cider.

Today, apprehensive over what was about to happen, I
didn't find the room comforting at all.

"Morning, Madison, Carter," said Mr. Williams. "What
brings you two out so early?"

"Good morning, Horace," said Pa. "My boy here's got
something to tell you. You might want to have Sara Jane
come down for this."

Mr. Williams looked perplexed.

"Okay. Let's sit here at the kitchen table. We can have
some breakfast whilst we hear what the boy's got to say.
Sara Jane! Come on down here!"

For the next half hour, Sara Jane and I recounted our
discovery from the evening before. When we finished, we
both looked apprehensively at Sara Jane's daddy to see how
angry he was going to be.

To our surprise, he let out a whoop and a holler, and
rocked so far back on his chair he almost fell over.

"I can see you two now," he said, laughing so hard he
could barely get the words out. "I bet you were both as
white as that old skeleton itself. And scared out of your
wits."

"Yes, sir," Sara Jane and I both replied at the same
time. I was sure relieved at how well he seemed to take all
this. I glanced at my daddy, and saw Sara Jane look at her
mother.

Grins spread across both their faces, as they, too, seemed to appreciate the humor in the scene we just described.

"Okay, come on," said Mr. Williams, still laughing. "Let's go take a look at this here skeleton."

∞

"By the way," said Pa as we made our way to the cemetery, "what happened to all those mushrooms you said you two found yesterday?"

"You know what, Pa?" I replied, realizing for the first time that neither Sara Jane nor I had thought to bring our sacks home with us. "They must still be there. I plumb forgot all about them with everything else going on."

"We'll remember to get them before we leave," said Pa.

As we approached the stone wall, Sara Jane stopped suddenly. "I don't think I want to go in," she said, softly. That darned braid was in her mouth again.

"Oh, I think you will," said Mr. Williams. "You were more than ready yesterday to go where you shouldn't have been. Today you're coming in with us." He took her hand in his and dragged her up and over the wall.

"There," I said, pointing at the base of the tree. "There it is."

The four of us walked over to the sycamore and stood in a semicircle around the skeleton.

"Sure enough is a skeleton," said Pa. "And from the looks of it, it's been here a spell."

I nodded. "Like I said—I think he's wearing a uniform. I reckon he could've been here since the war."

Pa knelt down next to the skeleton to take a closer look, while Mr. Williams bent to look over his shoulder.

"I think you might be right, son," said Pa. "Sure looks like a uniform to me, or at least what's left of one. Union, I'd guess. And look at these letters here on the collar: 'USA' on this one and—what does the other one say? 'CH'? What do you think, Horace?"

"I reckon you're right," replied Mr. Williams. "I cain't read, but I do recognize them letters. We got a pitcher at home of Athena's daddy in his uniform, and his jacket looks like this one, only, as I recollect, there's more letters on the left collar. But I don't know what they are. This here feller must've been in the same company or regiment."

"But this wouldn't be her daddy?"

"No, I knowed he got killed in a house fire."

"Okay, then," said Pa, straightening up. "First thing we got to do is to get the sheriff out here to take a look at this. Now, Carter, is everything just the way you found it?"

"Yes, sir, except I brushed some dirt and leaves off to get a better look. Oh, and I found this on him, so I took it off." I had a bad feeling in my stomach about having removed the medal. "I guess maybe I shouldn't have."

I took the medal from around my neck and held it out to my pa.

His eyes lit up. "Let me see that!" he exclaimed, as he grabbed it from my hand. His mouth dropped open as he stared at the medal, dangling from its chain. "Lord Almighty! I think I might know who this here feller is! Or was."

"You do?" said Mr. Williams.

"Who?" Sara Jane and I asked, almost in unison.

Pa was getting more excited by the minute. "I do believe this skeleton is my granddaddy, Owen McGlone. Him and my daddy and my Uncle Rufus, they was all with the Fortieth Kentucky. I know my granddaddy was at the second battle at Cynthiana. We didn't think he got killed in the fighting, but anyways, he disappeared right around then. That would have been in . . . '63, I think. Or was it '64?" he asked, turning to Mr. Williams.

"Sixty-four, I believe," said Mr. Williams.

"What makes you think this is him?" I asked. "This skeleton could be any old soldier."

"This," said Pa, holding the medal up for us all to see. "According to my daddy, my granddaddy wore two medals, both of them just like this one, ever since anybody ever knew him. Cousin Rupert's even got a picture of him with them on."

He turned to me. "Where's the other one?"

"The other what?" I asked.

"The other medal. Like I said, Grandpa McGlone always wore two medals, both exactly the same."

"Swear to God!" I exclaimed, forgetting for a moment my mother's admonishments about taking the Lord's name in vain. "There weren't but one medal! Was there Sara Jane?"

Sara Jane shook her head. "No, that's all there was, Mr. McGlone, honest, just the one."

"That's strange," said Pa, his eyes furrowing. "Anyway, I'm sure this one was his, and I'm betting this must be old Owen laying here now. Horace, why don't I stay here with the children, and you ride on into town and fetch Sheriff Furnish?"

While we waited for Mr. Williams to return with the sheriff, I asked my pa if he knew who the initials belonged to.

He thought for a minute, then said, "Only folks I know with those initials are Herman Johansen and Samantha Jackson. Oh, and Suzie Jaworski. But none of them are old enough to have been around in 1863. I reckon whoever carved those initials is long since dead."

About an hour later, Mr. Williams returned with Sheriff Furnish and another man whom I didn't recognize.

"Madison," said the sheriff, as he climbed down off his horse. "You know Doc Swinford, the county coroner? I asked Charlie to come along. I thought he might be of some assistance.

"So," the sheriff continued, as he knelt down to examine the remains, "why do you think this might be your granddad? I mean, it's a skeleton, pretty much like others I've seen over the years, dressed in what appears to be what's left of a Federal uniform. We find skeletons like this around here every once in a while, soldiers who got killed out here in the woods and were never found until years later, when someone happens on them."

"Because of this," replied Pa, holding up the medal. "See this? It's my granddaddy's. He always wore it around his neck. Wore two of them, just alike, except we found just this one. Carter here found it. That's what makes me think it's him. I've never seen another medal like this in my life."

"Any rumors your granddad might have been a horse thief?" asked the sheriff without looking up.

Pa's body stiffened and a hard look came into his eyes. "*What*? Why would you think that? What makes you think he was a horse thief?"

"How closely did you examine this skeleton?"

"Why, I looked pretty close, but I sure didn't do no autopsy. What're you getting at, anyhow?"

I knew by Pa's clenched fists he was getting even more irritated by the sheriff's questions.

"You see this?" said Sheriff Furnish. He placed his hand next to the skeleton's neck bone. "And this? And this? Those're pieces of a rope, what's left of it. And," he continued, placing his fingers on the neck bone, "I can tell from the way this bone is twisted, this fella died of a broken neck. My guess is he was hanged. Now it might *not* be because he was a horse thief, but . . . it also *might* be."

Dr. Swinford had also been examining the skeleton. "Madison, how old was your grandfather when he disappeared?"

"Why, late fifties, I believe. Why?"

"Then I don't think you have to worry about whether he was a horse thief or not, because I'm pretty sure this isn't him. My guess is this here fellow was probably in his twenties, maybe early thirties, when he died. Couldn't have been your grandfather."

"You sure?" asked Pa.

Dr. Swinford shrugged. "No, I'm not positive. Just an educated guess. We'd know more if we sent the remains to the university over in Louisville and let someone there examine them. Friend of mine works there. He's what they call a physical anthropologist, and he does this sort of thing."

"Let's do it, then," said Pa, cooling down a little.

"Now, Madison," said Sheriff Furnish, "I imagine there'd be some kind of expense involved with all this. I don't know if the county should—or even could—pay for it."

"That's okay," replied Pa. "I'll pay whatever it costs. I want to know for sure whether or not this is my granddaddy."

"All right, then," said the sheriff. "Charlie and I will take care of this from here on in, so the rest of you might as well go on home. I'll let you know what we find out."

"How long before we know?" asked Pa.

"I'd think by the end of the week," said Dr. Swinford.

"What's going to happen to him?" asked Sara Jane. "To the skeleton?"

"If Charlie here is right, and this ain't Madison's granddad, the county will take care of burying him," the sheriff answered.

"Where?" persisted Sara Jane. "Where will they bury him?"

"Indigents and unknowns are buried here in the darkies' graveyard, in the corner of the field over there," said the sheriff, pointing. "I imagine that's where we'll put him."

"Couldn't you bury him here where we found him?" I said. "Seems to me he rested here pretty peaceful-like for fifty years; he ought to just stay here forever."

Sheriff Furnish hesitated for a moment, and scratched his head. "I reckon maybe that would be all right," he said, finally. "But first thing is to make sure he's not your great-granddad."

"What about the medal?" It was a subject I'd been reluctant to bring up until now.

"As far as I'm concerned," replied the sheriff, "it's yours to keep. We sure don't need it for evidence, and there's no kin to claim it. Besides, your pa seems pretty sure it belonged to your great-granddad, so I guess it's up to him."

I looked at my father.

"There ain't no doubt in my mind this medal belonged to my granddaddy, no matter who this poor beggar was," said Pa. "So, yes, Carter, you found the medal, you can keep it. I reckon it'll be our 'family heirloom.'"

I started to grin, but it quickly disappeared as Pa continued. "Now, there's the matter of your punishment for being here in the cemetery in the first place. So, no more mushroom hunting for you this spring. And stay out of this cemetery!"

"And the same goes for you," said Mr. Williams, turning to Sara Jane.

For a brief moment, I thought about protesting what—in my opinion, at least—seemed to be an extremely harsh and unreasonable punishment. But then I realized both Sara Jane and I had gotten off pretty easy, considering. Besides, I got to keep the medal!

I slipped it around my neck. I silently vowed never to take it off again.

Although the telephone had been around for thirty-five years, there were very few of them in Harrison County, Kentucky in 1912. Doc Swinford had one, as did Mr. Clary at the general store. Telephones could also be found in the Mayor's office, the office of the *Democrat,* the local newspaper, and at the sheriff's office.

Only a few regular people had telephones, mostly those who were rich enough to afford one. Except us.

We weren't rich, but we had a telephone.

My mother had insisted on getting one last year, right after Pa had his second seizure. She said she wanted to have it to call Dr. Swinford in case Pa had another seizure. Strangely enough, Pa never had another seizure after that.

In fact, we had never used our telephone. We had never called anyone and no one had ever called us.

That's why it was such a jolt when it rang.

"What's that?" I asked.

"Why, I believe it's our telephone," replied my mother, jumping up and running to it.

She picked up the earpiece.

"Hello? Madison," my ma called out to Pa, "it's Sheriff Furnish."

Pa hurried into the kitchen and my mother handed him the earpiece.

"Louis? Did you hear back from the university?"

From the look on my pa's face it was obvious the answer wasn't the one he wanted.

"I see. Thanks, Louis. I'll let the rest of them know."

"What'd he say, Pa?"

"Looks like Charlie was right. That fellow was no more than thirty-five when he died, maybe even younger. Couldn't have been my granddad. Charlie says as soon as they get the remains back from the university, they're going to give him a proper burial out there by that tree, like you suggested."

"I'm sorry, Pa," I said.

So, I wondered, *if that wasn't my great-grandpa we found—who was it?*

Chapter Three

Time to Leave Home

1917

"I don't want you to go."

Sara Jane and I sat on the grass under the big oak tree in front of my house. Inside, the party was still going strong, a celebration of my graduation that day from high school. On a more somber note, it was also my going-away party.

Two months earlier, on March 12, a German submarine had sunk the merchant ship *Algonquin*, followed less than a week later by three more American vessels. On April 6, Congress declared war on Germany. We were about to be plunged into what would be known later as the "Great War."

Over my mother's objections, I had enlisted in the army, and was scheduled to be sent to Louisville at the end of the week to be processed.

I'd endured all the congratulatory back slaps I could, as well as slobbery kisses from Elsie and Gladys, my first cousins once removed on my father's side, not to mention their brother Rupert's wife, Molly, who kept hugging me, and telling me how proud I had made the whole family.

"Rachel," she'd said, "aren't we all so proud of him?"

"We certainly are," my mother replied. If the truth be known, though, she would as soon I'd not be going.

"Help me get out of here," I'd whispered to Sara Jane. "I can't take any more of this!"

Sara Jane grabbed my hand, then, looking around to make sure no one saw us, whisked me out the front door, making a successful escape to the front yard, where we now sat cross-legged facing each other. As usual, as soon as we hit the porch, Sara Jane shucked the shoes her mother insisted she wear to my party.

"I don't want you to go," Sara Jane said again.

"I'm not crazy about it myself," I said. "But it's something I have to do."

"I know," said Sara Jane, a note of resignation in her voice. "But I still don't want you to go."

"It's only for two years, maybe less. And then I'll be back, and it'll be like I never left."

"Ain'tcha scared? Boy, I would be."

I straightened my legs and leaned back. I thought for a moment before answering. "I guess I am, a little bit. But I know I'll be okay."

"Whatcha gonna do then when you get back? You gonna get a job in town, or help your daddy out here on the farm?"

I smiled. "Neither."

"Neither? What *are* you gonna do then?"

"Go to college."

Sara Jane's mouth fell open. "You are not!"

"I am," I said. "I've already been accepted at Berea. Got my letter yesterday. I called them and told them about my going in the army, and they said fine, I can still enroll when I get back."

"I'll be switched!" exclaimed Sara Jane. "Carter McGlone—a college boy! I always figured you'd come back here and settle down and marry Lucy Gregg." She grinned impishly. "You know, that girl in school you got such a crush on."

I felt the redness come to my cheeks. "I do not have a crush on her. Besides, she doesn't even know I'm alive."

"Uh-huh," said Sara Jane, still grinning. "So, whatcha gonna study there at college?"

"I'm going to become a teacher, so I can come back here and teach you how to talk right."

Sara Jane frowned. "Talk right? Ain't nothin' wrong with my talkin'! I talk just like my daddy."

"I know," I said. "But you *should* try talking like your momma. She talks real good."

Sara Jane lowered her head. I knew at once I had embarrassed her. I sat up and took her hand.

"I'm sorry. I was just funning with you. I think you talk fine."

She lifted her head and looked at me. "No, you don't. And you're right. I don't talk good like my momma. It's my daddy. He thinks it's highfalutin' to talk the way Momma does. You know, his family comes from down in the hills, and they all talk like him, Grandma and Grandpa, and all of them. I guess . . . I guess I felt like I should talk like that, too, so he don't feel embarrassed."

"I know," I said. "And I think it's okay that you speak the way you do."

"You do? Aw, no, you don't, you're just sayin' that."

"No, really. Because it's you. It's who you are. And I like who you are."

"Well, okay, then," said Sara Jane, brightening.

"How about you?" I asked. "You going to college after you graduate from high school?"

Sara Jane looked at me as though I had asked her if she were going to the moon.

"Now you are kiddin'. First of all, I'll be lucky to *finish* high school. And second . . ." she hesitated, ". . . well, my daddy don't believe a woman needs no education, so he wouldn't pay for me to go even if he had the money—which he don't. Or even if I wanted to go—*which I don't*."

"What'll you do then?"

"Why, I'm gonna do what every other self-respectin' girl in these parts does—I'm gonna find myself a rich, good-lookin' man to marry me, have three or four kids, and let my husband support me."

We both laughed so hard tears streamed down our faces.

When I regained my composure, I said, "I sure do appreciate your momma and daddy coming to my party."

"Heck, my daddy's always ready for a party," said Sara Jane, who by now had rolled over onto her stomach, and was sucking on a piece of grass she had picked. She'd graduated from chewing on her braids.

"I sure like your momma."

"Thanks, I kinda like her, too."

"I mean, she's real nice. And she's pretty, too."

Sara Jane turned her head and gave me a quizzical look.

"Well, she is," I said, feeling a little embarrassed. I decided to change the subject. "How old's your momma, anyway?"

"My momma? I reckon she must be . . . fifty? I know she was born in 1865. How old does that make her?"

"Fifty-two."

"That's about what I figured."

"And you're fifteen."

"Almost sixteen," she said, a big grin on her face.

I thought for a moment. "So, your momma was thirty-seven when you were born. That's kind of old to be having a baby, isn't it?"

"I don't think so," Sara Jane replied. "My cousin Jimmy's momma, my Aunt Mabel, she was in her fifties when he got born. And I weren't my momma's first baby, either. She had another baby way before me: my brother, Hank."

I looked at her, surprised. Then I remembered. "You're right; you told me about him once when we were kids. I'd forgotten."

"He died in . . . '97, I reckon, I guess a couple of years before either you or me showed up."

"How old was he?"

"Maybe ten, maybe eleven. I ain't real sure. Died of the fever. He was named after my great-granddaddy on Momma's side. I think his name was—"

My mother's voice rang out from the house. "Carter! Sara Jane! Come on inside. We're ready to cut the cake."

"Come on," said Sara Jane, jumping up from the grass, and smoothing out her dress. "I do *love* your momma's spice cake!"

Chapter Four

The War in Europe

1917

June 8, 1917

Dear Mom and Dad

Here I am in New York City! Actually, it's a part of New York City called Hoboken. I arrived this morning, and it looks like we'll be shipping out tomorrow for France (although nobody's supposed to know where we're going). I hear we'll be the first American troops to hit Europe.

It doesn't seem like only three weeks ago I left home. After a couple of days in Louisville getting processed and all, they shipped me off for two weeks of quick training. Then I took the train to New York. I got here yesterday and today joined up with the 1st Division. I'm in company F, 16th infantry. I met the commander, a Major General Sibert. He seems nice enough.

I haven't had a whole lot of time to see New York, but from what I have seen, I can tell you it's mighty big! And the people sure talk funny. Of course, I suppose they think I talk funny, too.

They say it will take us about three weeks to cross the ocean. I don't know whether I'm looking forward to the trip or not. I've never been on a big ship before. Hope I don't get seasick!
Say hi to Sara Jane for me. I'll write again after we land in France.

Your loving son,
Carter

"McGlone! Juh hear the news?"

I looked up from my mess kit to see Dickie Winters, a soldier I'd become friends with on the crossing. With almost 4,000 troops on board and only half as many berths, we'd slept in shifts. Dickie and I had shared the same bunk.

From Chicago, and as raw a recruit as me, Dickie was a likable guy, although I had the feeling there was a "shady" side to him. The ship had barely docked in Saint-Nazaire before he had organized a crap game on the sidewalk in front of a local restaurant, and proceeded to relieve four of our fellow soldiers and two of the local civilians of most of their money. Still, I liked him. He was outgoing, and a lot of fun to be around. He promised he would set me up with one of the local girls, a gift I wasn't sure I was ready for.

"What news?" I asked.

"We're going to Paris! Hot dog! Look out, sweet Marie!"

"What do you mean 'we're going to Paris'?"

"Pershing wants to make a big impression on the Frenchies, so he's sending a couple of companies and the band there to march in a parade on the Fourth of July. Our company's one of them."

"The Fourth of July? How come the French celebrate the Fourth of July?"

"Hell if I know! And I don't care. All I know is we're going to Paris!"

Once, in one of my geography classes in high school, we'd talked about Paris. The teacher passed around pictures of the Eiffel Tower, the Arc de Triomphe, Notre Dame Cathedral. But I never thought I would ever get to see them. Of course, that was before the country got into the war. In fact, I never thought I'd ever travel much farther than Louisville or Cincinnati. And now, here I was in France, on my way to Paris!

"Today's already the third. How can we be there by tomorrow?" I asked.

"By train. Taking off this evening. We'll be in Paris tomorrow morning. If we have some free time there, I'll set you up with some nice French girl, like I promised."

"Yeah, well, we'll see," I said.

We were all happy when the train pulled into Gare de Lyon station. The ride had proven to be not only a long one—fifteen hours—but uncomfortable, as well. As we swarmed from the cars like ants out of an anthill, women from the French Red Cross greeted us with hot coffee laced with rum. There was no time for anything else, not breakfast, nor even a chance to wash up.

We hurriedly formed up and marched from the station into the street. I stared in amazement at the huge crowd waiting for us, clapping and cheering, waving their hats. The French were ecstatic to see that the United States was now finally in the war.

We were a ragtag group at best. Our uniforms, while brand spanking new, fit poorly. Some of us had our rifles on our shoulders, others held them by their sides, and still others carried them at an angle across their chest. I don't even want to talk about how we marched. You would have thought we all had two left feet.

And yet—the French people still loved us.

Shouts of "Vivent les Americains," "Vivent les Etats Unis," "Vive Pershing!" accompanied us as we made our way—"marched" might perhaps be too generous a term—to Picpus Cemetery, the site of Lafayette's tomb.

Women rushed into the ranks, kissing us and placing wreaths of flowers around our necks. Children handed us bouquets. One young girl stuck a bunch of flowers down the barrel of my rifle. We looked like a flower garden on parade.

When we reached our destination, General Pershing spoke briefly. Then Lt. Col. Charles Stanton stood up.

"Lafayette, we are here!" he shouted.

People tossed their hats into the air, and the crowd erupted in a loud cheer.

I loved it. I loved the enthusiasm of the people, and I loved Paris. I hoped after the war I'd be able to come back and enjoy it as a civilian.

Dickie found me in the crowd.

"Carter, listen. Some of the guys are taking off to hit the bars. The sergeant said it's okay. You wanta come along? I'll find us some girls."

"I'll come along," I said. "But I'm not looking for any girls."

"Okay, let's go. Maybe I can get you to change your mind." Dickie winked and grinned deviously.

I wasn't sure how I got to the barracks. In fact, I wasn't even sure it *was* a barracks, since we went straight from the train to the cemetery when we arrived in Paris. All I knew when I woke up was I felt as though I'd been knocked over the head with a big iron skillet like the one hanging in my mother's kitchen. This must be what a hangover felt like, I thought. Up 'til now, I'd never gotten even a little tipsy before in my whole life.

I lay on a bunk, staring up at the bottom of another bunk some ten inches above me. I heard people moving around and, now and then, glimpsed someone pass by. Beyond that, I wasn't sure of anything. I couldn't lift my head. I couldn't even *turn* my head. *God, maybe I'm paralyzed!*

"How you doing, Carter?"

From somewhere beyond my line of sight, someone was apparently speaking to me.

"How you doing?"

Dickie knelt down by my bunk.

"I think I'm paralyzed." Did I say that? The words sounded slurred, like someone talking with a mouthful of grits.

Dickie laughed. "No, I don't think so. But you sure did get pickled last night. Took me and two other guys to drag you back here. I thought all you Kentuckians were hard drinkers, with all that moonshine and stuff."

I wanted to speak, but the effort proved too much. I just rolled my eyes.

"Okay, you lay there and sleep it off. I'll be back at supper time, and if you feel better by then, we'll go get some chow."

I shut my eyes. Food? No way was I about to eat anything. Maybe not ever again.

By the time Dickie showed up some hours later, I felt a little better. Two trips to the latrine, accompanied by two bouts of vomiting, left me weak, but considerably more sober. I was relieved to discover Dickie was right—I wasn't paralyzed.

"Man, you look a *lot* better."

"Yeah, well, I still feel like crap. Promise me you won't ever let me do that again."

Dickie laughed. "I'll do my best."

"Where are we, anyway?"

"They put us up in the Pipincerie Barracks. They've assigned a whole section for us. You ready for some chow?"

Amazingly enough, I was.

"Come on, then. I think we're having eggs sunny-side up along with turnip soup."

I turned and threw up again.

"What the hell is *this,* a barn?"

I eyed the building looming before us. It sure enough was a barn.

"This is where we're supposed to sleep?" asked Dickie indignantly, of no one in particular.

"Consider yourself lucky," replied one of the men standing next to us. "I understand some of the other guys are bivouacked in a stable down the road, along with the horses that pull our artillery."

"Well, crappy-do, that's all I've got to say," said Dickie. "Come on, Carter, let's see if we can at least find a dry spot in this shit hole."

I was all for that. Several days earlier we'd been loaded onto boxcars for the trip to Lorraine, where we were to begin our training.

It had rained constantly since we disembarked from the train. Everywhere we marched, it seemed, we found nothing but mud. No, I take that back. As we wended our way through the streets of the town, every house appeared to have a pile of manure in front of it. *Fumier*, the French called it. Between the rain, the mud, the manure, and the dampness that hung in the air like a wet dog, the whole area stunk to high heaven.

"This is the dirtiest, filthiest, crappiest place I have ever seen," Dickie complained, a sentiment shared by every other soldier there, myself included.

Over the next several days, we passed the time playing cards and reading old newspapers. When the rain finally stopped, we played catch outside. Dickie implored me to join him in town for a little "diversion"—namely drinking and women—from our dull, daily routine, but I declined. Damned if I was going to get soused again! Besides, I'd heard the stories going around of how a lot of the men had contracted some kind of disease from their little "adventures." Dickie, of course, was one of those lucky ones who had not gotten sick.

We found the French to be friendly enough, although there were occasions when we clashed with the local citizenry. Part of the problem was the language barrier.

"Don't any of these people speak American?" one of our men asked.

Having plenty of money and the willingness to spend it proved to be both a blessing and a curse. While the French merchants were more than happy to have the income, the fact that we seemed to have an abundance of those items long scarce in French civilian circles fostered a sense of resentment.

We heard the sound of guns at the front, but we knew it would be a while before our division ended up there. First, more training remained. Our instructors were members of the French Forty-Seventh Division—Chasseurs Alpins. Even before the actual training began, however, General Sibert instituted a regimen of drilling and physical conditioning, something most of the men badly needed—especially Dickie.

"Christ, I'm exhausted!"

Dickie collapsed onto the pile of straw that passed for his bed. "Why the hell do we have to do all this jumping up and down, and pushups, and running, and crap? They getting us ready to fight, or to retreat?"

"They want to make sure we're in good shape when we get out at the front line. It's not going to be as easy there as it is here," I said.

Dickie lifted his head and looked around. "Oh, yeah, we're living in the lap of luxury here, for sure. No beds, no mess hall, no jakes."

"Jakes?"

"Jakes. You know—latrines, shit holes."

"It'll be worse out there in the trenches," I said.

"I, for one, am ready to be out there," muttered Dickie. "Just let me go out and shoot some of those damn krauts, and I don't care what the living conditions are like."

I laughed. "Tomorrow we start training with the French. Maybe you'll find that more to your liking."

Over the next three months, we underwent arduous training, eight hours a day, five days a week, and a half day on Saturdays. We became familiar with our weapons: grenades, Hotchkiss machine guns, 37-mm guns, and the Chauchat automatic rifle. We trained in bayonet fighting, in using our gas masks to protect ourselves from gas attacks, and in the use of flame throwers, which Dickie and I, like many of the other fellows, considered a barbaric way to fight a war. Just how barbaric we were soon to find out.

We constructed trenches, ditches six to seven feet deep, dug into the earth, with twists and turns every thirty yards or so. Wooden planks were mounted against the sides to prevent them from collapsing inwards. Sandbags were piled about a foot high along the top of the trenches. In bad weather—which seemed to be every day—the trenches filled with water or snow or mud, always freezing cold. Trench foot was everywhere.

The only way to see over the trenches was by means of firesteps, crude wooden ladders placed along the sides about every six feet. Until Dickie showed up one day carrying a periscope.

"Where'd you get that?" I asked.

"Won it in a poker game. Now we won't have to stick our heads over the top and get them blown off."

On Saturday afternoons I wandered over to where the Twenty-Eighth infantry trained. I discovered the commander of Company G, a Lieutenant Huebner, had set up a rifle range where his men practiced. At first, I merely took target practice. My years of squirrel hunting served me in good stead. I was an excellent marksman. Before long, I was helping train the other men.

"McGlone, why don't you transfer to my company?" the lieutenant asked me one day.

"Sir, I appreciate the invitation," I replied. "But I'd as soon stay with the Sixteenth. I've made a lot of friends over there, and—well—it wouldn't seem right to leave them now, if you know what I mean."

"Sure, I understand," said the lieutenant. "Anyway, I appreciate the work you've done with my boys. You might have just saved some of their lives."

Chapter Five

The War Becomes Real

1917 - 1918

On October 21, 1917, the war became real to us for the first time, when the initial battalions moved into the front line. The first ten days were quiet, with no real fighting, although several "firsts" occurred for us: the first shot fired and the first man wounded. We even took our first prisoner when a German mail orderly from the other side got lost and wandered into our area.

On the night of November 2 our company's turn came to make our way to the trenches. The sky was moonless and pitch black, and a heavy mist hung over the entire area. To make matters worse, it had been raining, turning the whole landscape into one enormous sea of mud.

Everything was quiet for the first six hours.

Then it seemed as though the whole world exploded all at once.

Boom! Boom! Boom!

A heavy barrage from the Germans' guns began falling all around us. Within minutes, our telephone lines were cut off.

"Dickie, let me use your periscope."

He handed me the periscope, and I held it up to see over the top of the trench. A wall of fire spread across the landscape no more than a hundred yards away. I couldn't tell if it was coming toward us or not, but the roaring sound it made almost drove out the noise of the shells falling around us. Almost—but not quite. More explosions. The earth shook, as if trying to rid itself of the devastation being inflicted upon it. The shells exploded so close now, it seemed as though they were right there in the trenches with us.

At times, I wasn't sure if it was the ground shaking or me. I knew one thing, though: I had never been more scared in my whole life than I was at that moment. I grasped the medal hanging around my neck and held it tightly, as though it might possess some magical power to keep me safe. *Not likely,* I thought, as I remembered it hadn't done much good for the guy from whose remains I had taken it.

Suddenly, a large section of trench wall gave way; dirt, rocks, and duck-board tumbled down on Dickie and me.

"God damn!" shouted Dickie. "That was fucking close!"

"You said you wanted to get out here on the front lines," I shouted back, in an attempt to make myself heard over the din of the firing, at the same time rolling my body up into as tight a ball as I could.

"Yeah, but I didn't mean I wanted to get killed!" yelled Dickie.

I heard the terror in his voice, the same terror I felt. I shook uncontrollably. And I knew—it wasn't just the ground.

"Here they come!" We barely heard the voice of our company commander, First Lieutenant Willis Comfort, over the sound of the explosions.

Dickie picked up his periscope. It had been crushed by the falling duckboard.

"Crap!" he said, throwing it down.

We each climbed a ladder. Peeking over the sandbags, we saw the lights of the electric lamps fastened to the breasts of charging German soldiers: a raiding party, practically on top of us. I raised my rifle and fired at one of the blinking lights. The German took one more step, then fell face first into the mud. For a brief moment, I stared at the body sprawled out on the ground some twenty yards in front of me as the realization sank in that I had just shot a man. But there was no time to give too much thought to it. More Germans were coming.

I started firing again, but it was difficult to tell if I hit anyone through the smoke and fog.

In fifteen minutes, it was all over, and the raiding party retreated to their lines.

The trenches were eerily quiet. We weren't sure if the enemy would be charging right back or not.

I looked at Dickie. He had a glazed look in his eye.

"You okay?" I asked.

"I guess I'm still fucking alive," Dickie answered without looking at me. I knew he was as shaken by the whole affair as I was.

Finally he turned to me. "How you doing?"

"That's the first time I ever shot anybody," I said softly, pretty sure I had killed the German.

"Me, too," replied Dickie in a hushed tone. "Something, ain't it?"

I looked around. "I wonder if they got any of our boys."

"I reckon we'll find out when it gets to be daylight," said Dickie. "But at least you and me, we know *we're* still alive."

Exhausted, I sank back against the trench wall and drifted into a fitful half-sleep, filled with images of soldiers charging up a hill toward me, and spectacular fireworks lighting up the sky, interspersed with scenes of tranquil, rolling fields of corn and tobacco, bathed in sunlight, a light breeze gently moving the stalks back and forth.

Suddenly the dream changed.

Everything was still. The soldiers, the fireworks, the fields of corn and tobacco—all were gone. In their place lay a fine mist, like the one that covered the battlefield moments before the Germans had made their charge. Through the stillness, I thought I heard the faint cry of a bird, far off in the distance. Then, as the mist lifted, I made out the shape of a horse—and then a man, sitting on the horse, the same rider and horse I saw in my dream the night Sara Jane and I found the skeleton. Except this time I saw the color of the horse: gray. And the man's jacket—the same as the skeleton had been wearing. I raised my eyes and looked directly into those of the man's staring back at me and saw my father's face!

I awoke with a start and sat upright, shaking even worse than I had during the fighting. I looked at Dickie, sound asleep. I curled up in a ball in an effort to stop shaking, and after a while my body became still. But I slept no more that night.

As the sun crawled its way over the horizon, I could see a short distance down the line. Two men were slouched down, crying. I crawled over to them and saw what had upset them so.

It was the body of Merle Hay. His throat had been cut, the head nearly severed. Nearby lay the bodies of Tommy

Enright and Jimmy Gresham. Their throats had been cut, too.

I sank to my knees and sat back on my heels. It was all I could do to keep from throwing up. "My God," I muttered. "My God." I'd never seen someone I knew dead.

I heard Dickie shouting at me. "Carter! You ready to go?"

"Almost," I answered.

We had finished our frontline tour, and returned to our bivouac. The barn, which before seemed so wretched and inhospitable, now became almost tolerable after the cramped, muddy trenches we'd been living in.

Our company was hosting a Christmas party for the children of the village. The whole division had pitched in and come up with over 35,000 francs, which we sent with a committee to Paris to buy clothes and toys.

Dickie and I arrived at the party just as a sergeant in a makeshift Santa costume prepared to distribute the gifts. He stood next to a scrawny Christmas tree someone had cut, brought in, and decorated. Even Dickie was impressed at how much he looked like Santa.

In addition to a complete outfit of clothing—which was most appreciated by the parents—, each child also received what, to them, were the *good* gifts: fruit, nuts, candy, and—most importantly—toys!

As the gifts were distributed, I glanced at Dickie. My friend had tried to make everyone believe how tough he was, yet tears streamed down his face.

I knew that none of us who were there—soldiers, children, parents, civilians, myself included—would ever forget the Christmas of 1917.

∞

I found out later that the winter of 1917-1918 was one of the harshest ever experienced in Europe. I believe it. Every day, it seemed, we woke up to a drizzle of cold rain falling outside. Every day, that is, except for those days which produced either snow or sleet-storms. Mud, slush, and snow seemed to be everywhere. And cold! A bone-chilling, relentless cold that wrapped itself around one's body like a straight jacket and refused to let go.

One night Dickie came in late from one of his forays into town.

"God damn, it's cold," he said, his teeth chattering.

"How cold?" I asked.

"Colder than a witch's tit in a brass brassiere," he answered, setting off a chorus of laughter throughout the barracks.

∞

The next morning, I awoke to hear Dickie swearing, obviously distraught over something.

"What's wrong?"

"These damn shoes!" yelled Dickie. "I took them off last night, and now they're frozen stiff. I can't even get the fucking things on."

I reached down and felt my shoes. They were frozen, too, stiff as a board.

Just then, Andy Benton walked by.

"What's wrong, your shoes freeze up on you?" he asked.

"Hell, yes," said Dickie.

"Put some paper inside and set it on fire," said Andy.

"What?" Dickie and I asked at the same time.

Maybe I hadn't heard Andy correctly.

"What?" I asked again.

"Put some paper inside and set it on fire," said Andy. "Then, when the ice has melted, pour the water out."

We both did as Andy directed. It worked. But for the rest of that winter, we wore our shoes to bed.

I stared at the paper I held in my hand. "I've been transferred!"

"What do you mean, you've been transferred?" asked Dickie.

"I'm going over to the Twenty-Eighth. You remember last fall I told you Lieutenant Huebner asked me if I'd be willing to join his command, and I said 'no'? This time he didn't even bother to ask."

"You're kidding!"

"I wish I was. Here it is in black and white. I'm to report tomorrow."

"I'll be damned! What time do you have to be there?"

"0800, it says."

"Come on," said Dickie, grabbing his coat.

"Where we going?"

"I'm buying you one last drink, maybe more, maybe even get you drunk again. And don't even bother to say no, because you're going."

Before I knew what happened, Dickie picked up my coat, grabbed me by the arm, and dragged me out the door.

"McGlone, you're probably wondering why you're here."

I stood before Lieutenant Huebner, trying my best not to sway. True to his word, Dickie had succeeded in getting me drunk last night, and I still felt the effects of it this morning.

"Yes, sir," I answered, hoping I wasn't slurring my words too badly.

"I know last fall when I asked you about transferring, you didn't want to, and I respected that. Now, however, my company has been charged with putting together a sniper group, a bunch of sharpshooters we can use to pick off the enemy one by one. The rest of the squad came from my own men, the ones who had done the best at the rifle range. All but you. Because you're better than any of them. That's why I've had you reassigned to my command. The word is we'll be moving out in a few days to the front. Take the time to get acquainted with the other men. Corporal Rumsey will introduce you to the other squad members. That's all."

On January 15, we started out for the front. A cold rain that had been coming down as we left quickly changed to sleet. Our overcoats felt as though they were made of lead and the sleet increased the weight of the heavy packs strapped on our backs. It was like carrying another man. The temperature hovered around the freezing mark, turning the roads to treacherous sheets of ice. All in all, it was about as miserable as I remembered it ever being since I first arrived in France.

When at last we stopped for the day, we were happy to spread out and take refuge in several haylofts. At dawn we started off again, and after a long and grueling march, reached our destination: Ansauville.

For the first few weeks, everything was relatively quiet. The worst enemies were the lice and the rats.

February 6, 1918

Dear Sara Jane

I'm writing this from the trenches somewhere in France, near the town of Onsowville (I'm not sure I'm spelling it right). I'm also not sure just where this town is, either, except I think somewhere west of Paris.

Paris! How long ago it seems I was there, enjoying the warmth of the barracks, decent food, the overwhelming gratitude of the French people. A lot different than the wet, muddy trenches here at the front.

The worst part is the rats. No, I take that back. The worst part is the lice—cooties, the Brits call them. They're in our clothes, our hair, they get on our bodies. All of us are covered with sores and scabs that itch like crazy. The only way to kill the little devils is to snap them between your finger nails. I probably shouldn't be telling you all this— you'll get sick and puke.

Oh, but the rats. Some of them are over a foot long, and that doesn't even include their tails! And they have no fear of humans. Not only that but, well, I'm sure I've already told you more than you want to know. Don't tell my mom any of this. She'll be on the next ship over here to take me home!

It's been pretty boring since we got here. Not much fighting going on. But we got a new commanding officer yesterday, a General Bullard. Word is he's going to get things moving. I hope so. I'm okay, other than the cooties, the rats, and the damn cold. You tell my mom and dad I'm okay (but don't mention the rats and the cooties).

Love, Carter

Freezing mud oozed up around my boots as I watched a rat—at least a foot and a half long—make its way along the sandbags at the top of the trench on the opposite side of where I sat hunkered down. Fingering my rifle, I had about decided to see if I could stab the little sucker with my bayonet when Corporal O'Meara approached.

"McGlone, Captain Graves wants to see you."

"You know why?"

"Nope, only that he wants you over there on the double."

I squeezed myself out of the muck, and in a few minutes stood before Captain Graves.

"McGlone, glad you could get here right away. Look over there." The captain pointed to the German lines.

Squinting, I looked to where he pointed.

"What, sir? I don't see anything." *What the hell was I supposed to see?*

"About 500 yards out. You see that German soldier hanging up his laundry?"

I strained my eyes. Then I saw him. He was calmly tying up what appeared to be an undershirt.

"Yes, sir," I said. "I see him now."

"I hear you're one of the best sharpshooters the division has. I want you to take a shot at him."

I looked at Captain Graves. "Sir?"

"I want you to shoot at him. General Bullard says he wants us to stir things up around here. So, that's what we're going to do, by God!"

"But, sir, I don't think I can hit him from here."

"Jesus Christ, man, I don't care if you hit him or not! Just come close, so he'll know there's a damn war going on! The corporal here will spot for you with his binoculars. I figure you should be able to get a couple of rounds off before the kraut realizes what the hell's happening."

I shrugged and looked around for the least muddiest patch of ground. With the corporal giving rough coordinates, I got ready to take my first shot. *God, I hope I don't hit him by mistake.*

Crack!

"Twenty yards farther, and a little to the right," the corporal said quickly.

Crack!

I saw the German look around as if to say, *"What the hell was that?"*

"Ten more yards and dead on," said the corporal.

I ignored him, and shot at the same spot at which I had just aimed. I knew the corporal wanted to see the German go down, but I was damned if I was going to bushwhack a man from 500 yards away—while he's hanging up his laundry, no less!

This time the German flung himself over the parapet and into a trench. *He might be slow*, I thought, *but he sure isn't stupid.*

By now, several of our men had gathered around to watch the shooting exhibition. We heard angry voices of the

Germans in their trenches, cursing us ill-mannered Americans who had the indecency to shoot at them while they hung up their laundry.

"I think we made them mad," said Captain Graves, laughing so hard he had to sit down.

I laughed, too. But mine was more a nervous laugh, a laugh of relief—relief I hadn't actually killed the poor son of a bitch.

Over the next several months, the war consisted mainly of artillery fire between us and them. Our biggest concern was the one shell out of about every ten the Germans sent over filled with poison gas. The last week of February word got around that seven or eight men of the Third Battalion of the Eighteenth Infantry had died from gas poisoning, and more than seventy others had to be treated. The gas masks we were required to carry instantly received a lot more respect.

There were nightly patrols into the No Man's Land between our lines and the Germans, but for the most part, the war seemed to consist of the threat of poison gas, high explosives, and rain, snow, and mud. To make matters worse, more than one day passed when, for whatever reason, no food got to us. Any idea I might have entertained before I left home about the nobility and glory of war had long ago been replaced by the reality of cold, of rats, of lice, of death, of hunger, of fear, and the knowledge of just how miserable this whole damned experience was.

∞

I missed Dickie, but I had found a new friend in Al Montgomery, a farm boy like myself, from some place in Ohio.

"Aloysius Quincy Montgomery," he said.

"That's quite a moniker," I replied.

"I'm the third," said Al. "My grandfather, Aloysius Quincy Montgomery, was the first. He fought in the War Between the States. On the Union side."

"Did he make it out alive?"

"Oh, yes. In fact, my dad wasn't born until two years after my grandfather got out. But he did get wounded."

"Bad?"

"No, but he lost his right hand. Got it cut off. Would have gotten killed, except another soldier saved him."

It was a haggard group of men who made up our division as we arrived at the Montdidier sector, worn out, not so much by actual combat—of which there had been very little—as by the burdens of weather, boredom, and life in the trenches.

A month earlier, the German Army had overrun the British Fifth Army, and pushed its way westward. In response, our division had joined up with the French First Army near the small town of Cantigny.

Unshaven, dirty, foul, smelly, and weighed down by full packs, we resembled not so much fighting men as street beggars.

"Al, I gotta tell you something."

We sat by the side of the road, eating what passed for lunch. I stared at the glob on the fork suspended halfway to my mouth, wondering what it was. Aboard ship on the way over from New York to France, our main diet was yellow corn meal and stew, which we had grown sick and tired of after about six days. Now I'd give anything to have that over what I was about to eat. At least it had been recognizable.

I glanced at Al. "You stink!" I said.

"Yeah, well, you don't smell like any friggin' rose yourself," Al shot back.

We looked at each other, and started laughing.

"You know," I said, regaining my composure, "if my mom was here, she'd grab me by the ear and haul me off to the nearest river and give me a bath herself."

"My momma would use a bristle brush on me," said Al.

We bent over with laughter and the tears started up again.

The humor in this situation in which we found ourselves was the one thing that kept us going—and sane.

For the next two weeks, we endured what seemed like unending enemy artillery fire along the two miles of our front line. Day and night, hour after hour, the shells kept pouring in. All we could do was hunker down deeper in the mud of the trench and wait. It was like being locked in a tiny room while someone continually banged on a bass drum just inches from my head.

On May 28, everything changed.

Chapter Six

The End of the War for Me

1918

"What is all this stuff?"

I laughed. Al was puzzling over the array of supplies we had just been issued. We'd heard a major offensive was about to get underway early the next morning.

"Look at this!" exclaimed Al. "How do they expect us to carry all this stuff. And, what's this? A *lemon*? What the hell am I supposed to do with a lemon? Pretend it's a grenade, and throw it at the krauts? 'Watch out, here comes a yellow grenade!' Bang!"

"You'll be glad you've got all this when we go over the top," I said. But Al was right. There was an awful lot of gear here.

"Listen up, men," said Corporal O'Meara. "I'm gonna read down the list of what you're supposed to have. If you don't have something, let me know.

"Two-hundred and twenty rounds. Two grenades, and a rifle grenade. Two bars of chocolate, two iron rations, a pack of gum, a . . . a *lemon*? Okay, a lemon. Also—two water canteens, and a shelter half. Now, anybody who doesn't have everything they're supposed to?"

Several men raised their hands, and O'Meara proceeded to distribute the missing items.

"Corporal, what time you think we'll be going over?"

"Early. Colonel Ely says it'll be early. When you hear the guns start up, be ready."

"Al, I've got a favor to ask."

Al looked at me. Neither of us had said much since supper, as we were both deep in thought about the coming battle the next day.

"Sure, what is it?" asked Al.

"It's my medal, the one I wear around my neck."

"Yeah, I've wondered what that was for. Figured you'd tell me if you wanted me to know."

I told Al how Sara Jane and I had found the skeleton and the medal, the medal's connection to my great-grandfather, and that I hadn't taken it off since that day.

"The thing is, in case I don't make it through tomorrow—"

Al interrupted me. "We're *both* going to make it through tomorrow."

"Yes, but in case I don't," I said, "I'd like to make sure you see to it that it gets back to my dad. Would you do that for me?"

"Sure," answered Al. "But I wouldn't worry too much about tomorrow if I were you."

"You're not scared?" I asked.

Al looked me in the eye. "Shitless," he said.

At 5:45 the next morning, we heard the French artillery begin its assault on Cantigny. We climbed the firesteps and peeked out over the parapets: it looked as

though a huge tornado enveloped the town. Dirt, trees, pieces of buildings, equipment—even bodies—filled the air.

"Damn, would you look at that!" someone said in a hushed voice.

I couldn't speak. I had never seen such immense destruction. It seemed as though the whole town was being ripped apart.

For the next hour, shells continued to pour into the defenseless target. Then, at 6:45, the firing stopped.

"Let's go, men!"

As one, we were up and over the wall in seconds. Allied tanks lumbered from the woods on either side of us. Nobody seemed to be in a hurry, as we all rather casually walked toward what remained of the town. Suddenly, a number of German soldiers ran toward us from the ruins, wildly waving their arms in an attempt to surrender before some trigger-happy recruit panicked and shot them. I watched as some of our men escorted them back behind our lines.

French troops advanced along with us, using their flamethrowers to root out any German soldiers who might still be left in the many dugouts that surrounded Cantigny. I watched one Frenchie in particular. As he came across each dugout, he nonchalantly walked over to it, turned the nozzle on the tank on his back, aimed down the passageway, and sent a stream of fire exploding down the opening. Then, to make sure there were no survivors, he'd lob a grenade down the hole. The screams coming from the tunnels caused me to hunch my shoulders, as if in doing so I might shut them out.

I knew if there were any Germans in there, they would not be coming out alive.

By seven o'clock, we had taken the town—or what remained of it. The French artillery did its job so well we encountered hardly any resistance. In fact, nobody in my company had even fired a shot.

We barely arrived on the other side of town when . . .

Boom!

As one, we all hit the ground. All except Corporal O'Meara, who looked around for the source of the noise.

"What the hell?" someone shouted.

"German artillery," said O'Meara. "Guess they got tired of us firing at them, and now they're giving it back to us. You guys better get ready 'cause when the shelling stops, I've got a feeling we're going to see krauts coming at us."

O'Meara was right. Almost before the last shell struck, the German troops started rushing toward us.

"Here they come!"

I raised my rifle and began firing. This time I wasn't trying to merely come close. This was no guy hanging up his laundry to dry, but real-life enemy soldiers who would kill me if I didn't kill them first.

Then I saw him.

He was on top of me almost before I knew it, too close for me to get a shot off. I dropped my rifle, and grabbed the wrist of the hand holding a huge trench knife. The hair on the back of my neck stood up—I had never seen a knife that big before. With my free hand, I grabbed the German's throat and tightened my grip as hard as I could. But it wasn't enough. I couldn't apply enough pressure to choke him. I managed to wrestle him onto his back, but as I did so, a searing pain ripped through my left leg. At the same time, the German's free hand pounded my head. I let go of him, jumped up, and in the same motion kicked the knife out of his hand. Before I could pin him again, the German drew his pistol and aimed it at me. I heard the explosion of a gun, but—strangely enough—felt nothing.

Then I saw the bullet hole in the German's head, a trickle of blood running down his cheek. His hand, which lay lifelessly at his side, still held his pistol. I turned and saw Al, his rifle aimed at the dead soldier.

Blood gushed from my leg.

"Al, quick . . . a tourniquet."

Without a word, Al pulled a handkerchief from his jacket pocket, and tied it around my leg.

"Thanks, man."

I picked up my rifle, turned back toward the enemy, and resumed firing. No time now to even think about being afraid.

"Looks like your army career is over, son."

After the German attack had been repulsed, I was sent back to a dressing station, where a doctor tended to my wound.

"Appears the blade nicked an artery and cut partway through the muscle," said the doctor. "You're lucky you didn't bleed to death. Would have, if it hadn't been for the tourniquet. Nothing you won't recover from in time, but no more combat for you. I'm sending you back to the Frenchies' field hospital, but I imagine they'll send you on to a base hospital from there. All in all, you're a lucky young man—you're going to come out of this alive. The war's over for you, son."

Yes, I thought, *I sure as hell am lucky. And I don't ever want to fight in another war again, not as long as I live.*

Chapter Seven

Home to Kentucky

1918

I stared out the window and watched as the familiar hills and woods of central Kentucky passed by, listening to the rhythmic *clackety clack* of the wheels of the train as it carried me back to Harrison County. God, I was glad to be going home! I felt like the past twelve months had aged me twenty years. True, I was still only eighteen. But it felt like an *old* eighteen. I'd seen a lot, and done a lot, and I knew I would never again look at the world the same way.

As the train slowed down and neared the depot, I stuck my head out the window. Then I spotted them. Mom and Dad and . . . of course, Sara Jane! They were all waving at me. Sara Jane hopped up and down, as though she were standing on the metal plate that covered Mister Clary's root cellar on a blazing August day.

I didn't wait for the train to come to a complete stop. I jumped from the car and, forgetting for a moment the ache in my leg, ran, limping, to meet my mother, as she rushed toward me. She threw her arms around me, held me close, then gave me a lengthy kiss on the cheek. When she finally let go, my father grabbed me, gave me a hearty hug and a slap on the back. Then I turned to Sara Jane.

"My God," I said, "you've grown. You're so . . . so . . ."

"Beautiful," said my mother.

I picked Sara Jane up in my arms and twirled her around. "Beautiful is *exactly* the word I was looking for," I said. And it was true. If I had grown from a boy into a man during the past year, as I felt I had, so had Sara Jane changed from a girl to a young woman. Her hair, no longer in braids, fell freely down her back, reaching well below her shoulders. Her body had filled out; her waist was narrower, and her breasts fuller. She was quickly acquiring her mother's beauty and grace.

But she was still barefoot.

I was surprised at the feelings that stirred in me. Although Sara Jane and I both knew our families hoped the two of us would eventually get married, we had never thought of one another as anything more than best friends.

Sara Jane smiled, and then let out a loud "whoop," startling everyone on the platform, including other bystanders, who turned to see what the uproar was about.

"And you, Carter," said my mother. "Let me look at you. You are *so* handsome in your uniform."

"Take a good look, Mom," I said, "because this is the last time you'll see me in it. As soon as we get home, off it comes, and I'm back to civilian life."

"How's your leg, son?" my father asked. "I noticed you had a limp."

"My 'war trophy.' The doctor says I'll just have to live with it."

"Forever?" asked my mother. "Does it hurt?"

"No, Mom, it doesn't hurt. Well, yeah, it still aches a little. And, yes, I'll probably have the limp the rest of my life. But enough of that. I hope you've got a good dinner waiting for me at home.

"Pot roast, mashed potatoes, collard greens and cherry pie for dessert?" said my mother.

"Sounds great!"

My mother closed the door behind the last of the guests to leave and walked back into the kitchen, where my father, Sara Jane, and I sat around the table. Mom had wasted no time calling relatives and neighbors to spread the news of my return, and they had all stopped by to welcome me home.

Everyone was there, every family member who was present the year before at my going away party. All except for Cousin Molly and Clarence, Cousin Rupert's wife and son. Molly had died that spring, not long after they received word that Clarence, her youngest son, and my second cousin, had been killed in France.

"That's the last of them," said my mother, wearily. Happy I was home, and that everyone had come to welcome me back, it was also obvious she was glad the evening was almost over.

"I'm tired," she said. "I'll red up in the morning. I'm going to turn in now."

"Me, too," said my father, getting up from his chair.

"I'm going to walk Sara Jane home, and then I'll be right back," I said.

As we walked across the field, Sara Jane took my hand in hers.

"You missed a good mushroom year," she said.

"You found a lot?"

"Lordy, yes, they was everywhere."

"Did you find any in the darkies' cemetery?"

Sara Jane looked at me like I was crazy, and furrowed her brows.

"You think I'm nuts? I ain't never been back there since the day we found that there skeleton. Ain't about to be, neither. You still got that medal?"

I reached down the front of my shirt and pulled out the medal.

"Sure do."

She took my hand again and we walked for a while without saying any more. After a while she broke the silence.

"Was it bad over there?"

"Yeah, it was," I said. "It was bad."

"You want to talk about it sometime?"

"Maybe, sometime."

"You meet any pretty girls there?"

I looked at her and smiled. "Oh Lord, *yes*, they were all over the place. I had to practically beat them off with a stick."

"Oh, pshaw!" said Sara Jane, hitting my chest playfully with her free hand. "You may be good-looking, but you ain't *that* good-looking."

"You think I'm good-looking?" I asked, surprised.

"Oh, you're okay to look at. I mean, you ain't *ugly* or nothing."

I brought us to a stop so suddenly Sara Jane almost tripped and fell.

"What are you doing?" she asked.

I took her in my arms and kissed her, and was surprised when she kissed me back. I let go of her for a moment and we stood there, staring at one another.

Then we both burst out laughing.

"Ain't changed, has it?" she said.

"I'm afraid not," I answered. "It's just not there, is it?"

"Nope. It sure ain't. I guess we'll have to just go on being best friends 'stead of lovers."

"I guess so," I said. "Come on, let's get you home."

Chapter Eight

A Change of Plans

1923

After two years at Berea College I graduated in 1920 with a teaching certificate, after which I accepted a position teaching English and History at Millersburg Military Institute. For the next three years, my home would be in Paris.

Paris, Kentucky.

"They may share the same name," I told my parents, referring to the city I'd briefly passed through in France during the war, "but that's where the similarity ends."

I liked Paris. In many ways the town reminded me of Cynthiana. The people were friendly, and the pace of life relatively quiet.

I lived at the 130-year-old Duncan Tavern, now a boarding house. Though not luxurious, the accommodations were more than satisfactory. More importantly, they were affordable.

It was there one evening I met James Ledingham, a local attorney, who also owned and operated a small horse farm. Like me, he served in Europe during the war. Of course, unlike myself, he had been an officer. James invited me out to his farm for a Sunday afternoon barbecue and introduced me to his wife, Annabel, and their daughter, Missy.

I became good friends with the Ledinghams, and for the last year and a half that I lived in Paris, spent much of my free time at their farm. Occasionally Missy would be my date for social functions at the Institute although, as with Sara Jane, the relationship never progressed to more than a platonic one.

I'd also visit James in his office in town, where we talked about politics, local happenings, and law. I discovered that, while he serviced many wealthy white clients, a great deal of his time was taken up representing Negroes. He was one of the few local lawyers to do so.

The more we discussed legal matters, the more intrigued I became with the whole subject. Sometimes, when I knew James was arguing a particularly interesting case in court, I stopped by the courthouse to watch and listen.

After three years of teaching, I knew what I had to do.

"You're going to quit teaching?" My mother shook her head.

"I am, Mom. I've decided it's not what I want to do with the rest of my life."

"But, Carter, why not? I thought you loved teaching. You always wanted to be a teacher. And, it's a good job, a secure job."

"I know, Mom, but I want to do something else."

"What's that?" asked my father.

"I've decided to become a lawyer."

"A *lawyer*?" both my parents exclaimed in unison.

"Yes. The time I've spent with James has convinced me that's what I want to do—practice law. Teaching's been okay, but I . . . I don't have the passion for it I thought I would have."

"So, what does it take for you to be a lawyer?" asked my father.

"I'll have to go back to school. To law school."

"And where will you go for that?" asked my mother.

"Louisville. There's an excellent law school there, the same one James attended. He's already made inquiries about my getting in, and they've told him it shouldn't be any problem. I'll start next fall."

"How will you pay for it?" asked my father.

"I've got some money saved up and James said he'd be happy to make me an interest-free loan if I needed it."

"Well," said my mother, a twinge of resignation in her voice, "if this is what you want . . ."

"Thanks, Mom, it is. Dad?"

"I hope you know what you're doing, giving up a perfectly good job. But, I guess there's no sense doing something you don't want to do, if you can be doing something you do want to do. Besides, I guess lawyering can provide you a steady income, too, can't it."

I nodded. "I'm going to spend the rest of this summer working on James's farm to earn some more money before I enroll this fall."

My mother put her arms around me and kissed me. "I know you'll be a great lawyer."

Chapter Nine

Kiernan O'Doherty

1923

When my mother suggested I accompany my father into town for his weekly trip to pick up supplies, I jumped at the chance. It had been nearly a year since I'd been in Cynthiana.

While Dad went over my mother's list of provisions with Mr. Clary, the proprietor at Patterson's General Store, I wandered around, checking out what new items were in stock since the last time I'd been there. Absorbed in my explorations, I didn't hear the tinkle of the bell over the door as another customer entered the store.

A small metal flask at the back of a shelf caught my eye. I picked it up and read the inscription: "J. G. Kelly, SPIRITS, Maysville, K.Y." Even though prohibition was in effect, I assumed the flask was meant to hold alcohol of some sort. Whiskey, probably.

As I approached the counter, still studying the flask, I noticed a man stooped over, peering intently into a glass-topped case which held a variety of knives. I stand a few inches under six feet myself, but this man was a good five or six inches shorter than me, no more than five foot three or four. From the side, he appeared to be elderly, perhaps in his late seventies or early eighties. He wore a dark, old-fashioned frock coat. An equally out-of-date stovepipe hat rested, slightly tilted, on his head. I supposed its purpose was to make him appear taller.

I was a few feet away when the man straightened up, and turned to face me. For a brief moment, I was stunned by his appearance. The entire left side of his face, from his brow to his beard—and even under the beard, I assumed—was covered by a port-wine stain birthmark, which gave him the appearance of wearing a flame-red half-mask.

Our eyes met. His were cold as steel, and a chill ran through me. Never—not even in the war—had I seen such a look of anger, hatred even, nor felt such pure evil emanating from anyone as I did at that moment from that stranger. I thought I also saw what appeared to be a look on the man's face either of recognition, or of someone who had just seen a ghost—or both. I couldn't be sure.

He muttered something under his breath that sounded like "Jenkins," then quickly turned and bolted from the store.

"Do you know that man?" I asked Mr. Clary.

"Not someone you'd want to get on the wrong side of," he replied.

"Why, who is he?"

"Name's Kiernan O'Doherty. And he's about the most meanest, dangerous, disagreeable, man I've ever had the displeasure of knowing."

"You know him well, then?" I said.

"Aye. Sorry to say, I do. Our families both came from the old country together, back in '48. My da and his was friends there, and when the potato famine got too bad they decided to pack up their families, and try their luck here in America. I was three at the time, and Kiernan a year younger."

"So, he'd be in his seventies now?"

"Aye."

"Why do you say he's dangerous?"

"First of all, I got to tell you, his name fits him, that's for sure."

"How's that?" asked my father, lighting his pipe.

"In Ireland, Kiernan means 'black', and O'Doherty means 'hurtful,' and that man sure lives up to both of those definitions. Him and his da were both Fenians."

"Fenians?" I said.

"Fenians. The American arm of the Irish Republican Brotherhood. Them's the ones wants to rid Ireland of the British, make it a free country again, so to speak. They tried to recruit me and my da, but Da said he was an American now, *this* was his country, not Ireland. That didn't sit so good with the O'Dohertys, and we ain't been on real good terms since. That was back before the war—the Civil War. I was a little surprised when Kiernan came in here today. Hadn't seen him in about a year."

"But what's so dangerous about him?" I persisted.

"To understand Kiernan, you got to know a little about his da, who was as mean as Kiernan, maybe meaner. Terrence O'Doherty took up slave trading after he got here in America. He also chased down runaway slaves, and took them back to their owners, and collected the rewards. And he warn't too gentle going about doing it, neither. When Kiernan got old enough, maybe fourteen, or fifteen, he'd go along with his da, hunting for slaves. Hear tell sometimes when they caught up with one, old Terrence would have to pull Kiernan off the poor bastard before he beat him to death. You know, slave owners warn't too keen about getting back dead slaves.

"So, then, young Kiernan got himself in some sort of a mess, killed a colored, or something, and had to get out of the county, so he ups and takes off and joins the

Confederate Army. After the war, him and his da hooked up again, and became carpetbaggers. Made a small fortune, I hear, down in Alabama."

"What does he do now?" I asked.

"What else? He's a bootlegger. Comes up here to Kentucky 'bout every month or so, loads up his wagon with moonshine, and hauls it back down to New Orleans, where he sells it to the speakeasies there."

"Still, he doesn't sound all that dangerous," said my father.

"Oh, and did I forget to mention, he's got the reputation of having killed about a half dozen men, not counting no coloreds, most of them in cold blood, shot or stabbed in the back? 'Course, that was in his younger days. Still, all in all, I ain't about to turn *my* back on him."

"I got the impression he might have thought he recognized me," I said. "But I'm sure I've never seen him before."

"With any luck, son," said Clary, "you'll never see him again, neither."

Somehow, though, I had a feeling I had *not* seen the last of Kiernan O'Doherty.

Chapter Ten

Law School and Sam Jenkins

1923

It was my first day in Louisville. I'd spent the past two hours trying to find my way from the train depot to the apartment building I would call home for the next two years. Navigating downtown Louisville walking and toting a large suitcase hadn't been easy.

At length, though, I'd located the address, lugged my bag up the three flights of stairs to the fourth floor, and found the door to the apartment standing open. I walked in.

"Jenkins, Samuel—Esquire. You can call me Sam."

I took the outstretched hand of the man standing in the middle of the room. He stood a good three or four inches taller than me, and with his lanky frame, and an unruly mop of straw-colored hair, reminded me of the Scarecrow in one of my favorite books as I was growing up: *The Wonderful Wizard of Oz*.

"Hi. McGlone, Carter."

"So, where you from, Carter?"

"Cynthiana. And you?"

"Jasper, Indiana."

"Never heard of it."

"That makes us even. Never heard of Cynthiana." We both laughed.

"Is that here in Kentucky?" he asked.

"Uh-huh. East of here, and a little north of Lexington. So, I guess we're roommates."

"Looks that way," said Sam. "When old man Duffy rented me this apartment, he said there'd be another fella sharing it. Guess that's you. I took the bedroom over here. Hope you don't mind. You can have the one over there."

I looked to where Sam pointed. The door was open, revealing a room that appeared to contain the necessary furnishings: a bed, a desk, a washstand with a mirror and built-in drawers, and a wardrobe, where I could hang what few clothes I had. A window on the far wall extended almost from the floor to the ceiling.

"It's not much," said Sam, "but mine's the same. Understand from Mr. Duffy you're going to go to law school here."

"That's right," I said.

"Me, too," said Sam. "Maybe you can help me with my homework."

"Or the other way around," I said. We both smiled.

I walked into the bedroom and set my suitcase on the bed. While the basin was old and worn, the washstand sported handles and a faucet. *Running water!*

The wallpaper, like everything else, had seen better days, but appeared clean enough. While I unpacked, Sam hovered in the doorway and watched with intense interest, all the while keeping up a running commentary.

"I been scouting the neighborhood, and we're in luck. There's a nice little restaurant not two blocks away. Pretty good food, and the prices aren't too bad. In the back room, you can get something stronger to drink than lemonade—if you know what I mean." He winked. "'Course, we got a kitchen here, if you're the cooking type. I'm not, myself." He walked into the room and tapped on the radiator. "Got steam heat. Ought to keep us warm enough come winter. Bathroom's down the hall. Decent enough. Oh, and I found a garage out back to rent where I can keep my Duesy."

I stopped unpacking, and turned to face Sam. "Duesy?"

"Duesenberg. My car."

"You've got a *car*?" I asked. "A *Duesenberg*?"

"Yeah," answered Sam, somewhat sheepishly. "A graduation gift from my great-aunt."

"A *Duesenberg*?" I said again. I couldn't believe it. I rushed to the window to see. I'd heard of such a car, but had never even seen one, let alone known someone who owned one. "Where is it? I don't see it."

"Like I said, I got it parked in the garage. It's a Model A, eight-cylinder, hydraulic brakes. Why don't you finish putting your stuff away and we'll take a spin."

"Okay." I was anxious to see what a real Duesenberg looked like.

I removed my parents' photograph from the suitcase, and set it on a shelf of the washstand.

"Mom and dad?" asked Sam.

I nodded as I placed Sara Jane's picture on the other shelf.

Sam let out a whistle. "Please tell me that's your sister, and not your girlfriend."

I laughed. "No, neither one. She's my best friend. Sara Jane Williams. We grew up together."

Sam couldn't take his eyes off the picture. "You're joshing me! A great looking gal like this, and you're just best friends?"

"That's right."

"Ever kiss her?"

I grinned. "Yeah, once. That's when we knew for sure we were just friends."

"I assume you'll be inviting me to come home with you some time to meet the family? And all your friends?"

"Sure," I replied, chuckling. "The next time I go home, I'll be sure to take you along. We'll drive over in your 'Duesy.' And," I continued, "we'll make sure Sara Jane stops by."

Sam grinned.

"So," I said "your great-aunt's rich?"

"Filthy! So filthy rich it makes your skin crawl."

"How'd she get so rich?"

"Gold."

"Gold?"

"Yep, gold. Ever hear of the Klondike Gold Rush back in '97 and '98?"

"'Course I have," I replied. I remembered my father saying how one of his cousins had gone up to Canada to pan for gold, and was never heard from again.

"That's where my late great-uncle, Bertram P. Worthington, struck it rich. He was one of the first ones to make it to Dawson's Creek in the spring of '97. Took a fortune out of there. Came back to Indiana, built a mansion on Patoka Lake, a little ways outside of Jasper, and retired. He and my great-aunt Minnie never had any children, so I was kind of like a son to them. Uncle Bert died three years ago.

"But enough about me for now. Hurry up and I'll take you down to O'Neal's. That's the restaurant I told you about." Sam raised his eyebrows and smiled. "We'll see what's 'brewing' in the back room."

"After the drive in your Duesy," I said.

Chapter Eleven

A Visit Home

1924

"Carter! It's you!"

I smiled at the attractive young woman rushing to meet me, long hair flying behind her as she ran.

"Sara Jane, I always could count on you being here to meet my train!"

I dropped my suitcase and barely caught her as she threw herself into my arms.

"You know, if I was met like this every time I came home, I'd come home more often," I said.

"If you came home more often, maybe you might be met like this every time."

"How's my dad?" I asked. I'd been upset at first when I read my mother's letter informing me of my father's accident. He'd gone into a ravine to rescue a cow and slipped, breaking his leg in two places. But I'd been relieved when I read how all the neighbors had pitched in to work the farm.

"Oh, you know your daddy," answered Sara Jane. "He's not going to let a little thing like a broken leg keep him down for long. 'Course, your momma's trying to hold him back as best she can, keep him in bed where he needs to be 'til his leg at least starts to heal some. That's why she asked me to come and fetch you home from the train depot, 'cause she didn't want your daddy to have to be home by hisself. I know she's sure glad you're back.

"I was surprised when your momma said you was coming in on the train. I thought you was going to come with that roommate fella of yours in his fancy car."

"I was, but something came up at the last minute, and he had to go home."

"Nothing serious, I hope. I was looking forward to meeting him."

"He promised he'd come another time, maybe this summer, because he *really* wants to meet you."

"Yeah, right," Sara Jane replied, her face turning a light pink. "So, how was the train ride?"

"Long," I said, as I loosened my tie, unbuttoned the top button of my shirt, and slipped out of my coat. "And waiting to change trains in Lexington makes it even longer." I looked around. "Where's the carriage?"

"Ain't no carriage." Sara Jane's lips twitched into a little smile. "We're traveling first class today." She pointed to the shiny new Buick sitting in front of us.

"Wow!" I exclaimed. "Whose motor car is this?"

"My daddy's! He bought it last month."

"And he lets you drive it?"

Sara Jane laughed out loud this time. "He's got to. He don't know how, yet. I keep trying to teach him, but he cain't seem to get the hang of it."

"Okay," I said, hoisting my bag onto the back seat. "Let's see how it runs. And how are *your* mom and dad?"

"Thanks for asking. My daddy—well, he's doing fair to middling. You know, he took sick last month just right after Christmas, and he cain't seem to shake it."

"And your mom?"

"Oh, she's fine. Upset, 'cause I still ain't married."

I had to laugh. Sara Jane and I were like kinfolk, like the brother and sister neither of us had. In some ways, I felt even closer to her than I might have to a brother. Still, I thought it strange she hadn't found the right man yet. Of course, she was still young—only twenty-two. At the same time, I realized I had little room to talk. I knew women found me attractive, and I certainly didn't lack for their attention. A number of young ladies had made their interest in me quite clear. One girl even told me I looked like Douglas Fairbanks. But while I found much to admire in this one, or that one, I hadn't found myself even remotely serious about any of them.

"Any prospects?" I teased.

"Heck, no! All the boys around here are interested in is getting out of this place, heading down to Lexington, or over to Louisville, or up to Cincinnati. 'Course, you'd know all about that yourself, wouldn't you?"

She was right. I understood their desire to have something more in life than what Harrison County, Kentucky, offered.

"To tell the truth," continued Sara Jane as a slight flush spread over her face, "Randall Mason's been making sounds like he'd like to start courting me. 'Course, he ain't actually got up the nerve to say nothing, yet."

"And if he did?"

"If he did I . . . I might think about it. I mean, he ain't too bad looking, and his daddy does own the lumber mill over on Beaver Creek." She shrugged a little. "I don't know, though. I look at him and I think: 'He's okay . . . but is he the right one?'"

"And how will you know?"

My curiosity was aroused now, not just about Sara Jane, but about myself as well. How would *I* know? I wondered.

"How will you know when the 'right one' comes along?"

Sara Jane thought for a moment. "I think . . . I think when I meet him, something will happen to my heart. I'll feel something here," she said, holding her hand over her heart. "It'll be different, somehow."

She turned and looked at me. We both started to laugh.

"I sure enough wish it'd happen when I look at you," she said. "But it don't. It sure would make life a heckuva lot easier."

"I know," I said. "But then, you wouldn't have a brother, and I wouldn't have a sister."

"One good thing about Randall. He's the one who taught me to drive." We both laughed again.

"We missed you at Christmas," said Sara Jane. "We thought for sure you'd be home. It sure weren't the same without you."

The past Christmas was the first I missed being home since the one in Europe. But the opportunity to stay in Louisville and pick up some extra work clerking at a downtown department store, along with the expense of a train ticket from Louisville to Cynthiana, didn't make it financially feasible to get back. Sam and I had planned this current trip for some time, and when he had to cancel at the last moment, I decided to go ahead and splurge by taking the train.

"Yeah, I'm sorry I couldn't make it, too. Did you have a good Christmas?"

"Real nice," Sara Jane replied.

We rode on without saying anything for a while before Sara Jane broke the silence. "I told you my Grandma Mary come to live with us, didn't I?"

"You did. You wrote that in your last letter."

"She's not doing so good. Momma says she'd be surprised if she makes it through 'til fall."

"I'm sorry to hear that," I said. "I don't think I ever met your grandmother, did I?"

"I don't reckon so. When we was growing up, she lived most of her life over by Covington, with her brother. That'd be my great-uncle Edgar. She moved in with Momma and Daddy and me this past March, when he died."

"She was from around here originally, wasn't she?"

"Yeah, she was. She lived here until right after my momma married my daddy. That's when she and Mr. Pickens moved to Covington."

"Mr. Pickens? Your grandfather?"

"Oh, no. My granddaddy died right after Momma was born. Him and Grandma's younger brother got killed in a house fire. I guess the fire broke out in the brother's bedroom; a candle, they think it was, what started it. Granddaddy was on his way back from town when it happened. Grandma managed to get my momma out, and then she went back in for her brother. He'd told Grandma he had something important to get, a letter or something. But she couldn't get to him—the fire was too bad. She got burned real bad trying. Just then my granddaddy got home, and he tried to save the brother, but they both died. I guess Grandma lost almost everything in the fire. She and my momma moved in with Granddaddy's folks.

"A few years later she married Mr. Pickens. He was a little older than Grandma, maybe ten, fifteen years—I'm not for sure. From what Momma tells me, he worked in a dry goods store in Cynthiana until his daddy died, and left him some land outside of Covington. That's when he and Grandma moved there. She's never been back here since, 'til she moved in with us. Wouldn't of come then, I don't s'pose, 'cept she couldn't take care of herself no more."

Strange, I thought, how one could be so close to a
family, as I was with Sara Jane and her mother and father,
and yet know so little about other family members who
were so close to them. Of course, I knew Sara Jane's
Grandpa and Grandma Williams. They lived on a little farm
not far from Sara Jane's place. Many times, Sara Jane and I
dropped by for a glass of cider and freshly baked oatmeal
cookies.

"Do you know anything about your real grandfather?" I
asked.

"Not much. 'Course, I warn't around Grandma all that
much, only a couple trips we made up to Covington to see
her."

"I bet she's quite a woman," I said. I looked forward to
meeting her. "I imagine she's had a good long life."

"Yeah, and now it's almost over," said Sara Jane, her
voice catching. She began to cry. "I'm sorry, it's . . . it's
just that I hardly ever knowed my grandma, and now that
she's here, she's going to die. Sure don't seem fair
somehow."

She had pulled the car to the side of the road. Her head
was bowed, and tears streamed down her cheeks. I pulled
her to me, put my arms around her, and held her there for a
long time.

"I'm sorry," she said, as her crying subsided. "I don't
know why I do stupid things like that."

"It's all right," I said. "It's all right."

She straightened up, grasped the steering wheel firmly
with both hands, and guided the car back onto the road. I
knew she felt embarrassed, and when she changed the
subject, I didn't object. "Tell me something about your
family. Something I don't already know."

I thought for a few minutes. There *was* a family story I'd never shared with her. Maybe now was a good time. "I suppose I could tell you about the 'skeleton' in our closet," I said.

"Now, you ain't talking 'bout that skeleton we found when we was kids, are you?" she said, laughing.

"Kind of. It *is* about my great-grandpa, old Owen McGlone, the one who Dad thought the skeleton was at first."

"Okay," said Sara Jane. "I'm all ears."

"You remember what my dad said the time we found the skeleton? That my Great-grandpa McGlone up and disappeared one day back in '64? The 'official' story in our family, which I found out later, was that, despite what my dad told us that day, Great-grandpa might have been killed in the battle that took place here, maybe someplace out in the woods, and his body was never found. *Or*, that he was taken prisoner, and died in some southern prison. Thing is, Morgan paroled all the prisoners he took in that battle, didn't send any of them to prison. But, either way, Great-grandpa Owen was never heard from again after that.

"Now, the 'unofficial' story is, he got so fed up with the killing and all, he deserted the army, moved out west, got married again, and fathered seven more children before he died."

"Are you pulling my leg?" asked Sara Jane. "Where'd you hear that?"

"That's the story my Cousin Rupert told me after I got home from the army. I doubt it's true, at least the part about the seven children, because Great-grandpa was fifty-seven when he disappeared. It's unlikely he would have had seven more children before he died. And I don't think he would have up and run off, either. Although . . ."

"Although what? Come on, the suspense is killing me!"

"Although, Cousin Rupert still has the pistol my great-grandpa carried in the war. Whatever happened to him, wherever he went, or whatever he did, he didn't take his gun with him. So, I don't understand—if he was killed or taken prisoner, how did Rupert end up with the gun? Then, last fall, before I left for school, I heard another account from Rupert's son, Elroy."

"What was *that* one?" asked Sara Jane.

"According to Elroy, who said he got the story from his grandpa on his mother's side, Great-grandpa McGlone was ambushed by another soldier who killed him, and stole his horse and his pistol—oh, and his boots, too, I think. Then, when my grandpa and Elroy's grandpa—that would be my great-uncle Rufus—caught up with the guy, they hanged him from a tree. Lynched him right there on the spot. Of course, they never did find Great-grandpa's body. And there's no record of what happened to the body of the man they hanged. But if that story's true, it might explain the gun."

"You know what?" The words tumbled out of Sara Jane's mouth. "I'll bet the man they hanged was that skeleton we found! You remember, the sheriff said he looked like he'd been hanged? And he was wearing a Union uniform! And the medal! Your daddy said it was your great-grandpa's medal you found there. I bet sure enough it *was* him!" She was so excited she stopped the car in the middle of the road. "What do *you* think?"

"I have to admit I thought about that as Elroy told me the story. It sure would make sense. But there's no way to know for sure. And my grandpa and Elroy's grandpa are both dead now, so we can't ask them. I asked my dad about it when I got back home, but the only answer he gave me was, 'I don't know nothing about no lynching,' and then he went back to milking."

"Boy, it sure would be something to know," said Sara Jane. She started the car up again.

For a long time the only sounds were the car's engine and the *whoosh, whoosh, whoosh* of the tires on the road. I looked around, taking in the landscape whizzing by. The beauty of this land never ceased to amaze me. To my right stretched fields of burley tobacco, the most important cash crop in these parts. To my left were woods filled with hickory, and elm, and a dozen other varieties of trees. God, I loved this land! But not enough to want to stay here. Once I'd gotten a taste of city life in Louisville, I knew that's where I'd start my practice once I passed the bar.

I leaned back and enjoyed the sights, the sounds, and— yes—the smells. For most of the ride, I had been acutely aware of the distinct odor of spring; the pungent fragrance of last year's leaves that lay moldering on the ground. I smiled. *Mushroom time.*

We passed old Mr. Benson's pig farm. *There* was a smell I knew I'd never forget as long as I lived!

Once again Sara Jane broke the silence.

"Your momma tells me you're going to church on Saturdays. You ain't become one of them there Adventists, have you?"

I wrinkled my eyebrows. "Church?"

"Yeah. Your momma says you're going to some church up on a hill somewhere."

For a moment I didn't understand what she was talking about. Then I burst out laughing.

"No, I'm not going to no church," I said. "I'm going to *Churchill Downs*. It's a racetrack in Louisville where they race horses. Sam and I go out there most every Saturday when it's open, just to get out of our apartment."

"You bet on the horses? You ever win?"

"No, I don't bet. I don't have any money to bet. I just like to watch them run."

I pointed across the field. "Look. There's the old sycamore tree."

"Sure is. And see—there's the grave marker. You know, Carter, I still remember everything about that day. I was half scared out of my wits."

"I'd say more than half," I replied. "Pull over."

Sara Jane pulled the car over again and stopped.

"Let's walk over there," I said.

"You really want to? You know, even after all these years, I still remember my daddy's warning to stay out of there."

But I was already out of the car and heading toward the sycamore.

I heard Sara Jane turn off the engine and close the car door. When she arrived at the grave site a few minutes later, I was studying the initials carved into the tree trunk.

"You know," I said, as she stood next to me, "we never did figure out who belonged to these initials, did we?"

"Nope," Sara Jane answered. She knelt down at the grave, and placed on it a bouquet of flowers she had picked on her way across the field. "And we never found out who this here fellow was, neither, except now we know he was maybe the one who done killed your great-granddad."

I knelt down beside her. "I wonder if we'll ever know the answers."

We stayed like that for a long time. The air was still, much like that first day, the day we found the skeleton. The only difference now was the absence of any birds' cries. There were no sounds at all.

After a while I stood up, took Sara Jane's hand, and we retraced our steps to the car.

Chapter Twelve

Happenings in Louisville

1924

A broken leg was about the worst thing that could happen to my father, short of death. Never sick a day in his life, he had worked the fields of our farm from the time he was old enough to pick up a hoe. To be confined to his bed was an adversity he did not accept gracefully.

"Dad, what have you gone and done to yourself?" Even though I was concerned, I knew this was not a life-threatening injury, so I thought perhaps I might have a little fun with the situation.

"Now, Carter, I don't want to hear no 'smart mouth' from you. Your momma's already given me enough grief about how a man my age should be more careful."

"I remember how nimble you *used* to be," I said, laughing. "Like, when you'd hop across on those rocks in the stream that runs down through the lower meadow. I guess it gets harder when you get older, doesn't it?"

"Son, if I could get out of this bed, I'd come over there and give you a whuppin'. As it is, get on over here and let me shake your hand, and welcome you home. Good to see you. Catch me up on what's happening to you over there in 'Loo-ee-vill.'"

My mother and Sara Jane had been standing at the doorway, listening.

"We want to hear, too," said my mother, as she ushered Sara Jane into the room. "Tell us all about yourself, and school, and—well, everything."

For the next hour, I told them about life in Louisville. For three people whose own lives were pretty much confined to Harrison County, it was like being taken on a magical trip into a land they could hardly begin to imagine.

I told them about the big horse race Sam and I had attended the week before, a special race held once every year, called the Kentucky Derby, won this year by a horse named Black Gold. I described the gigantic structure called Churchill Downs, and the tens of thousands of people who came to watch the race, filling the grandstands and milling about in the infield.

They listened in amazement as I told them about the number of automobiles that jammed the downtown streets, the hundreds of thousands of people who lived in and around the city, and how tall and numerous the buildings were. "The new Brown Hotel built last year has fifteen stories," I said.

"Fifteen stories!" exclaimed my mother, shaking her head.

I told them about where I caught the train, Union Station, where better than sixty trains a day pass through. "It covers forty acres and—"

"Why, that's almost as much as our whole farm," said my father.

"I know," I said. "It's enormous."

I described the vast number of barges that made their way up and down the Ohio River, moving products such as coal, gravel, steel, and petroleum from one part of the country to another, not to mention the excursion boats that carried people on holiday to such places as Rose Island, where there's a zoo, where visitors could see all kinds of wild animals. I confessed Sam and I had taken the steamer *America* there one Saturday, and spent the evening dancing with all the young ladies at the dance pavilion.

I told them Sam and I and some other friends from school went to watch the Louisville Colonels play.

"You remember when they played here in Cynthiana a few years ago? That professional baseball team? I can't believe they get *paid* to play baseball!

"And guess what? One day one of our professors invited us over to his house, and we listened to his radio. We only listened one at a time, because we had to wear earphones to hear what was being said."

"What about school?" asked Sara Jane. "What's that like?"

"Ah, school," I sighed. That was another matter. "I love Louisville. I tolerate the school."

"Why? What's wrong with the school?" asked my mother.

"We meet in an old building on Armory Street downtown, close to the law offices and the courts. This is the first year the law school's been there. I'm somewhat older than most of the other students. Almost all of them came right out of high school into the law school."

I started to tell them about how the building was so ancient and decrepit, and how the students threw their textbooks at the huge rats that wandered fearlessly through the class rooms; and how one of my classmates declared the place so dirty it was like "breaking into King Tut's tomb." But then I decided they didn't need to hear all that— especially not my mother. "Let's just say I'll be glad when I'm finished.

"Sam and I both clerk part-time to make a little money. He's at the county courthouse, and I'm with Schuler and Morrisey—that's a big law firm."

"Tell us more about your roommate," said Sara Jane.

"You want to know about Sam?" I smiled at her, and she smiled back.

"Sam. Samuel Jenkins, to be precise," I said. "Or, as Sam likes to put it, 'Samuel Jenkins, Esquire.' First of all, he wanted me to tell you how sorry he was he couldn't come along this trip, but he had to go home unexpectedly. He'll come another time.

"Anyway, Sam's a farm boy, like me. He's from some little town in Indiana—Jasper, as I recall. He's a great guy, quite popular with the girls, and so smart it makes me envious." I looked at Sara Jane. "Say, maybe he's the one for you. He saw your picture on my washstand the day I moved in, and he thinks you're kind of cute."

"I bet," said Sara Jane. A slight blush spread over her cheeks. "If he's that smart, he sure wouldn't want nothing to do with an old backwoods girl like me."

"Any man would count himself lucky to have you as a wife," said my mother.

She looked directly at me.

"Now, Mom," I said, raising my hands as if in surrender. "You know Sara Jane and I are friends. And we both know that's all we'll ever be."

"Carter's right, Mrs. McGlone," added Sara Jane. "And I'm plumb happy to have Carter as my very best friend in the whole world."

"I just think it would be nice . . ." My mother didn't finish. "Go on. Tell us more about this Sam Jenkins, Esquire."

"Sam and I are talking seriously about becoming partners, and going into practice together when we finish law school."

"You mean he'd be willing to move here to Cynthiana instead of going back home?" my mother asked.

"No, Mom, he wouldn't be moving here. Neither would I. We'd be practicing law in Louisville."

A look of disappointment spread over my mother's face. "Oh, I . . . I see. I . . . I guess I thought all along you'd be coming back home and open an office here."

"Mom, I'm sorry to disappoint you, but Louisville is where the action is, where the money is. Neither Sam nor I want to be small-town lawyers. We're looking for more than that."

No one spoke for a few minutes. Then Sara Jane broke the embarrassing silence.

"How about the girls there in Louisville? What are they like?"

Thankful for the change of topic, I told them about the few women enrolled in the law school. Some of them were rather pretty. All of them were smart, though none as smart, or as pretty, as either Sara Jane or my mother, I quickly added. I told them about the fine ladies who spent their Sundays strolling through the parks, or going on picnics with their beaus, and described the elegant dresses they wore, and how all the women—and most of the men—wore hats. No, I didn't have any steady girlfriend, I said, but I'd dated several nice women, and, no, nothing serious was going on.

At last I was all talked out. Not that they were ready to quit listening. There was just nothing more for me to tell them.

"I reckon it's time we had a bite to eat, anyway," said my mother, though I sensed her reluctance to let the moment go. "Sara Jane, you'll stay for supper, won't you?"

"Yes, ma'am, I'd love to stay. Let me ring up my momma so she won't wonder I'm out somewhere doing something I shouldn't be doing, and then I'll help you get it ready."

"Ring her up?" I asked. "You don't have a telephone."

Sara Jane grinned.

"Yes, we do. Got it right after Grandma Mary came. Momma said she wanted one in case we had to call the doctor for her. Just like you got one after your daddy's seizure. At first, Papa said we couldn't afford it. Momma said if he could afford a new car, we could durn well afford a telephone. So we got one. We're even on your party line. So watch what you say when you're talking to your girlfriend!"

She grinned again.

"Carter," said my mother, "you help your daddy to the table, so he can join us."

After supper, my mother and Sara Jane cleared the table, while I helped my father out to the porch. I enjoyed the night sounds of life in the country, while my father smoked his pipe.

A few minutes later, Sara Jane and my mother joined us.

"Oh, Carter," said Sara Jane. "My momma wants to know if you want to come over tomorrow, and meet my grandma?"

"I'll be over first thing," I replied. I looked forward to meeting this woman whose impending passing had caused Sara Jane to break down in tears.

"For breakfast?" asked Sara Jane.

"Even though I'm stuffed right now, I'm sure I'll be ready for some of your momma's excellent cooking by tomorrow morning."

"We'll expect you for breakfast then," said Sara Jane, taking off her apron. "I reckon I'd best be heading home now."

"I'll walk you," I said. "First let me help my dad back into the house."

Chapter Thirteen

Mary Pickens

1924

The next morning I showed up bright and early at the Williamses' home.

"Carter McGlone! You are a sight for sore eyes!" Mrs. Williams put her arms around me and greeted me with a firm hug. "Sara Jane kept us up half the night going on about all those things you told her about Louisville. It sounds like an exciting place. Here, breakfast is on the table. Sit down and have a bite."

"Morning, Carter," said Mr. Williams.

"Good morning, Mr. Williams," I replied.

I never could make up my mind who was the better cook—my mother or Mrs. Williams. My mother's pork chops were delicious, but Athena Williams's cured ham? Well, it was beyond delicious. Of course, I had seconds of everything—everything, that is, except the buttermilk. My opinion of buttermilk is that it must surely be one of the most foul inventions ever devised by man or by God.

As I ate, I answered Mrs. Williams's questions, questions that had come to her from what Sara Jane had omitted from my accounts from the previous evening. While she had been to Covington a few times to visit her mother, she had never even gone across the river to Cincinnati. Nor had she ever been to Louisville, or even

Lexington. So every bit of information from me was like an adventure.

All the while, Mr. Williams said nothing, but I knew he was as intrigued as his wife and daughter.

"Oh, it must be wonderful to be there, to see all those sights!" Mrs. Williams exclaimed. "Just once I'd like to visit, to stay in one of those fancy hotels."

"Like the Brown Hotel," I said, caught up in her enthusiasm.

"Oh, yes!" she continued. "And to eat in one of those fancy restaurants. Oh, Carter, I envy you so!"

"Louisville's a wonderful city, no doubt about that," I said. "But it sure is good to be back home, too."

"And I know your momma's sure glad you're back," said Mrs. Williams. "I know your daddy's down now with his broken leg, but I hope he's getting along all right."

"Thank you, ma'am. He's doing pretty well. And, Mr. Williams, thanks for helping my dad out on the farm while he's laid up."

"And you can thank Athena, too," said Mr. Williams. "She was a big help to your ma."

"Yes, thank you, too, Mrs. Williams. You know, Mrs. Williams," I continued, "there's something I've always wondered about. I hope you don't think me too personal, but I've always been curious about your name. I mean, I like it, but I don't think I know of another person named Athena. Except the Greek goddess, of course."

"You'd like to know how I got it?"

"Yes, ma'am, if you'd care to tell me."

"Athena is a family name, a family *trait*, actually. I've been told the name means 'gray-eyed.' I don't know if you've ever noticed, but I do have gray eyes."

I looked, and saw for the first time that what she said was true—her eyes *were* gray. Funny, I had never noticed that before.

"Anyway," she continued, "like I said, it's a family trait. Women in my family have had gray eyes for at least since my ancestors came over here to America from England over one hundred and fifty years ago."

I looked at Sara Jane's eyes. No, hers were blue, a beautiful azure blue.

"But it doesn't happen to every generation," Mrs. Williams continued, noticing my look of confusion. "Just every *other* generation. For some reason, it skips those in between."

"So," I said, "your mother doesn't have gray eyes, but your grandmother did?"

"That's right. And it's so predictable my momma knew what she would name me even before I was born, and she knew for sure my eyes would be gray. That is, if I was born a girl, which I was, of course."

"That's amazing," I said. I'd heard of family traits being inherited, but not one that skipped generations, at least not on a regular basis.

"Speaking of my momma," said Mrs. Williams, "I know Sara Jane told you she's moved in with us now, come down here from Covington. She's not doing well at all. I'll be surprised if she makes it through the summer."

"Sara Jane told me that coming out from town. I'm mighty sorry to hear it, too."

"But, come. She's heard so much about you over the years. She's looking forward to meeting you. Her eyesight is pretty much gone, but her hearing is fine, and so's her mind. Sara Jane said she told you about the fire?"

"You mean the one where your father was killed?"

"Yes, that's the one. Momma's face was burned quite badly. And even though the scars healed pretty well, they're still visible. Just so you know."

She took me by the hand and led me into the bedroom. Sara Jane followed us.

Mrs. Pickens's bedroom, unlike the others, was on the ground floor, in what used to be the music room.

As I entered the room, the aroma of lavender swept over me, a pleasurable, almost sensuous, smell.

I approached the large four-poster bed which took up most of the room, and saw Sara Jane's grandmother for the first time. In spite of the obvious scars on her face, and even at eighty-four years of age, there was still an aura of loveliness around her. Her hair was as white as the albino fox my father had found in his trap when I was just ten. I wanted to keep it, Dad wanted to kill and skin it, but my mother made us set it free.

"A beautiful creature like that needs to be free," she had said.

I had little doubt that in her younger days, Mary Pickens, like that fox, must have been stunningly beautiful. And now she was about to be set free from this life.

"Mrs. Pickens?" I said.

"Yes? Who is it?" The voice, soft and mellifluous, carried a hint of huskiness—another result of the fire, I found out later. Like the lavender, it too was sensuous.

"It's Carter McGlone. I'm a friend of Sara Jane's."

"My very *best* friend," added Sara Jane, sitting down on the side of the bed opposite from where I stood.

"Carter McGlone!" The joy in her voice was obvious. "I've waited a long time to meet you, Carter McGlone. Come, take my hand and sit here beside me." She reached out her hand and I took it in mine. Gently, she pulled me

down to the bed. Her hands were smooth and soft, and I felt
a sense of . . . something . . . what? . . . as they touched
mine.

"When I lived over in Covington, and Sara Jane wrote
me, which . . ." she held up one finger and wagged it in Sara
Jane's direction, ". . . I might add, wasn't nearly often
enough, she would always tell me about her *best* friend,
Carter McGlone. For a long time, I thought perhaps she had
made you up, because it was hard to believe anyone could
be as perfect as she made you out to be. But then, when I
moved back here after my brother died, even Athena sang
your praises, so I decided you must be real. And here we
are; at last we meet. Now, you tell me all about yourself. I
want to hear firsthand everything about you."

At first I couldn't speak. The feeling when she took my
hand in hers was too much. A great sadness filled my heart
knowing the woman who lay here before me was living out
the last year, perhaps even the last months, of her life. As
Sara Jane had said, it wasn't fair.

When I regained my composure, I said, almost in a
whisper, "What would you like to know?"

"Everything," she replied. "I want to know everything."

Over the next several hours I told her my whole life
story: my childhood, my parents, my relationship with Sara
Jane, my time in Europe during the war, becoming a
teacher, then changing to the law. I told her about Louisville
and my first six months of law school. She had been to
Louisville once, she told me—a beautiful city, she thought,
but a little too crowded for her taste. She much preferred
Cincinnati. I told her about Churchill Downs, and how my
roommate and I liked to go there to watch the horses run.
She loved horses, she said, used to have several. Not
thoroughbreds—farm horses.

"No girlfriend?" she asked, smiling.

I chuckled. "I've never found a girl that compared to your granddaughter," I answered, glancing at Sara Jane. "She's the standard I judge all the rest of them by."

"And Sara Jane . . . ?" said Mary.

"Grandma," said Sara Jane, "Carter and I went through this last night with his momma. He and I are best friends. We're like brother and sister."

"She's right," I said. "Sometimes I wish that spark *was* there between us. Life would be so much simpler."

"I shall continue to pray for both of you," said Mary, now almost whispering, "that you will each find the right person for yourself. I know I did—once—a long time ago.

"I think I must rest now." Her voice became even softer. "But Carter, you will come back to see me again?"

"I will," I answered.

As I bent down to kiss her forehead, the medal fell out of my shirt, and hung dangling from around my neck.

"What's this?" asked Mary, taking it in her hands. Her voice became excited as she held the medal up as close to her face as possible in an attempt to better see it. "Where did you get this?"

The force of her question startled me. "Why, I found it," I answered.

"How? Where?" She became agitated.

I started to tell her about the skeleton, but Sara Jane interrupted me.

"Carter found it one day when we was out hunting mushrooms as kids, Grandma," she said, shaking her head slightly from side to side at me. "Just laying there on the ground."

"*Where* did you find it?" Mary persisted.

"Out in the darkies' cemetery," answered Sara Jane. "Why is it so important?"

"Never mind," answered Mary, as she sank back into the bed. "It's nothing."

She loosened her grip on the medal, and I started to straighten up. But she grabbed me by the shoulder and pulled me even closer to her than before. Her strength surprised me. She looked into my eyes and squinted, studying my face.

Then she let me go.

"I'm tired now. I think I do need to rest," she said. Then she looked at me again. "Carter McGlone, you take good care of that medal."

Once outside the room, I turned to Mrs. Williams. "Did I do something? Say something?"

"I don't think so," she replied. "And if you did, I surely don't know what."

"Me neither," said Sara Jane.

"Why did you stop me when I started to explain about how I found the medal?" I asked.

"I was afraid she might get upset, to hear about the skeleton and all."

"I suppose you're right," I said. "I wasn't thinking. I'm going to head on home. I'll see you tomorrow."

As I walked home, I wondered what it was about the medal that had so upset Sara Jane's grandmother. But the thought that occupied my mind even more was the feeling I had about her, that there existed some sort of bond between us, a *link* I didn't understand. Why did I sense it so strongly? Where did it come from?

And she was dying.

In spite of my promise to come back, I wondered if I would ever see Mary Pickens again before she died.

∞

"So, how are things back home? And how's your dad?"

I was grateful Sam had come to pick me up at the train depot, and I wouldn't have to walk the mile and a half to the apartment, carrying my suitcase as well as the box of food my mother sent back with me. 'Just in case,' she'd said.

"Fine," I answered. "And Dad's good. Champing at the bit to get out of bed and back to work. How's everything here?"

"Great," said Sam. "Some interesting cases came up in court while you were gone. I'll bring you up to date on them later. Is something wrong? You look like you're in another world."

I hesitated, not sure if I should tell Sam about Mary. And what, exactly, would I tell him?

"Something strange happened while I was home," I said, finally.

"What?"

I recounted how I'd felt when I first met Mary, her reaction to my medal, and my sense of sadness that she was dying, and I might never see her again.

"Wow," said Sam when I finished. "You're right—that *is* strange. And you're sure you've never met her before?"

"Positive."

"Come on. Let's go back to the apartment and get you unpacked. Then we're going down to O'Neal's. I'm going to get you drunk—*very drunk.*"

Chapter Fourteen

Sam Meets Sara Jane

1924

"So, this is Cynthiana."

Sam and I had been hitting the books solidly for the past month, studying for a series of important tests. Now that the exams were over, we decided to get out of town for a few days.

Even though we'd known each other as roommates for the past year, this was the first time Sam had been able to make it to Harrison County for a visit. We'd packed some clothes, jumped into the Duesenberg, and taken off.

Sam was letting me drive, since I knew the way.

"Yep, this is Cynthiana," I said. "Where I was born and grew up. A little northeast of here, actually. Here, I'm going to swing around the courthouse and show you something."

I turned left onto Pike Street and then right behind the courthouse onto Court Street.

"See that log house on your left," I said, pointing out a two-story building. "That's the oldest building in Cynthiana, over a hundred and twenty five years old. Henry Clay used to have his law office there. It's one of the buildings that didn't burn down."

"Burn down?"

"During the Civil War. There were two battles fought here in town, one in 1862, and the other in 1864. In the second one, almost the whole downtown went up in flames."

"Did you have any family in the war?" asked Sam.

"Three. My great-uncle Rufus, my grandfather, and their father, my great-grandfather, Owen. My great-uncle and my grandfather came through it alive, but old Owen just disappeared. Never was heard from again."

"I like your town," said Sam. "Reminds me of home. Any place to go for a drink?"

I shook my head. "I wouldn't know where." Since prohibition, no establishment in town sold liquor—at least, not legally.

"This is your town, isn't it? I'd think you'd know a place to get a drink in your home town—something stronger than soda pop."

"Sorry, I don't. As you know, I'm not much of a drinking man—except when you take me to O'Neal's."

Sam chuckled.

"Maybe when we get home, my dad'll know of someplace," I said, although I doubted it. To my knowledge, my father had never touched a drop of alcohol in his life.

"So, you're Sam. We've heard so much about you. I can't believe we've never had a chance to meet until now."

My mother was the quintessential hostess. No one remained a stranger in her home for long. A staunch Methodist and an avid reader of the Bible, her sense of hospitality mirrored that of people of the Middle East in biblical times: you offered the visitor whatever you had.

"Come in, come in," she said. "I'm so happy you were able to come."

"Hi, Mom." I had begun to think my mother forgot that I, too, had made the trip.

She turned and embraced me. "You, too, Carter," she said. "I'm glad *you* could come, too."

"Where's Dad?"

"Out at the barn. Why don't you show Sam to his room, and I'll go get your father."

∞

"This is a nice house," Sam said, as he unpacked his bag.

"I suppose it's not nearly as big as yours," I replied, thinking of the Duesenberg.

He glared at me. "It's not my *parents* who are rich," he said. "It's my aunt. Truth is, your house is probably a little bigger than ours."

"I'm sorry. I only—"

"It's okay," said Sam. "After nine months of living with you I know how thickheaded and insensitive you can be."

I grinned, and gave him a playful punch on the shoulder. "Come on. Let's go see if Dad's come in yet."

My mother called to me from downstairs. "Carter, Sara Jane called to see if you were home. She said she's coming over in a bit."

"So at last I get to meet Sara Jane," said Sam. "I'm anxious to find out if she's as good looking as that picture you have of her."

"That picture's over two years old," I said. "She's even better looking now."

∞

"You were right," said Sam, later that evening.

"About what?"

"About Sara Jane. She is prettier now than her picture."

"I told you so."

"Do you think she liked me?"

"What do you mean, *liked you*?"

"You know, thought I was good looking?"

"Confidentially, she told me she thought you looked a lot like John Barrymore."

"She didn't!"

"You're right, she didn't."

"Damn you, Carter, quit teasing me!"

"*I* don't know if she thought you were good-looking or not. Why don't you ask her yourself? We're going on a picnic with her tomorrow."

"We are?"

"I want to show you where we found the skeleton and the medal when we were kids."

"Good! I've always wondered if you made that story up. What time?"

"The picnic?"

"Yeah."

"After church. Mom's fixing us a lunch, and we'll meet Sara Jane at the old sycamore tree."

∞

She was waiting for us when we arrived. She'd placed some fresh flowers on the grave.

"Hey, Carter. Hey, Sam. Ain't this a beautiful day? I love springtime. What did your momma fix us for lunch? I brung us some cold lemonade."

"Fried chicken," I answered, "cole slaw, potato salad, and cold biscuits."

"So," said Sam, "I assume this is the grave of the famous skeleton you two found?"

"Yep," I said. Then, I pointed to the sycamore. "And there're the initials carved in the tree."

"Those are my initials," said Sam.

I looked. He was right. It had been so long since I'd paid any attention to the letters I had forgotten that one set read "S. J."

"I doubt it's you, though," said Sara Jane. "Unless you was around here in 1863."

"No, I don't think so," replied Sam, laughing.

"Okay, then, let's eat!" I said. "I'm starved."

As we ate, I noticed Sam casting sideway glances at Sara Jane. It was obvious he was smitten by her.

"Sara Jane, Carter tells me you work at one of the stores in town?"

"Yes. I clerk at Mr. Henley's dry goods store."

"Do you enjoy it?"

"Oh, it's okay. I don't reckon I'll do it my whole life, though."

"That's right," I interrupted. "Sara Jane told me one time her goal in life was to marry a rich man, and have lots of kids."

"Heck, he don't even have to be all that rich," said Sara Jane. "Just enough so's *I* don't have to work."

We all laughed.

"Any prospects?" asked Sam.

"Not yet," she answered, flashing him her most beguiling smile. "But I'm a lookin'."

Sam smiled back.

"I'm going over to Sara Jane's house when we're done here," I said, "so I can pop in and say hi to her grandmother.

You want to come along and meet her, or head back to the house?"

"I think I'll go on back to the house," replied Sam. "I don't do too well with sick people."

"Maybe Sara Jane could go with you, so you don't get lost," I offered.

Sara Jane blushed. "Sure, I'd be happy to."

"I enjoyed this weekend."

Sam and I were on our way back to Louisville, to the grind of classes the next morning.

"Yeah, me too," I replied. "I'm glad you came. So, did you find out if Sara Jane thought you were good-looking or not?"

"I don't know. Maybe. But the next time I visit," he said, a grin on his face, "I'll be a little more direct and find out for sure. Hey, listen, Carter, I've got a question."

"A question?"

"You and Sara Jane aren't, like . . . cousins, are you?"

"Cousins? No. What makes you think that?"

"I thought I saw a bit of a family resemblance between the two of you. I've got sort of a knack for spotting stuff like that."

"A resemblance?"

"It was the eyes, I think. You both have the same eyes."

"I've never noticed," I said.

"But I'm not always right," said Sam. "I just wondered."

Sam pulled the car over to the side of the road and turned off the engine.

"Why are we stopping?" I asked.

He pointed to a bed of flowers, about twenty feet in diameter, some thirty yards off the road. A marker on a post stood off to the side.

"I saw that on the way in and wondered what it was. Do you know?"

"Sure. Come on, we'll walk over and you can read it."

When we got to the marker, Sam read it out loud:

> *Site of*
> *Statehood Day Disaster*
> *May 31st, 1863*
> *Twelve friends and neighbors*
> *met their maker on this day*

"What kind of disaster?" Sam asked.

"People were celebrating Statehood Day, the day Kentucky became a state. There was a baseball game going on. All of a sudden, a storm came and a bunch of people took cover under the old oak tree that stood here. Lightning hit the tree and everybody under it was killed except for two people."

"Wow! So was the tree destroyed?"

"Not then. But the next day it was cut down and the lumber used to make the caskets for the people who were killed. Then they dug out the stump, filled the hole in and planted flowers. They've bloomed here every year since then."

"Do they still celebrate Statehood Day?"

"Nope, that was the last time. At least around here."

"So Kentucky became a state on May thirty-first?"

"No," I said, "actually it was June first."

"Okay, now I'm confused," said Sam. "Why were they celebrating it a day early?"

I shrugged. "Good question. And I have no idea. As a kid, I always wished I lived back then so I could fight in the war— the one between the states."

"And now?" asked Sam.

I chuckled. "I got my war over in Europe."

"You know the old saying . . ."

"Be careful what you wish for . . ."

". . . because it just might come true," Sam finished.

"Well, I can tell you, I no longer have any desire at all to go back in time," I said. "I'm satisfied to be right where I am."

Chapter Fifteen

An Odd Encounter

1924

Come on, Little Betty! COME ON, LITTLE BETTY!

I was glad Sam had talked me into coming to the track. It was a glorious day and we were at Churchill Downs. We'd both gussied up for the day. Sam had chosen an outfit from among the five in his closet, a three piece black and red pinstripe suit.

"Don't you think that's a little much for the track?" I asked.

"This is the kind of outfit we'll be wearing every day when we're practicing attorneys," he replied. "What are you wearing?"

"What else?" I answered. "I've only got the one outfit."

"Your blazer? You must have gotten that rag when you were in high school. Why don't you borrow one of my outfits?"

I smiled. "No, thanks. I think I'll stick to something a little more conservative."

Sam reached into his closet and pulled out a straw hat.

"You're wearing a skimmer with that outfit?" I asked, shaking my head.

"It's my lucky hat."

∞

I was happy I'd grabbed my cap on the way out of the apartment. It was hot in the grandstand with the sun beating down on us. I found myself shouting along with all the other people crowding around us, urging Little Betty on. Of course, I hadn't bet any money on the race. I didn't have any to spare. But Sam managed to come up with seven dollars, and had placed six of it on the nose of a twenty-to-one long shot, Little Betty, for no other reason than his current girlfriend, who had accompanied us, was named Betty.

As the horses came down the stretch, Little Betty, a small gray mare, lay in third place, a half length behind two other horses running neck and neck. As they neared the finish line, she began to gain on the front runners. Sam said something to me but I couldn't hear him over the roar of the crowd. He and Betty jumped up and down with excitement. He had taken off his skimmer and was slapping it against his leg, urging his horse on. I was surprised to find myself jumping up and down as well.

At the last moment, Little Betty put on a burst of speed and, to the three of us, as well as others around, appeared to lunge across the finish line, barely edging out the other two horses.

Betty and Sam hugged and kissed. Then Betty and I hugged, and I even got a kiss. Then Sam and I hugged—no kiss. Our celebration was interrupted by the public address announcer's voice.

"Ladies and Gentlemen. The results of the race are under review by the placing judges. Please hold all tickets. Final results will be posted as soon as the judges have a chance to make their determination of the winner."

A groan erupted from Little Betty's fans, including the three of us. The backers of the other two horses cheered and whistled. Some of them scurried around searching for the tickets they had just discarded, realizing there was a chance they might be winners after all.

Betty sat down and fanned herself with her program. Sam and I stood, our eyes fixed on the huge tote board located in the infield, waiting for the final results to be posted.

After many long anxious minutes, the official results went up. In first place—number seven—Little Betty! Sam pulled Betty up out of her chair, and the three of us went through another round of hugs and kisses. Then the payoff was posted: $42.40. Sam's six dollar ticket was worth $127.20.

"I'm rich!" Sam shouted. He threw his arms around Betty's waist and picked her up. "*We're* rich!" he cried out, giving her a big kiss. "Come on, Carter, come to the window with me. I may need a bodyguard! Betty, Honey, we'll be back in a few minutes. You want anything?"

"I'd love a beer," Betty replied, grinning. Prohibition might be the law of the land, but she still couldn't understand the big deal about having a drink now and then.

Sam returned her grin. "Yeah, so would I," he said. "Maybe later at O'Neal's. How about a soda pop for now?"

"Oh, okay," said Betty, a note of resignation in her voice.

Sam and I hurried through the exit doors to the betting windows which lined the wall in the cavernous area below the grandstand.

"Carter, here's a dollar. How about you getting our drinks while I get in line?"

"Okay," I said. I took the money and headed for the concession stand. "What do you want to drink?" I shouted.

"Sarsaparilla," Sam shouted back over his shoulder as he headed for one of the windows.

While I waited for the young woman behind the counter to pour our drinks, I looked around, soaking up the atmosphere: people hurrying from here to there, those standing in small groups replaying the just-completed race. I reveled in the ambiance of the building itself, the history, the mystique of the track. I loved all of it, I realized. And the best part was, I didn't even have to gamble to have a good time. Just watching the horses run, watching the bettors living and dying as their horses won or lost—that was what stimulated me. I especially enjoyed the paddock area where the horses were brought before each race, watching as they paraded by on their way to the track. I couldn't believe the size of some of them, and how small the jockeys were who rode them.

"Thirty cents, mister."

I turned around. The woman had placed the three drinks on the counter and was holding out her hand. I handed her the dollar Sam had given me.

She turned, got some change, and held it out to me. I took it, then took two dimes, and gave them back to her.

"Here, this is for you," I said. Heck, Sam just struck it rich. Why not a nice tip?

"Gee, thanks, mister." The woman smiled at me, then turned to the next customer.

I looked over to see Sam counting the small fortune he had won. At the same time I noticed a slightly-built, well-dressed, elderly man leaning against a side wall. He seemed to be staring at me. As I walked by, I was surprised to discover it wasn't a man after all, but a woman in men's clothing. I thought she was about to speak to me, but she just watched as I passed her. I continued on to where Sam was waiting for me, putting his winnings away in his billfold.

"Sam, can you take—"

I was interrupted by the woman, who had now come up behind me.

"Excuse me, sir, I'm sorry to bother you, but would you by any chance be Sam Jenkins's grandson?"

I turned around. Whoever she was, apparently it was Sam she was interested in.

"I *am* Sam Jenkins," replied Sam, stepping to my side.

"Oh, no, sir, I'm sorry," said the woman, looking at Sam. "I was asking the other gentleman here." She looked back at me.

"*Me?*" I said. I looked at Sam. "What makes you think I'm *his* grandson?"

"Oh, no, sir, not *his* grandson. I meant another Sam Jenkins I knew once, over in Harrison County, during the war—the Civil War. You see, you're the spitting image of him, so I figured you must be his grandson."

"You knew a Sam Jenkins during the Civil War?" asked Sam.

"That I did, sir. Perhaps, maybe *knew* him's a little much. We met briefly during the fighting there in Cynthiana in '64. Saved my life, he did. I was but twelve at the time, but I'll never forget him. Never forget his face, neither." Again she looked directly at me. "And, like I said, you're the spitting image of him. In fact, as I recall, he had a limp, like I noticed you do."

"I'm sorry," I said, "but my name's McGlone. I never had any ancestors named Jenkins. And after knowing this guy here," I grinned and looked at Sam, "I'd say I'm lucky not to."

Sam grimaced, and gave my shoulder a light tap, causing soda to slosh over the cup I was holding and spill.

"Oh, sorry," said Sam.

"Me, too," said the woman. "Sorry I bothered you two young gentlemen." She turned and began to walk away.

"What's your name?" Sam asked.

The woman stopped, and turned back. "Wilhemina. Wilhemina Overman. My friends call me Willie."

"Sorry Carter here's not your man," said Sam. "Hope you have a good day at the track." Then, turning to me, "We'd better get back to Betty. It won't be long 'til the next race starts. I want to get another bet down. I feel real lucky today.

"That was strange, wasn't it?" said Sam, as we walked back to our seats. "That you look like somebody who lived over sixty years ago with the same name as me. Hey, isn't Harrison County where we were?"

"Yes, Harrison County is where Cynthiana is," I said.
I thought the whole incident pretty odd, too.

"Hey, you know the initials on the tree?" said Sam. "Maybe they belonged to the Sam Jenkins that lady knew; 1863 would've been at the time of the Civil War."

"Maybe," I said.

"Where have you two *been*?" asked Betty, exasperation in her voice. "I've had to go to the ladies' room so bad I almost peed my pants. I didn't want to leave, in case somebody might take our seats."

"Sorry, Honey," said Sam. "You go ahead and go, and I'll tell you all about it when you get back."

Sam's luck held out the rest of the day, as he cashed winning tickets in three of the last six races. But my mind was still on our encounter with the old woman, and her thinking I was the grandson of a man with the same name as

Sam. I couldn't help but wonder if it was all merely a coincidence—or possibly something more.

Mary Pickens fooled everyone. She didn't die that year. In fact, following my visit, her health began to steadily improve. She was still bedfast—and always would be—and her sight continued to deteriorate, until the time came when she couldn't see at all. Otherwise, she seemed fine.

Over the next several years, whenever I came home to visit, I always made it a point to see her. We'd talk for hours, I about my life and school and, later, the law practice Sam and I had set up; she about her years in Covington. However, she never seemed to want to talk about her early life, the time before she left Harrison County. I sensed that, for some reason, the memories were too painful to relive. Accordingly, I never pressed her about it.

Chapter Sixteen

Home for Thanksgiving

1925

Thanksgiving was always my favorite holiday of the whole year. When I was a child, my father would hitch up the carriage early in the morning, Mom would load it with all the scrumptious food she had spent the previous two days preparing, and we would head out for my Grandmother McGlone's farm. My grandfather, Feargus McGlone, had died in 1896, three years before I was born. Grandma McGlone lived well into her seventies. All the McGlone clan, including Great-uncle Rufus's children and grandchildren, converged on Grandma McGlone's house for a day of feasting, storytelling, and socializing. But the part I liked best was when all the men and we older boys went out into the woods or fields hunting. We never failed to bring back a good number of rabbits, pheasants, and quail, which would later be prepared and placed in my grandmother's storehouse to see her through the coming winter. As I got older, I acquired a reputation as quite a marksman, a talent that proved itself very handy in the war.

This year, I had come home once more to celebrate Thanksgiving with my family. We no longer gathered at Grandma McGlone's, as she had passed away two years earlier. Nor did the whole clan even bother to gather together in one place anymore. It wouldn't have been the same. Each family now celebrated the holiday by themselves, or perhaps with a few other family members or neighbors who dropped by. Still, for me, it was the best holiday, if for no other reason than the memories it evoked.

But there was more to it than that. If spring was my favorite season, fall was a close second. To watch the leaves change colors from the various shades of summer green to violent splashes of reds and yellows and orange; to feel the crispness in the air, a portent of the winter which would be upon us all too soon; to know that, just as the seasons change, so, too, does life. I was no longer the little boy who hunted mushrooms in the spring; who swam in the pond in the summer; who hunted with his father in the fall; and who, on crisp, snowy, winter days stood outside with his face tilted upwards to the heavens, mouth open, tongue out, waiting for a falling snowflake.

I was now twenty-six years old. Sam and I had completed our time at law school, and opened our own practice in Louisville. Life had been good up to now. The future looked even brighter. But still, something was missing—and I knew what it was. There was no one with whom I could share all of this, a fact brought home to me this year even more sharply than in the past.

In September, Sara Jane had met the man 'with whom she was sure she would spend the rest of her life,' as she put it in her letter to me. Sam was crushed by the news, regretful he had missed his chance.

No, Sara Jane admitted, her heart hadn't done "flip-flops" when they first met. And, no, he wasn't all that rich, although his family was somewhat well off. But he was a good man, a hard worker, 'not too bad looking for a farmer,' she had added, and he loved her with all his heart. And she loved him. And that was good enough for her, she reasoned. As I read her letter, I realized—somewhat surprised—I was jealous. Not because someone else was marrying Sara Jane, but because she and her fiancé, Malcolm Richardson, had found what I, it seemed, could not: someone to love, and be loved by—someone to share my life with.

I wondered if my turn at love would ever come.

Chapter Seventeen

Kiernan O'Doherty . . . Again

1926

By the spring of 1926, business in the law firm of Jenkins and McGlone—Sam had agreed to drop the "Associates" at my urging—,though still barely enough to pay the bills, had improved to the point where we weren't able to keep up with the paperwork. We'd moved to a new location, one which afforded each of us our own private office, plus a reception area; and we had hired a young black woman, Esther Jones, a graduate of Oberlin College in Ohio, as a secretary and receptionist.

Sam balked at first about hiring a Negro, as most positions such as the one we looked to fill were strictly the province of white women. However, I convinced him Esther was far and away the best qualified applicant we'd interviewed. In fact, she was overqualified for the job, but other than teaching in the Negro schools, suitable positions for college-educated black women in Louisville were few and far between.

One result of having Esther as our secretary was that we began to get a lot of Negro clients. Her father, the Reverend Mordecai Jones, was the pastor of a large Negro church on the west side, and I suspected Esther had urged him— *pressured* might be too strong a word—to refer to us many of his parishioners, as well as others in the community.

Whether it was a blessing or not I'm not sure, because it soon became apparent that many prospective white clients would *not* hire us. But Sam and I decided, "What the hell—that was their loss." And so we built up a large Negro clientele—most of whom couldn't afford to pay us much.

I still wasn't sure why I had allowed Sam to talk me into having lunch at the Radford Hotel, as expensive as the place was. "We're celebrating," said Sam. "We can afford a luxury or two."

We had received the signed contract that morning from one of the city's largest Negro-owned life insurance companies, putting us on a retainer to handle a significant portion of the firm's legal work. It would mean a substantial increase in what, up to now, had been a very limited cash flow.

"Yeah, well I'd still like to have the cash in hand before we go out and spend it," I said.

"Oh, Carter, you're too . . . too frugal!"

"Too *frugal*?"

"I didn't want to come right out and call you 'cheap,' so frugal seemed the next best thing. Live it up a little, relax. Enjoy life. Bet on a horse the next time we go to the track!"

"Maybe you're right," I said. I had been frugal. But it had been out of necessity. Going through school had been an expensive proposition. Then, setting up the office, purchasing furniture and equipment, advertising, even hiring Esther. And the cases we had taken, mostly Negro clients, hadn't exactly been profitable.

But now—now, with this contract, and a pretty much guaranteed income well . . . maybe I *could* loosen up a bit, enjoy life a little more.

"I'm having the duck," I announced. "With polenta."

"Whoa!" exclaimed Sam. "I said live it up a little. I didn't say go hog wild!"

"Do you know I have never had duck in my whole life? And I've always wanted to. We have ducks on our pond back home, but my mom never let us eat them. 'They were too much like pets,' she said. So this is my chance. I'm going to have the Roast Duck *Bigarade.*"

"Hell, then," said Sam. "I'm going to have the Tripe a la Mode de Caen."

"What's *that*?"

"As I recall," said Sam, "the stomach of a cow."

I made a sour face. "I'm sorry but . . . that sounds *terrible.*"

"I understand it's quite delicious," replied Sam. "Besides, I didn't say anything about your duck, did I?"

"Yes, but you know, there's a big difference between a cow's stomach and a duck."

"Nevertheless, that's what I'm having," declared Sam.

"How was the duck?"

"Excellent!" I answered. "I'll have to tell my mother what she's been missing all these years. How about the tripe?"

This time it was Sam's face that looked sour. "Next time I'll stick to the outside of the cow," he said, pushing his half-eaten meal away. "Like a big juicy steak."

As we rose to leave, a disturbance a few tables away caught our attention. I turned to see a short man, his back to us, on his feet, castigating one of the Negro waiters, who towered over him by a good six or seven inches.

"You stupid-ass nigger! When I order soup here, I expect it to be hot!"

"I'm sorry, sir," said the waiter. "You ordered vichyssoise, which is normally served cold. We can, of course, bring you a bowl of hot soup if you'd prefer."

"Fishy-shwa shit!" shouted the man. "It's goddamn potato soup! Whoever heard of cold potato soup!"

"Yes, sir, I—"

"Don't interrupt me, nigger! And don't try to give me that shit about 'cold' soup! You were too damn lazy to get it out here when it was hot, and now you're trying to finagle your way out of it."

"Sir, I'd be happy to have the chef come out—"

"I don't need no goddamn *chef*!" the man exploded. "Probably a stupid-ass nigger like yourself. Don't know shit from apple butter. By God, boy, I'll teach you to sass me!"

The man raised the cane he'd been carrying in his left hand as if to strike the waiter, but before he brought it down I grabbed his arm and spun him around.

And saw the face of Kiernan O'Doherty!

"You!" he exclaimed.

The shock of seeing him again caused me to recoil, as I let go of his arm. He thrust his hand into the inside pocket of his coat, pulled out a small derringer, and aimed it directly at me. "You son of a bitch!" he cried. His eyes—small, dark holes—held the same look of hatred and anger I had seen that day in Mr. Clary's store.

I had no doubt he intended to shoot me then and there, but before he could pull the trigger, the manager, alerted by the fracas, arrived on the scene. He grabbed Kiernan's arm and shoved it upwards, causing the gun to go off. I heard the *thwock* as the bullet hit the ceiling above us, sending small bits of plaster raining down. The waiter grabbed O'Doherty from behind in a bear hug and Sam reached up and carefully removed the gun from O'Doherty's hand.

"I'm not calling the police," said the manager, twisting Kiernan's arm behind his back as he escorted him toward the door, "because I don't want any bad publicity. But don't ever let me catch you in my restaurant again."

As O'Doherty was hustled past me, he turned his head and, before I knew what happened, spit in my face. "The next time we meet," he hissed, "I'll kill you."

"Do you know that man?" asked Sam, as we watched them leave.

"I met him once before," I said, wiping my face with my handkerchief.

"You better hope you never meet him again," said Sam.

I didn't tell Sam Mr. Clary had said pretty much the same thing to me the first time I'd met O'Doherty. I'd had a feeling then he was wrong. I had that same feeling now.

Chapter Eighteen

Emmaline Jones

1926

"Mr. McGlone?"

I looked up to see an attractive, young, black woman standing in the doorway. She looked familiar, but I couldn't quite place her.

"Yes, may I help you?"

"Yes, sir, I'm Emmaline Jones. I'm looking for my sister—Esther?"

Esther's sister! Now I knew why she looked familiar. "I'm sorry, Esther had to run over to the courthouse to check on some records for me. I don't expect her back for, oh . . ." I glanced at the clock on the wall, ". . . probably another hour. Was she expecting you?"

"No, I just got into town on the bus. I thought I'd stop by and surprise her before I went home."

"I see. You're home from college?"

"Yes, sir. I graduated last week from Oberlin College."

"Oberlin. That's where Esther attended, isn't it?"

"Yes, sir, she graduated last year."

"It's nice to meet you. I've heard a lot about you from Esther."

"Thank you, sir. I've heard a lot about you, too, from Esther."

"I hope most of it was good."

She laughed. I liked her laugh—spontaneous and genuine.

"Oh, it was *all* good, Mr. McGlone. And I can see now Esther didn't exaggerate when she wrote me how nice you were. Although she did fail to mention how handsome, too."

Now it was my turn to laugh. "Look, it's almost lunch time. Since Esther won't be back for a while, can I buy you lunch? Then by the time we get back, she should have returned."

"I'd like that. It was a long ride to Cincinnati, with just a quick stopover there, and then nonstop here, so I haven't had a bite to eat since early this morning."

"Great. We could go to . . ." I stopped, realizing the places I frequented for lunch would not serve a Negro.

She seemed to sense my dilemma. "I have an idea," she said. "Why don't we go to Mr. B's? It's a short walk from here." She grinned. "And he doesn't care what color his customers are, even the white ones, as long as their money is green."

"Okay," I replied, hesitantly. I'd never been to Mr. B's. Never even heard of it, for that matter, but I assumed it to be an establishment that mostly Negroes frequented. If Emmaline thought it okay for me to be there, I was game.

"How's the meat loaf?"

"Great!" I answered honestly. After getting over the shock of walking into an establishment in which I was the only white person present, I soon felt at home. Emmaline introduced me not only to the waitress, a friend of hers from high school, but to about a dozen customers, all of whom she also knew. Several of them appeared to know me, or had at least heard of me and or Sam. It seemed our reputations as white lawyers sympathetic to the cause of the Negro were well known throughout the West End.

One man had even been a client of mine. I'd helped him settle a housing dispute when he moved into a previously all-white neighborhood and been threatened, not only physically, but with a lawsuit. I was almost embarrassed at how expressive he'd been in appreciation of what I had done for him.

Finally we'd been seated, and had ordered and received our lunch, and I was enjoying perhaps the most savory meat loaf I had ever eaten. No disrespect to my mother, or to Mrs. Williams, but something about this dish surpassed even their culinary accomplishments.

"Absolutely delicious," I said again. "You should try some. I doubt that tiny salad will hold you until supper."

"My momma tells me I have to watch what I eat, so I don't lose what she calls my 'girlish figure.' She says a man doesn't like a woman who's too fat. If you ask me, I'd think a man would prefer a woman who has a few pounds on her. It would be an indication to him that she's a good cook." She smiled, revealing a set of perfectly beautiful, white teeth that contrasted becomingly with the darkness of her skin. "Besides, I know Momma's going to have a big meal for supper tonight."

I had been all too cognizant of her figure from the moment I'd seen her standing in the doorway. Although calling it "girlish" did not nearly do it justice.

I'd always considered Esther attractive. She had a pretty face, was well-groomed, and her figure was nothing to be ashamed of. Her skin was a beautiful mahogany color, like Emmaline's. But I never thought of her as desirable, nor did I ever think of asking her out, not just because she was our employee and a Negro, but because I didn't think of her in that way.

Emmaline was different. There was something about her that attracted, even excited, me. It wasn't only that she was beautiful—though, certainly, she was. It was her attitude as well that captivated me. There was a sense of independence about her, and it was apparent she possessed a tremendous amount of self-confidence.

I knew I wanted to see her again—and realized how improbable, if not impossible, that would be. I was white. She was a Negro. That sort of thing didn't happen in Louisville. At least, not as far as I was aware.

"You're awfully quiet," she said.

"Sorry. I was just thinking."

"About?"

"Nothing important, some casework," I lied. I took my watch from my vest pocket, popped open the lid, and checked the time. "I imagine Esther's back by now. Are you ready to go? Did you get filled up on your salad?"

"No, I didn't get filled up, but I guess it will do until I get home. Yes, I'm ready to go."

I called the waitress over to the table.

"We're ready for our bill," I said.

"On the house," she replied.

"Excuse me?"

"Mr. Bartholomew—he's the owner—," said the waitress, indicating with a turn of her head a large man standing behind the counter, "he said it's on the house. No charge. He also said any time you want a good meal, stop back in—with or without your girlfriend." She gave me a big grin. "Okay, he didn't say that last part—I did."

"Oh, she's not my girl—"

Emmaline didn't let me finish. "Wendy, honey, you tell Mr. B thanks for us. And the food was delicious. And I'm *not* his girlfriend—at least not yet."

Wendy gave us another big smile. "Okay, Emmy. Y'all have a nice day now."

Once outside, I turned to Emmaline. "Why didn't I have to pay?"

"Because of who you are," Emmaline replied. "And what you've done. And what you're doing. My people appreciate that."

I was silent for a moment. Then I asked, "And the part about you not being my girlfriend, at least not yet?"

She frowned. "I'm sorry. I shouldn't have said what I said. I thought I'd give them something to talk about, something to liven up their day. Sometimes I talk before I think about what I'm going to say. It was wrong of me. I apologize."

I had to smile. "No need to apologize." It was the sort of spontaneity I found attractive in her—her lack of "*properness*," if there were such a word. "Besides," I added, "I was flattered."

She blushed. Or at least I think she did. It's hard to tell with Negroes. "Nevertheless, I shouldn't have said it."

By the time we got back to the office, Esther had returned from the courthouse. When she saw Emmaline, she jumped up from her chair, rushed to her, and hugged her.

"Did you just get in?" she asked.

"No, earlier. But you were at the courthouse, so Mr. McGlone and I went to lunch. We ate at Mr. B's."

Esther looked quizzically at her sister, and then at me. "At . . . Mr. B's?"

"Where else could we have gone?" asked Emmaline, smiling.

"I'm surprised . . . well, no matter. Here you are! How was the bus ride?"

"Long, boring, bouncing. I am *so* happy to be home."

"Listen," I said to Esther, "there's not much going on here today. Why don't you go ahead and take off, take Emmaline on home. I know she's had a long day."

"You're sure?"

"I'm sure. Now, go."

As the two women walked toward the door, I saw Emmaline whisper something to her sister. Esther shook her head, and Emmaline said something else to her. Then Esther turned to me. "By the way," she said, "we're having a welcome home party Friday night for Emmaline. Would you like to come?"

My heart raced at the thought of seeing Emmaline again. "I'd love to," I said. "What time?"

"Seven o'clock."

"I'll be there."

"You know the address?"

"It's in your personnel file."

I watched as they left, Esther in the lead. At the last moment, Emmaline turned and smiled—before Esther grabbed her arm and pulled her through the doorway.

It was enough to keep me distracted for the rest of the afternoon.

I could not have been more graciously accepted as a guest than I was by Esther and Emmaline's parents, Mordecai and Louisa. Three other daughters, Margaret and Rosemary, who were grown, along with eight-year-old

Beatrice, were there. The only children missing, it turned out, were the Joneses' two sons, Malachi and Clayton. Rosemary had brought her fiancé.

It didn't surprise me that all the Jones women—including little Beatrice—were exceedingly attractive.

Following the meal, Mrs. Jones took me by the hand and led me into the parlor.

"Mr. McGlone," she said, "I hope you found my food acceptable after having tasted real 'soul cooking.'"

Everyone laughed. It was apparent Emmaline had told them about our lunch at Mr. B's.

"I have to admit the meat loaf at Mr. B's was about the best food I've ever eaten," I said. I leaned toward her, as if speaking in confidence. "But not as good as your fried chicken."

Louisa giggled and placed her hand on my arm. "You smooth talker. You are definitely a lawyer, aren't you?"

I couldn't remember an evening when I'd had so much fun. Between the singing—mostly gospel hymns, but a few popular songs Esther and Emmaline threw in from their college days at Oberlin—and the one-woman show presented by Beatrice about Daniel in the lion's den, it was a festive time. The party was topped off with Louisa's peach cobbler, and homemade ice cream. The best part, however, was being in the same room with Emmaline. It was all I could do not to stare at her the whole evening, although I was sure I had probably done so in excess anyway. I hoped everyone was having too much fun to notice.

When I stood close to her during the singing, I couldn't help but smell the tantalizing scent of her perfume. Or perhaps it was the smell of her hair, shiny, and black, and clean. No matter. Whichever it was, I was entranced.

When the time came for me to leave, I reluctantly said my good-byes and headed for the door.

"I'll walk you to your car," said Emmaline.

"Okay," I said, relishing the thought of even a few more minutes with her.

When we reached the Duesenberg, she asked, "Is this your automobile? It's a real beauty."

"No, it's my partner's—Sam's. He's good about letting me use it when I have somewhere special to go. I don't have a car, but I'm thinking seriously of getting one."

"I think that's a grand idea," said Emmaline. "You should. I'm glad you came tonight. I . . . I was wondering—will I see you again?"

"Oh, feel free to stop in at the office anytime," I answered.

"That's not quite what I had in mind," said Emmaline, staring at the ground. "I meant, will I *see* you again."

"Oh," I said, as the meaning of her question sank in. "I . . . I . . ."

"I'm sorry," she said. "I'm afraid once again I've spoken out of turn. Sometimes I don't know when to be quiet. Please, forgive me. Good night, Mr. McGlone."

She turned to go back into the house, but before she could, I reached out and, taking her by the arm, turned her around so we faced one another.

"I'd love to see you again," I said. "I've been thinking of nothing else all evening."

She smiled. "You have?"

I nodded.

"Me, too," she said.

Then she cupped my face with her hands and, standing on tip toes, reached up and kissed me tenderly on the lips.

For a moment I was taken aback. At the same time, I was conscious of how soft and wet her lips were, and the surge of excitement that coursed through my body at their touch. I had kissed, and been kissed by, many women, but this was a feeling I had never before experienced.

"What about your parents?" I asked. "What would they think about this—about you and me?"

"You should know by now that *I'm* not too concerned with what anyone thinks about what I do," said Emmaline. "But I do understand your concern that Momma and Daddy might be opposed to it. You haven't met my brother Clayton yet, have you?"

"No, I haven't."

"And, of course, you haven't met his wife yet, either. Clayton is married to RuthAnn. You might have seen their picture in the parlor, and perhaps assumed RuthAnn to be a light-skinned Negro. She's not. She's as white as you are. They have two children, both quite beautiful, and both with very light skin. From the first day Clayton brought RuthAnn into this house, Momma and Daddy treated her like anyone else. You would have almost thought they were color blind, that's how little difference her skin meant to them. They love her like she was their own daughter. And I know from what Esther says, they think the world of you. So would they be upset if you and I see one another? What do you think?"

I grinned. "I guess not." Then I took her in my arms and gave her a kiss more passionate and less tender than the one she had given me a few moments earlier.

"I guess not, either," she laughed, when I finally let her go. "Now, I have another question for you. I'm curious. Have you ever kissed a black woman before?"

"Never."

"Was it different?" she asked, teasingly.

"Not because you're black. It *was* different, because I've never felt like this before when I kissed any woman."

"God, you've sure got all the right answers! Momma was right. You really *are* a lawyer." She brought her lips to mine once more.

As I drove home, I recalled the words to a poem by Francis Brooks I'd memorized in my English class at Berea:

> *Love's primal moments are his best,*
> *While yet a new and modest guest;*
> > *The first fleeting touch of fingertips,*
> > *The first soft pressure of the lips.*

The next day I bought myself a second-hand automobile.

Chapter Nineteen

My Dilemma

1926

Emmaline was right about her parents. They were delighted when the two of us started seeing one another. For the next two weeks, I was at her house almost every night.

Sam, though, expressed serious reservations about the whole affair.

"Carter, I don't believe you. You want to date a colored girl? Are you *sure* you know what you're doing? I mean, I'm as open minded as anyone—okay, anyone except for you, apparently—but . . . dating a *Negro*? Have you thought about how it might affect our business?"

"You know what, Sam? First of all, she's not a girl— she's a young woman. And, secondly, one thing I've learned from Emmaline is not to let what other people think dictate what I do. Personally, I don't give a damn how anyone else feels about this. I'm comfortable with it. She's comfortable with it. Her parents are more than comfortable with it. And, let's face it—as few white clients as we have, I doubt this will have any kind of serious impact on our business."

"Except, of course, some of our colored clients might not like what you're doing."

"I hadn't thought about that. But Sam was right. Prejudice worked both ways, although I had little doubt more whites would find the relationship offensive than would blacks.

"That may be the case. But I'm not going to let it stop me from seeing her."

"Okay. Let me ask you one more thing. What do *your* parents think about all this?"

I had to admit that was one hurdle I had not yet approached. I didn't want to tell them over the phone, or in a letter. I wanted them to meet Emmaline face to face when I broke the news to them. At the same time, I was apprehensive about what would happen if they reacted in a negative way. Not that I thought they would.

To complicate matters, Malcolm had asked Sara Jane to marry him; their wedding was in less than two weeks, on the Fourth of July. She had asked me to give her away, as Mr. Williams had passed away the previous winter. Should I ask Emmaline to make the trip home to Harrison County with me then, or not? It was a real quandary.

"Well?" said Sam.

"I haven't told them yet," I confessed. "I'm not sure how to."

Sam let out a sigh of exasperation. "Oh, great! You know, if this goes on for any length of time, or the two of you become serious, you're going to have to."

"I know."

"I'm glad I'm not in your shoes."

That evening, I called Sara Jane.

"Carter! Hey, how are you? How's the lawyering business? And how's Sam? And why are you calling? Something wrong? You're not chickening out on giving me away are you?"

"No, no, nothing like that." I laughed. "Yes, I'm fine, the business is going well, and Sam—well, Sam is still Sam. Listen, I called because I needed to get your advice on something."

There was absolute silence on the other end of the phone. Finally, Sara Jane spoke. "You know what Carter? I can't remember you ever, at any time since I've known you—which is all my life—ask me for advice."

"I know," I said. "I'm in a real pickle here, and I want to know what you think."

"Okay," said Sara Jane. "Fire away."

"I've met this girl—"

"You didn't get her pregnant!"

"No, not that. We haven't even slept together."

"What is it then?"

"I thought about inviting her to come along next week when I come home for your wedding."

"I think that's wonderful! So . . . what's the problem?"

The next part was the hard part. I decided to just come out with it. "She's colored. She's a Negro."

This time Sara Jane didn't answer at all. "Sara Jane, you still there?" I asked. "Did you hear what I said?"

"I heard," she replied, slowly. "I'm letting it sink in." Then, after a brief pause: "Have you told your momma and daddy?"

"No," I said. "I'm not sure how to. I don't know how they'd take it. What do you think?"

"I think they'd take it the same way I'm taking it. After they got over the initial shock, they'd be thrilled to death you've found someone you like. And you *must* like her if you're wanting to be with her, even if she's colored."

I let out my breath. "God, I'm so happy to hear you say that. Do you mean it? You wouldn't have a problem with it?

Or Mrs. Williams?"

"Not now that I think about it, I know I wouldn't. And I know momma wouldn't, either. If you like her, I know she must be a special person."

"She is," I said. "She really is. And . . . I've got to say this—she is *so* gorgeous! Wait 'til you meet her!"

"So, when do you plan to tell your momma and daddy?"

"I hoped to do that after we got there. I wanted them to meet Emmaline, to see how special she is."

"Is that her name—Emmaline?"

"Emmaline Jones. Her father's a preacher here in Louisville. One of the best. And her sister is my secretary—mine and Sam's, in our law firm."

"You think that's the best way, springing it on them like that, instead of warning them in advance?"

"I've thought about it. But, yes, I think this is the way I want to do it. One thing, though—I don't want this to create any problems for your wedding."

Sara Jane laughed. "Don't you worry. This man's been after me long enough, ain't nothin' about to stop this wedding!"

"So you think it'll be okay?"

"I *think* it'll be okay with your momma and daddy, but I don't know for sure. But I do think maybe you should call them and tell them before you come. And, I've got to be honest with you, I'm not so sure about some of the other folks around here, how they'll take it."

"I don't care about anyone else," I said. "As long as you approve, and my mom and dad do, nothing else matters."

"And you'll be bringing her to the wedding?"

I hesitated. "How do you feel about that?"

"You darn well better bring her! I sure as heck ain't going to let you drag her all the way out here from Louisville, and then leave her sitting at your house by herself while you go traipsing off to my wedding!"

I smiled. "Thanks. I hoped you'd say that." Then I remembered Malcolm. "But, how about Malcolm and his family? How will they feel?"

"He won't say nothing. He knows better. Besides, she's *my* guest, not his. *I* get to decide who my guests will be. So you ain't slept together yet, huh?"

I had to laugh again. "No, I've only known her for a few weeks. And, to be honest, with her dad being a preacher and all, I'm not sure she'd go to bed with me even if I asked her to."

"She a virgin?"

That was a question I'd asked myself. "I'd put money on it," I said.

"Good for her. Then it's settled. You and Emmaline come on over here, and we'll have one heckuva party."

"Okay. And, Sara Jane—thanks. You don't know how much better you've made me feel."

"One more thing, Carter."

"What's that?"

"Just in case—*just in case*, mind you—there's a problem with your momma and daddy about Emmaline— and I'm sure there won't be—but *just in case there is,* know it's okay for her to stay here with us."

"And you're sure your mother wouldn't mind?"

"I know she wouldn't. She thinks the world of you, you know."

"Sara Jane, you're a sweetheart."

"You got that right. And don't you ever forget it."

"Carter, are you sure about this?"

When I first asked Emmaline to go with me to Sara

Jane's wedding, she said it sounded like a wonderful idea. Then, I guess reality set in. Everyone there, or at least *almost* everyone, she realized, would be white. She'd stick out like a blackbird in a flock of white swans, she said.

When I admitted I hadn't yet told my parents she was black, she became concerned.

"What happens if we get there and they go crazy? What happens if your friends won't talk to you because I'm with you? What if—"

"First of all, my parents will love you. And, second of all, I thought you didn't care what people thought."

"I don't care all that much what they think about *me*. I *do* care what they think about *you* because of me."

"Well, I don't," I replied, with as much finality as I could muster. "And, anyway, Sara Jane would never forgive me now if I didn't bring you along."

Emmaline smiled. "She must be one good friend."

"The best."

"And the wedding's next Sunday?"

"I figured we'd drive over on Saturday and come back on Monday."

"And we'd be staying at your house?"

"Yes."

"Separate bedrooms, of course."

"Of course." Not what I'd prefer, but I knew it was the only way.

"You know," she said, becoming very serious, "this is a good time to talk about that subject."

"What subject?"

"*That* subject."

"Oh, *that* subject," I said. Now I knew what she was talking about.

"My daddy's a preacher, and I still believe and practice what I learned in church. I also honor the family I was brought up in, and the morals my momma and daddy instilled in me. So, I guess you might as well know from the start I don't believe in sleeping with a man until I'm married to him. I'm still a virgin, and I intend to remain one until my wedding night."

My immediate feeling of disappointment was quickly replaced by a sense of admiration and respect for this young woman who evidenced such strength of character.

"Fair enough," I said. "I can respect that. But we can still kiss, can't we?"

"Oh, yes!" said Emmaline, beaming. "Ain't nothin' wrong with kissing!" And with that, she flung her arms around my neck and pressed her lips to mine. I loved the taste of her, the feel of her. I kissed her back, and felt her body tremble. When she let me go, she smiled again, and in a low voice said, "But no sex."

I cupped her chin in my hand. "You never know," I said. "You might change your mind."

"You never know," she replied. "But I sure wouldn't bet on it if I were you."

Chapter Twenty

An Unwelcome Homecoming

1926

I arrived at Emmaline's home at nine o'clock Saturday morning, and fifteen minutes later we were on the road.

"You said we were going to Harrison County, didn't you?"

"Uh-huh. Why?"

"My daddy asked me last night, and when I told him I thought it was Harrison County he said that was odd, because that's where my Granddaddy Jones lived as a slave before he ran off and joined the Union Army during the Civil War."

"No kidding!"

"Yes, I thought it strange that's where we're going."

"What's your grandfather's first name?"

"Was. He's dead now. His name was Malachi. My oldest brother is named after him."

"Does your dad know whereabouts your grandfather lived?"

"Only that Granddaddy and his brother, Lucius, both had the same owner. Apparently he gave them their papers, making them free men, and then they both took off together to join the Union army. Daddy got out some old records of Granddad's. It appears that after he and his brother went up north, they joined the Eighteenth Corps. Great-uncle Lucius was killed at the battle of New Market Heights in Virginia, but Granddad came out of the war alive and settled in Cincinnati, where he met my grandma. My daddy was born there and met my mom there, and then they came to Louisville when Daddy took the church here."

"So you don't have any relatives still living in Harrison County?"

"I doubt it. Daddy said Granddad's momma died a few years before he and Lucius took off, and as far as he knows there wasn't any other family living anywhere around there."

"What was your great-grandmother's name? Do you know?"

"Daddy wasn't too sure about that. According to Granddad Jones, it was either Rose, or Rosemary. That's my sister's name, too, you know, Rosemary, the one who teaches at Central."

"So you and I sort of share the same roots," I said. I turned to her and smiled.

"Who knows," she replied, "maybe your ancestors were my ancestors' owners."

For some reason I found the idea unsettling. Then I felt ashamed for feeling that way.

"Maybe," she continued, "you and I might be related. You know how things were back in those days."

I liked that idea even less.

"So you're Emmaline. Carter was right. You *are* beautiful!" Sara Jane encircled Emmaline with her arms, and gave her a warm hug.

"It's so nice to meet you," said Emmaline. "Carter has told me so much about you. And he was right about you, too, when he said how lovely *you* were."

Sara Jane blushed. "Carter said that?" she asked, cocking her head to one side and looking at me. I grinned back at her and shrugged my shoulders. "Well, come on in," she said. "Meet my momma and my grandma. Momma! Carter and Emmaline are here!"

As Mrs. Williams entered the room, I was struck again by how attractive she was. *God, every woman in my life is good-looking*, I thought.

"Carter, it's so good to see you again. And this is Emmaline!" Mrs. Williams gave Emmaline a big smile and extended her hand, which Emmaline accepted. "I'm so happy you could come for Sara Jane's wedding," said Mrs. Williams. "And, I'm so excited!" She looked at her daughter with delight.

"Have you eaten? We were getting ready to sit down for lunch."

"We'd love to have lunch with you," I answered. "First, though, I want to go in and say hi to Mary, and introduce Emmaline to her."

The drawn shades made the room seem almost like a cave, albeit a friendly, inviting cave. The scent of lavender, now so familiar, gave it a distinctive identity. It was Mary's personality. This was her room, and the imprint of her essence filled it.

"Mary," I said softly.

"Carter! I thought I heard you out in the other room. I'm so happy you're here. I've missed you."

"And I've missed you, too. Mary, I want to introduce you to my girlfriend, Emmaline. Emmaline, this is Mrs. Pickens."

"Mary," said Mary, reaching up her hand. "Please call me Mary."

Emmaline took it, and Mary drew her closer until Emmaline sat down on the side of the bed. Mary placed her hands on either side of Emmaline's face.

"May I?"

"Of course," replied Emmaline. I'd told her Mary could no longer see.

Gently, Mary explored Emmaline's features, gliding her hands over the high cheekbones and the full lips. She lovingly caressed Emmaline's hair, feeling the silky smoothness of it.

I was suddenly conscious of the fact that the two women for whom I felt the greatest attachment in the whole world—not counting my mother and Sara Jane—were here together in the same room. Different in some ways—one white, the other black; one old, the other young—they were also much alike. Strong-willed, with minds of their own, intelligent, well-read, and educated. At least I assumed Mary to be from the time I'd spent with her. I knew Emmaline was. Both were kind, gentle, and considerate.

"Yes," murmured Mary, "you are quite lovely. Exquisite. Carter, you've done well. Do you know that you are the first lady friend Carter has ever brought to meet me? And . . . how long have we known each other, Carter?"

"Two years," I replied. "It was two years ago last month when I first met you."

"Two years," sighed Mary. "Is that all? Why does it seem so much longer?"

"Because you and I are a good match."

Mary smiled. "Yes, we are, aren't we? But I have a feeling you have found another, even better, match here. And one more your age.

"Now, I know you've been on the road for a long time, and Athena has lunch waiting for you. But I'll look forward to talking with you both again before you go back to Louisville. Emmaline, I'm so happy we had a chance to meet."

"Me, too," said Emmaline.

"We will see you before we leave," I promised.

∞

"She seems to be doing well," I said, as we sat down at the kitchen table.

"Yes, she is," replied Mrs. Williams. "And it's all because of you."

"Me?" I said, surprised.

"When Mother first came here two years ago this past spring, she came here to die. As you know, we didn't expect her to last the summer. Then you came along. And she changed. All of a sudden, she seemed to revive, and she's been like that ever since. Oh, we know she's not going to get any better, and she'll never get out of her bed, but to see the spirit she has now . . .," Mrs. Williams placed her hand on her heart and sighed. "I can't tell you how it makes me feel."

"She thrives on your visits, you know," said Sara Jane. "She gets so excited when she knows you're coming. She doesn't show you, but we can tell."

I was stunned. I knew Mary and I had a special relationship, one I couldn't completely understand, but which, I knew, affected me greatly. But I never suspected I might have this kind of effect on her. I vowed to return home more often, and to spend more time with her on each visit.

Mrs. Williams asked Emmaline about college, about her family, and about life in Louisville. "Carter used to tell us all about Louisville when he'd come home on visits from law school, but I guess he's so used to the big city now, he doesn't realize we country folk still find all of that fascinating."

"Are you all set for tomorrow?" I asked Sara Jane.

"All set for what?" she answered, trying to act innocent.

"For your *wedding*," I said. "You remember? You and Malcolm?"

"Oh, yes," answered Sara Jane, airily. "That is this weekend, isn't it? I'd almost forgotten."

We all laughed.

"Yes, I'm quite ready. Do you know what time you're supposed to be here?"

"Four o'clock," I said. Then I remembered I was to drive Sara Jane and Mrs. Williams to the church in their car. "What about Emmaline?"

"What about Emmaline?" asked Mrs. Williams.

"Will she be riding with us?" I realized I hadn't quite thought this through all the way.

"If she'd like to, she's welcome," said Sara Jane. "Or, she can ride in with your momma and daddy."

Everyone was quiet for a moment. Then Sara Jane asked, "Are you nervous about meeting Carter's parents?"

"I'd be lying if I said I wasn't," replied Emmaline. "I hope they can accept me half as graciously as you, and your mother, and your grandmother have."

"Don't worry," Mrs. Williams reassured her. "I've known Madison and Rachel for a long time. They're good people, and they're open minded. I think you'll do fine."

"How about me?" I asked. "Isn't anyone concerned about whether I'm nervous or not?"

"Oh, pshaw!" said Sara Jane. "You can take care of yourself."

"*Are* you nervous?" asked Mrs. Williams.

"A little," I confessed, looking at Emmaline, guiltily.

"This is a fine time to finally admit it!" said Emmaline, half serious.

Mrs. Williams reached out both of her hands, taking mine in one and Emmaline's in the other. "Everything's going to be fine," she said. "Trust in the Lord."

I honked the horn as we drove up the lane to the house, knowing it would bring my mother running out to greet us.

"Carter, it's about time! We were expecting—" My mother stopped short when she saw Emmaline sitting in the passenger's seat.

I got out of the car, and hugged my mother. Then I went around the car and opened the door for Emmaline.

"Mom, this is Emmaline. Emmaline, this is my mom, Rachel McGlone."

"Mrs. McGlone, it's a pleasure to meet you," Emmaline said.

I detected a trace of apprehension in her voice. She reached out her hand for my mother to take, but to the surprise of both of us, my mother embraced her, and gave her a warm and friendly hug, as Sara Jane had done earlier.

"Emmaline. So you're Carter's new girlfriend. When he wrote us a few weeks back, and told us he had met someone, he didn't tell us—"

"That I was black?" Emmaline interrupted.

"That you were so *beautiful*," said Rachel. Then, with a broad smile, she added, "And a Negro. Carter always was one for surprises."

The two women laughed. I breathed a sigh of relief.

"Where's Dad?" I asked.

"Out in the barn. We had about given up on you."

"We stopped by Sara Jane's first, so I could introduce Emmaline to them."

"And get Athena and Sara Jane's thoughts on how your father and I might react to Emmaline?" My mother knew me all too well.

"That, too," I admitted, with a grin. Then I got serious. "How about Dad? Is he going to be okay with this?"

A worried look came over my mother's face. "Carter, I have to be honest with you. I . . . I don't know. I would hope he'd be, but . . . well, I'm not sure."

I saw concern on Emmaline's face. I was sure she saw it on mine as well.

"I guess we need to find out, then," I said, taking Emmaline's hand.

"I guess so," replied my mother.

As we came around the side of the house, my father was coming up from the barn. He stopped short when he saw the three of us. Slowly, he started walking again, and when we met, grabbed me in a bear hug.

"Carter! Where've you been, boy? We expected you hours ago. We started to get worried maybe your automobile broke down, or something."

I took a deep breath. "Dad, this is Emmaline Jones. Emmaline, my dad, Madison McGlone."

"Mr. McGlone, I'm so pleased to meet you," said Emmaline. "Now I know where Carter gets his good looks."

My father looked at Emmaline, but didn't smile, or

offer his hand. For a split second his eyes narrowed, and then his gaze shifted away from us and to the barn.

"Let's go on up to the house," said my mother. "Have you eaten yet?"

I told her we ate at Sara Jane's. I also told them how Sara Jane, her mother, and Mary liked Emmaline so much.

"I can understand why," said my mother, turning to Emmaline, although it was obvious her words were more for the benefit of my father. "She seems to be a delightful person."

"I still have some work to do," said my dad brusquely, as he turned and walked back toward the barn.

Anger, mixed with disappointment, welled up in me as I watched him walk away. "Not what you'd call a warm reception," I said.

"I'm sorry about that," said my mother. "Carter, why don't you get your bags, and bring them on in the house."

I got the two suitcases from the car, carried them into the house, and deposited them in the parlor. I was still fuming over my father's rudeness.

"I need to get some fresh air," I said, turning to Emmaline. "Come with me."

For the next half hour we walked, Emmaline struggling to keep up with me. Perhaps I thought if I walked fast enough I could outdistance the anger churning inside me.

"Carter, wait," she said. "I can't keep up."

I stopped and turned. Feelings of guilt and shame, and, at the same time, affection, washed over me. I felt guilty I hadn't told my parents in advance about Emmaline, which might have prevented the scene that had just taken place; shame, because I was so wrapped up in my own hurt feelings I hadn't given much thought to how Emmaline must be feeling; and affection, as I realized with even more certainty how much she meant to me.

"I'm sorry," I said. I walked back to her, put my arms around her, and held her close. "I'm sorry."

"It's okay," she said. "It's okay."

"Come on," I said. "I want to show you something."

Another five minutes, and we were at the old sycamore tree. I showed her the grave, and recounted the story of how Sara Jane and I found the skeleton and the medal. I lifted the medal out of my shirt to show her. Then I pointed out the initials carved into the tree.

"This is fascinating," said Emmaline. "Do you suppose you'll ever find out who the skeleton was, or who S.J. or H.J. were?"

"I doubt it," I answered. "I suspect their identities will remain a secret forever."

As we walked up the road to the house, I spotted my mother on the porch. She was crying.

"What's wrong, Mom?" I asked when we reached her.

"Carter, I'm sorry. I'm sorry, Emmaline," she said, putting one arm around Emmaline's shoulders. She started crying again. "It's your father, Carter. Emmaline can't stay here, he won't allow it. I tried and tried to talk to him, but he seems set on this."

"Because she's a Negro," I said, with no attempt to hide the tone of bitterness in my voice.

My mother nodded.

"Carter, it's okay," said Emmaline. "I understand." She was crying now, too.

"By God, I don't!" I exploded. "I never took my father for a God damned racist!"

"I'm sorry," said my mother, again.

"Emmaline, you go get in the car," I said. "I'll get our bags. And I'll call Sara Jane before we leave to tell her we're coming over there for the night—someplace where we're welcome."

"Emmaline, I feel so bad," said my mother.

"I know." She put her arms around my mother. "I know."

∞

"So, things didn't go too well at home, huh?" Sara Jane had come out to meet us as we drove up to the house.

"You might say that," I said. I was still seething with anger.

"You okay?" Sara Jane asked Emmaline.

"I think so. In fact, I might be doing a little better than Carter."

"What happened?"

"My dad," I said. "He said Emmaline couldn't stay in the house."

"Gosh, that surprises me. And your momma?"

"Mom's okay about Emmaline. She's upset over my Dad's being such a horse's ass."

"Carter!" said Emmaline, reprovingly.

"Anyway, you're welcome here," said Sara Jane, hugging Emmaline.

Mrs. Williams joined us on the porch. "Come on, let's get you two settled," she said.

Chapter Twenty-One

Sara Jane's Wedding

1926

We had all been to church that morning. Emmaline and I sat with Mrs. Williams, Sara Jane, and Malcolm. My parents sat on the other side of the aisle. I purposely avoided my father and he made no effort to talk to us.

Now we were back at the Williamses'.

Today was Sara Jane's wedding day.

I knocked on her bedroom door. Finding it ajar, I peeked my head in. She sat on the bed, staring at the wall.

"How you doing?" I asked.

"Hey, Carter," she said, turning to me. "Come on in."

"So, how're you doing?"

"I'm scared out of my wits," she replied.

I smiled, went over, and sat down next to her. "Everything's going to be fine," I assured her. "You're going to have a beautiful wedding."

"Heck, I ain't scared about the wedding," she said, flopping back on the bed, her arms extended out over her head. "It's the dadgum *marriage* part I'm worried about."

Her words surprised me. "You do love him, don't you?"

"Oh, yeah, I love him. It's . . . it's . . . well, I ain't never been married before. I don't know if I can be a good wife or not. And besides, I ain't never . . . well . . . you know, *done* it before. I'm afraid I won't be no good at it."

"When you say, 'done it', do you mean . . ." I didn't finish the sentence. I knew what she meant, but I thought a little teasing might loosen her up some.

"Heck, Carter, you know darn well what I mean. I ain't never been with no man before!"

"Oh, I see," I said, suppressing a laugh.

"Darn you, you're making fun of me," said Sara Jane, as she rolled over and punched me in the stomach.

"I'm sorry," I said, after getting my breath back. "Listen, you don't have anything to worry about. It'll come natural to you. Trust me."

"Yeah, I suppose you've had lots of practice yourself."

"A little," I answered. "Now, since I have the honor of giving you away today, I think it's also my responsibility to see to it you show up at the church—and on time. So, hop to. Get your wedding dress on, and let's be on our way."

"Okay," she said, slowly getting up from the bed. "Would you ask my momma to come up and help me?"

Thirty minutes later Sara Jane took my breath away for the second time when I saw her coming down the stairs. This time not from being hit in the stomach, but from how beautiful she was.

Although Sara Jane and her mother sewed most of their own clothes, for this special occasion Mrs. Williams had hired Nettie Shoemaker, the best seamstress in Cynthiana, to design and sew her daughter's wedding gown.

Made of Normandy lace, it had a high neckline and long-fitted sleeves. The veil was ecru-colored tulle and lace, attached to a headpiece consisting of a large cascade of plastic flowers wound on a wired headband—all of which I found out later from Emmaline.

"Wow!" I exclaimed. "You look fantastic!"

"Oh, shut up!" said Sara Jane, a big grin on her face.

"I mean it," I said. "I'd say Malcolm is one lucky guy."

"He certainly is," said Mrs. Williams, who had followed her daughter down the stairs. "I wish your daddy was here to see this."

Sara Jane turned and hugged her mother. "Yeah, me too, Momma."

Mrs. Williams used her handkerchief to wipe a tear from her cheek.

"I love your veil," said Emmaline.

"I know," said Sara Jane, beaming. "Ain't it neat? See how it's a double layer? This here top layer goes over my face—that's so's Malcolm cain't see me during the ceremony—and then the bottom layer makes the train. But look—it's so darn long I hope I don't trip over the dang thing."

We all laughed.

"Where'd you get the pearls?" I asked.

"They belonged to Malcolm's momma. She got 'em from her momma and both of them wore them at their weddings. Since she didn't have no daughter to give them to, she give them to me."

"And they look great on you, don't they Mrs. Williams?" I said.

We all turned to Mrs. Williams. Huge tears streamed down her cheeks.

"Oh, Momma, come on," said Sara Jane. She, too, was crying. "It ain't like I'm moving out of the country, or nothing."

"I know," said Mrs. Williams. "That's not it. It's that my little girl . . ."

She couldn't finish. She blew her nose with her hankie.

"Enough of this blubbering," said Mrs. Williams. "Carter, I appreciate your driving us. I don't know how, and I didn't think it would look right for Sara Jane to be behind the wheel in her wedding gown as we pull up to the church."

"Besides," added Sara Jane, "as nervous as I am, I might wreck us."

"We ready to go?" I asked.

"One last thing," said Sara Jane. "I want to go in and see Grandma Mary for a minute. Y'all go on and get in the car, and I'll be right there."

∞

Most guests were already inside when we arrived at the church. I drove the car around to the back to allow Sara Jane to go into the pastor's study, where she would remain until time for her to walk down the aisle.

"I don't want him to see me beforehand," she said.

"That's traditional," Mrs. Williams reassured her.

"Yeah, well, I don't want him to see me and think 'What the heck am I getting into?' and chicken out and run."

"Honey, don't you worry," said Mrs. Williams. "When Malcolm Richardson sees you he's going to think he's died and gone to heaven, and is marrying an angel."

Sara Jane grinned. "Yeah, right," she said. But I knew she knew how beautiful she looked at that moment.

"I'm going to walk Emmaline around to the front of the church, and get her settled, and then I'll be right back," I said.

"Sara Jane, you look lovely," said Emmaline, as she left the pastor's study with me.

We no sooner got outside when Emmaline turned to me and said, "I think maybe I should stay in the car."

"Why?" I asked, taken aback.

"You know why. I don't know anybody here except Sara Jane's mother and your folks, and I don't have anyone to sit with. I'd feel out of place."

I started to protest, but at that moment Mrs. Williams emerged from the pastor's study. At the same time, my mother came around the corner of the building.

"Emmaline," said Mrs. Williams, "I'd like you to sit with me, if you would. After Carter gives Sara Jane away, he'll be sitting with us, too."

My mother smiled. "I was about to offer the same thing."

"See," I said. "Now you've got two invitations."

Emmaline smiled. "Thank you both. But I'm not sure how it would look if I sat in the front row, where family usually sit. And how would Mr. McGlone feel about me sitting with you?" she asked my mother.

"If Mr. McGlone doesn't like it, he can sit someplace else by himself," replied my mother, a note of defiance in her voice.

"I don't want to cause any trouble."

"Honey, you're not the problem," my mother assured her. "It's that misguided husband of mine."

"If you're sure," said Emmaline. I could tell she was still not at all sure herself.

"I'm sure."

I stood in the doorway and watched as the two of them walked down the aisle. A murmur ran through the congregation. A few people turned to look. Mrs. Broadhurst

lifted her nose into the air, then turned away. Neither my
mother nor Emmaline gave any indication they noticed, but
I knew they were both acutely aware of the stir they were
creating. Some of Malcolm's male friends whispered among
themselves.

When they reached the aisle where my father was
sitting, my mother entered first and sat down, and
Emmaline followed. A look of surprise and disapproval
came over my father's face, but he said nothing. Nor did he
move.

Mrs. Williams joined me and took my arm. I escorted
her to her seat in the front row. As I retraced my steps back
up the aisle, I felt the eyes of everyone on me, just as they
had been on my mother and Emmaline moments earlier.

I reached the doorway, walked down the church steps
and around the building to the pastor's study. It was time for
me to perform my role in giving my best friend away on her
wedding day.

∞

" . . . And wilt thou, Sara Jane Williams, have this man,
Malcolm Lloyd Richardson, as thy wedded husband, to live
together after God's ordinance in the holy estate of
matrimony? Wilt thou love him, comfort him, honor and
obey him, keeping him in sickness, and in health, and,
forsaking all others, keep thee only unto him, as long as ye
both shall live?"

"I will." Sara Jane's grin stretched from ear to ear.

"Please join your right hands. Forasmuch as Malcolm
and Sara Jane have consented together in holy wedlock, and
have declared the same before God, and in the presence of
this company, I pronounce them man and wife. In the name
of the Father, and of the Son, and of the Holy Ghost,

Amen. What God hath joined together, let not man put asunder. Young man, you may kiss the bride."

Malcolm carefully lifted the veil from Sara Jane's face and gently kissed her.

"Give her a *real* kiss!" shouted someone from the back of the church.

Malcolm looked around, then took Sara Jane in his arms, bent her half-way over, and gave her a long, passionate, kiss.

Cheers and whistles and applause filled the church.

"Now that's the way to kiss her, Malcolm!" shouted out the same voice that had motivated the groom moments before.

As they walked down the aisle, Sara Jane glanced over at us. Mrs. Williams was beaming and crying. I raised my fist halfway in the air in a salute.

Following the ceremony, all the guests headed for the Williamses' farm. Malcolm had talked Mrs. Williams into allowing him to open up the third floor, and he and a number of his friends had completely refurbished the place, painting, cleaning, and making repairs where needed. I was especially taken by an American flag, easily ten by twenty feet, and containing thirty-four stars, painted on the ceiling.

"I'm fascinated by that flag," I told Malcolm.

"I understand from Mrs. Williams that it's been there a long time, as long as she can remember," he said. "I just wish we'd had time to spruce it up some."

The flag had seen better days. The paint was faded and in some places was absent altogether.

"Still in all," I said, "I think it's great."

I strolled over to one of the tables that held an assortment of food prepared by Mrs. Williams and a few of her neighbors: fried chicken, ham sandwiches, pickles, sourdough bread, three or four different kinds of cheese, crackers, mini-peach cobblers, gingerbread, applesauce cookies, potatoes sliced into strips and fried, hard-boiled eggs, apples, peppered pecans and other nuts, candies, egg nog, and punch.

Malcolm had arranged for a local band to provide music. He'd also ensured that his cousin, Harvey, brought along a sufficient quantity of his homemade moonshine. I suspected some might have ended up in the punch.

Keeping with tradition, Malcolm and Sara Jane had the first dance. They were soon joined by the other guests. In my role of having given the bride away, I was dancing with Mrs. Williams. I'd left Emmaline with my mother.

"Are you happy?" I asked Mrs. Williams, knowing full well what her answer would be.

"Deliriously!" she responded.

"I understand Malcolm's a good man, and a hard worker," I said. "He'll make Sara Jane a good husband. And I know she'll make him a good wife."

Mrs. Williams looked up at me. "You're right." She put her mouth close to my ear and whispered, "But I still wish it had been you."

I chuckled. "Yes, well, maybe I'll be next."

"You could do worse than Emmaline," said Mrs. Williams, smiling at me.

When the dance ended, I took Mrs. Williams's hand and kissed it. "For the beautiful mother of the beautiful bride."

Mrs. Williams blushed. "Quit that! Get over there and dance with my daughter. The second dance is always for the man who gives the bride away."

I grinned. "But promise me, you'll dance with me again, later?"

"I promise," she said.

I walked over to Sara Jane and Malcolm, and tapped his shoulder.

"Mr. Richardson? This is my dance, I believe?"

Malcolm grinned, gave me a little bow, and stepped aside as I took Sara Jane in my arms.

"So, how are you feeling now?" I asked.

"A lot better. Except I still got to . . . you know . . ."

"You've got nothing to worry about," I said. "It'll be as easy as falling off a log."

She punched my shoulder. "You know darn well the last time I fell off a log I broke my arm!"

"Oh, right," I said, with a little laugh. "So, are you going to be staying at your place, or living with Malcolm's parents?"

Sara Jane looked at me and grinned. "Neither," she said. "Malcolm done built us our own house, up toward Kelat."

"No kidding?" I was duly impressed. "Will you invite me over after you get settled in?"

"You'll be our first guest. You and Emmaline."

I gave her a little squeeze. "I do wish you all the best, you know."

"I know," she said. She reached her face up and gave me a quick kiss on the cheek. "Thank you."

When the dance ended, I started to make my way to where Emmaline was waiting. I was concerned she might be feeling uneasy. But before I got there, I saw my father walk up and speak to her. A chill ran through me. Was he going to make a scene?

What happened next caught me by surprise. My father took Emmaline's hand and led her out to the middle of the room. I stared in disbelief as the two of them circled the dance floor. I noticed other guests watching them, as well.

When the dance ended, I waited anxiously as Emmaline wound her way back to me.

"You danced with my dad?" I asked. I still couldn't believe it.

"Yes. He told me he was sorry for the way he'd acted yesterday, and asked me to forgive him. Then he asked me to dance with him."

"How does he dance?" *What a dumb question*, I thought, as soon as the words left my mouth. But I couldn't think of anything else to say.

"I was happy when the dance ended," answered Emmaline. "And so were my feet."

"Not too good, huh?"

"He could use some practice. But, hey, you know, it meant a lot to me that he *did* dance with me; even more, that he apologized."

"Me, too," I said, wondering what brought about this change of heart. "So, is it my turn now?"

She smiled and nodded.

As I took her in my arms, I realized this was the first time I had ever held her in public. Our eyes met, and then we seemed to float across the floor to the strains of the music. I wasn't surprised she felt weightless in my arms, or that she was an excellent dancer. I felt her body brush against mine, and wondered how long our "no sex" agreement might last.

I felt the eyes of most of the guests on us, as they had been a few moments earlier on Emmaline and my father, but I didn't care. Whether Emmaline felt the same way, I wasn't sure. I pulled her closer to me. She didn't resist.

After the next three or four dances, I felt a tap on my shoulder and turned to find my mother standing there.

She smiled at Emmaline and then said, "Miss Jones, might I have this dance with my son?"

Emmaline flashed a smile in return and answered, "You certainly may, Mrs. McGlone."

I took my mother's hand and led her onto the dance floor.

"She is quite beautiful, isn't she?" she said.

I looked down at her. "Are you talking about Sara Jane or Emmaline?"

"They're both beautiful," said my mother. "But I'm talking about Emmaline. How serious is this?"

"What do you mean?"

"I mean, is she just your current girlfriend, or do your feelings for her go beyond that? You've never brought any other girl home."

I thought for a moment before I answered. "I think there's a possibility I may be in love with her."

My mother looked up at me. "Know this, Carter," she said. "If it comes to the point where the two of you end up getting married, I will love her like she was my own daughter. Colored or white—makes no difference. But you must also know such a marriage brings with it many problems, many trials and tribulations. It will be a far more difficult marriage to make work than if she was white. And, I'm not sure how your father would accept it—or her. I have to be honest with you about that."

"I know," I said. "But believe me, Mom, we are a long way from that point." I wanted to ask her what had happened with Dad, how he had come to apologize to, and then dance with, Emmaline. But just then he tapped me on the shoulder and, with some reluctance, I relinquished my mother to him.

Chapter Twenty-Two

The Mugging

1926

At seven o'clock, the band announced they were taking a break.

Sara Jane and her maid of honor, Vera, approached Emmaline and me.

"Emmaline, Vera and I are going to go powder our noses," said Sara Jane. "You want to come along?"

"Yes, I would," answered Emmaline.

"I'll be here when you get back," I said.

"I should hope so," replied Emmaline over her shoulder as she hurried off with the two women.

"Sir?"

I turned to find an elderly man at my elbow, the violin player from the band.

"Yes," I said.

"I believe I met your grandfather once."

"Oh?"

"It was right here in this house. In this very room. And it was exactly sixty-three years ago today. I was only seventeen, and it was my first time playing with a band. We were playing for an Independence Day party."

"And you met my grandfather?" I asked.

"I'm sure it was him. You look just like him."

"I do?" I'd seen pictures of both my grandfathers and I didn't think I looked like either of them.

"Yes. He came over during one of our breaks and complimented us on our playing." The man smiled. "That's when he gave me my nickname."

"Your nickname?"

"Fiddler. He said I was quite a fiddler. The other fellers in our band jumped on it and I've been Fiddler Jack Hawkins ever since."

"You do play well," I said. "The whole band does."

"Thank you, sir. I just wanted to tell you 'bout your grandfather. Today's my final performance. I've got arthritis in my hands, you see, so it's getting harder and harder to play. Kind of fitting, I think, that my first and last performances were both here in this house, in this very room, and your grandfather was here for one and you were here for the other."

"Do you know which of my grandfathers you met?"

"No, sir, he didn't give me no name. But, as I said, you look just like him."

"Well, good luck to you, Jack."

"*Fiddler* Jack, sir, thanks to your grandfather."

I decided to step outside for a breath of air. On my way down the stairs, I stopped to once again admire the huge stuffed deer head mounted on one wall. It had been there as long as I had been coming to this house. Mrs. Williams told me once her uncle had shot the deer, and that its rack was the largest ever seen in these parts.

I continued downstairs and out onto the porch. As I watched the last rays of sunlight drain from the western skies, George Burnett and Sid Mulroney, two men a few years younger than myself, and whom I knew to be friends of Malcolm's, joined me, along with an older man whom I had never met.

"Nice party, huh?" said the stranger

"Yes, it is," I replied. "I'm happy for Malcolm and Sara Jane."

"Nice looking gal you got there, too," said George.

"Thanks," I said. I felt my stomach muscles tighten.

"Why don't we take a little walk?" said the stranger.

"I—" I didn't finish, as I felt the tip of a knife blade in my ribs.

"This way," said George.

I followed George and Sid down the stairs, then down the lane, with the stranger close behind me. We'd gone about fifty yards when they led me off the road and into the woods.

"What's this all about?" I asked, trying to appear calm, in spite of my concern.

Sid spoke for the first time. "It's about you and that nigger," he said.

"My relationsh—" I stopped short, as I again felt the knife tip pressed to my side.

"We ain't asking for your opinion," said George. "We're a tellin.'"

The older man, the one holding the knife, stepped around in front of me and pressed the tip of it to my Adam's apple.

"You don't know me, son. My name is Courtland— Jonah Courtland. I'm the head of the Klan in this county."

"The Ku Klux Klan?" I said. Now I was *doubly* concerned.

"That's right," said Jonah. "And, son, I'm telling you, we don't put up with white boys screwing 'round with nigger bitches anymore than we do with niggers fooling 'round with our white women. I don't know who you think you are, coming to this party and parading your nigger whore around like she was something, but, son, you done made a big mistake."

"Yeah," said George. "Malcolm is our friend, and you done embarrassed him by bringing that nigger here. Man, you ain't got good sense, have you?" George slapped me hard on my cheek, and I staggered back a few feet.

Jonah spoke up again. "So, son, here's what we're going to do." He reached down, grabbed my right hand and pulled it up in front of my face. "You see that there little pinkie? We're going to cut that little pinkie off, and give it to Malcolm as a wedding present. Then you're going back to the party, you're going to tell whoever you need to tell you fell out here, and that's how you lost your little finger, and then you're going to get your nigger whore and get out of Harrison County *tonight*."

I had about decided I would have to make a fight of it, when I heard the rustle of bushes behind me, followed by the sound of Malcolm's voice.

"Hey, boys, what's going on out here?"

"Looky here, Malcolm," answered George. "We was just getting ready to give you a wedding present from ol' nigger lover here." Jonah and Sid laughed.

"Oh? What kind of present?"

"His little pinky," giggled Sid. "And then he's going to get his nigger pussy and get the hell out of here."

When Malcolm came around in front of me, I was dismayed to see two more of his friends with him. *Hell*, I thought, *there's no way I'm getting out of this now.* I felt the perspiration on my forehead; little rivulets of sweat ran down one side of my face.

"I've got a better idea," said Malcolm. "Let me have the knife."

Jonah grinned and handed it to him. But the smile quickly faded as Malcolm grabbed him by the front of his shirt and held the knife to his throat.

"Carter is my wife's guest," he said, fairly growling the words. "And mine, too. And so's his date. So he and I are going to go back to the party, and we're going to enjoy ourselves. You three are going to get your asses out of here. And Jonah," he said, emphasizing each word as he pressed the knife hard enough against the man's windpipe to cause a thin line of blood to form, "if I *ever* see you on this property, or on my property, again, I'll shoot your ass. You got that? And that goes for all your damn Klan members, too."

Jonah blinked his eyes, too afraid to nod his head as Malcolm held the knife pressed to his throat.

Malcolm loosened his hold on Jonah and turned to George and Sid. Instinctively, they backed away from him. "And boys," he said, "that goes for you, too. Don't ever let me catch you on our property again."

"But, Malcolm," George protested, "we're your friends."

"Ain't no friends of mine would treat a guest like this at my wedding reception. Now, get the hell out of here."

As the three of them scurried off, Malcolm turned back to me.

"You okay?"

I nodded. I was still so shaken I didn't trust myself to speak.

"Let's get back to the party, then. And, Carter," he added, "I think it's best if the girls don't know nothing about this."

∞

"Where you two been?" asked Sara Jane, as Malcolm and I returned to the ballroom. "We's beginning to think you done took off."

"No, I went out for a cigar," said Malcolm, "and Carter joined me. Couldn't get him to smoke one, though."

"Carter, are you all right? You look a little pale," said Emmaline.

By now I had recovered my voice. "I'm fine. I think it was Malcolm's cigar smoke that made me a little dizzy. I'm not used to it."

"Okay, then!" said Sara Jane. "Let's dance!" She grabbed Malcolm's hand and rushed him out to the dance floor.

"Do you want to dance?" asked Emmaline.

"Let's, uh . . . let's go out and get some air," I said.

"Sure. You look like you could use some."

After about fifteen minutes on the second-floor porch, I assured Emmaline I felt much better. "Perhaps we should go back up and rejoin the party."

I danced most of the dances with Emmaline the rest of the evening, but also squeezed in a few with my mother and Mrs. Williams, and one more with Sara Jane. It pleased me to see that while I danced with the latter, Emmaline was being whisked around the dance floor by Malcolm.

When I tried to bring up the subject of my father with my mother, she said she'd tell me all about it later.

A few minutes after midnight, Newt Carpenter, Malcolm's best man, and one of the ones who was with Malcolm in the woods, asked the band to stop playing. He had an announcement.

"In case y'all hadn't noticed, our bride and groom have abandoned their guests. You know what that means? That rascal Malcolm has spirited our sweet Sara Jane off to their new abode. And you know what *that* means? *Shivaree!*"

A loud cheer went up from the younger men and women.

"Come on!" shouted Newt. "Let's go welcome in the newlyweds!"

The words were no sooner out of his mouth than several dozen people rushed down the stairs to their cars. The night was still young. The party had only begun.

Emmaline and I didn't join them. I knew it was the custom, but somehow I didn't feel comfortable participating in this ritual for a woman who had been my best friend my whole life. I also still felt the effects of my encounter earlier with Jonah, George, and Sid.

"Do you mind if we don't go?" I asked Emmaline.

"That's fine," she said.

"Mom, what happened last night?" Although I'd wanted to get an early start back to Louisville, I couldn't leave without knowing what caused my father's apparent about-face regarding Emmaline, so I'd called my parents' house from the Williamses'.

"You mean with your father?"

"Yes. Why the sudden change of heart about Emmaline?"

"Oh, that. Well, your father and I had a little talk on the way out to the Williamses' farm yesterday after the wedding."

"You must have put the fear of God into him," I said. I knew my mother could be persuasive. At the same time, I also knew how stubborn my father was.

"It's not that your father has anything against coloreds. And he sure doesn't have anything against Emmaline. He just doesn't believe in the races mixing. And then, he was so shocked when Emmaline turned out to be colored, he didn't know what to think. So, he didn't handle the situation well. I reminded him in our little talk that, no matter how he felt, you are our son, and Emmaline was not only your girlfriend, but our guest, and there was no excuse for the way he'd acted. He agreed."

"Why didn't he say anything to me?"

"Too ashamed, I reckon. Give him time, and he will. I don't know if he'll change his mind about you and Emmaline, but he did say that if you brought her back again, she'd be welcome to stay here."

"I don't know she'd want to go back there," I said. "I don't know *I'd* want to, if she were with me."

"I understand. And I wouldn't blame either of you. But tell her anyway."

"I will. Is Dad there now?"

"He's outside."

"Okay. Tell him I'm glad he's changed his mind. About some things, at least. Love you, Mom."

"I love you, too, Carter. You be careful driving back to Louisville. And say goodbye to Emmaline for me."

Chapter Twenty-Three

Battle Grove Cemetery

1926

I took a deep breath—October, and the smell of fall was definitely in the air. Emmaline and I were going away for the weekend. Over the past several months my workload had increased significantly, which meant many more hours in the office, to the point of working almost every Saturday, and some Sundays. Emmaline's new position as a teller at the American Mutual Savings Bank kept her almost as busy. As a result, few opportunities presented themselves for the two of us to spend much time together.

But this weekend, I'd set aside all of my work—except that which I'd been able to persuade Sam to handle for me—and had convinced Emmaline to go away with me. Not that she'd required much coaxing.

It was our first trip back to Harrison County since Sara Jane's wedding. My mother assured me that, even though my father had still not completely accepted the situation, there would be no problem this time with the two of us staying there.

As we drove up the lane to the house, I saw my mother hanging laundry in the side yard. I honked the horn. When she turned and saw us, she hastily pinned up the shirt she'd been holding and ran to meet the car.

"Carter!"

I brought the car to a stop, jumped out, and gathered my mother up in a bear hug.

"Oh, let me go!" she exclaimed. "You're squeezing the breath out of me!"

"Emmaline, let me look at you," Mom said, when I finally let her go. "How are you?"

"Fine, Mrs. McGlone, thank you."

"We weren't sure what time you'd get here. What time did you leave?"

"A little after noon," replied Emmaline.

"How's Dad?" I asked. Not so much a question as to how my father was physically, as to how he would take Emmaline's presence. My mother understood.

"He's fine, Carter. Don't expect him to be falling all over himself with hospitality, but he'll be okay. Let's get you settled in your rooms, and then I'll put supper on the table."

Mom was right about my father. During the meal he was polite, but reserved. Give him time, my mother told me.

After supper, Emmaline offered to help with the dishes, but my mother made it clear that, as a guest, she could just forget about doing any house work.

"Why don't you take Emmaline for a drive?" she said. "Maybe she'd like to see Battle Grove Cemetery."

"Mom, I can't imagine—"

"Is there something special about the cemetery?" asked Emmaline.

"It's located on the site of a big battle fought here during the Civil War," said my mother. "A lot of men who died in the battle are buried there. There are some unusual gravestones and monuments, and it's a lovely cemetery."

"Oh, yes, let's do go!" exclaimed Emmaline. "I love old cemeteries."

"If you're sure," I said. I couldn't imagine why she'd want to go traipsing through an old cemetery.

"I am, I am! Let's go now, while it's still light."

Dusk was settling in as we arrived, but Emmaline wanted to take a quick walk around.

"Do you know many of the families of these men?" she asked.

"Some," I answered. "Of course, a lot of the men who are buried here died in the fighting that took place here, and they were from somewhere else."

We came to a tall, marble monument, at least twenty feet high. In the last glimmer of the sun's rays, I watched Emmaline struggle to read the inscription:

ERECTED

MAY 27, 1869

BY THE

CYNTHIANA CONFEDERATE

MEMORIAL ASSOCIATION

IN MEMORY OF

THE CONFEDERATE DEAD WHO

FELL IN DEFENSE OF

CONSTITUTIONAL LIBERTY

Emmaline stepped back as though she had encountered a snake.

"This is a Confederate monument," she said, disbelief in her voice. "Why on earth would there be a Confederate monument here? I thought Kentucky fought on the side of the Union."

"As I recall," I said, "during the war there were a number of Southern sympathizers here in Harrison County, and some men fought on the side of the South. In some cases, families were split, some for the North, some for the South. And the other thing is that the Confederate soldiers who are buried here probably died right here in the battle, like the Union soldiers who are buried here."

"Yes, but . . ." She still had trouble believing the people of this county would have erected—or at least allowed to have been erected—a Confederate monument.

"Come on, it's getting dark," I said. "We should be going."

As we made our way back to the car in the gathering darkness, I heard the sound of voices close by. We had almost reached the road when three men stepped out from behind a large bush and blocked our way. Even in the failing light, I recognized two of the men as the ones who had threatened me at Sara Jane's wedding reception: George and Sid. I didn't recognize the third man.

"Well, looky who's here," said George. I could tell from his slurred words and the smell of his breath, he'd been drinking. "If it ain't old nigger lover, and his nigger whore!"

"Let us pass," I said.

"Let us pass," mimicked George. "Let us pass. Let us pass, my ass! What you two doing out here in the dark, anyway? Fucking? In the cemetery? Damn, that's just disgusting!"

I felt anger begin to build in me. I had to restrain myself from punching George in the mouth. I realized that, even in their drunken condition, the three of them together were easily more than a match for me. Common sense told me the best thing was to get the hell out of there. Emmaline moved to my side and wrapped her arms around one of mine. I felt her body tremble.

Then a fourth man emerged from the shadows. My heart sank: Kiernan O'Doherty! The anxiety I'd felt before due to the presence of the three men who stood before me and Emmaline paled in comparison to what I felt now, as I recalled Mr. Clary's account of the man's past, and his reputation as a cold-blooded killer. In an instant, I realized what Emmaline and I had stumbled upon: a moonshine transaction which had probably just been consummated, with O'Doherty buying, and George and Sid and the other man the sellers. Now they were finished, and celebrating, already drunk.

"We're on our way back to our car," I said. "Then we'll be out of your way, and you boys can go on with your drinking."

"Go on with our drinking," George repeated. "Well, now, maybe we're ready to do more than just go on with our drinking."

"Thass right," said Sid, slurring his words. "Maybe we're done drinking."

"Shut up, Sid!" George commanded.

Sid slunk back, like a whipped dog.

O'Doherty never said a word, just stood by and watched, hands behind his back.

The third man, who had also been standing quietly by the whole time, stepped forward, and brushed Emmaline's hair back from her face. "She's kinda purty," he said. "In a nigger sort of way."

"Keep your hands off of her!" I said, anger rising in my voice. "And get out of our way. *Now!*"

I glanced back at George in time to see the gun handle as it slammed into the side of my head. I staggered backwards, and heard Emmaline scream. I caught myself and stumbled forward, only to feel an excruciating pain as the gun handle once again caught me across my right temple. This time my knees crumpled, and I fell to the ground.

When I looked up, I saw O'Doherty standing over me, a wide grin covering his birth-marked stained face. In his hand he held a derringer, the same one he'd pulled that day in the restaurant, pointed at my chest.

"I knew your granddaddy, boy. You're the spittin' image of him."

It was the same thing Willie said to me that day at the track.

"He was a real son of a bitch, too." Kiernan's voice was smooth and cold, like the water in a mountain stream. "I tried to kill him, but they pulled me off him. Ain't nobody here to stop me from killin' you."

I heard the blast of the gun, then felt the impact of the bullet. A searing hot iron seemed to blaze its way up my cheek.

The last thing I remembered before I passed out was the sound of Emmaline's screams.

When I came to, I saw the vague figure of a man hovering over me. The first rays of the morning sun were beginning to spread across the ground. I tried to get up, but couldn't.

"Easy son," said the man. "I got help on the way. Looks like you've taken quite a hit there."

I raised my hand to my head. It came back swathed in blood.

"What happened?" I asked.

"Beats me," replied the man. "I'm Josh Tinker, the caretaker. Found you here this morning when I came to work. Called for the doctor—should be here soon."

Then I remembered. "Emmaline? Where . . . where's Emmaline?"

"Who?"

"Emmaline. My girlfriend. Where is she?"

"Don't know. Didn't see nobody here but you."

I tried to get up again, and this time partially succeeded.

"They must have taken her somewhere," I said.

"Who?" asked the caretaker again.

"George and . . . and Sid. And . . . oh, God! O'Doherty!"

"I don't know nothing about that. Oh, look, here's the doc now."

After a quick glance at my scalp, the doctor said I'd have to go to the hospital and get stitches.

"Mom, what about Emmaline?"

The hospital had called my parents as soon as I'd been admitted. They had been up all night, worried because we hadn't returned. They'd gotten the sheriff out of bed in the middle of the night. He found my car parked at the entrance to the cemetery, but no sign of Emmaline or me. When he came to talk to me, I told him what happened.

"I don't know," said my mother. "They searched the cemetery, but she wasn't there. Sheriff McKee has men out now looking for her, as well as George, Sid, and the other two men. And Malcolm and his friends are out looking, too. As soon as anyone knows something, they'll tell us."

"I'm scared for her. I've got to get out of here and go find her."

"I know, Carter, I know. I have to admit—I'm scared, too. Your daddy and I don't know those boys personally, but he says he knows their reputation. And your daddy told me about the conversation with Mr. Clary. That Mr. O'Doherty sounds like an evil man. But there's no way you can leave here now. The doctor says you've had a concussion, and you need to stay in the hospital another night."

At the mention of O'Doherty's name, I remembered that while he fired his gun at me point-blank, it didn't appear as though I'd actually been shot.

When I mentioned it to my mother, she said, "The doctor thought it odd you had a bullet hole in your shirt, but, like you said, you weren't shot. He finally figured out that the bullet must have ricocheted off of your medal, and struck you up alongside your cheek and knocked you out. He said if it hadn't been for that medal, you'd be dead, now."

I took the medal in my hands and held it up, studying it. It appeared just as it always had: the bullet hadn't damaged it at all.

I told my mother about what happened the night of Sara Jane's wedding. She shook her head and began to softly cry. "I can't believe people act like that nowadays."

"Have you called Emmaline's parents? Do you need their number?"

"Not yet. We wanted to wait a few hours to see if there was any good news to give them. But if we haven't heard anything by this afternoon, then I'll call. And, yes, I will need their number."

"Where's Dad? How come he didn't come with you?"

"We figured one of us should stay at home in case Emmaline called, or in case one of the men looking for her tried to call the house. He'll come in to see you later, after I get home. He's as sick about all this as I am. Sara Jane's waiting outside. She'd like to see you."

"Sure. Tell her to come on in."

"Carter," exclaimed Sara Jane, hurrying into the room. "You okay?"

"I'll be okay," I answered. "I'm more concerned about Emmaline."

"They haven't found her yet?"

"I guess not. At least, that's what my mom said."

"They will. I know they will. And she'll be okay; she'll be fine."

"I hope you're right," I said. But my gut told me something different. "Listen, I've got to get out of here. I can't just lay here in this bed, not knowing what's happened to Emmaline. I've got to try to find her."

"You sure you know what you're doing? Your momma said the doctor's planning on keeping you another night."

"That may be the doctor's plan, but it's not mine. Now, if you don't mind, I've got to get dressed."

By the time I reached the corridor, Sara Jane had already told my mother what I was up to.

"Carter, you can't—"

"Come on, Mom, we're leaving." I took my mother's arm and firmly walked her out of the hospital, Sara Jane right on our heels.

∞

We didn't find Emmaline that day.

On Sunday afternoon, Mordecai arrived from Louisville.

"Tell me again what happened," he said, the calmness of his voice masking the anxiety I knew he must have been feeling.

I recounted how we had gone out to the cemetery and encountered the four men; the ensuing fracas, and how I'd been knocked unconscious by the bullet from O'Doherty's gun. I decided to omit my previous run-in with George and Sid, as well as what I knew about O'Doherty. I didn't want to upset Mordecai unnecessarily. My father assured him the whole sheriff's department along with most of the townsfolk, were out looking for his daughter, and for the four men.

I felt consumed with guilt that I was the one responsible for Emmaline's disappearance. "Reverend Jones, I can't tell you how sorry I am that I got Emmaline into this."

"Carter, this isn't your fault. And I don't blame you for it."

"If anyone's to blame, it's me," said my mother. "I'm the one who suggested they go to the cemetery."

"No one's to blame," Mordecai reassured her. "No one's to blame. Let's have faith she's all right."

That night my mother put Mordecai up in the guest bedroom that would have been Emmaline's.

∞

My father, Mordecai, and I spent the morning looking for Emmaline. Finally, we decided to return to the house, to see if there was any news.

When I turned the car into the lane that led up to the house and saw Sheriff McKee's car parked there, a sinking feeling hit me. She's dead. As sure as I was alive, I knew Emmaline was dead.

We were met on the front porch by my mother and the sheriff.

"Reverend Jones, Carter, Madison. I'm . . . afraid I've got some bad news," said the sheriff. "We found Emmaline's body a little while ago."

"*Nooo . . .*" I cried. I reached out and put my hand against the wall to steady myself.

Mordecai slumped into the rocking chair without speaking.

"Whereabouts?" asked my father.

"Down by the river, the other side of Abdallah Park Road. Some young boy fishing there discovered it on the riverbank. Looks like they might have raped her first, and then killed her."

"Oh, no!" moaned my mother. "Oh, no!" She put a hand over her mouth, and leaned back against the wall for support.

"I'm real sorry about all this," said the sheriff.

"Is there any sign of the men who did this?" asked my father.

"Not yet. I'm pretty sure they've cleared out of the county. According to George and Sid's moms, they never have come home since that night. They might be anywhere by now. We put out notices on Saturday to all the law enforcement agencies in Kentucky, also in Ohio, West

Virginia, and Tennessee. We'll get them; don't you worry about that."

"What about the other two?" asked my mother.

"Still don't know who the one was," answered Sheriff McKee. "Could have been somebody passing through and hooked up with those two boys for a drinking party. Ain't nobody else missing as far as we know. As for O'Doherty, we'll find him, too."

Mordecai spoke for the first time. "It's God's will," he said. "He must need her up in heaven more than we need her here."

"Amen," answered my parents almost simultaneously.

My mother came to me and put her arms around me. I sobbed uncontrollably. I wasn't at all sure I shared the same viewpoint as Reverend Jones and my parents about it being God's will, and all. I just knew I would never see Emmaline again.

That night, my dream returned. This time, though, there was something different about the rider: it was a skeleton sitting astride the horse. Slowly, the bones took on flesh, and clothes began to appear, until a whole man materialized. The face was the last thing to take shape. When the man turned to look at me I shuddered. It was Sam's face.

Emmaline's funeral was held on Friday, the twenty-second of October, five days before her twenty-third birthday.

The church was packed to capacity. Sam was there, as were a number of people Emmaline had worked with at the bank. Even my parents came all the way from Harrison County for the service, the first time either of them had ever been to Louisville.

Emmaline's brother, Clayton, led the service. Mordecai said he didn't think he could do it.

Louisa invited me to go back to the house with them after the service at the graveside and I'd accepted.

But as I walked into the living room, memories of Emmaline flooded over me. I stayed long enough to eat a ham sandwich, and then made my apologies to go. As I got ready to leave, Louisa spoke to me.

"Carter, even though Emmaline's not with us anymore, you know you're still always welcome in our home."

I looked at her and gave a weak smile. "Thank you, Mrs. Jones." I hugged her and then shook Mordecai's hand. But as I walked down the steps, I knew in my heart I would never again go back into that house.

Chapter Twenty-Four

The Other Side of Yesterday

1926

I arrived home the week before Christmas to find my mother had taken ill. The doctor feared she might have tuberculosis. By Christmas Day, however, she had improved considerably. The doctor concluded it was probably some form of virus that had caused her to get sick.

My first few days back, I didn't leave the house. I felt I should stay and take care of my mother.

"When will you be returning to Louisville?" she asked me.

"I'm scheduled to go back the day after tomorrow, but I think I'll stay around a little longer."

"Didn't you write me that Sam was putting together a big party for New Year's Eve?"

"Yes, but I don't have to be there."

"Nonsense. *Here* is where you don't need to be. I'm feeling much better now, and the doctor says it's only a matter of time before I'm out of bed and up and around. In the meantime, Athena has agreed to look in on me and help with whatever I need. I want you to go back to Louisville, and go to the party, and have fun."

"But, Mom—"

"No buts! Besides, maybe you'll meet a nice young girl there . . ." My mother hesitated. The memory of Emmaline's death a few months earlier still weighed heavily on all our minds.

"Maybe you'll meet a nice young girl there, and you'll fall in love and get married, and give me the grandbaby I've always wanted."

"I'm not sure I'm ready for another relationship yet," I said.

"Nevertheless, I want you to go back and go to the party. I'll be fine."

"If you're sure it's okay. I'll take the train out on Tuesday. I haven't had a chance to see Sara Jane or Mary since I've been here. I'll go over to Malcolm and Sara Jane's tomorrow after church, and then when Mrs. Williams comes over here on Monday, I'll go visit Mary."

"My God, woman, what did you do? Swallow a watermelon?"

I hadn't seen Sara Jane since she broke the news to me several months earlier that she was expecting, the reason she wasn't able to travel to Louisville for Emmaline's funeral.

"Oh, don't even talk to me!" she said, throwing her hands into the air. "Do you know how miserable I feel? And I'm only five months along!"

"By the time that baby comes they'll have to roll you around in a wheelbarrow."

"You know, if it didn't take so much energy, I'd get up out of this chair and come over there and whop you one!"

"I'm sorry," I said. I walked over, knelt down beside her, and kissed her cheek. "I didn't mean to make fun of you. But," I continued, rising and moving out of her reach, "you are pretty huge."

"Okay, let's talk about something else besides how big I am," said Sara Jane. "How's your momma doing?"

"She's a lot better," I replied. "Maybe your mother told you, it wasn't tuberculosis after all, probably something she picked up."

"That's good. It's bad enough to be sick, but to be sick around the holidays—well, that's even worse. And how're you doing?"

Sara Jane knew from talking with my mother how much I still missed Emmaline.

"I'm doing okay," I said. "It's hard, knowing I'll never see her again."

"You liked her a lot, didn't you?"

"Yeah, I did."

"Did you love her?"

"I think so . . . yes, I know so."

We both fell silent. Thoughts of Emmaline, mingled with Kiernan O'Doherty, kept running through my mind.

Sara Jane's words brought me back. "You going to see Grandma Mary while you're here?"

"Oh, yes," I replied, relieved not to have to talk any further about Emmaline. "I'm looking forward to it."

"I know she sure is looking forward to your visit. She's always a lot peppier after you've been there. Sometimes I think there's something going on between you two." She grinned.

"Well, if she were—let's see—if she were about thirty years younger, and I was about thirty years older, there might be."

"Between you and me, if my grandma was just *fifteen* years younger, and you was still twenty-seven, I'm not sure you could handle her."

I laughed. "You may be right. So, back to the upcoming event—and I promise not to say another word about how much weight you've gained—what are you going to name the baby?"

"If it's a girl, we'll name her—"

"Athena," I interrupted, remembering my conversation with Mrs. Williams.

"Yeah," said Sara Jane, smiling. "Our family tradition, you know."

"And if it's a boy?"

"Then we'll name him after his daddy—Malcolm, Jr."

"That's a good, solid name."

"I'll be glad when this is over."

"Just four more months."

"Oh, shut up! Besides, maybe it'll be sooner."

"Listen, I'm going to drive down to your mom's house now to see Mary. I have to leave early tomorrow, and I haven't packed yet. All kidding aside, you look good. Tell Malcolm I said he's a lucky guy."

"I will. You take care of yourself. Carter?"

"Yes?"

"I love you."

"I love you, too, Sara Jane."

∞

"Carter, your momma tells me you're going back to Louisville tomorrow."

"Yes, ma'am." I was always happy to see Mrs. Williams if for no other reason than I imagined in her the Mary of thirty years ago. "My mother's doing much better, and she insisted I go. And I do appreciate your looking in on her."

"Not at all. I'm heading over there as soon as Sara Jane shows up. It's a good excuse for her to come over here and stay with Momma. Not that she needs an excuse. She loves that woman dearly. And, of course, Momma is always happy to see you, too."

"I just left Sara Jane's. She didn't say anything about coming over."

"No, she knew you'd be here. She'll come later. Now, go on in. I think she's awake. If not, you wake her, because I know she won't want to miss you."

When I entered the room, Mary lay in the large fourposter, her hands clasped to her chest, her unseeing eyes staring at the ceiling, and apparently oblivious to my presence.

"Mary?"

"Carter?" She turned her head toward me and a smile graced her face. "Dear me. I fear I was daydreaming."

"And where did you go on your daydream?" I asked, sitting down on the side of the bed.

"Oh, it's not a question of *where*—it's *when*. I was visiting one of my favorite times—the other side of yesterday."

"The . . . other side of yesterday?" I didn't understand. "You mean the day before yesterday? Saturday?"

"Oh, no, Carter. I mean long before then. Whenever my grandmother reminisced about something, or someone, from the past, she would always say she was 'visiting the other side of yesterday.'"

"And to what time did your visit take you?"

She gave a playful laugh and looked again at the ceiling. "To a time when I was young and beautiful, and madly in love, head over heels, with a most handsome young man, a love, I must admit, I can still feel here, even now." She placed her hand on her heart.

"Your first husband?" I asked.

"Oh my, no," Mary replied quickly. "It was during the war—the Civil War—and my young man . . . well, I know he wasn't killed in the fighting, but something happened to him afterwards, because he never made it back to me. We had such a very short time together. And yet, it was the most beautiful time of my life.

"Please don't misunderstand," she hastened, turning back to face me. "I did grow to love my first husband. But, I have to admit, not with the same passion I felt for my first love."

"You never found out what happened to him?"

"They never found his body," replied Mary. "And he never returned to me. I know if he could have come back, he would have. He promised he would. You remind me of him a great deal."

I took her hand in mine and gave it a gentle squeeze.

She smiled. "Now, enough of my daydreaming. What have you been up to in Louisville?"

I told her about a big case Sam and I were involved in, and how busy our practice kept us. "Seems like all we do is work. Okay," I added, somewhat sheepishly, "I guess that's not entirely true. We still find time to go to the track when the horses are running and, occasionally, out drinking at a speakeasy." I felt guilty, not because Sam and I were breaking the law, but because somehow it didn't seem right to be having fun with Emmaline gone only two months.

Mary seemed to sense my uneasiness. "That's good," she said, "that you're getting out. You're both young men. You *should* be having fun. Are you on your way back to Louisville?"

"Yes," I replied. "The trial for this case comes up a week from today, and I still have a lot of preparation to do. Since my mother seems to be getting along much better now, I feel it's okay for me to go."

"I'm sure she'll be fine," said Mary.

"Is there anything I can do for you before I leave?" I asked. "I think Sara Jane will be here shortly."

She smiled. "You are so kind and considerate. I don't … well, as a matter of fact . . . there is something you could do for me. If you have the time."

"Whatever you want."

"Would you read to me?"

Her request caught me by surprise. I knew both Mrs. Williams and Sara Jane read to her, but in all the times I had visited her over the last several years, she had never asked me to read before.

"Of course," I answered. "What would you like to hear?"

"On the shelf on the wall behind you there should be a book of poetry by William Yeats. I'd very much like for you to read from that."

I stood and looked at the books lining the shelf. Finding the book Mary mentioned, I took it down, and looked at the title: *The Secret Rose.*

"I used to have many books," said Mary. "But I lost most of them, first in the fire, and then more in the flood of 1913—all except this one. I collected more later, but this is still my favorite. Do you like Yeats?"

"I can't say I'm familiar with him," I admitted.

"He's Irish, one of our modern poets. Much of his writing is extremely nationalistic, but I prefer his romantic, melancholy works. He won the Nobel Prize a few years ago, you know. Carter, you really must start reading something other than those musty old law books," she said, teasingly.

"You're absolutely right," I replied, laughing. "Is there anything in particular you'd like to hear?"

"You choose."

For the next hour, I read at random from the book. I understood why Mary liked Mr. Yeats's writing so much. I enjoyed it, too.

"I have time for one more," I said, at last. I heard Sara Jane rummaging around out in the kitchen.

"Yes, I know you must go. One more would be fine."

I turned the page and read out loud the title of the next poem: "When You Are Old and Grey." I paused, not sure if I should read the poem or not.

Mary seemed to sense my hesitation. "Please," she said. I began:

> *When you are old and grey and full of sleep*
> *And nodding by the fire, take down this book,*
> *And slowly read, and dream of the soft look*
> *Your eyes had once, and of their shadows deep;*
> *How many loved your moments of glad grace,*
> *And loved your beauty with love false or true;*
> *But one man loved the pilgrim soul in you,*
> *And loved the sorrows of your changing face.*
> *And bending down beside the glowing bars,*
> *Murmur, a little sadly, how love fled*
> *And paced upon the mountains overhead,*
> *And hid his face amid a crowd of stars.*

I closed the book, and laid it on my lap. I looked to see tears streaming down Mary's face.

"Oh, Mary, I'm so sorry!"

"No, no," she said, dabbing at her eyes with her handkerchief. "It's just . . . every time I hear that poem, I feel as if it were written just for me."

"I know," I said. And I did. I had no doubt of the beauty that was once hers, hidden now to some extent by the scars from the fire, the soft eyes now clouded by age and disease. I knew of her lost love, the one she spoke of that same afternoon. And I almost felt *I* was the man who had loved her pilgrim soul, had seen the sorrow in her face, the same sorrow I saw now.

"Carter," she said, her sightless eyes looking deep into mine, as though searching for something there, "before you leave, I want you to make me a promise."

"Anything."

"Promise me *you'll* come back."

"Mary, you know I always come to see you when I'm back home. And I'll be back at Easter, maybe before." I was confused by her request.

"Promise me," she said, as she closed her eyes, drifting off to sleep. "Promise me."

Carefully, I laid her hands back on her chest. I stood, and kissed her gently on the forehead, then placed the book back where I'd gotten it. I looked again at her, her face a vision of serenity.

"I'll be back, Mary," I whispered. "I promise—I'll come back."

Chapter Twenty-Five

It's Twins!

1927

The ringing of the phone woke me.

"Carter, this is Athena—Athena Williams."

"Mrs. Williams! Sorry, I didn't recognize your voice. Is anything wrong? Sara Jane . . . ?"

"No, no, she's fine. She wanted me to call you and let you know she had her babies."

"Oh, wow, that's gr . . . babies?" I stopped as the words sank in. "Babies? She had more than one?"

"Twins! Twin boys . . . and they're both doing fine."

"Twins . . . no wonder she looked so big when I saw her at Christmas. Did you all know she was going to have twins?"

"No, it surprised everyone."

"Has she named them yet?"

"The oldest one is named after Malcolm—Malcolm, Jr."

"And I'll bet she named the other one after Mr. Williams."

"No, Horace is his *middle* name. His first name is Carter."

I was stunned—and speechless.

"Carter?" Mrs. Williams prompted.

"Yes, ma'am, I'm here. She named the baby after me?"

"She said that way, even though you live in Louisville now, she'll always have a Carter around."

"Mrs. Williams, I don't know what to say. I'm flattered—and flabbergasted. How's Malcolm taking all this?"

"Oh, he's beside himself with joy. Strutting all around, like a peacock."

"How does he feel about Sara Jane naming one of his sons after me?"

"Carter, he is so happy to have two sons, and to have one named after him—why, I doubt he would have objected if Sara Jane had named the other one after me!"

I laughed. "That'd be a heckuva moniker for a boy to be stuck with: Athena. When were they born?"

"This morning. About seven o'clock."

"Today?" I looked at the calendar, then burst out laughing.

"What is it?" Mrs. Williams asked.

"Do you know what today is?"

"No, I . . . I guess I hadn't paid any attention with getting Sara Jane to the hospital and all."

"It's April first. April Fools' Day! I guess that's pretty appropriate, considering how Sara Jane got fooled when she had *two* babies, instead of one."

This time it was Mrs. Williams's turn to laugh. "I hadn't even realized the date. I don't imagine Sara Jane has either."

"She still in the hospital?"

"Yes, she'll be there for another week, and then she'll go home. Carter, Sara Jane wanted me to see if you're for sure coming home at Easter."

"Most definitely. I want to see those new little Richardsons."

"The reason I asked is because she wants you to be their godfather, and they're planning on having the babies christened on Easter Sunday."

For the second time in the conversation, I found myself at a loss for words. Finally, I managed to speak. "Mrs. Williams, I'd be honored. You tell Sara Jane I will for sure be there. I wouldn't miss it for the world. And tell her I'll give her a call next week, after she gets home from the hospital."

"I will, Carter. She'll be so pleased. Oh, and Carter, your momma wanted me to tell you she and your daddy are both doing fine. And I'll let them know you'll be here for Easter."

Chapter Twenty-Six

A Sad Homecoming

1927

I arrived home the Thursday before Easter, but the homecoming was not a happy one. Mary had passed away the previous day, and the funeral was scheduled for Saturday.

Sara Jane had telephoned me to give me the news. When I heard it, I broke down in tears. I felt as though something had gone out of my life, some spark I knew Mary had kindled there. In a period of less than six months, I had lost two of the women who meant the most to me in the whole world.

A handful of people attended the funeral, held at the graveside: Mrs. Williams; Sara Jane and Malcolm; Malcolm's mother and father; my parents and I; a brother of the late Mr. Pickens, who had taken the train down from Cincinnati; the Reverend Marvin Cartwright, who led the service; and old Mr. Heggebohm, the cemetery caretaker.

Immediately after the service, Mr. Pickens left to return to Cincinnati, while the rest of us, with the exception of Mr. Heggebohm, retired to the Williamses' farmhouse for refreshments.

Sara Jane and I sat on the front porch for a long time without speaking, each of us lost in our own thoughts, our own memories of the woman whose body we had just seen laid to rest. Inside the house, in addition to those who attended the funeral, were a number of neighbors who had come by to extend their condolences to Mrs. Williams.

Sara Jane broke the silence. "Grandma left me her diary."

"She kept a diary?"

"I guess she did, up until when she couldn't see anymore to write in it. It was one of the few things that survived both the fire and the flood."

"What does it say?"

"I don't know—I ain't had a chance to read it, yet. We didn't even know she had one. She kept it locked up in her trunk, with some of her other things. Before she died she told me it was there, and that I should have it. She said I could also have all the jewelry in there—a ring, a locket, and a pendant, she said. She said I'd also find a picture of my grandpa in the locket. My *real* grandpa. I don't know what she meant by that, but maybe the diary will explain it."

I wondered if it could be a reference to her first love, the one she told me about the last time I saw her. But before I could say anything, Sara Jane continued. "I almost forgot. Grandma give me this to give to you just before she passed."

She reached into the pocket of her dress, brought out a small pouch with a drawstring, and handed it to me.

"What is it?"

"I don't know. Grandma said it was for you, and she didn't want anyone to see it before you got it."

I opened the pouch, turned it over, and spilled its contents out into my open palm. I gave a short gasp, as did Sara Jane.

"Carter! It's a medal just like the one you wear!"

I stared at the medal in my hand, speechless. Even the chain was like mine. When at last I found my voice, I asked, "Did she say anything about it? Where it came from?"

"No. All she said was, 'Tell Carter to make sure he comes back.'"

"Comes back?"

"Yeah, comes back. Ain't that weird? I don't know, maybe she thought you might make it back before she died."

"Why didn't you call and tell me she was dying?" I was upset that I *hadn't* gotten back before Mary's death, had not been able to see her one last time.

"There weren't time. It happened so sudden like. And she gave me the pouch to give to you the night she died. I called you right after."

Tears filled my eyes again. I felt a pain—a loss—that was almost unbearable. I hadn't even felt like this when *my* grandparents died. Sara Jane moved closer to me and put her arm around my shoulders. Neither of us spoke. There was nothing to be said.

After a few minutes, I stood up. "I'm going for a walk."

"Would you like me to come with you?"

"If you'd like." I took the medal and placed it around my neck, along with the one I had taken from the skeleton fifteen years earlier.

We walked for a long time. Sara Jane spoke of her new sons, the joy they brought into her life, and how much work they were. She talked about Malcolm, and what a good and caring man he was. I told her of the law practice, and how well it was going.

It was dusk when we at last found ourselves at the old sycamore tree. We hadn't come that way on purpose. It just happened. We stood at the foot of the grave, marked by a plain marble stone:

Unknown soldier
died ca 1862 - 1864

I stared at the stone and remembered the day Emmaline and I stood there, and I told her the story of the skeleton and the medal. Only six months ago, but it seemed much longer.

Sara Jane seemed to be fascinated by the two medals now hanging around my neck. She took them in her hands and turned the chains so that the medals lay on my back.

"You know, Carter," she said, "both of these medals got that groove on the back of them."

I vaguely listened to what she was saying. My attention was drawn to the carving still visible on the tree trunk:

S.J. + H.J.
1863

"I wonder if they go together somehow," she said.

As she spoke, I turned and suddenly felt myself floating, as though I were flying through the air. My body spun around and around, caught up in what seemed to be a slow-moving tornado. Everything was white—or clear. I couldn't tell which.

Then—there was nothing.

Chapter Twenty-Seven

What Year is This?
April, 1863

"Whatcha doing here?"

Carter heard the voice as though it were coming from a distance, floating somewhere above him. His eyes were open, but he seemed to be in a kind of heavy fog, a milky blanket that obscured everything from sight.

The voice spoke again.

"Whatcha doing here, mister? Who are you?"

Focusing his eyes, Carter made out a vague figure. Gradually, the form became clearer and took on the shape of a person—a young boy, perhaps ten years of age. A large dog stood by the boy's side. Carter lay on the ground; the boy stood over him.

"Where's Sara Jane?" asked Carter.

"Who?"

"Sara Jane Will . . . Richardson," said Carter.

"I don't know no Sara Jane. I sure don't see no one else around. Just you and me and old Red here."

Carter struggled to his feet and looked at the boy. His clothes were old-fashioned, far different from anything Carter had ever seen. The lad was handsome, with coal-black hair that fell over his shirt collar. The dog at his side looked to be mostly legs and not much else.

"What happened?" asked Carter. "Who are you?"

"Name's Russell Jones. This here's my dog, Red. We live tuther side of that hill yonder." He pointed his finger. "As for what happened, I sure don't know. Red and me, we're out hunting for ginseng, and all of a sudden here you was, all sprawled out under this old sycamore, like you was dead. Heck, I thought you *was* dead."

Carter turned around. It *was* the old sycamore tree. Or was it? It looked like it except . . . except not as big as he remembered. There was something else strange about it, too. But what? Then it hit him. The initials and the date! They weren't there. They had disappeared.

Carter looked around and saw the stone wall was also gone, as were the gravestones. Missing, too, was the marker at the base of the tree where the skeleton had been buried.

"I . . . I don't understand," he murmured.

"You okay, mister?"

Carter turned back to the boy. "What day is this?"

"Why, it's Thursday."

"You mean Saturday, don't you? This is Saturday, and tomorrow's Easter Sunday?"

"Mister, I reckon I ought to know if today's Thursday or if it's Saturday. My sister always makes me go to church on Sunday, and if today was Saturday, I'd be going to church tomorrow, which I ain't. Besides, ain't Easter anyway. Easter was two weeks ago. And I know that, 'cause she made me go to church then, too."

"But it is the sixteenth of April?"

"Sure is. April 16, 1863."

Carter had turned to look once more at where the carving had been, but abruptly turned back. "What year did you say?"

"Eighteen and sixty-three," replied the boy. "Why, what year did you *think* it was? Juh get hit on the head by something falling out of this tree?"

It can't be! thought Carter. If this really was 1863, that meant he had traveled back through time more than sixty years. How could that be? It wasn't possible!

And yet—and yet, that could explain some things. Why the tree looked younger and smaller; why there was no carving; why the grave was missing; why *all* the graves were apparently missing; why there was no stone wall; the clothes the boy had on. But how? How could this have happened?

"Listen, mister, you don't look too good. Ain't acting quite right neither, I don't reckon. Why don't I take you to the house and let my sister have a look-see at you?"

"Perhaps . . . perhaps that would be a good idea," said Carter. He didn't know what else to do. He needed some time to figure this out, to try to determine how he had gotten here—wherever here was. "We are in Harrison County, Kentucky, aren't we?" he asked.

"Man, you're addled, for sure," said the boy. "'Course we're in Harrison County. Where'd you think we was?"

"I . . . I just wanted to be sure."

"So, what's your name?" the boy asked again.

"Uh, my name is Car . . ." Carter hesitated. Should he use his real name? If this was Harrison County, and the year 1863, there would probably be McGlones living around here now, mostly his relatives. It might be best that, until he figured out what had happened, he didn't use his real name. He blurted out the first name that came to his mind.

"Jenkins. Sam Jenkins." Sam wasn't from here. He'd have no relatives here.

"Can I ask you another question?" said the boy.

"What?"

"How come you're wearing those funny clothes? That necktie you got on—and your shirt and pants and shoes? I ain't never seen nothing like that, not even from old Reverend Moundtree."

Carter looked down at his clothes. They were the same as when he and Sara Jane stood talking under the sycamore tree; the clothes he'd worn to the funeral. His tie was loosened at the collar, and he saw with some relief both medals still hung around his neck.

"They're, uh . . ." it's a new style, that's all."

"They sure do look peculiar. Okay, Mr. Jenkins, come on and let's get you over to the house."

∞

Carter followed the boy across the field to a dirt road. As they walked he looked around. Nothing seemed familiar. The woods were thicker than he remembered them.

"I guess you're not from around here, are you, Mr. Jenkins?" asked Russell.

"Actually . . ." Actually, Carter thought, no I'm not from around here—not from this time, anyway, if he were to believe what the boy was telling him. "No, I'm . . . I'm just passing through."

"How did you get your limp?"

"It . . . it was an accident. Something fell on it."

"Where you heading for?"

This kid sure asks a lot of questions! "I'm . . . I'm not sure exactly."

"Bet you forgot when you got hit in the head."

"That could be," said Carter.

As they rounded a bend in the road, a modest, two-story frame farmhouse, not unlike the one Carter grew up in, came into view. A porch ran the length of the front of the house. Carter didn't remember ever seeing the place before. He spotted four other structures, one of them a barn. From the appearance of the other buildings, he assumed they included a chicken coop and a smokehouse. Behind the chicken coop, he saw the corner of what appeared to be a log cabin.

A woman stood at a well in the side yard, pumping water into a bucket.

"This way, mister. Helen!" Russell shouted, as they walked down the lane to the house. "I got somebody here who done hurt hisself."

As the woman turned toward them, Carter stopped. Her beauty almost took his breath away!

Her dark hair was put up in a bun at the back of her head, accentuating a long, graceful neck. She wore a flowing skirt that came down to her ankles and a white cotton blouse not quite adequate to hide the firm curvature of her breasts. When Carter reached her, he saw her eyes were a stunning greenish blue, like turquoise, and her skin tanned from long hours of working in the fields. In her late twenties, he thought, and, all in all, one of the most beautiful women he'd ever seen. Perhaps *the* most beautiful woman he'd ever seen, even including Emmaline.

He had the strangest feeling he had met her someplace before, not unlike the one he'd experienced the first time he met Mary. Something about her seemed familiar. When she spoke, it was a voice Carter was positive he knew. But that was impossible. This was 1863, if what Russell told him was true. There was no way he could know this woman.

"Russell says you've hurt yourself?"

"I'm afraid your brother has exaggerated somewhat," said Carter. "I feel all right, except I'm a little disoriented."

"I found him sprawled out under that big sycamore tree in the field down the road," said Russell." Thought he was dead at first. Then I thought maybe something fell out of the tree and hit him in the head. Anyways, he didn't seem quite right to me, so I brung him back here."

The woman held out her hand. "My name is Helen Jones. Are you sure you feel all right? Perhaps you'd like a drink of cold water. We finished supper, but there's leftover in the pot. I can fix you a plate."

"Perhaps a drink of water would be good," said Carter. He found it hard not to stare at her.

"I didn't get your name," she said as she handed him a dipper of water from the bucket.

"Oh, I'm sorry. It's . . . Sam, Sam Jenkins."

"And what brings you to these parts, Mr. Jenkins?"

That's a good question. What the hell did bring me to these "parts"? "I'm . . . just passing through, ma'am."

"It's getting on near dark," said Helen. "You'd be welcome to stay the night in the barn, if you like. I could—"

"What's wrong with the cabin?" interrupted Russell.

"Oh, I don't think Mr. Jenkins would want to stay in the cabin."

"Why not?" Russell persisted.

"Because of Mornin."

"Mornin?" said Carter.

"Mornin's an old Negro, a former slave of ours," said Helen. "My daddy gave him his freedom a couple of years ago, but he still lives here on the farm. He helps out as best he can."

"You're right," Carter said. "He probably wouldn't want anyone invading his privacy."

"Oh, it's not that," said Helen. "He loves company. We don't get much around here. It's . . . well, like I said, he's a Negro, and—"

"And you thought I'd be offended if you suggested I spend the night in a cabin with a Negro."

"I guess so," she replied, smiling.

Carter turned to Russell. "Which one's better, the cabin or the barn?"

"Shucks, the cabin," replied Russell, in no uncertain terms. "The barn stinks."

Carter smiled at his forthrightness. "Then, ma'am, if you don't think Mornin would object, the cabin would be fine with me."

"Very well, then. And, please, Mr. Jenkins, you can call me Helen."

"Thank you . . . Helen. And, please, call me Car . . . Sam."

Carter suddenly realized that, indeed, he *was* hungry. He hadn't eaten since noon, had not even had anything at the Williamses' home following the funeral.

The funeral—although it had only been a few hours ago, now it seemed like a million years.

"Ma'am—Helen—I guess I'd like to accept your offer of something to eat. I reckon I'm hungrier than I thought."

"Good. You can wash up here at the pump. Then come on in the house, and I'll have a plate ready for you. I'll get you some blankets, too."

As Carter splashed water over his face, he tried to comprehend what had happened: He *had* traveled back in time! How? Why? And why to this time? It just didn't make sense.

Chapter Twenty-Eight

Mornin

Carter sat at the table eating the stew Helen had placed before him, glancing around now and then. The kitchen contained a fairly new cast-iron cook-stove, the table he sat at and four chairs. Against the wall facing the barn stood a sink with a pump and handle. To his left there was no wall; rather the kitchen opened up into a parlor which, along with a few chairs and a long wooden bench, held a square, grand piano, the type he remembered seeing in Sara Jane's Grandmother Williamses' home. Stairs led to a second floor. He knew the stone fireplace was on the wall next to the stairs; he had seen the chimney from the lane.

The other two walls contained several doors, all closed, so he wasn't sure where they led. The whole scene reminded him of his grandmother's home, like something from another era. Then it struck him—it was! This wasn't 1927—it was 1863.

Even more troubling was the realization that he had no idea how he might get back to his own time—or if it was even possible. He wondered what Sara Jane was telling— had told, will tell?—hell, he didn't know which!—everyone about his disappearance. He knew they'd all be worried sick over what had happened to him.

Helen busied herself at the stove, her back to Carter. In spite of his concern over the situation in which he found himself, it was difficult to keep his eyes off her. *Damn, she's beautiful*!

Russell entered just as Carter finished his stew.

"All my chores are done."

"Very good, Russell. Thank you," said Helen. "Now it's time for you to go to bed, so say good night to Mr. Jenkins."

"Aw, Helen," pleaded Russell, "let me stay up a little bit longer. I want to talk with Mr. Jenkins here. It ain't like we get company every day."

"I don't . . ." Helen saw Carter raise his eyebrows and shrug his shoulders.

"It's okay with me, if it's okay with you," he said.

"All right, then. For a little while. And you better not pester Mr. Jenkins with too many questions."

Russell plopped down on a chair across the table from Carter. "So, Mr. Jenkins, where *are* you from?"

"Russell!" snapped Helen.

"No, that's okay," said Carter. "I was a kid once myself. I know how curious they can be. I'm from Louisville, Russell. And you can call me Sam, too. Have you ever been to Louisville?"

"Louisville?" exclaimed Russell. "Shucks, no, I ain't never been nowhere. But I sure would like to go to Louisville. My Uncle Teddie told me a lot about it. He's been there."

"Your uncle?"

"My brother," said Helen. "Right now, he's off fighting with the Sixth Kentucky Cavalry. We're not sure exactly where." Carter saw the obvious concern in her face. "We're praying he'll be safe, and come back to us soon."

1863? Sixth Kentucky? Of course . . . the War Between the States! In all the confusion of finding himself in another time, he hadn't even thought of that.

"I'm sure he'll be okay," Carter said. "So . . . just you and Russell here to take care of this farm? And . . . Mornin, was it? Your parents . . .?"

Helen sat down at the table. "My mother died three years ago, giving birth to our little sister. She died, too. Daddy was killed last year when the Confederates attacked Cynthiana. He was a member of the Home Guard."

"I'm sorry," said Carter.

"My Grandma and Grandpa Swaney still live over in Morgan County. I have a couple of uncles there, too. It's been a spell since I've seen them. My uncles and their wives came over for Daddy's funeral, but Grandma and Grandpa weren't able to make the trip because of their age and all."

"That's your mother's side of the family?"

"That's right. She was from Morgan County originally. Daddy met her when he was over there one time buying some cattle. They met each other, and fell in love and within a year they were married, and she came back here to Harrison County with him to live."

"Are you a Johnny Reb?" asked Russell. It was obvious he had been stewing on this for a while.

"No, Russell, I'm not a Rebel," answered Carter. "I never was for the South seceding." He racked his brain trying to recall what he'd learned in school about the war and what happened here. At the time it hadn't seemed too important. Now, it did.

"Enough questions, Russell. Time for bed," said Helen.

"Oh, okay," said Russell reluctantly. He stood up and headed for one of the doors at the back of the room. "So, Mr. Jenkins—Sam—you still going to be here in the morning? Will I see you then?"

Unless this is all some kind of a dream, I'll still be here, thought Carter. "I reckon so. I'll see you in the morning."

"I think it's time for me to turn in, too," said Helen. "Here are the blankets. I think you'll be comfortable tonight. Let me walk you out to the cabin and introduce you to Mornin."

Carter smiled, stood, and took the blankets from Helen's hands.

"Mornin's a strange name," he said. "How did he come by it?"

"I'll let him tell you," answered Helen. "He loves to tell the story."

As they walked the short distance from the house to the cabin, Carter couldn't help but steal a glance at Helen. *God, she's even more beautiful than I first thought.* Better he turn his mind to other matters.

"How long has Mornin been with you?"

"He was my daddy's slave even before I was born. He's quite old and not in good health. I've been thinking of having him move into the house, into Teddie's room while he's gone. The thing is, I never know when Teddie might show up, and then he might get angry with me. Then, too, Mornin is so fiercely independent, I'm not even sure he would agree to moving into the house. I can't even get him to take his meals with us.

"After daddy made him a free man, Mornin said he had to 'take responsibility for himself,' now. So, I don't argue with him. I'll let him live out his life here on the farm, if that's what he wants."

Unlike the farmhouse, the one-story cabin was constructed of logs, and chinked with mortar. A stone chimney jutted out from one end. Carter spotted the old man through the window, sitting at a table eating supper. Helen knocked on the door, and almost at once it was opened. Helen said he was elderly, but in spite of a full head of white hair and a neatly-trimmed white beard—making him look somewhat like a taller, thinner, black Santa Claus, Carter thought—it would have been difficult to guess his true age.

"Miz Helen. What brings you out heah dis time o' night? Everting all rot?"

"Good evening, Mornin. Yes, everything's fine. Mornin, this is Mr. Jenkins. He's passing through, and has no place to spend the night, and I've invited him to stay here. I hope it's no imposition if he sleeps here in the cabin tonight."

"Oh, yas'm, dat would be jus' fine. Wit da boys gone now, dere's plenty room. And ah could use da company. Come on in, Marse Jenkins."

"Very well," said Helen. Then, turning to Carter: "I'll have a good hot breakfast ready in the morning, if you'd care to join us."

"I'm sure I will," Carter replied. "Good night, and thanks, again."

While Mornin cleared dishes from the table, Carter made his bed, one of three bunks set side by side against an end wall, two feet from one another. Glancing around, he guessed the building to be perhaps twenty feet long and fifteen or sixteen feet wide. Three wooden chairs surrounded the table where Mornin was sitting when they arrived. Next to the fireplace were shelves that held dishes and cups, and a small table sat in the other corner with a wash pan on it. Pegs fastened along the wall behind the beds held what Carter assumed to be Mornin's clothing. In addition to the front door and two windows at the front of the cabin, the back wall contained two more windows. Unlike many cabins of its time, this one had a wooden floor.

"I asked Miss Jones about your name, because it was so unusual," said Carter. "She said you'd tell me about it."

The old man beamed, showing a mouth full of gleaming white teeth.

"Yas suh, dat's a good story. Seems dat when mah momma was gettin' ready to born me, dere was dis big storm, a hurrycane iz whut it was, comin' tru. Da night she was havin' me, da storm hit. Daddy say da wind, it was blowin' sometin fierce. An rain . . . lawdy, ain't nevah seed rain like dat befo or since, he say.

"Anyways, mah momma, she was in a terrible fix all naght, cause ah didn' wanta come out. And den, too, she was afeard o' da storm—da wind, and da rain, and da thundah, an lightin'. It was jus terrible bad.

"Finally, jus as da sun was startin' to come up, ah decides to be borned. And rot den, dat's when da storm quit. No more wind, or rain—nothin'.'"

Mornin's voice got softer. "Got reeeal still like. Daddy thought it was mebbe jus da eye of da storm, but no, it weren't. Da storm was over, gone.

"So Daddy, he turns to Momma and says, 'Iz a brand new mornin'.' And she says, 'Den dat's what we name him—Mornin.' And dat's how ah got mah name."

Carter leaned back in his chair and laughed. "You're right, that is a good story. And you mentioned some boys—who are they?"

"Dey's da otha two niggahs use to live heah. Dey up an tuck off rot aftah Marse Jones got kilt. Went ta join da Union army, dey said. Don' reckon dey'll evah be back."

"What about their parents? Did they live here, too?"

"Don' rightly know who dere daddy was. Dere momma, Miz Rose, she lived up in da house. She died jus 'bout a month aftah Miz Helen's momma died. And dat little baby, too. Ah tink she was jus too heartbroke to go on livin', 'cause she loved dat woman almost as much as she loved dose boys."

Carter stretched out on his bunk. "Are they kin of yours?"

"Oh, no suh. Marse Jones done bought dem when dey was jus young'uns. Dem and dere momma. Some famah ovah in Buhbon County was gonna jus buy dere momma, an let somebody else buy da boys, cause dey was jus young an skinny. Marse Jones, he say no way he gonna let dat man split up dat family, so he jus bought all tree of dem, da whole bunch. Ah tink Lucius was jus' two or tree, an Malachi mebbe five. Dat was nigh on to fifteen yeahs ago. Dey been heah evah since. Until dey left. Marse Jones, he gave dem dere papers las' year, same as me, so dey's free niggahs now. Marse Jones, he was a good man. And Miz Helen, she be a good woman."

Carter sat straight up. "I'm sorry. What did you say the boys' names were?"

"Malachi was da oldes', an da younga one was named Lucius."

Malachi? Lucius? Rose? Could these be Emmaline's ancestors?

"What was their last name, Mornin?"

"Oh, dey didn' have no las name, Marse Jenkins. Lots of us slaves don' have no las' name."

"But when they joined the army, wouldn't the army have asked for a last name?"

"Whut a lot of slaves do, dey take dere mastah's las' name. So ah s'pose if Malachi and Lucius did dat, dey'd take da name of Marse Jones."

Malachi Jones! They had to be one and the same.

"Now, Marse Jenkins, I don' mean to be rude, but if y'all don' mind, ah believe ah'll turn in. Ah's feelin' kinda tired. 'Iz been a long day."

Carter didn't answer. He was too deep in thought. *So Emmaline's grandfather, Malachi, was a slave on this farm.* If that were the case, it would seem to answer the two questions that came up on their first trip to Harrison County: Carter's ancestors were not Emmaline's ancestors' masters; nor were he and Emmaline related. Not, he thought, sadly, that it made any difference now.

Carter yawned. It had been a long—not to mention—unusual day. He had awakened in 1927, and now here he was about to go to sleep in 1863.

He lay back down on his bunk. Sleep came slowly, but come it did at last.

Chapter Twenty-Nine

Carter Decides to Stay

Even before he opened his eyes, the pungent aroma of chicory coffee mingling with the savory smell of crisp bacon drifted into Carter's nostrils. He rolled over, lifted one eyelid, and saw Mornin standing in front of the fireplace.

"Good morning, Mornin."

Mornin turned and looked at him and grinned. "Mornin', Marse Jenkins. Ah hope ah didn' wake you wif all da noise ah make."

"No, not at all. It was the smell of your coffee that woke me. Chicory, isn't it?"

"Yas suh, dat's da way ah lak it. Oh, would you lak some?" Mornin quickly pulled down a cup from the shelf and filled it without waiting for an answer.

"Yes, thank you that would be great. And, please, call me Sam."

"Yas suh, if dat's what you want."

Carter got out of bed, put on his pants, shirt, socks, and shoes, walked over to the table, and sat down.

The coffee tasted as good as it smelled.

"You brew some mighty fine coffee," said Carter.

"Tank you, Marse Sam. When a man lives by hisself, he got to learn to take care of hisself. Ah learnt to cook a long time ago, when ah was da only niggah heah, befo' Rose and her boys come.

"'Course, when she was heah, she lived up in da main house, stayed in dat back room where Marse Russell sleeps now. Da boys, dey stayed out heah wit me. Dere momma would come out each day an fix dere meals, but ah always fixed mah own. Miz Rose was a good cook." Mornin grinned. "But ah ain't sure maybe ah'se a bettah cook."

Carter returned the grin. He liked the old man.

"So, since you're a free man, will you be staying on here, or do you have family somewhere that you're going back to?"

"Oh, no suh, ah'll stay heah. Ain't no family no mo. Leastways, if dey is, ah don' know where ah'd find dem."

"I take it from the story of how you got your name, with the hurricane and all, you're not from around here originally?"

"No suh, ah'se from Loo-see-ana. Nawluns. Ah belonged to da Breaux family dere. Mebbe you heerd of dem?"

"No, can't say that I have," said Carter.

"Marse Breaux, he was a judge dere. Good man. He bought me when ah was—oh, ah tink mebbe twenty, somethin' like dat."

"How did you end up here?"

"Well, suh, one year Marse Breaux, he made a trip up ta Louavul for somepin'. Ah don' know what. Anyways, him and Marse Jones, dey was good friends, and Marse Jones axed Marse Breaux over to his fahm heah fo a visit. Marse Breaux, he had brung me along wit him to Louavul, and so off we went. We hadn' been heah but two days, an ah come down wit da fevah. Marse Breaux, he got to git back to Nawluns, but ah coulden travel, so Marse Jones he say why don' ah stay heah 'til ah better, den he send me back down to Marse Breaux. So dat's what we did.

"'Cept Marse Breaux, he changed his mind later on, said why don' ah stay up heah wit Marse Jones, and ah be his slave. An so *dat's* what we did."

"So, Mr. Jones bought you from Mr. Breaux?"

"Oh, no suh, Marse Breaux he done give me to Marse Jones for a present. Ah didn' cost him nothin'."

"How old are you now, Mornin?"

"Don' rightly know fo sure, but ah s'pect ah's 'bout sixty-five, mebbe sixty-six."

"Miss Helen and Russell seem like nice people."

"Oh, dey's da best," said Mornin. "Dey treat me real nice. And dey's nice to otha folks, too."

"Listen, Mornin, you've been around here for a while. Have you ever heard of a family named 'McGlone'?"

"McGlone?" Mornin wrinkled his brows in thought. "No suh, cain't say as ah have."

"I was won—" A knock at the door interrupted Carter.

Mornin quickly opened it. Russell stood there, holding a basket.

"Hi, Mornin."

"Hi, yoself, Marse Russell."

"Sam, Helen says breakfast will be ready in a little bit. And she wants to know how you slept last night."

"Morning, Russell. I slept fine, thank you."

"You can wash up out at the pump if you want. I got to go get some eggs."

"Okay, I'll be right there."

Russell ran out the door, on his way to the hen house. Carter turned to Mornin and put out his hand.

"Mornin, it was a pleasure meeting you. Thanks for the coffee. And I enjoyed our talk."

"Yas suh. An' good luck to you, suh."

Carter walked out to the well pump, brought up some water, and was washing his face when Russell came racing from the chicken coop, Red close at his heels.

"Hurry up, Sam. Ain't gonna be but a minute 'til Helen has these eggs frying."

"I'm on my way," said Carter.

Carter stood there for a moment, seeing the house for the first time in the daylight. It was a well-built home, two stories, constructed of wood with a room added on at the rear, which he now knew must be Russell's bedroom. Carter surmised the second floor probably contained two or three bedrooms. Smoke curling out from the chimney told him there was a fire in the fireplace. Even though it was April, the air had a chill to it.

As soon as Carter opened the door the savory aroma of baked ham and biscuits came wafting from the cast iron stove. Helen stood with her back to him. Her hair wasn't up in a bun this morning, but lay gracefully on her back, falling almost to her waist. Like Russell's, it was jet black, as black as the inside of the big cave on old man Rickett's farm. She turned to Carter and he was struck again by how beautiful she was, the fine lines of her face, the eyes that seemed to both blaze and sparkle at the same time. Carter remembered what Sara Jane said once when he asked her how she would know when the right man came along: "I think when I meet him, something will happen to my heart. I'll feel something here."

She had held her hand over her heart. "It'll be different, somehow."

Carter felt that way now. There *was* something going on in his heart, a sensation he had never experienced before, not even with Emmaline. And it was this woman who stood here before him who was the cause of whatever it was he was feeling.

She interrupted his reverie. "Good morning, Mr. Jenkins. I hope you slept well. Are you hungry?"

"Yes, ma'am, I sure did. And I sure am."

"Sit down and I'll bring you a plate. I hope you're partial to baked ham, fried potatoes fried eggs, and biscuits, because that's what's on the menu for breakfast. We also have some nice fresh milk—unless you'd prefer buttermilk?"

"Oh, no, ma'am, plain old milk is fine. Everything else sounds fine, too."

Russell came in and sat down at the table. As he reached for the biscuits, Helen placed her hand over his. "Did you wash your hands?"

"I did."

"Then let me sit down, and we'll say our grace before we have our meal."

Carter jumped to his feet, pulled Helen's chair away from the table and held it for her. "Thank you, Mr. Jenkins," she said. Carter thought he detected a slight blush in her cheeks.

"Let us join hands," said Helen, bowing her head. "Heavenly Father, we give you thanks for this day, and for all the many blessings you bestow upon us in this life. We ask you to be with our Teddie, to keep him safe in your care. And we pray this terrible war may soon be ended, and all of our men, both those fighting for the Union and those fighting for the South, may return home to their loved ones. We give you thanks for bringing Mr. Jenkins to share our meal with us, and we give you thanks for this food, and ask that it might be used to strengthen us as we do your work in this world. In Jesus's name, Amen."

"Amen," said Russell and Carter in unison.

Throughout the prayer, Carter's heart had been racing. The touch of Helen's hand, soft and gentle, even though strong from farm work, sent a charge of electricity through his whole body. With some reluctance, he let go.

"So, Mr. Jenkins," asked Helen. "What are your plans? Will you be staying around here for a while, or will you be on your way to wherever it is you're going?"

"What are my plans?" Hell, he didn't know. "To tell you the truth, I . . . I'm not quite sure right now."

"Why don't you stay, then?" Russell jumped in. "You could tell me more about Louisville."

"Well," said Helen, "if it's work you're looking for, I could use some help around here on the farm. I'm afraid with my daddy's death, and Teddie gone, Russell and I haven't been able to keep up with all the repairs that should have been done. Mornin tries to help, but he's not able. I'm a bit concerned that, with planting time upon us, we're not going to be able to get everything finished when we should. I couldn't pay you anything, of course, but I could provide you with a place to sleep, along with your meals."

Carter had watched her face as she spoke. At first, she looked directly at him, but then busied herself moving the food around on her plate with her fork.

"Sure," Russell joined in again. "Helen's a real good cook, and you could sleep out in the cabin, like last night!"

Carter mulled over the offer in his mind for a few minutes. If he didn't stay here, where would he go? Where *could* he go? He had no family—at least none that knew him. He knew no one. He didn't even have a job anymore. At least this would give him a place to live until he decided what to do. And, he admitted to himself, the thought of being around Helen was inviting.

"I reckon I could stay," said Carter. "I don't have anyplace I have to be right now."

"Then it's settled," said Helen, with a smile.

A wide grin spread over Russell's face.

"I don't mean to be presumptuous, but can I assume you don't have any clothes with you other than the ones you have on?" asked Helen. "I didn't notice a bag or valise when Russell brought you home."

Carter felt a sense of embarrassment as he looked down at his clothes, which at this point didn't look too presentable. Nor were they the proper style for this time period he somehow found himself in.

"I'm . . . afraid you're right," said Carter. "These are all I have with me."

"I think we can fix that," she said. "There are plenty of Teddie's clothes upstairs, and I judge he's pretty much the same size as you, maybe a tad shorter. After breakfast, we'll see what we can find."

"Do you play the piano?" asked Carter, noticing again the instrument in the other room.

"I do," Helen replied, her face brightening. "My mother taught me how to play."

"Do you play?" asked Russell.

"Not the piano," Carter answered. "But I do play the guitar."

"The guitar!" exclaimed Helen. "We don't have a guitar, but my daddy's old banjo is upstairs. Teddie planned to take it when he left, but then he thought it might be too much to lug around, along with everything else. Besides, he doesn't play all that well. Can you play the banjo, Mr. Jenkins?"

"I've played the banjo on occasion. My cousin Rupert had one, and he let me play it sometimes."

"How wonderful!" exclaimed Helen. "Perhaps one of these evenings we can have some music in the house."

Chapter Thirty

Carter Settles In

Helen was right about Teddie and Carter being close to the same size. Carter chose a few cotton shirts, two pair of overalls, one of Teddie's straw hats, and a pair of work boots.

"Don't forget socks," Helen reminded him. "And, of course you'll need some, uh . . ."

"Underwear," said Carter, sparing her the embarrassment of having to say the word.

"That's what I was trying to say," said Helen, a redness creeping to her cheeks.

"Let me take these out to the cabin and get changed. Then you can give me an idea of where I can start working."

Mornin was delighted to hear Carter would be staying around for a while. Over Carter's protestations, he promised to clean the cabin and make it more presentable.

"It's fine the way it is," said Carter.

"Oh, no suh, when'iz jus' me heah, ah sometimes git a bit careless 'bout keepin' it clean, but ah'll do a bettah job now dat you heah, too. 'Sides, it give me someting to do."

As Carter changed his clothes, he kept wondering about how he had arrived in this time. *It must have something to do with the medals*, he thought. He took them in his hands and carefully studied them. Sara Jane had been right—there were grooves on both of them. Did they go together? Perhaps. But what would happen then? Would he return to his own time? Or some other time? After all, he had no idea why, or how, he had come to this particular year of 1863. It didn't make sense.

He placed the medals back to back. But uncertainty prevented him from locking them together. He didn't want to chance ending up in the Middle Ages, or the Stone Age, or—who knows when?

Besides, there was Helen. Carter wasn't certain he wanted to leave yet, even if he could.

Slowly, he brought the medals apart. He could always try later if he decided to.

Over the next two days, Carter kept busy plowing the fields. He needed to get the corn planted right away. Russell walked along beside him when he wasn't doing his own chores. Carter told him about Louisville, being careful to remember the Louisville he knew was not the one that existed in this time. In return, he got Russell to tell him more about Harrison County: the people who lived there and what was happening. Did Russell happen to know a family named McGlone?

He didn't think so, he said. Williams? No, that name wasn't familiar either. "But," said Russell, "I sure don't know everybody in this here county, so they might be here, and I don't know them."

Finally, Carter got up enough courage to ask Russell the question he *really* wanted the answer to.

"So, Russell, is there anybody courting Helen? I mean, does she have a boyfriend?"

"Helen?" Russell replied, as though he couldn't believe anyone *would* want to be courting his sister. "Not that I know of. Although . . ."

"Although?"

"Now that you mention it, I always did wonder if old Dieter took a shine to my sister."

"Dieter?"

"Uh-huh—Dieter. I never can say his last name. German, I think. Roomhustle, or something like that. I know him and Helen, they was best friends growing up. And anytime we go into town or church, or anywhere Dieter's around, he's always talking to Helen. He *might* be sweet on her."

"Is Dieter a farmer?"

"Sort of. His folks have a big tobacco farm over that hill yonder," answered Russell, pointing. "I guess you could call it a plantation. They own the mill, too."

"How old are you, Russell?"

"Twelve."

"And Teddie?"

"I reckon he's about twenty-five, or twenty-six."

"And Helen?"

"Helen? She's a couple years younger than Teddie, so I reckon she must be about twenty-two, twenty-three."

"I would have thought her a little older," said Carter.

"How old are you, Sam?"

"Twenty-eight." *Except*, Carter realized, *I'm not even going to be born for another thirty-six years.*

"Sam. Russell." Helen called from the house. "Time for supper. Get washed up, and come on in."

That evening, after supper, Helen played the piano while Carter accompanied her on the banjo. He was a little rusty, but no one said anything. Russell clapped his hands in time to the music or hummed along to the songs he knew.

During a break for a treat of lemonade, Helen asked, "Mr. Jenkins, Russell and I will be going to church tomorrow. Would you care to join us?"

Carter thought for a moment before answering. "I appreciate the invitation, but I don't think so, not this time." He had too much thinking to do. And he didn't feel ready to meet other people right now.

"Very well," said Helen. "Perhaps another time." Carter thought he detected a hint of disappointment in her voice.

"Perhaps. And, I do have a request."

"Yes?"

"Would you please call me . . . Sam?" He had to think for a moment before getting the name out. "I've been calling you Helen, and you've been calling me Mr. Jenkins. I'd like for you to call me 'Sam', if you wouldn't mind."

"Of course," replied Helen, with a smile. "I'd be happy to call you by your given name, if that's what you prefer."

"Russell, don't you play an instrument?" asked Carter.

"No. Never had any hankering to."

"Russell does have his talent, though," said Helen. "He's quite an artist."

"Is that right?"

"Oh, I'm okay," said Russell, a blush coming to his cheeks.

"You're more than okay," admonished Helen. "He has a true gift. Maybe you can get him to show you some of his work."

"I'd love that," said Carter. "Do you paint with oil? Water color?"

"Naw. Cain't afford none of that fancy stuff. I use charcoal. Make it myself in the fireplace."

"Do you want to be an artist when you grow up? Make your living that way?"

Russell looked at Carter the same way Sara Jane had looked at him when he asked her about going to college.

"Make a living? Who the heck could make a living drawing pictures? I want to be a fireman."

"A fireman? Do you have a fire department around here?"

"We got us a volunteer fire department. But I'm planning on heading up to Cincinnati to join the fire department there."

"Last year," said Helen, "when Morgan's men came through Cynthiana, there were a group of soldiers—"

"*Firemen*," interrupted Russell.

"All right, then, firemen—"

"And they had big fire engine horses with them," Russell interrupted again.

"May I continue?" asked Helen.

"Sorry," said Russell.

"This group of firemen were sent here from Cincinnati with a big cannon, and eight fire engine horses to help fight against the Confederates. To be perfectly honest, they didn't accomplish much, but Russell was so impressed by the horses he has now decided to move to Cincinnati and become a fireman when he's old enough."

"Which ain't going to be too long from now," said Russell, emphatically.

"I think that's an admirable thing to aspire to," Carter said, trying hard not to show how amusing he found the whole idea to be.

"Please," said Helen. "Don't encourage him."

"Seriously. I think it's great."

"Thanks for your help." Helen gave Carter a scorching look.

"Perhaps it's time for some more music," said Carter, sensing the best thing now might be to lay the subject to rest.

The following day, after Helen and Russell left for church, Carter spent the next hour exploring the rest of the farm. What few buildings there were all well constructed although they needed a considerable amount of repair. He made mental notes of the major jobs that would be required. He checked out the livestock: the usual assortment of chickens, a few pigs, about a dozen cows, and one other horse besides the one Russell had hitched to the wagon to go to church in, plus the usual assortment of cats—good mice catchers, essential on a farm.

At one time the place had been much more flourishing than it was now. However, a small tobacco patch, and a good-sized garden were already planted behind the barn, which stood next to the smokehouse, a low-lying stone structure with a wooden door and no windows.

Carter finished his tour of the farm, saddled up the second horse and set off down the lane. When he reached the road he turned and headed in the direction where he knew his home to be—or, at least, would be—in 1927. Was the house there in 1863? He wasn't sure.

Between Helen's farm and Carter's home sat his Grandmother McGlone's farm—or where it should have been. But when he came to the site, he was disappointed to find only woods—no buildings. Apparently the home hadn't yet been built.

A few more miles brought him to the site of his own home. He was relieved to see that, indeed, it did exist, almost as he remembered it. But who lived here now? His grandparents? Strangers? He remembered it was 1864 when Great-grandpa McGlone disappeared, which meant now, in 1863, he must still be alive. Was this his home? Or was he off fighting the war someplace? Carter didn't know.

He thought about hanging around to see who might go in or come out, then realized that, even if it were one of his ancestors, he might not recognize the person. Reluctantly, he turned and headed back toward Helen's farm. Then he stopped: *Sara Jane.* Her family's farm lay but another half mile away. He turned back and set off again in that direction.

Approaching the house, Carter was almost blinded by sunlight reflecting off what appeared to be a fresh coat of white paint. By Sara Jane's time, the white had turned a dismal gray. To the right of the house, he noticed a building that was no longer there in the 1920s—perhaps the kitchen, he thought.

The place looked much as he remembered it—nicer, of course, better maintained, with more buildings than when Sara Jane lived there, but her home, nonetheless.

Carter knew the house was solidly built from yellow poplar. The floors were all constructed from pine, although by the 1920s, the years had been no kinder to them than to the house's exterior. He had asked his mother once how Sara Jane's parents could afford such a grand house, as run down as it was, when her father was a plain old dirt farmer, like his own. She explained that before Sara Jane was born, her family had been quite wealthy, but they lost much of it in the stock market in 1899, the same year Carter was born. And what little they didn't lose then, they lost in 1907, when the market again plummeted.

Carter wondered who lived in this house now, and if they might be Sara Jane's ancestors.

He glanced up at the sun. Near one o'clock, he reckoned. He reined the horse around and headed back.

∞

As he neared the farm, he saw Helen and Russell coming down the road in the wagon, Red running alongside. They all arrived at the lane leading to the house at the same time.

"How was church today?" asked Carter.

"Boring, as usual!" exclaimed Russell. "I would of gotten a nice nap if Helen hadn't kept poking me in the ribs."

"Church was fine," said Helen. "Reverend Moundtree gave an excellent sermon, and the choir sang . . . well, the choir sang with great vigor."

They all laughed at this somewhat less than enthusiastic endorsement of the choir's effort.

"They sounded worse than that old rooster in the morning," said Russell, still laughing.

"I must admit," added Helen, "they could surely stand some improvement. But they try. How did you spend your morning?"

Carter told her he had looked around the farm. And, as she could see, he'd gone for a ride.

"I hope you don't mind that I borrowed the horse." He said nothing about checking out the various homes.

"Anytime," said Helen. "So, what do you think of the place now that you've had a chance to look it over?"

"It's a good farm, the land is good and rich," said Carter. "The house is certainly well built, and a few minor repairs will have it in tiptop shape. The outbuildings may need a little more than minor repairs, though, especially the barn roof."

"My Grandfather Jones built the house and the barn in the early 1800s," said Helen, "when he and my grandmother came to Kentucky from Tennessee. My family's been farming here ever since."

"And the cabin?"

"Grandfather Jones built that when they first got here, to live in until they built the house. They didn't need much room; it was only him and Grandmother Goldie, and my father and uncle Lou. Uncle Gardner didn't come along until after they got here.

"Russell and I have been invited to go over to some dear friends of ours, Henry and Hilda Ruehmschuessel, for dinner next Sunday. I talked with Hilda after church today and told her about you, that you're staying here for a while, helping out around the farm. She insisted you come also. Would you like to go?"

"Ruehmschuessel?"

"That's Dieter's family." Russell had climbed up onto the saddle behind Carter and wrapped his arms around Carter's waist. He gave him a little squeeze.

Carter smiled. "I would very much like to go."

"Do you know Dieter?" asked Helen.

"Russell mentioned him to me once. I've never met the man."

"It's settled then," said Helen. "We'll be coming back here before we go, so you won't need to go to church with us unless you want to."

"No, I do want to. I'd like to go to church." Carter figured he might as well start meeting the other people who lived around here. This might turn out to be his home for the rest of his life, if he was unable to return to his own time. Besides, he wanted to see what Dieter was like.

Then Carter remembered he didn't have any clothes suitable for church.

"Don't worry," said Helen. "We'll find you something of Teddie's you can wear."

Chapter Thirty-One

Dieter Ruehmschuessel

Carter decided Russell was right about church—it *was* boring. Reverend Moundtree was one of those preachers who believed he hadn't earned his keep if his sermon wasn't at least forty-five minutes long. It didn't help that he spent the first fifteen minutes telling you what he was *going* to say, the next fifteen minutes *saying* it, and the last fifteen minutes telling you what he had just said. It was all Carter could do not to doze off, as he noticed Russell doing on several occasions before Helen nudged him awake with an elbow to the ribs.

The small church was packed. Sunday services, as in Carter's day, were an essential part of the life of the community, a gathering place for folks who might not see one another the rest of the week. Church was a social, as well as a religious, experience.

Outside, after the service, Carter looked around at the small groups of people milling about. *Are any of these my ancestors?* he wondered.

His thoughts were interrupted by Helen's hand on his arm.

"Hilda, Henry, I'd like you to meet Sam Jenkins. He's the gentleman I told you was staying at the farm. Sam's going to be helping get some repairs done around the place."

"Sam, a pleasure to meet you," said Henry.

"And we're so delighted you'll be joining us later today for dinner," added Hilda.

"Thank you Mrs. Ruehmschuessel." It was apparent from the couple's heavy accents they had come to America from the old country. "I'm looking forward to it," said Carter. "And, I'm looking forward to meeting the rest of your family." *Especially Dieter.*

"I'm impressed," said Henry. "You pronounced our name exactly right. Not too many people do on the first try."

"Helen was a good instructor. And, I have to admit, I practiced a little bit." They all laughed.

"I think Karl is off someplace with Russell," said Hilda. "And I suspect Gertie is with that young Michaels boy. But here's one you can meet right now: our oldest son, Dieter."

Carter turned and saw what might only be described as a young Viking god approaching them. He appeared to be somewhat taller than Carter, and moved with long, easy strides, the walk of a man possessed with an abundance of self assurance. A shock of blond hair fell carelessly over his ears, framing a ruggedly handsome face, and a set of magnificent mutton chop sideburns that, in turn, flowed into a full mustache. Carter swore he saw a glint in the man's eyes, which were perhaps the bluest Carter had ever seen.

The frock coat he wore couldn't hide his broad shoulders, nor muscular body.

"Sam," said Helen, "I'd like you to meet—"

"Dieter Ruehmschuessel," Dieter interrupted, thrusting his hand out toward Carter. His smile was genuine and, Carter noted with a twinge of jealousy, extremely charming. In fact, Dieter Ruehmschuessel was quite possibly the most striking man he had ever met.

"Nice to meet you," said Carter, shaking Dieter's hand. It was a strong hand, a farmer's hand.

"And you," replied Dieter. "So, I understand you're staying over at Helen's farm?"

"For a while, yes. She was kind enough to take me in and give me a place to sleep and my meals, in exchange for my helping out with some repairs around the place."

"Sam's staying in the cabin with Mornin," Helen added quickly.

"If you have any big jobs where you need another hand, let me know," said Dieter. "I'd be glad to come over and help."

"Thanks," said Carter. "I'll remember that."

"Dieter and Helen were best friends growing up," said Henry. "We always figured some day they'd be more—get married, have children, give us grandchildren. Might still happen—one never knows."

Carter sneaked a look at the two of them. They were both blushing, though neither said anything.

Hilda broke the embarrassing silence. "Henry, we need to be getting home. I want to get Chessie started on dinner right away."

"Chessie?" said Carter, looking at Helen.

"Hilda and Henry's cook," she said.

"Oh."

"I'll go round up the children," said Henry.

"So, Sam," said Dieter, "we'll see you later today, then."

"We'll be there about four," said Helen. "And don't forget, I'm bringing pies."

"Helen makes the best apple pie in the county," said Dieter.

"Not only the best apple pie, but the best sweet potato pie, too," added Hilda. "We'll see you in a little bit, then."

Carter watched as Dieter and his mother walked away. *How could I possibly compete with him?* Then the realization of what he was thinking hit him. *Compete? Is that what I thought? Compete for Helen?*

Well, why not? Why not, indeed?

"Are you ready to go?" asked Helen. "I see Russell heading this way."

∞

"How many slaves do the Ruehmschuessels have?" Carter asked as the wagon bounced its way down the road.

"Oh, they don't have any slaves anymore," replied Helen.

"But, Chessie . . .?"

"They used to have slaves, but Henry freed them all after Mr. Lincoln issued his proclamation."

"The Emancipation Proclamation?"

"That's right. Earlier this year."

"But," said Carter, confused, "that only applied to slaves in the Confederacy. Kentucky wouldn't have been affected."

"Dieter persuaded his father to do so. He never did believe in slavery, and he said if slaves in the rest of the South were being freed, so should all of them."

"Dieter sounds like a fine man."

Helen nodded. "He is the finest man I've ever known. Except for my father and Teddie, of course."

Carter wondered just how fine Helen thought Dieter was.

Helen commented that the choir had outdone themselves. Their rendition of, "We Praise Thee, O God

Our Redeemer, Creator" was, in her opinion, the best she'd ever heard them sing, and a vast improvement from the previous week's effort.

Carter enjoyed the choir's performance, also. But the song that struck him most was the final hymn, "Now Thank We All Our God." Verse two, in particular seemed to speak directly to him:

> *O may this bounteous God*
> *   Through all our life be near us,*
> *With ever joyful hearts*
> *   And blessed peace to cheer us;*
> *And keep us in his grace,*
> *   And guide us when perplexed,*
> *And free us from all ills*
> *   In this world and the next.*

There was no question Carter was perplexed. Nine days had passed since he had traveled back in time to 1863, and he still didn't understand how, or why. He could but hope and trust God *would* guide him and, in time, make everything clear.

As Carter combed his hair before the small piece of mirror hanging on the cabin wall, his thoughts turned to Mary. She'd been much on his mind ever since he arrived in this time period. From what Sara Jane told him, he knew her grandmother had spent her whole life in Harrison County up until the time when she moved to Covington. That meant she must be alive now, here in 1863 and, in all probability, living somewhere close by, perhaps even in Sara Jane's house. Carter realized how little he knew about her. She was

eighty-seven when she died in 1927; that meant she would
be twenty-three now in 1863. He knew she had a brother
named Edgar, and her second husband was named Perkins.
But he didn't know her maiden name, nor her first
husband's name, nor anything else about her. He berated
himself that he'd never found out Mrs. Williams's maiden
name.

At church that morning he studied—not too obviously,
he hoped—all the women who appeared to be about the
right age. But none looked as though they might be her, or
at least what he imagined she might look like at this age,
before she'd been scarred by the fire. He realized that with
all the churches in the county, chances were she did not
even go to this church. And if he did see her, would he
recognize her? After all, she was in her eighties when he
knew her.

Carter decided the first place he would look for her
would be Sara Jane's house. Beyond that, he wasn't sure
what to do, other than to hope their paths might cross.

Carter's eyes opened wide in surprise when the wagon
pulled up to the Ruehmschuessel farm: it was Sara Jane's
home, the one he'd seen last Sunday on his ride. Sometime
during the next fifty years, apparently, the Ruehmschuessels
would sell the property, and Horace Williams would obtain
it. And what of the Ruehmschuessels? What would happen
to them? He couldn't remember any families by that name.
And Mary. Any hope he harbored this might be where she
lived quickly evaporated.

Besides the main house, Carter saw a large tobacco
barn, what appeared to be stables, and a number of other

buildings. In Sara Jane's time, only the barn and the smokehouse still stood.

When they reached the house, Henry and Dieter came out to meet them, followed closely by two young children, a boy and a girl, whom Carter took to be Karl and Gertie. There was no mistaking their relationship to Dieter. They both sported the same attractive head of blond hair and were just as handsome. Carter estimated Karl to be about the same age as Russell, and Gertie a year or two younger. A Negro servant accompanied them.

Russell and Red flew out of the wagon and took off running towards the creek with Karl. Dieter helped Helen down from the wagon, holding her hand a little longer than Carter thought necessary.

"Hi, I'm Gertie," the little girl said. "You must be Mr. Jenkins."

"I am. But you can call me Sam."

"My momma says I have to call grown-ups by their last name," replied Gertie, very serious.

"That's a good rule. But I'll tell you what. I'll ask your momma if it's all right to make an exception in my case."

"Okay," said Gertie. She gave Carter a big grin.

Carter liked her perky manner. She reminded him of Sara Jane when she was Gertie's age.

"Can I take the pies in?" asked Henry.

"Yes, please," replied Helen. "They're right here in the back of the wagon."

The servant reached out to take the halter, but Dieter stopped him. "It's okay, James, I have it. Sam, you want to walk with me to the stable?"

"Sure," replied Carter.

"I understand from Helen you're just passing through," said Dieter.

"I thought so, but I guess I'll stay for a while, now."

"Oh?" Dieter looked surprised.

"I don't have anywhere else to go. And, staying over at Helen's farm, at least I'll have a place to sleep."

"It's a nice community," said Dieter, leading the horse into the stable. "And the folks around here are all decent, God-fearing people. Of course, most of them are Southern sympathizers."

"And you?" Carter asked.

"I'm strictly in favor of the Union," replied Dieter. "Never believed in slavery. I was glad when my daddy set them all free earlier this year."

"I understand from Helen that you had something to do with that."

Dieter smiled. "It's not always easy getting my daddy to see things my way."

"How many acres does your family have here?"

"A little over 500. But we're only farming about 350 now. It takes a lot of hands to produce tobacco and when daddy freed our slaves about a fifth of them left. It's been hard on us working the farm without them. And now we're paying the ones who stayed. They're not slaves anymore; they're hired hands."

"And how many stayed?"

"About seventy of the field hands and eight in the house. I suppose Helen told you her two young bucks left to join the army, too?"

"Mornin told me. Helen did tell me her father was killed last year, and that Teddie's off fighting somewhere."

"Teddie? Oh, you mean Helen's brother. Yes, he's with the Sixth Kentucky Cavalry. Rumor is they're somewhere in Tennessee, maybe south of Nashville. But I don't think anyone knows for sure."

"How about you, Dieter? Were you in the army?"

"Not exactly. I'm a member of the Home Guard. We stay here in the county to protect it from the Confederates. Like when Morgan came through here last year. How about you?"

"I served in . . ." Carter stopped. He couldn't tell Dieter he'd served during the big war in Europe. A war that hadn't even happened yet. "I served in a unit in Louisville," Carter lied.

"Union?"

"That's right."

"Well, if you stay around here long enough, we may try to draft you into the Home Guard. We can use some more men."

"How many stalls are there in here?" asked Carter.

Dieter looked around. "Twelve. Couple of them aren't filled right now, though. Let's head on up to the house, to see if supper's about ready."

"Tell me, Dieter," said Carter as they made their way to the house. "You familiar with a family hereabouts by the name of McGlone?"

"McGlone? No, can't say as how I've ever heard the name."

"How about the farm east of here about a half mile? Do you know who lives there?"

"That'd be the Schroeders. They came to America about the same time as my parents did. Why do you ask?"

"Oh, no reason. I noticed it on the way over here, and I was curious."

Carter couldn't tell him that some thirty-six years in the future that would be *his* home. But for now, it was the Schroeder home, a family he'd never heard of. *Where does my family live now*? he wondered.

∞

The house was pretty much as Carter remembered it. Oh, the furniture was different, of course. And sometime over the years not one, but two, indoor toilets had been added. But, all in all, it was Sara Jane's house, just no Sara Jane.

"I hope you boys are hungry," said Hilda. "Chessie says we'll eat in about fifteen minutes."

Carter looked at the long table that took up most of the room, piled high with more food than he remembered ever seeing, even at his grandma McGlone's house when his family used to have Thanksgiving there. Perhaps not more, but certainly a lot.

"Dieter, you call the children," said Hilda. "Tell them it's time to get washed up."

∞

As everyone held hands for the blessing, delivered quite eloquently by Dieter, Carter had the overwhelming sense that this time period in which he now, somehow, found himself, was where he was destined to remain. He wasn't going to be able to go back. He didn't have the courage to try the medals, not knowing where—or when—they might take him. This would be his home, his time, his new name, his life from now on and, strangely enough, the possibility did not upset him nearly as much as he thought it might.

Henry and Hilda were as curious about Carter as Dieter had been, so he repeated what he'd already told Dieter and, before him, Helen: that he was passing through, he was from Louisville, and he might stay around for a while.

The remaining time was taken up, for the most part, with talk of the war: why it was being fought; which families were on which side; Morgan's raid into Cynthiana the year before; what the prospects were for either side to emerge victorious; and when would it all end. Carter couldn't tell them he knew the answers to the last two questions. Hilda, in particular, empathized with those families who had men away fighting, and their concerns about the safety of their sons, husbands, fathers, and brothers.

As the conversation went on, Carter found that, in spite of himself, he liked Dieter Ruehmschuessel. The man was intelligent, moral, a good conversationalist, and had a great sense of humor. Not only did he know farming, he was also knowledgeable about politics in general, and the war in particular.

"Enough talk about the war," said Hilda. "It's time for dessert. Would you like some pie, Sam?"

"Yes, please."

"Apple or sweet potato?"

"Or both?" asked Henry, grinning.

"I think maybe Henry has the right idea," said Carter. "Let's try a piece of each. Let's see just how good a pie maker Helen is."

He sneaked a look at Helen. She looked back at him, a smile on her lips.

Hilda turned to one of the servants. "Mary Louise, please bring Mr. Jenkins a piece of each of Helen's pies. And see what everyone else wants."

Hilda was right. Both pies were delicious. But then, having eaten Helen's cooking for the last week, it was no more than Carter expected.

After supper, the men retired to the parlor. Henry settled into a rocker while Dieter chose one of the sitting chairs. Carter found a place on the sofa.

He studied the numerous paintings that adorned the walls, particularly the large one above the fireplace depicting what appeared to be a castle. A German castle, Carter supposed. That one would still be there in Sara Jane's time, although the colors then were not nearly as vivid as what he saw now, the result, he surmised, of age and smoke. He didn't remember any of the other pieces.

Carter watched as Henry and Dieter filled and lit their pipes. He was fascinated by Henry's, which had a beautiful amber hue. A bear rearing up on its hind legs had been carved onto the bowl.

"You fancy my pipe?" asked Henry.

Carter looked up. He hadn't realized he was staring. "I've never seen one like that before."

"It's a meerschaum," said Henry. "My father brought this back with him from one of his many trips to Turkey. Gave it to me just before he died. I plan on giving it to Dieter before I die."

"No need," said Dieter. "I'm quite content with my own pipe."

Carter looked at Dieter's pipe. It was plain, dark brown, but polished to a shine.

"Yours isn't a meerschaum?" said Carter.

"Briarwood. Much better material for a pipe than meerschaum."

Henry grunted and inhaled. "Shows what you know."

"Do you smoke, Sam?" asked Dieter.

"No, I never took it up."

"Chew?"

"No, not that either. But I'll enjoy the smell of the smoke from your pipes. Reminds me of my father and my grandfather. Both of them smoked pipes."

"Where're your folks from?" asked Henry.

"They're from . . ." Carter hesitated. "They're from Indiana."

"And is that where you were born?" Henry continued.

"No. I . . . I was born in Louisville."

"I see," said Henry.

Thankfully, the rest of the conversation consisted of more talk of the war, and not of Carter.

Presently, Helen came into the room. "I do believe it's time for us to be going. We have to get home so Russell can tend to his chores."

It didn't take long to get the horse hitched up. Everyone waved good-bye as they started down the lane.

"It was wonderful having you here," Hilda called out. "Come back again, all of you."

On the ride back to the farm, Carter thought about the day and how pleasurable everything had been: the food, the conversation, even church that morning. The most pleasurable thing of all, however, was being with Helen.

Chapter Thirty-Two

The Statehood Day Disaster
May, 1863

The next few weeks passed quickly. Carter put in numerous hours every day planting and making repairs to the buildings, the fences, and stone walls. He discovered that, in spite of having grown up on a farm and performing the hard work that entailed, his years of being a lawyer and working in an office had caused him to grow soft. At the end of each day, he collapsed onto his bunk, exhausted from his efforts. His whole body ached; his feet hurt; blisters covered his hands, and his face was sunburned, despite the broad-brimmed hat he wore.

Dieter came by to help put a new roof over part of the barn. He and Carter became good friends, talking about many things: farming, the war, the weather. One thing they never discussed, however, was Helen. Carter was sure Dieter suspected he had feelings for her, and he was even more sure Dieter did, too.

On Sundays, Carter attended church with Helen and Russell. While he felt Reverend Moundtree's sermons were considerably longer than they needed to be, and the man was not the most eloquent speaker Carter had ever heard, nevertheless, he found what he had to say worth hearing. Plus, Carter enjoyed the music. Helen said his presence must have inspired the choir, because they never sounded so good before he started coming. His circle of acquaintances grew as Helen introduced him around following the services. And, finally, he no longer had to answer questions about where he'd come from, why he was here, or what his plans were. At the same time, his discreet inquiries regarding the McGlone family proved fruitless. Nor was he able to obtain any information about Mary.

So Carter settled into a life not too dissimilar from the one he had known growing up on his family's farm. And yet it was different. There was no family here now, no mother or father, no Sara Jane.

On the other hand, there was Helen.

Helen stood at the kitchen window, the plate in her hand suspended half in and half out of the dishwater. What held her attention was the sight of Carter out by the barn, replacing a fence post that had partially rotted away.

The day was hot, and he had removed his shirt, revealing a body that had, over the past month of working on the farm, regained the hardness lost during the years of practicing law.

From the moment she laid eyes on him that first day, coming up the lane with Russell, she felt an attraction toward him, a feeling different than anything she had ever experienced. She told herself what she felt was preposterous, that she didn't know anything about him— who he was, where he came from, why he was here. Over and over she questioned her lack of prudence in asking him to stay on and help out around the farm. Oh, there was no question she needed the help—the work had become much more than she and Russell alone could handle with Teddie being gone. And she hadn't wanted to ask for Dieter's assistance. She wasn't sure why, exactly, unless it was that she might feel uncomfortable at the thought of him earning her gratitude. As much as she cared for him—as a friend— she didn't want to be beholden to him. But she knew the need for another hand wasn't the only reason, not even the real reason. She hadn't wanted to see him leave. There it was, pure and simple.

Helen lowered the dish back into the pan and leaned on the window sill, resting her chin in her hands. *Good Lord, he's handsome!* she thought.

She watched as he strained to lift the old post out of the ground, the muscles in his back flexing with the effort. Even from here, she saw tiny beads of sweat as they glistened on his skin, forming rivulets down his spine, eventually disappearing beneath his trousers.

She felt herself grow moist in a place that told her *watching* him was not enough—she wanted to be with him, to experience his body against hers, to feel him inside her.

She trembled as she watched Carter pick up the new post and jam it into the yawning hole. Then he moved extra dirt in around the post, tamping it down with the stamper, a round piece of heavy metal attached to a wooden handle. Helen felt herself becoming more and more flushed.

When he finished, Carter picked up his shirt and disappeared into the barn.

She waited a few minutes for him to return, but he didn't. Finally, she turned back to her dishpan. Maybe someday, she told herself. Maybe.

"Hey, Sam, you play baseball?"

Carter turned away from the shutter he was repairing to find Russell standing behind him.

"Baseball?"

"Yeah, baseball. You know what baseball is, don't you?"

Carter set down the hammer, removed a handkerchief from his pocket and wiped his brow. "Baseball? Sure, I know what baseball is. Why?"

"There's gonna be a game next Sunday at the big meadow over by the Laramee farm. Dieter's team is playing the team from Oddville. They can always use another player. You any good?"

Carter smiled. "I'm not too bad. Sure, I'll play—why not?"

From his position in left field, Carter watched as dark clouds rolled in from the west. A few light sprinkles of rain began to fall.

Better than a hundred people were gathered around the makeshift baseball diamond, most of them cheering for the Cynthiana team, but a sizable number who had come down from Oddville with their team rooted for their home club. The game was close, eighteen to sixteen, in the top of the seventh. Carter had had a good day, with three hits in five turns at bat, including a triple. Dieter had done even better, hitting successfully in all of his at bats, including two home runs.

Just as the Oddville first baseman came to the plate, the heavens opened up, as though God had pulled the plug on his bathtub.

A wild scramble ensued as spectators and players alike rushed for the shelter of a tobacco barn a few hundred yards away. About a dozen others scurried off in the opposite direction, seeking protection under a huge oak tree. Streaks of lightning lit up what was now a blackened sky.

No sooner had everyone taken cover, than a loud *boom* reverberated through the clouds, causing the barn to shake.

Carter looked around for Helen and Russell, but they were nowhere to be seen. He spotted Henry and hurried to his side. "Did you see Helen or Russell?"

"I saw them take off for the big oak tree," replied Henry. "They'll be okay."

Carter looked toward the barn entrance. He saw the tree, some 300 yards away.

"This sure is messing up the holiday," Henry continued.

Carter turned to Henry. "Holiday? What holiday?"

"Why, Statehood Day. When Kentucky became a state. We have a big celebration every year."

Carter's face blanched. "Henry, what's the date today?"

"The date? May 31st, why?"

"Isn't Statehood Day June 1st?"

"Yah. But that'd be tomorrow, Monday. We'll all be working the fields tomorrow."

May 31—the Statehood Day disaster!

He looked through the barn door. And that's the oak tree, the one where everyone was killed!

Carter bolted through the crowd and out the door, running as fast as he could. Rain, like bits of glass, stung his face. Lightning crisscrossed the sky. As he got closer to the tree, he began shouting. "Get out! Get out from under the tree."

But the sound of the rain drowned him out. People

stared at him as he ran toward them, but no one made a move to leave the safety of the tree.

"Get out!" he shouted again.

Then he saw Helen running toward him, with Russell close behind.

"Sam, what is it? What's wrong?" she shouted.

They'd gone no more than twenty yards when a massive bolt of lightning struck the oak. Fingers of electricity leapt from the trunk like fireworks, striking every person still there, knocking them all to the ground.

Helen and Russell both stopped and turned to see what had happened. Helen's hands flew to her mouth.

"Oh, no," she cried, just as Carter reached her and wrapped his arms around her.

Russell stood frozen in place.

Small patches of grass were on fire, but the rain quickly extinguished them.

"Come on," said Carter. "We've got to see if we can help."

He grabbed Helen by the arm and they ran back to the smoldering tree, leaving Russell behind, still not moving. Bodies lay strewn about. They hurriedly checked each one for a pulse.

But no one had survived.

By this time, a large crowd had arrived from the barn. Carter shook his head.

Those whose family members had taken cover under the tree ran to find their loved ones. The sound of crying soon overcame even the noise of the rain, which was coming down now even harder.

A wagon appeared and most of the bodies were placed in it. But a few men picked up others of the deceased and carried them back to the barn.

Helen and Carter stood and watched as the site cleared out. Russell joined them. Helen turned to Carter. She was shaking.

"You saved our lives."

"I wish I could have saved all of them. I thought you'd be coming to the barn."

"I started to," said Helen. "Then I looked around and saw Russell following little Jasper Smart. They were headed toward the tree. So I turned and ran with them. I didn't want to leave Russell alone. How did you know? You did know, didn't you—that this was about to happen."

Carter looked at her. "It was just a feeling," he said. "I just had a feeling."

Over the next four days, funerals were held in three different churches. Carter, Helen, and Russell attended every one.

"Is it true they made the coffins from the oak tree?" Russell whispered to Carter during the Reverend Abercrombie's eulogy for the boy who had been with him under the tree.

"Every one of them," Carter whispered back. "Even the fellow from Georgetown."

"Serves the damn tree right," whispered Russell, albeit not softly enough that Helen couldn't help but hear what he said.

She glared at him. Then her face softened as she saw his eyes were filled with tears.

The following week Carter, Helen, and Russell watched, along with the other town folk, as Cyrus Milton hitched up his two large draft horses to what remained of the oak. Half a dozen men had spent the previous two hours digging dirt from out around the stump and now it was the horses' turn.

At first, it seemed the stump would win. Then, bit by bit, the tree began to budge and finally, with one final lunge, heaved up out of ground. As the horses dragged the stump away, six more men started filling in the hole with dirt brought over from Henry's farm. When they finished, a number of women started planting flowers.

By four o'clock, it was all over.

Everyone went home.

Chapter Thirty-Three

Independence Day Hop
June–July 1863

"Do you dance, Sam?"

"What?" Carter had been too busy sharpening an ax to pay attention to what Helen asked him.

"I said, 'Do you dance?' Hilda and Henry are having an Independence Day hop at their home Saturday after next. She said I should invite you to come and join us." Helen grinned. "There'll be any number of lovely young ladies there, all of them dying to meet you."

Carter looked at her, not understanding. "A hop?" he said.

"Yes, a hop. A ball, a party, a *dance*. You do dance, don't you?"

"Yes, yes, I dance." His eyebrows furrowed. He still didn't understand. "Why should lovely young ladies be dying to meet me?"

"Why, it's no secret you're staying here now. And— you're single. And you're not bad-looking. And look around you. Do you see many other eligible bachelors? Other than Dieter, and a few others who are still neutrals or with the Home Guard, most of the men are off to war. The others that are left are, for the most part, either ugly, or stupid, or already taken. You'd be a real catch."

"You think I'm good-looking?" He hadn't heard much of what Helen said after she said that.

Helen blushed. "Oh, you're *all right*," she said with a giggle. "And I didn't say you were *good*-looking—I said you weren't *bad*-looking. At least you don't have any big wart on your nose."

Carter laughed. "Sure. I'd love to go to the 'hop.' What's the dress to be?"

"*Very* formal," announced Helen, her nose tilted upwards, affecting an air of pretentiousness. "We may be country folk out here in the backwoods, but we can be finely dressed country folk when we want to be."

"I don't suppose my work shirt and overalls are appropriate then?" said Carter, teasingly.

"Only if you wish to embarrass me, and ensure none of those lovely young ladies will have anything to do with you."

"I must say, the latter would be all right by me; at the same time, I most assuredly do not want to embarrass you. What would you suggest I do for something appropriate to wear?"

"You're in luck," said Helen. "Teddie happens to own an elegant coat and pair of pants, which are just going to waste hanging there in his wardrobe. You'll look quite handsome in them."

"Lovely young ladies, you say?" said Carter, grinning.

"You'll love it," Helen shot back, tossing her head as she strode toward the house.

Helen was right: he did love it. The party provided a welcome break from the hard job of working the fields and making repairs around the farm.

Hilda met them at the front door. "Helen, you are so beautiful. And Mr. Jenkins—my, how handsome." Carter took Hilda's hand, bowed, and gave it a light kiss. She blushed and covered her mouth with the fingertips of her other hand. "Mr. Jenkins, you are quite *der Ehrenmann*." Carter's brows wrinkled. Had he just been complimented or chastised?

"The gentleman," said Hilda, sensing his confusion.

Carter smiled. "*Danke*," he said, making use of one of the few German words he knew, eliciting a big smile from Hilda. "And you, Mrs. Ruemschuessel, look quite lovely this evening."

Hilda blushed even more.

"Come in, come in," she said, reluctantly removing her hand from Carter's.

The Ruemschuessels had gone all out in decorating the house for their gala affair. The octagonal ballroom, the same room in which the dancing had been held following Sara Jane's wedding, took up the entire third floor, with windows all the way around providing a 360-degree view of the surrounding countryside. What little furniture there was had been removed to provide more space for dancing.

Carter looked up at the ceiling. There was the flag, the same American flag with its thirty-four stars that, sixty-three years later, he would see at the reception. Except this flag was new, the reds, whites, and blues practically bursting forth in their brilliance.

The food was in keeping with the gaiety of the occasion: generous helpings of fried chicken, roast beef, heaping bowls of boiled potatoes, vegetables and fruit; and, of course, pies and cakes. A large punchbowl sat on the sideboard—although Henry was quick to inform Carter that a 'beverage more to a man's liking' could be found down in the pantry on the main floor.

A string quartet, musicians who had come by train from Cincinnati to provide the music for dancing, had finished tuning their instruments.

While Carter knew a number of the guests, primarily from church, the rest were strangers to him. As Helen introduced him around, he felt somewhat relieved, and at the same time perplexed, that there were no McGlones present.

A number of military officers, close friends of Henry's had come up from Lexington on the train for the occasion. And, as Helen promised, a bevy of young women were in attendance, all of whom seemed most anxious to meet Carter. Oh, they paid a good deal of attention to the officers, too, but, as Helen explained, "Those men will be going back to Lexington, and you'll still be here. Who do you think the girls are most interested in?"

Carter noted two young women named Mary. But it was evident from their appearance neither was "his" Mary.

The quartet began playing. Carter thought the tune vaguely familiar, but couldn't place it. "That's 'Happy Hours at Home' by Stephen Foster," Helen told him when he inquired as to the title.

"The Stephen Foster who wrote 'My Old Kentucky Home'?"

"The very same. Although I believe the actual title of that song is 'My Old Kentucky Home, Good Night.' I have the sheet music at home. I love his music. Sometimes it's...

moving, sometimes romantic. But I especially like pieces like this one, which are fun!"

"Would you care to dance?" asked Carter.

"I thought you'd never ask," Helen replied, offering her hand.

Carter led her out to the middle of the room, took her in his arms, and they began to glide across the floor. As he imagined, she was as light as fairy wings. Even through the gloves they both wore, Carter felt the warmth of her hand.

"You dance quite well, Mr. Jenkins," said Helen, in a facetiously formal tone of voice.

"As do you, Miss Jones," Carter replied, smiling.

Carter felt a tap on his shoulder and turned to find Dieter standing there. Once again, he was struck by the man's good looks, made even more pronounced by the black formal jacket and white tie he wore. Carter felt a twinge of jealousy.

"May I?" asked Dieter, flashing his engaging smile.

"Of course," replied Carter, doing his best to be gracious, even though he resented the intrusion.

Carter watched for a few moments as Dieter—much more gracefully than himself, he realized—waltzed Helen around the dance floor. He decided to avail himself of some of the "special" beverage Henry had told him about.

Two other guests with the same idea were lounging in the pantry when Carter entered. One he recognized from church, but the other was a stranger.

"Sam," said Eli Strong, one of the church members, "have you met Warren Pickens?"

"No, I don't believe . . ."

Carter stopped short. Pickens? Could it be the same one? Mary's second husband?

"Warren, this is Sam Jenkins," continued Eli. "He's new to the county. Sam's staying and working over on the Joneses' farm with Helen and Russell. Sam, Warren Pickens. Warren runs the dry goods store in town."

As they shook hands, Carter studied the man's face. Of course, he had never met him. Mary's husband died before she had returned to Harrison County. But he *had* met his brother at the funeral. The family resemblance was unmistakable. This had to be Mary's second husband. At last—Carter's first real link to her!

"Warren, nice to meet you."

"And you, Sam."

After a round of small talk, Eli took a pocket watch from his vest pocket. "Oh, my," he said. "I've been hiding out here far too long. My wife's going to kill me!" He returned the watch to its place and hurried out to join the other guests.

"Are you married, Warren?" asked Carter.

"Me?" said Warren, somewhat surprised. "No. With this war and all, I've been much too busy to get married. Although I must say that seeing all the attractive young ladies at this party, the idea gets much more appealing all the time."

"So, no one special in your life yet?" Carter wasn't quite sure how to broach the subject of Mary.

"No, no one. You?"

"No, not right now. I don't suppose you know any young ladies named Mary, do you?" *What a stupid question*, thought Carter as soon as the words were out of his mouth. Everybody knows *somebody* named Mary, a fact quickly confirmed by Warren.

"Mary? I know several Marys. In fact, two are here at this party. Does your Mary have a last name?"

"I'm sorry, but . . . I don't remember her last name. I . . . I met her once, and I thought I remembered her mentioning your name—or perhaps your store. I may have been mistaken."

"Could you describe her, perhaps?"

"Um, no. It was a rather brief meeting."

"Sorry I can't help. But if you should remember her name, let me know, and I'll be happy to tell you if I know her. I should be returning to the party. Perhaps I can entice one of those lovely young ladies to dance with me. Nice meeting you, Sam."

"Yes, you, too," said Carter.

When he returned to the ballroom, Dieter and Helen were still dancing. He felt like breaking in, as Dieter had earlier, but thought better of it. He felt a hand on his shoulder, and turned to find Henry standing there.

"They make a fine couple, don't they?" said Henry.

"Yes, yes, they do." He couldn't deny it. There was no finer looking couple on the dance floor.

Henry removed his glasses, placed one lens near his mouth, breathed on the glass, then proceeded to wipe it with his handkerchief.

"Sam, did you have a chance to see the second floor on your way up here?"

Carter started to reply that he had seen the second floor many times. Then he remembered that was when Sara Jane lived here. He hadn't been there since coming to this time period, except passing through on his way up the stairs to the ballroom.

"No, I'd love to," he said.

It was much as he remembered it from Sara Jane's day, although in considerably better condition. He even recognized some of the furniture as belonging to the

Williamses, and thought it strange the Ruehmschuessel's furniture should end up in Sara Jane's home. Perhaps when her family bought the house some of the furniture stayed with it.

"It's a magnificent home," said Carter, as he and Henry climbed back up the long, curving staircase. "Did you have it built?"

"Thank you," replied Henry. "Ja, we had it built when we first arrived here. Of course, what it needs now are some grandchildren running around." He smiled.

"Yes," Carter agreed, halfheartedly, "that's what it needs." Carter thought of Helen and Dieter together upstairs, and decided it was time he broke in and reclaimed his dancing partner. But just as he reached the dance floor, the music stopped.

"Ladies and gentlemen," said the cello player. "With your permission we're going to take a short break."

Carter strolled over to the group. "I enjoy your music," he said.

"Why, thank you," replied the cello player.

Carter turned to the fiddle player, a young man of about seventeen.

"And you're quite a fiddler, young man."

"Fiddler! That's it!" exclaimed the bass player. "We've been studying on what to call young Jack, here."

Jack shuffled his feet and looked away.

"This is Jack's first performance in public," said the cello player.

"You're Jack?" asked Carter. "What's your last name, Jack?"

"Hawkins, sir," Jack answered.

Carter grinned. "Hawkins! So you're Jack Hawkins. *Fiddler* Jack Hawkins. Well, son, I predict that you're going to have a long career ahead of you."

"Thank you, sir."

"Now if you gentlemen will excuse me," said Carter. "I'm going to see if I can reclaim my date."

Carter turned and walked away, his eyes searching the room for Helen.

But she was nowhere to be seen.

Nor was Dieter.

Chapter Thirty-Four

A Proposal

"This was a good idea, to get some fresh air," said Helen.

Dieter had suggested perhaps a stroll through the apple orchard might be in order, to escape the stuffiness of the ballroom. Hot July days might not be the most perfect time for such indoor activities, he said, especially in the third story of a home.

As they walked along the path, Helen marveled, as she always did when she came here, at the sheer beauty of the place: the house, the grounds, the barns with their many stalls for the fine horses the Ruehmschuessels owned.

"You do have a lovely home," she said.

"I think so, too," replied Dieter, taking her hand as they walked.

They came to a small bench, partially hidden under the apple trees.

"Let's sit and rest a bit," said Dieter.

"Are you tired already?" she teased.

"No. But let's sit anyway."

They sat down, and Dieter took both of Helen's hands in his. "It is a lovely home," he said. "But it is missing one thing."

"What's that?"

"You. It's missing you."

Helen looked perplexed. "I don't understand. What do you mean, 'It's missing me'?"

"You should be living here. With me. As my wife."

For a moment Helen was speechless. Then she burst out laughing. "Oh, Dieter," she said. "You had me going there for a minute. I thought you were serious."

Dieter didn't smile, but continued to hold her hands. "I am serious. I'm quite serious."

Helen looked at him, searching his face. "You are serious," she said, at last.

"Helen, I love you. I've always loved you, but I didn't realize how much until . . ."

"Until?"

"Until . . . Sam came on the scene."

"Sam?"

"I've seen the way he looks at you. And I've seen the way you look at him. I don't think you're in love with him yet, but I can see it happening. And, when I realized it might happen, that's when I realized how much you mean to me. I knew I couldn't wait any longer to tell you how I feel."

"Dieter, I am fond of you. I mean, we grew up together. You were like an older brother to me. You still are. And I do love you—but not in that way. Not the way a wife should love a husband."

"But you could learn to, I know," said Dieter.

"And, besides," Helen continued, without acknowledging his comment, "there's nothing between me and Sam."

"And you believe that?"

She hesitated, unsure how to respond. Unsure because, in her heart, she knew she was attracted to Sam.

"We should be getting back to the party," she said.

Dieter rose to his feet and helped Helen to hers, and they retraced their steps back to the house.

When Carter discovered Helen and Dieter were gone, he decided to look for them on the second floor porch. *Perhaps they stepped out for some air*, he thought.

But they weren't there.

He descended to the first floor porch, where a number of young ladies and officers were mingling and, as Carter's mother would have said, doing their "mating dances." But Helen and Dieter were not among them.

"Well," muttered Carter, "I'll be damned if I'll embarrass myself like some love-sick school-boy by going out looking for them."

For the next half hour, he found himself engaged in conversation with a pretty young thing by the name of Sally O'Rourke. Under other circumstances, he might have had a go with young Sally. But now, his mind was fixed on Helen. Where the hell was she? Where the hell were *they*?

Then he saw them walking toward the house as they emerged from the apple orchard. His heart sank. He didn't want to think about what they might have been doing. No, he thought, Dieter's too much of a gentleman, and Helen's too much of a lady, for anything to have happened. Besides, they're friends, childhood friends. *Keep telling yourself that, Carter.*

"Helen. Dieter."

"Oh, hello, Sam," said Dieter. "You've met Miss O'Rourke, I see."

"Yes, Mr. Jenkins and I have been having such a lovely conversation," said Sally, in a southern drawl. "I was about to ask him to dance, if he didn't ask me first."

"Why, Miss O'Rourke," said Dieter, "I do believe this next dance is mine."

Sally smiled and brought her fan to her lips. "Why, I do believe you're right, Mr. Ruehmschuessel." Turning to Carter, she said, "Perhaps a later dance, Mr. Jenkins?"

"I'd love to," replied Carter, relieved at having been spared.

As Dieter escorted Sally back inside, Helen turned to Carter. "So, it looks as though you've lost your dance partner."

"So it appears. I wonder where I can find another."

Helen held out her hand. Carter took it, and they followed Dieter and Sally into the house and up to the ballroom.

The remainder of the evening, Helen alternated her dances between him and Dieter. A few of the young officers tried their hand at acquiring a turn, but she graciously declined each of their invitations.

At ten o'clock, the music stopped. Henry raised his hand for silence, and the servants handed out glasses of champagne to everyone.

"My dear friends," he said, "you have come here today to celebrate the birth of our great nation. I love this country. I loved Germany. I still love Germany. But I love America, too, for *this* is my country now. And it saddens me to see we are at war with one another. When I left the old country almost thirty years ago, I thought I had seen the last of war and fighting. Sadly, I was mistaken. But this war will not last forever. One day soon it will be over, and we will once again be one nation. And so, I invite you to join with me now in raising your glasses in a toast. To the Union."

Carter, along with most of the others gathered there, raised his glass. "To the Union."

"And now, friends, if you will," said Henry, "please to retire to one of the front porches, as I have arranged for a magnificent display of fireworks to celebrate this occasion."

As they filed out, Carter found himself next to Dieter.

"Dieter, I noticed during the toast several men either set their glasses down, or held them in their hands, without toasting. What was that all about?"

"Oh," answered Dieter, "they're secseshes."

"Secseshes?"

"Secessionists. Southern supporters."

"You mean, they're against the Union?"

"Yes. There were a lot more of them around early in the war, before Morgan came through here. The way he and his men handled themselves changed the minds of quite a few of them."

"That's right. I remember you telling me the county was—*is*—kind of divided in its sympathies."

"Like the whole state. We've got Kentuckians fighting on both sides in this war. We've got *brothers* fighting on both sides. Hell, there've even been people arrested here in this county for being southern sympathizers."

"But I don't understand, then," said Carter. "If those men in there are secessionists, why did they come to the party? They must know where your father stands on this. In fact, why did your father even *invite* them to come?"

"The answer to your first question is they came because my father *did* invite them, and because they have to stay on his good side for business reasons. Why did my father invite them? Because he wanted to make it clear to them that, even though a great many people in this county are Southern sympathizers, my father is staunchly for the Union."

"And yet, they still didn't toast."

Dieter grinned. "Yes, give them credit, they've got nerve. But my father likes that, he respects that. Look, they've started."

Carter looked up to see the first of the fireworks as they lit up the night sky. Then he saw Helen on the top step, her hand on the shoulders of her brother who was standing on the next step down, along with Karl and Gertie, the eyes of all four of them riveted to the display of pyrotechnics. He'd forgotten Helen told Russell he could come for the fireworks. He joined their gaze as more fireworks splashed their bright colors and patterns against the black backdrop of night. He was glad he had come to the party. He was proud to be an American. And, he admitted to himself for the first time, yes! I *am* in love with Helen!

Helen watched as the wagon disappeared behind the trees bordering the road. She had sent Sam and Russell into town to pick up some supplies she needed.

She turned, climbed the steps to the porch, and sat down in the rocking chair.

Her mind still raced with what had happened two nights earlier when Dieter asked her to marry him. It wasn't a total surprise, she realized. Yes, they had been childhood friends. But she was aware that, over the years, Dieter began to think of her as more than a friend. And, she admitted, she did find him quite attractive.

But she didn't love him. Not enough to marry him, anyway. She certainly didn't have feelings for him like those building in her for Sam.

Sam. What was she going to do about him? More and more, every time she looked at him, she experienced an almost overwhelming desire to take him to her bedroom, where she envisioned him throwing her onto the bed and making love to her. She knew she shouldn't be thinking thoughts like that, but—there they were, nonetheless.

She had never been with a man. But she felt sure that, in spite of what everyone said, having intercourse would be a wonderful experience, not the dreaded ordeal others made it out to be.

She placed her hand on her breast. She yearned for the touch of a man's lips on it. She wanted to feel the closeness of a man's body next to hers. She wanted Sam. And, she thought, I think perhaps he feels the same way about me.

She couldn't be sure, of course, but she saw the way he looked at her at those times when he thought she wasn't watching. And she knew from his demeanor Saturday night he seemed to be more than a tad jealous over the attention Dieter lavished on her. But it wouldn't be proper for her to take the initiative. She'd have to let him do it. The best she could do, she thought, would be to give him enough encouragement—without being obvious about it—so that if he were interested, he'd make the first move.

But what if he did make the first move? What if he wanted to take her to bed? How would she respond? Propriety dictated she wait until she was married before having sex. Her mother, if she were still alive, would tell her the same thing.

And yet, at this point, she wasn't sure marriage was what she wanted, at least not right now, because she wasn't positive—absolutely positive—she was in love with Sam. She knew she was tremendously attracted to him, and that she desired him. Maybe that was enough. She didn't know.

The sound of a wagon passing by on the road brought her out of her reverie. She looked up, gave a deep sigh, then stood, and walked into the house.

Chapter Thirty-Five

A Birthday Party
August, 1863

Carter and Helen sat on the kitchen stoop and watched Russell as he chased fireflies around the side yard. While the weather in late August could sometimes be miserable, with the heat and humidity, this year had been unusually pleasant. Carter listened to the chirping of a cricket under the porch, counting the number of chirps in fifteen seconds and adding forty to that number. He reckoned the temperature to be an approximately sixty-two balmy degrees.

"Sam, do you know what next Saturday is?"

"Next Saturday? Uh . . . the day before Sunday?"

"Next Saturday is the twenty-second," said Helen. "A special day for you, I understand."

"My birthday!" exclaimed Carter. "How did you know?"

"Russell told me. He said he asked you once how old you were, and when your birthday was. He said you also asked him how old I was."

"He said you were twenty-two or twenty-three."

"He also said you said I looked a lot older."

Carter was glad it was dark, so Helen couldn't see the redness coming to his cheeks. "No, wait," he said, defensively. "I didn't say you looked a *lot* older. I said I thought you were a *little* older."

Helen laughed. "Don't worry, I'm not offended. And I know Russell has a tendency to exaggerate. Anyway, it's your birthday, and I'd like to get you a present."

"A present? What kind of present?"

"That's what I'm asking you. What would you like?"

"I . . . I hadn't thought about it."

"Is there anything you need?"

"Well, I don't *need* anything. However . . ."

"What?"

"I guess . . . well, I guess I'd like to have a book."

"A book? What kind of book?"

"Maybe something by . . . oh, maybe—Elizabeth Gaskell," said Carter.

"Elizabeth Gaskell? The British author? Do you like her writing?"

"I do, very much. My favorite is *Cranford.* I used to have copies of almost all of her works but I . . . I don't have them anymore."

"She's also one of my favorite authors," said Helen. "In fact, I have *Cranford.* I have two of her other books, too, *Mary Barton* and *North and South.* I think the only one I don't have is *Ruth.* And, you know, I understand she's published a new book. I think it's called *Susan's Lovers.*"

"*Sylvia's Lovers,*" said Carter.

"That's it!" cried Helen. "*Sylvia's Lovers.* I might be able to pick up a copy at the book store in Cynthiana. If not, I'm sure Charles would order one for me. And, listen, Sam, you can borrow the other books anytime you want to."

"Thanks. I'd like that."

"I think a little party next Saturday might be in order, too," said Helen.

Carter grinned. "Thanks, again. I'd like that also."

She stood and headed for the door. "I think I'll turn in. Don't let Russell stay up too late, will you not?"

"Okay. By the way, when is your birthday?"

"Next March," she said, closing the door behind her. "And I'll be twenty-four then."

The party was a fun occasion. Helen had invited the Ruehmschuessels to join them. Even Mornin came in for some cake and ice cream. Russell and Karl volunteered to man the handle of the ice cream churn, but Dieter soon took over when the two boys complained it was too hard to turn.

Helen had located a copy of *Sylvia's Lovers*, which Carter was pleased to have. Hilda had knitted him a pair of gloves. "You'll need these when the winter comes," she said.

"What do you say we have some music?" Helen always liked to have music in the house anytime the opportunity presented itself.

"I hoped you'd say that," said Henry. "I've got my fiddle out in the carriage."

"How about you, Mornin? Do you play an instrument?" asked Carter.

"Yas suh, Marse Sam, as a mattuh of fac, ah do play da hamonica."

"Go get it then!" Helen was bouncing with excitement.

While Mornin retreated to the cabin for his harmonica, and Henry retrieved his fiddle from the carriage, Carter took the banjo from the shelf where he'd been keeping it, and began tuning it to the notes of Helen's piano. He asked Dieter if he played an instrument.

"'Fraid not," Dieter replied. "But I love music. I've always enjoyed Helen's playing."

Carter got a strange satisfaction knowing there was at least *one* thing he could do that Dieter could not.

For the next hour the four of them—Helen, Henry, Mornin, and Carter—collaborated on everything from "The Battle Cry of Freedom" to "Dixie's Land" to "Laura Lee," while Hilda, Dieter, Russell, Karl, and Gertie provided an appreciative audience. Mornin surprised everyone when he laid aside his harmonica on one song and broke forth in a beautiful baritone voice.

Finally, Hilda called a halt to the festivities. "We all have to get up and go to church tomorrow," she said. "So I think it's time we started for home."

"Thank you all for coming," said Carter.

"We'll see you tomorrow," said Dieter.

Everyone was gone. Russell had begged to spend the night with Karl, and Helen had reluctantly given in.

Once again, Carter and Helen found themselves on the kitchen stoop. The fireflies were out in force tonight, without the threat of Russell chasing them.

Helen sat, hands folded in her lap, staring up at the sky. After a long silence, she turned to Carter. "What are you thinking about?" she asked.

"Oh, I don't know," Carter answered, without looking at her. But, of course, he did. Having the party reminded him of the wonderful birthday parties he and Sara Jane shared as children. It set him again to wondering how he got here, what had happened. Unconsciously his fingers went to the two medals hanging suspended from the chains around his neck. Would he ever get back to his own time? What had everyone thought about his disappearance—his mother and father, Sara Jane, all of his friends—and how were they handling it? The *real* Sam Jenkins. What did he think of his partner—his friend—having vanished into thin air?

In spite of all that, however, Carter's thoughts were even more on Helen, and the emotions stirring in him. He was in love with her, there was no denying it. He'd felt a special connection with Mary, and tremendous affection for Emmaline, which at the time he thought was love. But now, for the first time in his life, he realized, he was totally and completely in love. And with a woman who was alive, here and now, some thirty-six years before he would even be born.

"Let me ask another question," said Helen. "What are you *really* doing here, Sam?"

"What do you mean?" This time Carter did look at her.

"It's clear to me that, even though you know a lot about farming, and you're pretty good at repairing things, you're also a lot more educated than any farmer I know. The way you talk, the way you were dressed the first day when you showed up here, the books you like to read. And it was obvious when you first came, whenever we said grace and we joined hands, you hadn't touched a plow handle or an ax in a long time. They were too smooth, too soft, not hard, and calloused like a farmer's. You said you were passing through, and you were from Louisville. I'm wondering where you were passing through *to*?"

She was quiet for a moment. Then she said, "I'm sorry, I shouldn't pry. I have no right asking you to explain yourself."

"Oh, no," Carter quickly replied. "You have every right. You took me in and fed me, gave me a place to sleep. I'm a little surprised you've done what you've done *without* knowing anything about me. In fact," he chided, "you probably shouldn't have. I might have been an escaped convict, or a deserter, or a murderer for all you knew."

"Are you?" She looked Carter in the eyes. "Are you an escaped convict, or a deserter, or a murderer?"

He laughed. "No, I'm not any of those. I'm a simple man trying to make sense out of life." That much was true, he thought. "I . . . I *was* a farmer growing up. And, yes, I have been to school, and I am pretty well educated. I'm a . . . a lawyer. Although I'm not practicing right now."

"A lawyer!" replied Helen, leaning back, impressed by this revelation. "Well, I knew you were no farmer. A *lawyer*. Did you practice in Louisville?"

"I did."

"And now?"

"Now? Now I'm a hired hand, working on a farm for a beautiful woman."

As soon as he spoke, Carter realized what he'd said, and regretted having said it. Why he said what he did, he had no idea. He feared he might have offended Helen.

"I'm . . . I'm sorry. I didn't mean it that way."

"No, I'm . . . I'm flattered," said Helen. "At least I think I am. What did you mean when you said you didn't mean it?"

"I meant . . . I meant . . . well, I shouldn't have said what I said."

"But did you mean what you said? Do you think I'm beautiful?"

For a moment he hesitated, not knowing how far he should go. *What the hell*, he thought. *I might as well admit it*. "Yes, I do think you're beautiful. In fact, I think you're the most beautiful woman I've ever met." There. Now it was out.

Helen looked into his eyes and smiled. "I thank you, Sam Jenkins, for thinking so. And for saying it. It's nice for a woman to know men find her attractive. And right now, with a lot of our menfolk away at war, there aren't too many left around here who might say so. And the ones who are here either don't have the courage to say it, or they don't agree with your assessment."

"Dieter does," said Carter.

Helen laughed. "I know how he feels about me. And I'm fond of him. He's quite a handsome man, also kind and hard working. But, as far as I'm concerned, I doubt we'll ever be more than best friends."

"And how do you feel about me?" He wasn't sure he wanted to hear the answer.

"I like you, I truly do. But I don't know you. I know hardly anything about you except you used to be a farmer, and now you're a lawyer—except you're not a lawyer anymore, you're a farmer again. And you're not an escaped convict, or a deserter, or a murderer." She smiled again. "But I really *don't* know you. I don't know who you are, or why you're here, or where you've come from—except Louisville, I guess—or where you're going when you leave here."

"To tell you the truth," said Carter, "I've kind of been thinking about staying around here, maybe putting down some roots."

"That would be nice. So, would you go back to lawyering?"

"I hadn't thought that far ahead."

For a while neither of them spoke. Finally Helen said, "I think I'll turn in now. Will you be going to church tomorrow?"

"Yes. And, thanks again for the party. It meant a lot to me."

"You're welcome. Good night, Sam."

"Good night, Helen."

Carter remained on the steps for another half hour, enjoying the night sounds he knew so well. Then he stood and headed for the cabin.

Chapter Thirty-Six

A Letter from Teddie
October, 1863

Sept 24, 1863

Dearest Helen & Russell

I'm sorry I have not been able to write you sooner but we have been moving around a lot. Today were camped at some place called 7 Springs. I'm not even sure what state were in whether its Georgia or Tenesee. Our unit has been in a terrible battle the worst one we've seen so far. It mostly took place in some little town in Georgia called Chickamaga which is not too far from Chatanooga. I am sorry to say we did not emerge victorious. However I am happy to say I was not wounded or killed (in which case you would not be getting this letter—ha ha!) Unfortunately Lieut Mead got killed. I liked him. He was a good officer. Oh & Chaplain Clark got wounded. About 1/2 dozen of our boys got killed too & we got quite a few missing who we figure must have been captured. Don't think I wrote you back in July we lost 5 of our boys including Lieut. Murphy. I'll be lucky if I get out of this dam war alive. I'll be happy when the war's over & I can come back home & take up farming again. It is still a mystery to me how we lost this battle. From what I here there was over 40000 of our boys in this last battle & only 30000 graycoats. So I can't figure out how they won when we had them outnumbered. But they did. I know our unit done itself proud. We was held back til the end then all of a sudden it seemed like the rest of our troops was falling back & they called us in to help. We kept fighting & falling back, fighting & falling back cause them dam rebs kept flanking us. Col Watkins said we did one hell of a job. He's right too. Hope you & Russell are doing okay. Tell Mornin I said hi. Dieter too. Is he still there or has he changed his mind & joined up yet? Or is he still with the Home Guard. That's what I should have done, joined the Home Guard! Next time (if there is a next time) I won't be so goldarned fired up to go off to war. There's a rumor we might get home for Christmas. I'll write & let you know as soon as I here anything.

Your loving brother

Teddie

Chapter Thirty-Seven

Christmas...And a Kiss

December, 1863

"What would you like for Christmas?"

Carter looked up from the gate he was repairing to see Helen standing there. He hadn't heard her come up behind him. She seemed to like to sneak up on him. "What?" he asked.

"I said, 'What would you like for Christmas?' You do know Christmas is next week?"

"I . . . I hadn't even thought about it."

"Well, it is," said Helen. "And I—that is, Russell and I—want to give you something, a present."

A gift. Of course! He'd have to get a gift for Helen, and one for Russell, too.

"Is it something you'd be buying or making?" he asked.

"Either way. Depends on what you'd like."

"What I could use would be a scarf. Now that the weather's getting colder, a scarf would be nice."

"I can do that," she said.

"What would you like for Christmas? And Russell—what would he like?"

"Oh, you needn't get us anything. I know you don't have much money."

That was true. In fact, he didn't have *any* money. He'd had a few bills in his wallet, along with a few coins in his pocket, when he showed up last spring. Unfortunately, the bills had been printed, and the coins minted, after the 1890s, a fact embarrassingly brought home to him shortly after his arrival, when he'd given Russell a Walking Liberty half-dollar, which turned out to be dated 1921, to take into town to buy some pomade. "What's this?" Russell asked. Carter had quickly retrieved the coin, and told Russell he'd changed his mind—he didn't need any pomade. Later he'd taken the money and hid it under a loose floorboard in the cabin.

"I know, but I'm pretty good with my hands. I could make something between now and then."

"If you'd like. I know Russell would love to have a kite. And I . . . I'd like to have a new sewing box. My old one is practically in pieces."

"Done. I can do both of those."

"Why don't you wash up and come on in the house?" said Helen. "Supper's almost ready."

Carter couldn't remember a Christmas Eve like this one of 1863. When he was a child, Christmas had always been a magical time, with great family get-togethers at Grandma McGlone's home, similar to the ones at Thanksgiving, where he and his parents, along with the family of his great-uncle Rufus, his children and grandchildren, all gathered at Grandma's house. There would be an immense spread of food, and all the children—Elroy, Clarence, Carter, and the five children of his cousin, Elsie, and her husband—would each get to open one of their presents before everyone piled into the wagons, and headed off for Christmas Eve service at the Methodist church. But, as a man, as an adult, Carter felt Christmas had lost some of its wonder. Last Christmas—the one in 1926—had been particularly difficult because of what had happened to Emmaline two months earlier.

This year, along with Helen and Russell, Carter attended the Christmas Eve service, where Reverend Moundtree gave an inspirational—if still too long—sermon about the three wise men and their gifts; and where the choir outdid themselves with their rendition of "We Three Kings."

At the same time, the evening had been a disturbing one, too.

Earlier that day Helen, Russell, and Carter exchanged the presents they'd made for each other. Carter was delighted with the scarf Helen knitted for him with yarn she unraveled from an old sweater. Russell and Helen were equally pleased with the gifts he'd made for them, the kite and sewing box. Later, before going to church, they had gone to the Ruehmschuessel farm for supper.

Russell was entranced with the slingshot Karl received as one of his gifts, while Gertie was engrossed with the new doll given to her by Dieter.

"I have a present for you, Helen," said Dieter, a smile on his face.

"What is it?" asked Helen, excitement in her voice.

Dieter handed her the box which, Carter was certain, Hilda had wrapped. When Helen opened it, she smiled broadly at Dieter, and then stood on her tiptoes to kiss his cheek.

"You dear," she said. "How did you know I wanted this?" She held up a beautiful heart-shaped locket on a gold chain. The front of it held a place for a photograph. Carter was crestfallen. Dieter's gift was much nicer than the sewing box.

"I saw you looking at it the day we were in Rieckel's store," said Dieter. "And I knew from the way you were eyeing it it was something you wanted."

A frown covered Helen's face.

"What's wrong?" asked Dieter.

"I can't accept this," said Helen.

"Why not?" Dieter was confused by Helen's sudden shift of emotion.

"Because your giving me this locket is the same as asking me to marry you," she said. "And I can't say yes to that."

Dieter's face turned red. "I'm sorry. That wasn't my intention. I bought it only as a gift, nothing more."

Helen still wasn't sure. She turned to Hilda for support.

"I think, ja," said Hilda, nodding. "It's just a gift. Go ahead and take it."

"Are you sure?"

"Ja," Hilda reassured her again. "We're all witnesses." She laughed.

Helen's face brightened. "Very well then, I accept," she said to Dieter.

"May I put it on you?" he asked.

She turned, and he deftly latched the hook to the loop. Placing both of his hands gently on her shoulders, he turned her back around.

"It's beautiful," said Helen, admiring her gift.

"And yet, not half as beautiful as you," Dieter replied, a slight catch in his voice.

Helen looked up at him and blushed. "Thank you," she said, and kissed him again on the cheek. Quickly she turned to Hilda. "Isn't it beautiful, Hilda?"

"Ja, it is."

"You can open it and there are two more places inside for pictures," said Dieter.

"May I see?" asked Gertie, willing to neglect her doll for the moment to examine the exquisite gift her brother had given Helen. "Whose pictures are you going to put in it?" she asked

"I don't know," said Helen. "We'll see."

"If we're going to make it to church on time, we're going to have to sit down to supper," said Henry. "Chessie has it on the table."

Following the service, the three of them rode back to the farm in near silence. Russell had fallen asleep in the back of the wagon, while Helen softly hummed the Christmas hymns they'd been singing a short time before. Carter's thoughts alternated between the joy he'd experienced during the service, with Helen sitting beside him, and the jealousy he felt now, knowing how much grander Dieter's gift to her was than his had been.

When they arrived at the farm, Helen ushered Russell in and put him to bed, while Carter led the horse into the barn, unhitched it, and stowed the harness. Instead of going on to the cabin, he walked to the house, and sat down on the stoop. He stared at the full moon, which hung like a silver plate against the blackness of night.

Minutes later, Helen came out and sat down next to him. He scooted over a few inches to give her some room, but continued staring at the moon.

"What are you thinking?" she asked.

"About tonight. About the service. About last Christmas."

"What about last Christmas?"

He didn't answer right away. There was no way he could tell her about being home, and seeing Mary for the last time. Or about Emmaline.

"Oh, it's . . . it's so different now from last year—in more ways than you can imagine."

"Better or worse?"

"I'd say . . . better."

"It was better for me, too."

"How so?"

"Having you here."

Carter looked at her. Her head was turned away from him.

"Having me here?"

She turned back and looked at him. "Yes."

"I guess that's good, then?"

She smiled that beautiful smile of hers. "That is *very* good, Mr. Jenkins."

For a brief moment they looked at each other. Then Carter tipped his head and kissed her tenderly on the lips.

He was both surprised and delighted when she kissed him back.

"I—"

Helen cut him off. "No, don't say anything." She kissed him once more, then rose, and walked to the door. "I'll see you in the morning," she said, then entered the house, closing the door behind her.

Carter sat there a long time, not believing what had happened. He kissed her. And she kissed him back. And then she kissed him again! The feeling was there in his heart, all right, he knew. Sara Jane was right. *"You'll feel it,"* she had said. Boy, did he ever!

Chapter Thirty-Eight

Something More Than a Kiss

Carter awoke Christmas morning to the sound of rain pelting the cabin roof. Whereas the day before had been nice, even somewhat balmy, today was one of those cold and rainy late December days, the kind that sends a chill through the skin all the way to one's bones. It reminded Carter of his time in France. He threw Teddie's raincoat over his shoulders and ran to the house.

As soon as he walked into the kitchen, he felt the comforting heat from the huge stone fireplace. Helen sat at the table, cutting strips of dough into noodles. She looked up and smiled, but it was evident she was concerned about something.

"Good morning, Sam," she said.

"Good morning, Helen."

"Breakfast will be ready in about half an hour."

"Helen, about last night . . ."

She brought both of her hands up to her mouth, as though in a praying position. "Yes," she said, "I suppose we should talk about last night."

"Helen, I—"

"No," she interrupted. "Let me go first. Sam I . . . I'm not sure what came over me last night. I don't usually do things like that." She looked up at him. "I think maybe what we did last night—what *I* did—was wrong, was a mistake."

This wasn't what Carter had expected.

"I don't think what happened was a mistake," he said. "And I don't think it was wrong, either. I told you once I thought you were beautiful—the most beautiful woman I've ever known. That's true. What I didn't tell you—I wanted to, but . . . I couldn't then—is that I've fallen in love with you." Helen started to speak, but he put his fingers to her lips. "When I first met you, when I first saw you, it was as though I knew you already, that you and I shared a history that had already begun somewhere, sometime. I'm not sorry for what happened last night. I believe it was meant to be. You told me you're not in love with Dieter, that you'd never be more than friends. Is that true?"

"Yes," she replied, softly.

"Then I must ask you this. Do you . . . do you have feelings for me? Do you . . . love me?"

Helen was quiet for a long time. She stared at the mound of dough in front of her.

What she said next caused Carter's heart to leap.

"Yes," she said, her voice even more hushed than before. "I do have feelings for you. I do love you."

Carter moved around the table to where she sat, took her hand and helped her to her feet. She turned and faced him. "God, how beautiful you are," he whispered. Then he took her in his arms and, with an intensity he didn't know he possessed, kissed her. They stayed like that for a long time, their lips embracing each others'. Carter felt the beat of her heart as her breasts pressed against him. Her body quivered. He inhaled the fragrance of her hair, surprised to find it was a scent he knew: lilac, perhaps. Or lavender. He wasn't sure.

The sudden sound of Russell's boots on the stoop brought them back to reality.

Hastily, they let go of one another. Helen brushed the hair back from her face and sat down, while Carter stepped quickly around to the other side of the table.

"Sam! Merry Christmas!" Russell sang out as he came into the kitchen.

"And Merry Christmas to you," Carter replied.

"Don't look like I'll get to fly my kite today. Too much rain."

"Yes, I doubt it," said Carter. His mind still reeled from what just happened between him and Helen. "Maybe tomorrow."

"We going to fix that broken stall in the barn?" asked Russell. "Don't look like we'll be able to do nothing outside, 'cause I think this rain's going to last all day."

Before Carter could answer, Helen interrupted. "No work today. It's Christmas. A day to relax. Russell, after we have breakfast, why don't you go over to Karl's and play with him?"

"You mean it?" Russell was excited at the prospect, not only of not having to work, but getting to go to Karl's, too. He didn't even mind having to walk in the rain for a half hour to get there. Although, more likely, he'd be running.

"Yes. Now, both of you go get washed up. We'll eat in about fifteen minutes." Helen looked at Carter and smiled. "I'll fix us a real nice breakfast."

Helen stood at the window and watched Russell as he ran across the field toward Karl's house. When he was out of sight, she walked back to the table where Carter still sat and eased herself on to his lap. She cupped his chin in her hands and tenderly kissed him.

"You know why I sent Russell over to Karl's?"

"I think so."

"It's because I wanted to be alone with you."

"Do you want to talk about what's happening?"

For a moment she didn't speak. When she did, her words came out softly. "No, I want you to make love to me."

This time it was Carter's turn to be silent. He wasn't sure he heard what he thought he had heard.

"Are you sure?" he asked, finally.

"Sam, I have loved you from the first time I saw you coming up the lane with Russell. I can't explain it. I heard this voice in my head saying, *Helen, this is the man you've been waiting for*." She giggled. "Why do you think I invited you to stay the night, and then offered you a job the next day?"

"I wasn't sure. I thought maybe you felt sorry for me."

"Now you know," she said. She kissed him again, then got up. "Come with me."

She took Carter's hand, and led him up the stairs and into her bedroom.

She turned to him. "This is my first time. I wanted you to know that."

For a moment he was taken aback, but then realized he shouldn't be surprised. It was what he would have expected of her.

"I know this probably isn't your first time," she said. "And that's all right. I wouldn't expect a good-looking man like you—especially one who's lived in Louisville—to never have been with a woman before. And I don't need to know. All I need to know is that you love me—and I love you. And I want you to make love to me."

Carter took her in his arms and kissed her lips. Then he kissed her neck, and found his senses delighted at how pleasing her skin felt to his touch, how sensuous was the smell and the taste of her. He unloosened the belt around her waist, while she unbuttoned the top of her dress and let it slip from her shoulders to the floor.

"You don't wear a corset?" asked Carter, surprised.

"It's not practical for farm work. Why? Do you think I need one?" she added, smiling.

Carter shook his head. "Definitely not."

By now Helen had removed her stockings and shoes and stood before Carter dressed only in her chemise. Carter's heart pounded. He felt himself getting hard.

"Are you sure about this?" he said.

"No . . . yes," she answered softly. She hesitated for a moment, then, with both hands, lifted the chemise straps from her shoulders and let the garment slide gracefully down her body to join the dress which lay at her feet.

Carter sat down on the bed and stared at her now naked body, marveling at the perfectly formed breasts, voluptuous and inviting. She was the most beautiful creature he'd ever seen, perfect in every respect. He drew her near and lifted his head slightly to nuzzle a nipple, alternately kissing and sucking it. He felt her body trembling in his hands. A faint moan escaped her lips. His penis, now fully enlarged, strained against his pants.

He stood up and Helen helped him remove his clothes. When he, too, was completely naked they embraced and held each other for a long time. The touch of Helen's hand on his penis sent a shiver through his body.

Gently, Carter laid her down on the bed, then lay down beside her, and took her in his arms.

And they made love.

∞

Helen spoke first. "I never knew anything . . . I never knew anything could be so incredible. I feel . . . I feel like . . . well, I can't even describe how I feel."

"I know," said Carter. "I feel the same way."

He propped himself up on one elbow and looked at her next to him. Her long black hair lay over her shoulders, partially covering her breasts. Her blue eyes sparkled as she looked back at him. "Did I ever tell you how beautiful you are?" he asked.

She laughed. "Yes, but I don't mind hearing it again." She propped herself up an elbow. "And did I ever tell you how much I love you?"

Carter smiled. "I think I remember you mentioning it in passing before we made love. But I couldn't tell what you were saying *while* we were making love. It sounded like a lot of moaning and sighing."

"Oh, you!" She gave him a playful punch on his shoulder.

"It's a good thing Russell wasn't here," said Carter. "He would have thought I was beating you or something."

Helen sat upright in the bed. "Oh, my goodness! Russell might be home any minute. It's almost dinner time. I've got to get up. You've got to get dressed!"

She started to rise, but Carter caught her and pulled her back down beside him. She looked at him and smiled. Then she kissed him. He felt himself getting hard again. "If I know young boys," said Carter, "having been one myself, it'll be a while before Russell and Karl get their playing all out." He returned her kiss. And they made love again.

∞

Carter was buttoning up his shirt when they heard Red barking in the yard, closely followed by Russell as he stomped his boots outside the kitchen door.

"Helen," he shouted, "where are you? Where's dinner? I'm starved."

Helen came down the stairs. Russell was busy dipping a cup of milk from the milk jug.

"Did you have a good time at Karl's?" she asked.

"Uh-huh. Where's dinner? Ain't we eating today?"

"I'll have it ready shortly."

"Okay," said Russell. "Where's Sam?"

"I'm . . . not sure," Helen fibbed. "Perhaps out in the barn. Why don't you go see?"

"Okay."

As soon as Russell left, Carter came down the stairs. He walked over to Helen and put his arms around her waist.

"Sam, not now!" she said. "Let me get dinner ready. Why don't you go out and talk to Russell while I'm doing that?"

"You want me to tell him about you and me?" he asked, teasingly.

"No!" replied Helen. "I don't want him to know anything about you and me. Not yet, anyway."

"Relax. I'm going to ask him how Karl's new slingshot worked." He gave her a quick peck on the cheek, and left to find Russell.

Chapter Thirty-Nine

Teddie Comes Home
January, 1864

Jan 10th, 1864

Dearest Helen & Russell

As you could see I weren't there for Christmas. But were getting a 30 day furlough in a couple of weeks! At least that's what Lieut Roper tells us. I know I sure am looking forward to being back there & seeing you all. I reckon I'll be home before the end of the month so you best get busy baking up some of your sweet potato pies for me. I got the letter you sent me & the package of goodies. I especially appreciated the tobacco! You'd think being down south here we'd be able to get tobacco but no. I think where we are right now is some town called Rossville. It's in Georgia. Oh how I long for Kentucky & home! I'm looking forward to meeting Sam. He seems like a nice fellow from what you write. No I didn't mind him borrowing some of my clothes. They sure weren't doing me no good. My best friend Ben Fleck took sick a couple of days ago. Think maybe he's got food poisoning from what the doctor says. I wouldn't doubt it with the kind of food they got for us to eat. I sure am looking forward to your cooking! I think he'll be okay. Looking forward to seeing you all again. I guess I wrote that already. Well there it is again!

Your loving brother

Teddie

Unusually warm weather marked the end of January, as winds continued to come in from the south. The sky was clear and pale blue with no clouds. Carter heard the breeze as it whispered its way through the woods behind the cabin.

Helen was up early to hang out the laundry. She was pinning up one of Russell's shirts when a gust of wind caught it, and blew it up and over the line. Just then Carter saw a man on horseback coming down the road at a trot. Then Helen saw him. At first, he was too far away to make out who he was. But as the rider drew nearer, Carter heard Helen cry out.

"Teddie! Teddie!"

She dropped the shirt and started running. At the same time, Teddie jumped from his horse and ran to meet her. She flung herself at him, and he caught her and twirled her around, her feet inches off the ground.

Carter, on the porch, could overhear their conversation.

"Teddie! It's really you!"

"Hey, Helen," said Teddie, a big grin on his face. "How you doing, sis?"

"How am I doing? I'm doing great now that you're home."

"You know I have to report back to my unit the twenty-second of next month."

"The twenty-second? That's only three weeks!"

"We got thirty days leave," said Teddie. "But I had to run an errand first."

"What kind of errand?"

"Friend of mine, Jackson Krenshaw, got wounded in the battle at Missionary Ridge. He hung on for a long time, but then he upped and died 'fore we was set to go on furlough. Before he went, I promised him I'd take his personal belongings to his folks up in Ludlow. It's outside of Covington."

"I'll bet that was hard."

"It was. And the worst part was, I had to be the one to tell them 'bout him dying, 'cause the captain heard I was going there and thought it'd be best if he sent the letter with me telling Jackson's folks 'bout his death."

"Oh, I'm so sorry."

"One good thing came out of it, though," said Teddie, brightening some. "I met Jackson's sister."

"Oh?"

"He had a picture of her with him. He showed it to me all the time, said I should look her up when the war was over. Unfortunately, I didn't have to wait 'til the war was over, but I did meet her."

"And?"

"She's real cute."

"So you took a fancy to her?"

"Reckon I did. Anyway, I told her I couldn't stay this time 'cause you all was expecting me home, and I didn't have much time anyway."

"I wish you didn't have to go back at all," said Helen. "I'd think after two years, you'd given enough time. Why do you have to go back?"

"'Cause there's still a war going on," replied Teddie. "And we're going to win this damn thing, but it's going to take every man we can muster up to put in the field."

"Well, come on up to the house. You look real good. A little skinny, maybe. You haven't had breakfast yet, have you?"

"No, I ain't. But I'm ready." He smiled.

"Okay, come on then. Russell's been dying for you to get home. And you'll finally get to meet Sam."

Teddie took Helen's hand in one of his and the horse's reins in the other, and they started for the house. "Speaking of Sam," said Teddie, "how serious is this between you and him? From your letters, it sounds like you're kind of sweet on him."

Helen looked at him and grinned. Carter saw the blush come over her face even from where he stood.

"Kind of serious," she said.

"Then I guess I better meet him, and ask him what his intentions are."

Helen frowned and stopped. "Don't you dare."

"Why, I think as the head of this here family, it's my solemn duty."

"You're joshing me, aren't you?"

He laughed. "Sure. You're a big girl now. You don't need me to tell you who to fall in love with. But I tell you this," he continued, his voice serious now. "He damn well better treat you right, or he *will* have me to answer to."

Helen grinned. "Come on," she said.

They'd just started up the lane when Red exploded from behind the back of the house, Russell hard on his heels.

"Teddie! Teddie! You're back!"

"Russell! My God, look how you've grown! You're almost as tall as your sister." Teddie grabbed him in a bear hug. "It's good to be home," he said.

"Where's Sam?" Helen asked Russell.

"Why, he's right up there on the porch," he answered.

Helen and Teddie looked to where Carter was standing. He waved. He didn't know whether or not they knew he'd overheard their conversation.

It was apparent from the start, Teddie and Carter would get along fine.

"Sam Jenkins. I sure have heard a lot about you from Helen."

Carter glanced at Helen. Her face turned a little red.

"I hope what you heard was good."

"Oh, for sure," answered Teddie, sitting down on the porch steps and pulling his boots off. "For sure." He turned to Russell. "Hey, Russell, you s'pose you could fetch me a dipper of water?"

Russell ran off towards the pump.

"You don't know how excited everyone's been around here since your letter saying you'd be coming home," said Carter. "How long will you be able to stay?" Of course, he'd heard him tell Helen, but he thought by asking they might assume he hadn't heard their conversation.

"I have to report back to my brigade in Lexington the twenty-second of next month. Those clothes fit you pretty good," said Teddie, giving Carter the once-over.

Carter looked down. He'd forgotten he was still wearing Teddie's clothes.

"I hope you don't mind," said Carter, feeling somewhat embarrassed.

"Shucks, no. No sense in them hanging there doing nothing. 'Course, when I get back for good, we might need to share."

Carter smiled. "I'll be happy to give them back to you when you're home for good."

Over breakfast Russell plied Teddie with questions about the war. Had he seen anybody die? Had he killed anybody? Where all had he been? Where was he going when he left here?

Yes, answered Teddie, he had seen a lot of men get killed. And, yes, sorry to say he killed some himself. Since his first taste of battle at Cumberland Gap a little more than two years ago, he had fought in other battles in Kentucky, as well as Tennessee and Georgia, including the big one at Chickamauga.

"And how about you?" he asked Russell. "You taking good care of the farm while I'm gone?"

"Doing my best," answered Russell.

"He's doing a great job," said Helen. "And with Sam's help, we're getting things whipped back into shape."

"So, Sam, tell me a little about yourself," said Teddie.

Carter gave Teddie the same story he'd given everyone else who had asked since he mysteriously showed up on Helen's doorstep almost a year before.

"And are you planning on settling down in these parts?" asked Teddie.

"I think so." Any hopes he might have harbored of returning to his own time had slowly been fading away, not only because he wasn't sure how to get back, but also because, since falling in love with Helen, he wasn't sure he *wanted* to go back, even if it were possible.

"Helen says you was a lawyer. Is that what you plan to do here?"

"I'm not sure. Right now, I'm content to be a farmer again."

"Where's Rascal?" asked Russell.

"Rascal?" said Carter.

"Rascal was the horse Henry gave Teddie when he went off to fight. Yes, where is Rascal?" Helen asked, turning to Teddie. "That wasn't him you rode in on."

"Sorry to say Rascal didn't make it through that last battle. I'm riding Queenie. She was Jackson's horse. Figgered I'd ride her up to his home and see if the family would sell her to me."

"So you bought her," said Helen.

"Nope. Jackson's sister wouldn't sell her to me."

"So how come you got her now?" asked Russell.

"Jackson's sister said she'd loan me the horse, but she made me promise I'd bring it back after the war was over. I reckon I'll have to go back for sure," said Teddie, grinning.

Carter and Helen both laughed.

"What's so funny?" asked Russell.

"One of these days you'll understand," said Helen. "Teddie, if you're finished eating, you want to take a walk out to the graveyard? Sam, you could come along if you want to."

"No, you three go ahead. I'll clear the table."

For the first few days back, Teddie did little but eat and sleep, catching up on the two things he'd been most deprived of for the past two and a half years.

On his third day home, a Sunday, Helen persuaded him to accompany herself, Russell, and Carter to church.

"People know you're back," she told him. "They want to see you, to say hi, and wish you well. Besides, there's a social at church tonight, and I want all of us to go. It wouldn't look right if you didn't go to church, but showed up at the social."

"Okay, okay," Teddie said finally, throwing his hands into the air. "You win. I'll go."

$$\infty$$

Helen was right. All of Teddie's friends were anxious to see him, especially Dieter. "Teddie, you're a sight for sore eyes. You're looking good!" exclaimed Dieter.

Teddie grinned. "You should have seen me a few days ago when I first got here, before Helen began fattening me up with her cooking."

"How's the war going, in your opinion?" asked Dieter.

"We're going to win. It's just a matter of time. The South's getting wore down. I don't see how they can last another six months."

"I sure hope so," said Henry, joining the two of them under the tree where they were taking refuge from a light drizzle. I think we're all ready for this to be over with."

"You coming to the social tonight?" Dieter asked Teddie.

"Oh, yes. My sister made it a point to tell me I *would* be there."

They all laughed.

"Henry! Dieter! Come on!"

The two men turned to see Hilda motioning to them. "It's time to go home. I've got a lot to do before we come back this evening."

"I guess we'd better go," said Henry. "We'll see you tonight."

$$\infty$$

Carter watched as Russell and Karl filled their plates from the multitude of dishes covering the serving tables, then headed outside to find a place where they could eat in peace, away from the young girls who liked to pester them, especially Gertie. A few minutes later, plate in hand, he joined them under a large willow tree.

"So, how's it feel having Teddie home?" asked Karl.

"Ain't hardly seemed like he is home yet," answered Russell. "All he does is eat and sleep. But he said tomorrow me and him are going out hunting. You want to come along?"

"You sure it'd be all right?"

"Oh, sure. Come on over after breakfast. See if Dieter wants to come, too."

Karl and Russell went back in for seconds, but Carter decided he'd had his fill, so he stretched out on the grass.

A few minutes later, he heard Teddie and Dieter's voices coming from the nearby woods.

"Dieter," said Teddie, "I didn't have a chance to ask you this morning after church, but what's the story with Sam? What do you think of him?"

At first Dieter didn't answer. Then he said, "As far as I can tell, he's a decent fellow. He's a hard worker. I know— I've been over to the farm and seen what he's done there. I don't have anything bad to say about him."

"And what about him and Helen? What about you and Helen?"

"I love Helen. But she doesn't love me." He told Teddie what happened at the Fourth of July party at his home, the first Carter had heard of it, too. "Between you and me," continued Dieter, "I think she's in love with Sam. And I'm pretty sure he's in love with her."

Neither of them spoke for a while. Carter thought maybe they'd left. Then Teddie said, "I think you're right. I think they are in love with each other. I'm a little bothered we don't know more about him. Maybe I'll get to know him better over the next couple weeks.

"Enough of this talk. Russell and I are going out hunting tomorrow. Why don't you and Karl come over and go with us?"

"Okay," said Dieter. "Sounds like fun."

When Carter was sure they'd gone, he got up and went back inside.

Chapter Forty

A Fourteen Point Buck

Russell sat as still as he could, hardly daring to breath. He thought when Teddie agreed to go hunting with him they'd be looking for the usual game: squirrels, wild turkeys, and rabbits. But Teddie said no, he wanted to see if they couldn't bag a nice big buck. So, here they were, sitting amongst a stand of cedars, waiting for a deer to come down the trail. Karl and Dieter were upwind, making their way slowly down the hill.

He was sorry Sam decided not to come along. He'd been out hunting with him and knew he had a good eye, better, perhaps, even than Teddie's. But Sam said he wasn't feeling well—something he ate at the church social last night. Russell suspected the more likely reason was he wanted to be alone with Helen. They probably thought he didn't know something was going on between the two of them. Shoot, he wasn't blind! Well, he didn't care. Sam was a real nice guy, and Russell liked him a lot.

He looked up at his big brother. Teddie was listening intently for the telltale rustling of leaves or trees which would signal the approach of their quarry.

"Teddie—"

"Shush."

"Do you hear something?"

"I maybe could if you wasn't talking."

They sat there for another fifteen minutes, not moving or speaking. For the last five of those, Russell realized he had to pee. Bad. Finally, he could stand it no longer.

"Teddie—"

Teddie held up his hand. "Get ready."

Russell looked around.

Suddenly a figure exploded from the underbrush thirty yards away, then came to a sudden stop, its nose lifted to the wind. Russell's mouth fell open. It was the biggest buck he'd ever seen: ten, maybe twelve points. Maybe more, even.

"This one's yours," whispered Teddie.

Russell looked at him, disbelief on his face. His? This monster? Why wasn't Teddie going to bring him down?

"You ready?" asked Teddie, still whispering, never taking his eyes off the buck.

Russell nodded, then turned his attention to the buck. He raised his musket and sighted in on the target.

"Shoot whenever you're ready," said Teddie, quietly. "Steady . . . steady."

Russell said a silent prayer and pulled the trigger. The smoke from the powder momentarily blinded him. When he looked to where the deer had been standing, it was gone. His heart fell. He had missed!

"You got him!" shouted Teddie, jumping up from his place on the ground. "You got him!"

"I did?" said Russell, more than a little doubt in his voice.

"Come on," said Teddie, grabbing Russell by the arm and dragging him to where the buck had fallen.

When they got there, Russell's mouth fell open. God, it was huge!

"Nice shooting, Russell."

"What's all the commotion?"

Dieter and Karl had heard the deer moving, followed by the sound of Russell's musket. They had come running to see what had happened.

"Russell shot him dead," said Teddie, a bit of a boast in his voice.

"I guess he did," said Dieter, admiringly. "Put that minie ball right through his neck. Great shooting, Russell. God, he's big!"

"Fourteen points," said Teddie.

"Jumpin' jingo!" exclaimed Karl. "I ain't never seen a deer that big!"

Russell stood there, still speechless. He couldn't believe how big the deer was, or that he had been the one to bring him down!

"Come on," said Teddie. "Let's gut him and haul him back home."

"Sam! Come quick! They're back!"

Carter knew from the sound of Helen's voice that something had happened. He hoped it wasn't something bad. Rounding the corner of the house, he saw Dieter and Teddie, Russell and Karl emerging from the woods. They had bagged a deer!

Teddie and Dieter were dragging the buck behind them, each one holding on to one set of antlers.

"So, Sis, what do you think?" asked Teddie, when they reached the house. Helen looked at the enormous buck lying on the ground.

"Teddie, it's . . . it's wonderful! Who shot it?"

"Why, the man of the house," replied Teddie, grinning. "Russell."

Carter and Helen both looked at Russell; he had a grin on his face even bigger than Teddie's.

"Good for you, Russell!" exclaimed Helen, clapping her hands. "Okay, let's get it cut up, and into the smokehouse."

For the next hour, all six of them worked on the buck, keeping out enough for the evening's meal, as well as one hindquarter for Dieter and Karl to take home.

When they finished, Helen went inside to start dinner. Dieter and Karl, carrying their portion, headed for home. Russell went with them so he could tell Henry, Hilda, and Gertie all about his big day.

Teddie and Carter sat on the front steps holding cold drinks Helen had prepared and brought out.

"What is this?" Carter asked Teddie.

"Oh, it's switchel. We usually have it in the summer, when it's hot. But I like the taste of it, and since we'd been working so hard and sweating so much, I asked Helen if she'd make some. It's some vinegar and sweetener, and chilled water. Ain't bad, huh?"

"It's quite refreshing."

"So, Sam, what about you and Helen?"

For a moment Carter was taken aback by the directness of his question. "What do you mean?" he said.

"She tells me it's kind of serious between you two."

"She did?"

"That she did. Is that true?"

Carter was quiet for a moment. "Yes, it is," he said, finally.

"You thinking 'bout getting married?"

"We . . . we haven't talked about it."

"Treat her right," said Teddie. "That's all I've got to say. Treat her right."

∞

The day for Teddie to leave and rejoin his unit seemed to roll around in no time.

"Teddie, you be careful," said Helen. "Don't get shot."

"Sis, I'll certainly try not to. Russell," he said, looking at the boy, "you and Sam here have done a good job keeping the farm going. I'm proud of you.

"Sam, good meeting you. And thanks for all your hard work around the place."

"It's been my pleasure, Teddie," said Carter, shaking his hand.

"When will you be back?" asked Helen.

"My enlistment's up in October. I don't reckon I'll be back 'fore then, unless the war ends."

"October!" Helen cried. "That's eight months from now!"

"It'll be gone before you know it," said Teddie.

Helen threw her arms around Teddie. "You take care of yourself. And, God speed."

Teddie mounted his horse, turned, and galloped down the lane. When he reached the road, he looked back, waved, and blew a kiss.

Chapter Forty-One

A Picnic and a Second Proposal
March, 1864

While February's weather had been relatively mild, temperatures in the thirties—and sometimes even lower— still brought cool days and chilly nights. The trend continued into March, but by the month's end, the days had turned considerably warmer.

One morning Carter turned over in bed and looked up to see Helen standing over him, watching.

"Good morning," he said, rubbing his eyes. "To what do I owe this most pleasant visit?"

She sat down next to him and took his hands in hers. "I was watching you sleep. I enjoy watching you."

Carter looked around for Mornin.

"He's gone into town," said Helen. "Won't be back until this afternoon."

Carter relaxed. "Did I snore?"

"A little." She giggled.

He sat up and reached over and kissed her, then began to ease her down onto the bed with him.

"Wait!" she said. "I've got an idea."

"I've got an idea, too," said Carter, as he continued to pull her down. "I hope it's the same as yours."

"No, mine's better. Let's go on a picnic today."

Carter frowned. "I still think my idea's better."

"Please?" pleaded Helen. "It will be so much fun!"

He loved her enthusiasm. Helen was what his mother would have called a "free spirit."

"All right. Today's Sunday. What about church?"

"Oh, we'll still go to church. Then we can come straight back here, pack up our basket, and take off."

"Where shall we go?"

"I know the perfect place. Do you want to know why I want to go on a picnic today?"

"Why?"

"It's my birthday!" squealed Helen. "I love birthdays—especially mine!"

Carter frowned again, but this time more seriously. He'd forgotten her birthday was this month. He felt bad that he had no present for her, especially after she had given him the book on his birthday.

"So, today's your birthday. And you're . . . twenty-four?"

"That's right. And Russell's birthday is next Sunday, April third; a week after mine."

"So, we'll make this a birthday picnic for both of you," said Carter.

Helen hesitated. "I was thinking . . . the two of us . . . you and me." Then she flashed the smile that told him she was in a playful mood.

"Okay. I hope he won't be disappointed."

"I'm sure he won't. Now, get up, and let's get the chores done, and get ready for church."

Although the day started out a little cool, by the time they returned from church, the temperature was in the low seventies, the kind of day that fairly shouted out to the world that winter was finally over, spring had arrived, and summer would not be far behind. As Helen and Carter walked through the fields, he thought about how lucky he was the way everything had turned out. If he hadn't somehow been transported back to 1863, he would never have met Helen. Now, he couldn't even begin to imagine life without her. He marveled at the fact he didn't miss his law practice at all—although he *did* still miss all the people he had left behind. He was content to work around the farm.

And, Carter acknowledged to himself for the first time, he would be Sam Jenkins for the rest of his life. Carter McGlone no longer existed. There was no way at this point he could tell Helen or anyone else his real name.

Helen squeezed his hand, looked at him, and smiled. *God, she is so lovely.*

When they reached their destination, Carter knew exactly where they were: the old sycamore tree, the same tree where he and Sara Jane found the skeleton and the medal; and where Russell found him when he somehow jumped back in time sixty-four years.

"Why here?" Carter asked.

"Because this is where Russell found you," replied Helen. "This is where you came into our lives, into *my* life. This is where I want to celebrate my birthday—with you."

He took her in his arms and held her, their eyes locked on each other's.

"You're such a romantic," he said.

"Yes, I am," she replied. "And you know you love it."

Carter spread out the blanket they'd brought, as Helen unpacked the picnic basket. A soft breeze blew from the southwest, heralding even warmer days ahead. As they sat and ate the fried chicken and potato salad Helen had prepared, they talked. Not about anything important; just talk.

When they'd finished eating and everything was put away, Carter stretched out on the blanket. Helen lay down beside him.

"I brought a book of poetry to read to you," said Carter.

"Oh, good!" said Helen, excitement in her voice. "I love poetry! Who's it by?"

"Edgar Allan Poe."

Helen sat upright and wrinkled her nose in disgust. "Edgar Allan Poe! Isn't he the one who writes all those strange stories?"

"Yes, but he also writes poetry. And I discovered a poem he wrote for you."

"A poem for me? What's it called?"

"To Helen."

She laughed. "All right, read it to me."

"To Helen," said Carter.

> *"Helen, thy beauty is to me*
> *Like those Nicean barks of yore,*
> *That gently, o'er a perfumed sea,*
> *The weary, way worn wanderer bore*
> *To his own native shore.*
> *On desperate seas long wont to roam,*
> *Thy hyacinth hair, thy classic face,*
> *Thy Naiad airs have brought me home*
> *To the glory that was Greece*
> *And the grandeur that was Rome.*
> *Lo! In yon brilliant window-niche*
> *How statue-like I see thee stand,*
> *The agate lamp within thy hand!*
> *Ah, Psyche, from the regions which*
> *Are Holy Land!"*

Helen thought for a moment, then asked, "Do you understand all of that?"

Carter laughed. "I have to admit, I don't. But I understand the part about your being beautiful. I see your classic face. And I do feel like *I* was that weary, way-worn wanderer, whom *you* took in. Through you, I *have* come home, not to Greece, and not to Rome, but to you."

She leaned over and kissed his forehead.

"I love you," she said.

She lay back down beside him and took his hand in hers. For a long time, they lay there together, staring up at the first spring leaves beginning to appear.

After a while, Carter broke the silence. "How long has this tree been here?"

"As long as I can remember," answered Helen. "I don't remember it never having been here."

Carter wished he could tell her about everything that had happened to him here on this very spot. That it was here he'd found the skeleton and the medal. It was here something happened that thrust him back in time into her world. But, of course, he couldn't tell her. How would he explain it? He didn't even understand it himself.

"A penny for your thoughts."

Helen's voice brought Carter back from his reverie. He turned and looked at her. "You," he fibbed.

She rolled over on top of him, peppering his face with quick kisses. He felt her breasts press against his chest, and her pelvis against his. He was becoming aroused.

"What are you doing?" he asked, teasingly.

"If you don't know, you're dumber than I think," answered Helen, between kisses.

"What if someone should come by?"

"I'm trusting they won't."

"But I—"

Carter didn't get to finish, as Helen brought her lips full on his, kissing him with a passion he wasn't sure he'd ever felt from her before.

What the hell, he thought, returning her kisses with a passion of his own.

Later, they lay together side by side once more, drained from the intensity of their lovemaking. After a while, Carter got up.

"Where are you going?" asked Helen.

"Nowhere. I want to do something."

He took a penknife from his pocket, and began carving on the tree trunk. Helen sat up to see what he was doing.

"Are you carving our initials?"

"Yes," he replied, without stopping his work.

"Now who's the romantic?" She laughed.

When he finished, he stepped back so she could see.

S.J + H.J.
1863

"I hate to tell you this, Sam, but that's the wrong year. This is 1864, not 1863."

"No, the year's right," he said, sitting down next to her. "1863 was the year I met you. It's the right date. That's the year *my* new life began."

"Mine, too," said Helen, tears coming to her eyes.

"Helen, I have something to ask you."

"What is it?"

"Will you marry me?"

"Oh, Sam!" She threw her arms around his neck, tears flowing even more freely now. "Oh, yes, yes! I wondered if you would ever ask! I hoped you would!"

"I've been hesitating because . . . well, because I don't have anything to offer you. I don't own any property. I don't have any money, and I don't have a job. Although I suppose I could go back to being a lawyer."

"Would you want to?"

"Maybe. I've been thinking about it."

"Whether you do or not, it wouldn't make any difference to me. I love you. And, yes, I *do* want to marry you. And if you decide you don't want to be a lawyer again, there's always the farm. It belongs to me, and Teddie, and Russell, and when we're married it will be yours, too. Oh, Sam, I'm so happy!"

"Then let's get married right away."

Helen was silent for a moment. When she spoke it was with some hesitation. "I . . . I'd like to wait, if that's all right with you."

"Wait? Wait for what?"

"I want to wait until Teddie gets back from the war. His enlistment is up in October. He's the one who should give me away. You understand, don't you?"

No, he wasn't sure he did understand. If she loves him as much as she says she does, why wait? But he wasn't going to argue with her.

"I guess . . . I guess if that's what you want, we can wait."

"It is, Sam, it really is. I wouldn't feel right doing it before Teddie gets back."

"Okay, then," said Carter, resigned to the inevitable. "We'll wait."

"Oh, thank you, Sam," gushed Helen. "I love you so much!" She leaned over and kissed him again. "I can't wait to tell everyone!"

Suddenly her mood became more serious. "Or maybe we shouldn't, not yet."

"Tell everyone? Why not?" He was ready for the whole world to know about them.

"People might talk, since you're living at the farm."

"You mean they might get the *right* idea," he said, grinning.

"I don't want them to get any more of an idea than they already have. Let's wait for now."

"If that's what you want. I wish I had remembered it was your birthday," Carter continued. "I would have gotten you a present."

"Having you in my life is present enough," said Helen. Then a thought struck her. "Wait! I know what I want."

"What?"

"I want us to go into town tomorrow and have our picture taken."

"Our picture?"

"You know—a photograph? Of the two of us together. Mr. Tillman has a little shop where he does photographs. Oh, please say yes! That would be the best birthday present! I could put it in my locket."

Carter wasn't at all sure he wanted their picture in the locket Dieter had given to her for Christmas. Besides, if Helen wanted to keep the relationship secret, was having their picture taken together a good idea? "But what if this Mr. Tillman goes blabbing all around town that we're having our picture taken together?"

"No, he wouldn't do that. He's an old, old friend of our family. I'd make sure to tell him we want to keep it to ourselves, and he'd honor that."

Carter still had his doubts. But Helen was so enthusiastic about the idea. "All right," he said. "We'll go in first thing."

"Oh, thank you, Sam!" Helen squealed and kissed him again.

Carter smiled at her. He loved it when she was happy.

"Sam, I have a question for you. The two medals you wear—you never take them off, even when we make love. What are they for? Where did you get them?"

Carter knew eventually she would ask him about the medals. Even so, he wasn't ready when she did. There was no way he could tell her the truth, that one he had taken off a skeleton and the other had been given to him by a woman sixty years in the future. He decided the best thing to do was to bend the truth a little.

"I found the one medal when I was a young boy, about Russell's age. The other one was given to me by a friend before I met you."

"By a *lady* friend?" asked Helen, a slight frown on her face.

"That's right." Carter laughed. "A lady friend who happened to be eighty-seven years old, and the grandmother of my best friend."

Her face brightened. "Okay, then. Are the medals identical?"

He looked down at them. "Exactly the same. You know what? We should be getting back. Russell will wonder what happened to us. Besides, it looks like it's getting ready to rain."

Chapter Forty-Two

Carter Gets a Job

Carter found himself settling more and more easily into his new life. The farm was up and running again. His love for Helen grew stronger every day. And he loved making love to her. The year 1927 seemed a long way off now, another time, another life. Not only had he reconciled himself to the fact that he was here in this time to stay, he found himself quite content with the reality of it.

Through his involvement in the church, he was now friends with an ever-widening circle of people.

And he and Dieter, especially, had become the closest of friends.

"Sam, over here! I think I've found the spot!"

Carter looked upstream to see Dieter bringing in what appeared to be about a five-pound bass. They had come out in late afternoon to try their hand at fishing in Wolford's Creek, but for the first hour hadn't had even a nibble. Then Dieter decided to move up the river bank about a hundred yards to where he knew some old tree stumps lay buried under the water. It was there that he was now landing his catch.

"Hurry up!" he said. "I can see them out there in the water! They're jumping over each other to get to my bait!"

Carter ran along the bank until he reached Dieter, who by now had landed the bass and was tossing his line back into the stream. For the next forty-five minutes, they pulled fish out almost as fast as they could cast their lines. Then, the feeding frenzy was over. The fish were gone.

They counted their catch: a couple dozen bass and eight crappies. A good day's haul.

Back at Dieter's house, Chessie set about cleaning their catch for supper, while the two of them sat on the porch, each with a cup of whiskey from a batch Henry had brewed.

"I love Kentucky," said Dieter.

"Excuse me?"

"I said 'I love Kentucky.' I haven't traveled much— Ohio, Tennessee, once to Virginia. That is, before that part became West Virginia. But no matter where I've gone, I've never found a more beautiful place than right here."

"I know what you mean," said Carter. "I'm like you. I haven't been to too many other states. But if there's a more beautiful land, I'd like to see it."

"You know, my ma and pa came to America from the old country before I was ever born. They were looking for a new way of life, a life of freedom and opportunity. They loved Germany. But I know they love Kentucky even more. I hate to think what it would be like if they had stayed in Germany. That's where I'd be living now." He looked at Carter and smiled. "Of course, if that had happened, I wouldn't know what I'd be missing, would I?

"And I love the Union," Dieter continued. "It distresses me to see it so divided. And no place is that more evident than right here in our own state. I'm sad thinking about how we have men fighting on both sides, North and South. I'll be so thankful when this war is over. And I pray to God the

North will be victorious, for if the South is, I don't know how the nation can survive."

"The North will win," said Carter.

"You sound so certain," Dieter said, turning to look at him.

"I am."

"I wish I could be as certain as you."

"Helen said you're a 'neutral'?"

"Because I'm not off fighting somewhere?"

"I guess."

"Kentucky was a neutral state when the war broke out. We all hoped it would stay that way. We were wrong, of course. It's too strategically located not to be on one side or the other. But I vowed right from the start I would never go off to war against my fellow countrymen."

"But you're in the Home Guard."

"Yes, I am. And, I'm not real happy about that. But I see the Home Guard as different from being off somewhere fighting. The reason we exist is to defend what we have right here, in this county. I know some Home Guard units in other counties have gone off to fight somewhere else, but I wouldn't do that."

Neither of them spoke for a while.

Then Dieter broke the silence. "Sam, I have to know. Are you in love with Helen?"

Carter was somewhat taken aback by Dieter's question, as he had been when Teddie asked him the same thing. He knew Dieter was sweet on Helen but, still, he wasn't prepared for the question.

"I have to know," persisted Dieter. "Are you?"

"Yes," said Carter, after a moment's hesitation, "I am."

"And how does she feel about you?"

"She loves me, too."

"She told you so?"

"Yes." He hoped Dieter wasn't going to ask if they'd slept together, because if he did, he'd have to lie. He didn't.

Carter looked at Dieter. "You love her too, don't you?"

Without looking up, Dieter replied, softly, "Yes."

"I'm sorry," said Carter. And he truly was. For he knew how much Helen meant to him, and he imagined how Dieter felt about her. More than that, he felt almost guilty that, here Dieter had known Helen his whole life, grown up with her as childhood friends, and then, from out of nowhere, a complete stranger comes along who steals her heart.

After a while, Dieter spoke again. Carter was thankful it was on a different subject.

"I know Helen's not able to pay you anything for helping out around the farm. If you're looking for work, I know there would be a job for you at our mill. In fact, Pa told me the other day he needed some help in the office. He's a good man to work for, and he'd pay you a fair wage."

"Thanks," said Carter. "I've been thinking I need to do something to earn some money. I'll go over and see him tomorrow."

"There's something else I wanted to talk to you about," continued Dieter. "You know there's been rumblings the Johnny Rebs are getting ready to invade Kentucky again."

"Yes, I've heard those rumors."

"It's the Home Guard's primary responsibility to guard the railroad tracks to make sure the Confederates don't blow them up. We also do some training over at Camp Frazer. If the Rebs do come through here like they did in '62, we'll need all the help we can get. What do you think about joining up? It doesn't pay anything, but they do provide you with a rifle."

Carter had already considered joining the Home Guard. He knew the story of Morgan's raid two years ago, how the Confederates were victorious in a small skirmish. And he had begun to feel a little guilty he'd played no part in this war raging in both the North and the South.

"I think I'd like to do that."

"Good," replied Dieter. "We're getting together next Wednesday at eight o'clock in the morning to do a little drilling and get better organized. Why don't we go over together?"

"That would be fine."

"It's settled, then."

Carter sat at his desk by the window, every once in a while glancing out to see another wagon bringing grain to be ground. He would have preferred to have continued working at the farm, and being around Helen, rather than sitting here in the office at the mill tending to Henry's accounts. Still, he was grateful for the job. At least now he had some money coming in, which allowed him to buy his own clothes. He wouldn't have to continue wearing Teddie's.

He leaned back in his chair and watched as the next wagon arrived. Two young boys, one white, the other black, sat on the seat next to the driver, who was himself white. Carter guessed the white boy to be perhaps sixteen or seventeen, the Negro a few years younger.

As the boys climbed down from the wagon, the horse suddenly reared, causing the Negro to lose his balance and fall against the other boy. Both of them crashed to the ground in a tangled heap.

"You dumb-ass nigger!" shouted the white boy, pushing the Negro off of him. "You black son of a bitch!"

The white boy jumped up, grabbed a cane from the wagon, and brought the rod down full force on the other boy's back. A scream of pain exploded from his lips. The white boy raised the cane and again struck the Negro as hard as he could. Another scream. The Negro rolled up into a ball, trying as best he could to protect himself from the blows raining down on him. He started to cry. The driver stood to one side, arms folded, laughing.

Carter had seen enough.

Jumping up from his chair, he flew down the stairs two at a time and out the door, coming up behind the white boy as he was about to land yet another blow. He grabbed the boy's wrist, spun him around—and came face to face with Kiernan O'Doherty. A young, teen-aged Kiernan O'Doherty. There was no mistaking the birthmark. Carter felt the hair on the back of his neck stand up.

O'Doherty's dark eyes, full of hatred, bore into him. A snarl erupted from his lips, as he smashed his free fist into Carter's cheek, causing him to release his grip and stumble backward.

Kiernan raised the cane to strike Carter, then abruptly stopped it in midair, his eyes locked on something—or someone—behind Carter.

Carter turned his head to see what had distracted O'Doherty. Henry stood there, a ten-gauge shotgun in his arms pointed straight at the youth.

"Get off my property," said Henry. "*Now!*"

The boy slowly lowered the cane, then dropped it to the ground.

"*Now!*" repeated Henry.

Kiernan's mouth curled up in a sneer as he gave a slight nod of his head. He looked at Carter one more time, mouthed the word "later," then turned, and leisurely walked away.

"Are you all right?" asked Henry.

"I'm fine," replied Carter, though he felt a knot in his stomach. "Thanks. How's the boy?"

By this time, the young Negro was on his feet. Although huge welts had begun to appear on his back as a result of the beating, he seemed to be okay otherwise.

"Do you know him?" Carter asked Henry, as they watched Kiernan stride off into the distance.

"Ja," said Henry. "He's no good, that one. I told old man Farnsworth already I didn't want that boy back on my property. I reckon I'll have to tell him again."

"Do you know where he lives?"

"The kid? Ja, him and his daddy have a place over on Raven Creek Pike, but I don't know where. From what I hear, the boy spends most of his time at the Yellow Roof Tavern."

A shiver ran through Carter. He remembered O'Doherty's face in the store that first time, its sheer ugliness, the look of hatred he'd seen there. And then, again, at the restaurant.

But it was the third meeting, the one in the cemetery, he recalled most vividly, the look in O'Doherty's eyes when he aimed his derringer at Carter and fired.

The night they raped and killed Emmaline.

Chapter Forty-Three

Saving Emmaline

May, 1864

Carter sat at the kitchen table, his eyes fixed on the sheet of paper in front of him. It had been a long time since he'd thought about Emmaline, but his run-in with Kiernan a few days earlier brought back all his memories of her.

Helen and Russell had gone out to pick berries. They'd asked Carter if he wanted to go with them, but he'd declined, saying he had some chores he couldn't put off.

The real reason, though, was that, in reliving Emmaline's death, Carter began to wonder if, knowing now it was going to happen, might he somehow prevent it? After some deliberation, he came up with two plans he thought might work.

First, he would write a letter to her.

Dear Miss Jones:

What I am about to tell you may sound strange, but please trust me that I know whereof I speak.
I know you are currently seeing a man by the name of Carter McGlone. In October, Mr.

McGlone will invite you to go with him on a second visit to his parent's home in Harrison County. You must not go! If you do, something terrible will happen. I cannot explain how I know this; however, please believe me, I do. As proof, I offer the fact I know you will receive his invitation. If I did not know that, I could not know the other. Use whatever excuse you must to decline this invitation.

A Friend

Carter laid the pen down for a moment, then picked it up again and resumed writing.

Dear Reverend Jones,

The enclosed envelope is for your daughter, Emmaline.Please give it to her today before she begins her new job at the bank tomorrow.

A Friend

He took two envelopes and addressed one to Emmaline Jones, the other to Rev. Mordecai Jones, along with the church's name and address. On the front of Mordecai's envelope, he added "Please do not open until June 14th, 1926."

Carter placed Emmaline's letter in her envelope, sealed it, then placed it, along with the note to Mordecai, in the other envelope. He sealed the second envelope, then stood and walked over to his jacket hanging by the door and placed both envelopes in one of the pockets.

Carter knew Dieter well enough now to know that if he were willing to agree to what Carter was about to ask of him, he could count on it being done.

"Dieter, I have a favor to ask of you."

"What's that?"

"I know this is going to sound strange, crazy even. But I had this . . . this *dream* the other night. It was so strong I knew I had to act on it. But I'm not sure I can do it by myself."

"What kind of dream?"

"In my dream, I was delivering a letter to a minister in Louisville. Except the minister won't be there for almost another fifty years." Carter remembered Emmaline told him once that her father had become the minister of his church in 1912. He remembered the year, because it was the same year he and Sara Jane found the skeleton. He also remembered her saying that the church itself celebrated its fiftieth anniversary earlier in 1926.

"And," Carter continued, "the church itself won't even be built until twelve years from now." Carter felt embarrassed at how ridiculous it all sounded.

Dieter stared at Carter as though he had lost his mind.

"You're going to deliver a letter to a church that doesn't yet exist, for a minister who won't be there for another fifty years? You're right—that sounds crazy."

"I know," said Carter. He was determined to see this through. "The thing is, I'm not sure I'll be around in twelve years when the church is built."

"Why wouldn't you be?"

"You never know. With this war going on, who knows who will be around in twelve years." Besides, he knew, his second plan to save Emmaline's life might well get him killed.

"That's true," said Dieter.

"That's why I want you to promise me if I'm not here in 1876, you'll go to Louisville and make sure the new minister gets this envelope." Carter took the envelope from his jacket pocket and held it up for Dieter to see. "I've written the name and address of the church on the outside, along with the name of the minister who should get it, and the date it's to be opened. What I need the first minister to do is to put it in a safe place, and to make sure Reverend Jones gets it when he replaces the current minister. Or, if there's another minister—or two or three—between the first minister and him, that each of them are made aware of the envelope's existence, and that it gets passed down eventually to Reverend Jones."

"Sam, you *are* crazy. Besides, what makes you so sure *I'll* be around twelve years from now?"

"I don't know for sure either one of us will. But you could put the envelope in a safe place, and let someone else know how important it is, so if something should happen that neither you nor I are here, that other person could make sure it gets delivered."

Dieter stared at him for a long time. Finally, he said, "You feel strongly about this, don't you?"

"I do. It's a matter of life and death. Literally."

"Okay. I'll do what you ask. But now if you're still here in 1876—and I'm sure you will be—you'll be the one to go to Louisville, is that right?"

"Yes. You'll only need to do this for me if, for some reason, I'm not around."

"Okay. Give me the envelope. I've got a box at home I keep some valuable papers in. I'll put it in there."

"And who will you tell that it's there?" Carter wanted to make sure if something happened to both of them, the envelope would still get delivered.

"I'll tell Karl," said Dieter, "and Russell. They're both old enough to grasp the importance of this—whatever *this* is—and by 1876, they'll be plenty old enough to go off to Louisville by themselves."

"Good. Dieter, I appreciate this."

"Sam, I do this only because we're friends. And—because I'm curious to find out if this church will be there twelve years from now."

As Carter lay on his bunk that night staring at the darkness, he thought about his second plan. Helen had sensed something was wrong, had asked what was troubling him. He explained what happened at the mill, but of course couldn't tell her the rest, about his encounters with O'Doherty in his other life, and especially about Emmaline.

If O'Doherty were to die before that fateful night when Emmaline was raped and murdered, thought Carter, perhaps the incident wouldn't even take place. After all, the only reason those men were there, he was sure, was to buy and sell moonshine. If he killed Kiernan—if the man didn't even exist in 1926—then he couldn't be in the cemetery that night. In all likelihood, then, neither would George nor Sid nor the third man. Between this plan and the letters, which were his back-up plan, he might have a chance of saving Emmaline from harm.

But could he kill him? Murder the boy in cold blood, even if it meant possibly saving Emmaline some sixty years from now?

He'd killed men before, of course, during the war. But this was different. They were anonymous and, except for the last incident—his hand-to-hand combat with the German that got him out of the army—none were at close range.

Carter swung his legs around and sat up on the edge of the bed. Where did Henry say he hung out? The Yellow Roof Tavern? Carter knew the place—he'd seen it one day on his way into town.

Quietly, so as not to disturb Mornin, Carter got dressed and tiptoed to the cupboard, where he knew Mornin kept a large Bowie knife for cleaning fish. Carter found the knife, wrapped a towel around it, and slid it down the inside of his right boot. He removed his jacket from the peg by the door, slipped it on, opened the door, and left.

Carter was surprised at the number of soldiers in the tavern. He knew a lot of military training was done in the area, but hadn't thought about how many of those men would be here drinking.

Altogether, he counted twenty or so patrons, including a few civilians; but no Kiernan O'Doherty.

Carter bought a glass of beer at the bar and found an empty table at the rear of the room that gave him a clear view of the door. If O'Doherty came in, he'd be sure to spot him.

An hour passed, and still no sign of him. Carter walked back up to the bar and ordered another beer.

"Excuse me," he said. "But do you by any chance know a young boy by the name of Kiernan O'Doherty?"

The bartender wrinkled up his nose. "Uh-huh, I know the little snot. He's a real turd, that one. Why, you a friend of his?" The tone of the question was not a friendly one.

"No, I need to give him something. Do you know if he might be coming in tonight?"

"Not tonight, nor any time soon, if we're lucky."

"Why's that?"

"'Cause he's gone—hightailed it out of the county. Ran off down south to join up with the Confederates."

Carter was stunned. "Somehow, he didn't strike me as the military type," he said.

"I don't reckon he'd have left if he'd had a choice."

"A choice?"

"That's right. After he beat that poor little nigger boy to death, old man Farnsworth came looking for him with a shotgun. I guess O'Doherty figured it best he clear out. He was right, too, 'cause the old man would have shot him dead without ever blinking an eye."

"He beat someone to death?"

"Yes, sir. Seems he had a run-in with some feller at old Henry Ruehmschuessel's mill who stopped him from beating up on the nigger. When the nigger got back to the farm, young Kiernan took the poor bastard out behind the barn and beat his head in with an ax handle. He's a mean one, that kid is.

"One of the boys he runs with was in here last night talking about him, told me all about it. Said Kiernan was hightailing it as soon as he took care of one last thing. Say, you're that Jenkins fellow from over at the Jones place, ain't you?"

Carter nodded.

"Heard your name mentioned, too. Something about 'unfinished business.' If O'Doherty's involved, you might want to watch your back."

"Thanks for the warning," said Carter.

Carter felt a sense of disappointment, mixed with relief. He hadn't looked forward to killing the boy. He would have, though, if it meant saving Emmaline. Now, it seemed, he'd missed his chance. Or had he? Had O'Doherty already left the county? Or was he still around, taking care of that "one last thing?"

Carter wondered what the chances were their paths would cross again.

∞

Carter wasn't sure what it was that woke him. Perhaps the squeak of the cabin door. *Mornin must be going out to relieve himself,* he thought.

He started to roll back over when he heard a sound like someone being hit, and being hit more than once—*thud, thud, thud*—followed by a low moan. He sat bolt upright in his bunk and tried to adjust his eyes to see in the semi-darkness of the cabin. A flash of moonlight on something bright caught his eye as the object ascended, then descended rapidly, followed by another *thud.* He knew instantly what it was—a knife!

"Hey!" the word erupted from his throat.

The knife, which had already been raised again, stopped in midair.

Carter jumped up from his bed. He saw what appeared to be a boy or a short man, standing over Mornin's bunk. But before he knew what happened, the man lunged at him, and once again he saw the flash of silver as the blade arced through the air. Instinctively, he reached out his hand and managed to grab the assailant's wrist as the blade was about to plunge into his chest. They struggled, knocking over the table and chairs.

Their wrestling around brought them close to the window where, by the moonlight coming in, Carter could finally recognize his attacker: Kiernan O'Doherty. Carter locked his foot behind O'Doherty's leg and pushed him with his body. They both fell hard against the wall and the window, shattering the glass. Carter heard the knife clatter to the cabin floor, and somewhere, off in the distance, Red was barking.

Kiernan bolted for the door in an attempt to escape. Carter caught him from behind and together they fell, tumbling out of the cabin onto the ground. Kiernan rolled over on top of Carter and grabbed his throat in a stranglehold. Carter put his hands around O'Doherty's neck in an attempt to stop him. The strength of the young boy surprised Carter.

A shotgun blast rent the air, followed a moment later by Helen's voice: "Whoever you are, you better get the hell out of here before I aim this shotgun at you!"

Kiernan hesitated for a second, then, in a quick movement, released his hands from around Carter's throat, jumped up, and took off running for the woods. Carter still lay on the ground, trying to catch his breath, when he heard O'Doherty's voice coming from the safety of the trees.

"The next time I *will* kill you, you son of a bitch!"

Helen knelt down beside Carter. "Are you all right?"

Carter nodded, still trying to catch his breath. Then he remembered—Mornin!

"Mornin," he said, feebly.

Russell had joined them, and he and Helen helped Carter to his feet.

"Mornin," Carter said again. "I'm afraid he's hurt."

They ran into the cabin. Helen quickly found a lamp and lit it.

"Oh, my God!" she exclaimed.

The old man lay still on his bunk, covered in blood. Carter put his fingers to Mornin's neck—there was no pulse.

"He's dead," said Carter.

"Oh, no," moaned Helen. She and Russell both began to cry.

"Do you know who that was?" asked Helen, between sobs.

"Yes," said Carter. "That kid I had the run-in with at the mill last week—Kiernan O'Doherty."

"Will he come back?" asked Russell. Carter heard the fear in Russell's voice.

"I doubt it. He knows we're on to him, now. He's probably well on his way out of the county. We'll wait 'til daylight, and I'll ride into town and get the sheriff."

"He was after you, wasn't he?" said Helen.

Carter nodded. "I imagine he thought it was me lying there. He didn't know about Mornin, didn't know he lived here, too."

Helen came and put her arms around Carter's neck and looked up at him. "He said the next time he'd kill you."

"I'll be more careful from now on. But I doubt we'll see him again."

How many other times had he thought that, he wondered.

Chapter Forty-Four

Preparing for Morgan's Return

June, 1864

Sunday, the fifth of June, was one of those rare, pleasant days as far as the weather was concerned in that part of Kentucky. Normally the temperature would be in the mid to high nineties, and the humidity almost unbearable. Today, though, a gentle breeze blew out of the north, bringing with it an unusual coolness for this time of year.

They had been to church that morning. Reverend Moundtree gave his usual stirring—but far too long—sermon. Carter enjoyed going to the Lutheran church with Helen. It was a lot different from the Methodist church he had always attended with his parents.

The sermon topic was one of Reverend Moundtree's favorites, and one on which he often spoke: love. The text was Paul's first letter to the Corinthians, chapter thirteen, the famous "love" passage.

Although Carter had read that passage many times, and heard more than one sermon preached on it, this day one verse in particular stood out for him, as Reverend Moundtree quoted the scripture: *For now we see through a glass, darkly. But then, face to face. Now, I know in part. But then shall I know, even as also I am known.*

Will I ever know fully? Carter wondered. Know what brought him to this time, and for what purpose. And even though he had long ago reconciled to the fact he would never return to his own time, he knew in the back of his mind there was always one little thought that maybe—*maybe*—he might, somehow, go back. But now, having fallen in love with Helen, would he even want to?

They'd decided to walk to church that day, rather than hitching up the buggy, and now took their time as they strolled back to the farm. Russell ran on ahead, letting off some energy pent up while sitting on a hard wooden pew for the last hour and forty-five minutes listening to Reverend Moundtree drone on and on about love, and burning bodies, and cymbals crashing.

"What does all that have to do with love?" Russell had asked, without receiving a satisfactory answer.

"Sam, I've heard Morgan might be back in Kentucky." There was concern in Helen's voice.

"I know," said Carter. "I think it's more than a rumor. I hear he's got Federal troops chasing him, and he's looking for the easiest route out of the state. That way could be right through our backyard."

Helen stopped and turned to face him. "I'm frightened," she said. Her chin quivered ever so slightly.

"You'll be all right," Carter tried to assure her, although he wasn't so certain himself how safe she might be if they couldn't hold off Morgan's troops.

"I'm not frightened for me," said Helen. "I'm frightened for you—and, for us. I don't know what I'd do if something happened to you."

"I'll be careful," Carter reassured her. But deep down, he was concerned, if not frightened. He couldn't believe he had traveled so many years to meet the one woman whom he now knew to be his soul mate, only to possibly lose her by being killed in some goddamn war. A war that happened thirty years before he was even born. Well, he'd survived the big war. He was determined to come out of this one alive, too.

∞

There was no news of Morgan and his men over the next few days. *Perhaps the rumors were false*, thought Carter. *Morgan wasn't in Kentucky after all.* And yet, he knew, sooner or later he would come.

On Wednesday, he and Helen were sitting at the kitchen table when Russell rushed into the house, almost out of breath. "Sam, Helen, it's Dieter—he's coming up the road like the devil's chasing him!"

Dieter was already dismounting by the time they reached the front yard.

"What is it?" cried Helen.

"It's Morgan," said Dieter, catching his breath. "Two men rode into town with news Morgan and his raiders are in Kentucky for sure, and they've captured Mt. Sterling. Word is he's got over 1,800 men with him. Not only that, he's already got advance units in Paris, at Ruddles Mills, and Talbott's Station!"

"Paris!" cried Helen. "That's not even fifteen miles from here!"

"There's a train leaving for Covington about noon," Dieter continued. "I'm putting Ma and Gertie on it. We wanted to put Karl on, too, but he won't go. Listen, Helen, we can get you to the depot in time to catch it. Russell, too, if he wants to go."

"I ain't going if Karl ain't going," declared Russell.

"How about it, Helen, will you go?" Dieter looked at her, pleadingly.

"I can't go. I need to stay here and mind the farm."

"Helen, I think Dieter's right," said Carter. "You should go. Forget about the farm."

"No." Her voice was firm now, and steady. "I'm staying. I'll be all right. Russell will be here with me."

Carter and Dieter both knew that when Helen made up her mind, it was not easily changed. Dieter turned his attention to Carter. "Sam, Colonel Berry wants all the Home Guard to meet at the courthouse this evening at five o'clock. We'll find out then what's going on.

"I've got to go and put Ma and Gertie on the train," Dieter continued, climbing back on his horse. "I'll see you later at the court house."

"Helen, are you sure you don't want to go?" Carter thought he should take one last stab at getting her to change her mind. "It's hard to tell what might happen around here over the next few days. If I'm off fighting, I won't be able to help."

"We'll be fine. Won't we, Russell?"

"We sure will be," said Russell." I'll take care of things around here."

"I'm going to make us some dinner," said Helen. "And then we've got a lot of work to do before you leave to go into town."

$$\infty$$

When Carter arrived at the courthouse, he spotted Dieter talking with several men and walked over to join them. He noticed they all wore what appeared to be military jackets.

"What's this?" he asked, putting his hand on Dieter's shoulder.

"The jacket?" said Dieter. "It's a uniform jacket. Two years ago, when we got the word Morgan was headed this way, Ma sewed some shirts for me and a couple of the boys at the mill. Designed them after the regular army shirts. Said if we were going to be fighting as soldiers, we should look like soldiers, and not some ragamuffins."

Carter remembered seeing Dieter's picture in the upstairs hallway of the Ruehmschuessel home, wearing this jacket.

"She did a good job," said Carter. "They look like real uniforms. Nobody could tell any of you from regular soldiers."

Carter noticed the letters "USA" embroidered on the right collar of each jacket and "HCHG" the left.

"What's the 'HCHG' stand for?" he asked.

"Harrison County Home Guard," replied Dieter. "Ma said we should be proud we're members of the unit protecting our own homes."

"Colonel Berry's getting ready to talk," shouted someone. Everyone quieted down.

"Listen up, boys," he said. "My scouts tell me Morgan and his men have bedded down for the night. So, I want all of you to go on back home, and meet back here tomorrow morning, early. I'm going to meet with Colonel Garis, to find out what his plans are. When you come back tomorrow, I'd suggest you bring a rations kit with you. No telling how long we may be here."

Chapter Forty-Five

A Startling Revelation

Breakfast the next morning was a quiet affair.

Afterward, Russell went outside to play with Red. Helen was clearing the table.

"I'm leaving soon for town," said Carter. "I'm going to go ahead and walk in. Helen, I think Russell should take the horses into the woods and tether them there. That way, if Morgan's men should come by here, they won't be able to steal them."

"I think that's a good idea," said Helen. "And I'm taking these five cured hams and burying them out behind the barn. I'll be damned if they're going to eat my hams!"

Carter laughed, not only at the defiance in her voice, but in her choice of words. The one time he'd ever heard her curse before was the night she ran O'Doherty off with a shotgun.

"What are you laughing at, Sam Jenkins?" she said, turning and facing him, a scowl on her face.

"You." He laughed again. "I sure wouldn't want to be a Confederate soldier trying to steal anything from you."

"You sure wouldn't want to be. 'Cause it might be the last thing you ever tried to steal in your life!" Then she smiled. "I'm tough, aren't I?"

"You sure are." He took her in his arms. "You sure are."

Suddenly her mood became serious.

"Sam, I have something to tell you."

"And I have something to tell you. You are the most beautiful woman I have ever met, and I am madly in love with you!"

"Seriously," continued Helen, blushing. "I have to tell you this."

"What is it?" Carter was concerned now at the gravity of her tone.

"I don't think we're going to be able to wait until Teddie gets back before we get married. I'm with child, Sam. I'm going to have a baby."

For a moment, Carter just stared at her. Then the impact of her words sank in. "You're going to have a *baby*? *Our* baby? Are you sure?"

"Of course, our baby, you idiot," she giggled. "It's not something I could have done by myself, and I've never been with any man but you. And—am I sure? Well, I've never *had* a baby before but—yes, I'm sure."

"This is great!" exclaimed Carter. A baby! "Have you thought about a name?"

"Yes. If it's a boy, I want to name him after you—Samuel Jenkins II."

But my name's not Samuel, he thought. *Not even Jenkins.* But how could he tell her this now? How would he explain it? And, did he even have to?

"And if it's a girl," Helen continued, "I'll name her after my mother—Athena."

For a moment, Carter was stunned. Had he heard her right? "Athena?"

"Yes, it's a name that's been in our family for generations. It means—"

"'Gray-eyed,'" Carter interrupted, as questions began to swirl through his mind. "It means 'gray-eyed.'"

"Yes," said Helen, surprised. "How did you know that?"

Carter sat there, still unable to believe what he was hearing.

"Helen," he said, "your first name is 'Helen' isn't it?"

"Well, no. Actually my first name is Mary. My full name is Mary Helen Jones. My family all call me Mary— my Grandma and Grandpa Swaney, all my aunts, and uncles, and cousins. 'Course my mother and daddy did, too, when they were still alive. But I always preferred Helen. And Helen is what Russell and Teddie both call me. Even though the rest of our family insisted on calling us by our proper names, Teddie and I called each other by the names *we* liked. Why? Why do you ask?"

"But, is Teddie your brother's actual name?" Carter asked, ignoring her question. A knot started to build in his chest.

"No, his given name is Edgar. But he likes Teddie, and I like Helen, and that's what we've always called ourselves. Why?" she asked again.

Carter let go of her hands and stood up suddenly, startling her.

"Sam? What's wrong? What did I say?"

"I . . . I have to go," he stammered. "I have to go."

"I know you do," replied Helen, alarmed by his abrupt change of mood. "But not right away. Please—tell me what's wrong!"

Athena. Helen. Mary. Edgar. Teddie. *No, it can't be*! he thought. And yet—the evidence was all there. Now he knew why she seemed so familiar to him when they first met, why he felt such a connection. He knelt down, and held her hands again, studying her face. He saw it now. It *was* her! Mary—Sara Jane's grandmother, Mary! How could he have not seen it until now? And if Athena was their daughter—his and Helen's—then Sara Jane would be his granddaughter! Quickly, he let go of her hands again.

He couldn't tell her the truth—at least not yet. He needed to go, to get out of the house, to think, to sort this all out. What excuse could he use?

"I . . . I have to be at the courthouse in a little bit." He stood, picked up his rifle and the ration kit Helen had prepared for him, and moved toward the door.

"Sam, what is it? What's the matter? You look like you've seen a ghost."

"I have to go," he said again.

Her words brought him to a halt. "Sam, please come back. Promise me you'll come back to me."

Come back. The same words she would give Sara Jane to pass on to him sixty-three years from now as she, Helen—Mary—lay on her death bed.

Carter turned, walked back to her, and knelt in front of her again. He placed one hand alongside her face. "Remember this. No matter what may happen, I know that in this life I have been blessed to be loved by you. And you have my promise. One way or another, I will come back to you. Here, I want you to have this."

He took one of the medals from around his neck—the same one she had given him—or would give him sixty-three years in the future—and placed it around her neck. "As long as we each have one of these, we will never truly be apart."

Then, cupping her chin in his hand, he gave her a long, tender kiss. He stood, turned, picked up the rifle and ration kit, and this time walked out the door.

As he walked the four miles into town, thoughts swirled through Carter's mind. Sara Jane said her grandfather died in a fire. Was that him? Would he survive this upcoming skirmish—as well as the Great War—only to die in a house fire? Knowing what would happen, could he avoid it? And could he save Russell? Sara Jane said Mary's younger brother was also killed in the fire. But Mary said her young man—and Carter knew now she must have been speaking of him—had been lost in the battle, his body never found.

It was more than he could comprehend. There were just no answers.

When Carter arrived at the courthouse, a throng of people were already gathered. Dieter was again talking with some of the men of the Home Guard.

"Dieter, I have to talk to you."

"What is it?"

"Not here. Let's go down to the river. We've got time before we have to assemble."

"We're expecting the 168th Ohio anytime now," said Dieter as they walked. "I'll feel better when they get here."

"Uh-huh," murmured Carter. His mind was on what he was about to tell Dieter.

When they arrived at the riverbank, Dieter turned to Carter. "So, what did you want to tell me?"

Carter hesitated for a moment, unsure now if he should tell Dieter of Helen's pregnancy. Finally, he decided he must.

"Helen's with child," he blurted out.

"You bastard!" cried Dieter. Before Carter could react, he felt the force of Dieter's fist as it smashed into his nose. The next thing he knew he was on the ground, with Dieter hovering over him, his fist still clenched. "Get up, you bastard," he shouted, "so's I can knock you down again!"

"Wait," said Carter, feeling what he was sure was blood running down his chin. "Wait, Dieter, you don't understand. I love Helen, and she loves me. You know that. And we're going to get married."

Dieter relaxed his fist, and took a step back. Warily, Carter got to his feet.

"You know we love each other," he said, again. "When you told me I should ask Helen to marry me, I realized that's what I wanted. So I did ask her before this happened, and she said yes. But she wanted to wait until Teddie gets back to give her away. Now, I don't think we can wait."

Dieter didn't say anything at first. Then he took out his kerchief and offered it to Carter.

"Here. I'm sorry I hit you. But I was so damned mad. Yeah, I know you love Helen. And I know she loves you. You didn't even have to tell me that the day we were out fishing. I saw it in both of your eyes long before then. I . . . I didn't think about the two of you sleeping together."

"The thing is," said Carter, holding the kerchief to his nose, "I've got a feeling I may not come out of this battle alive."

"That's crazy," Dieter replied. "Why would you think that?"

"It's just a feeling. I can't explain it, but it's there nonetheless."

"Well, I'm gonna stick close to you, and make sure you *do* come out alive."

Carter smiled. "Thanks, I know I can count on you. But I want to make sure I can count on you for something else, too."

"What's that?"

"If I don't make it, I want you to marry Helen and raise our daughter as your own."

Dieter looked stunned. For a moment, he didn't answer, then he said, "But . . . I . . . ."

"You love Helen. Maybe even as much as I do. And I know she cares for you. She'd say yes if you asked. I want you to promise me you will."

"I . . . all right, I will, if that's what you want. And if that's what Helen would want, I'd be proud to be her husband, and raise your child. But it's not going to happen, 'cause you *will* be okay. And what makes you think it will be a girl?"

Carter couldn't tell him he knew the baby would be a girl, that her name would be Athena, and that she would be the mother of his childhood friend, Sara Jane Williams.

"I . . . I don't know for sure. Another feeling that I have."

A shout rang out from the direction of the courthouse.

"I reckon we better get back up there," said Dieter. "Sounds like something's about to happen. How's your nose?"

"It hurts," Carter answered, grinning.

Chapter Forty-Six

Al and Willie

When they got back to the courthouse, they found everyone had moved to the train depot. The 168th had arrived and was setting up camp. Over the next several hours, everyone kept busy cleaning their rifles and ensuring everything was in order.

Carter was restless, still unsettled from what he'd learned from Helen. He laid down the book he'd been reading. Dieter was shining his boots.

A man from the 168th sauntered over.

"You fellows want to throw some paper?" he asked.

"Throw some paper?" Carter didn't understand.

"Play cards," explained Dieter.

"Oh, no thanks. I'm not much of card player," said Carter.

"I'll pass," said Dieter.

The man turned and began to walk away.

"Wait a minute," said Carter.

The man turned back to him.

"Do I know you?" asked Carter. There was something strangely familiar about him.

"I don't think so," replied the man. "Don't think we've ever met." He turned and started to walk away again.

"What's your name?" asked Carter.

Without stopping, the man turned and said, "Aloysius—Aloysius Quincy Montgomery."

Aloysius Quincy Montgomery—no wonder he looked so familiar! Al's grandfather! The grandfather of the man he'd served with, been friends with, the man who saved his life in the Great War. And now it seemed the two of them would be fighting side by side in this war, more than fifty years before that other war.

Carter shook his head. It didn't seem possible, or make any sense.

He decided to go for a walk, to try to clear his head. When he told Dieter he was leaving, he merely nodded and went on shining his boots. *Always the impeccable dresser*, thought Carter.

As Carter walked around to the back of the depot, he spotted what at first he took to be a young boy, a lad no older than twelve.

"Son, what are you doing here?"

When the youth turned around, Carter was surprised to find it wasn't a boy after all, but a young girl, with short hair, dressed in men's clothing.

"I'm the *vivandiere*, sir," the girl replied.

"The what?"

"The vivandiere, sir."

"What the hell is that? And how old are you, anyway?"

"I'm twelve, sir. And I'm not sure what vivandiere means, except that's what Colonel Garis calls me."

"And what does a 'vivandiere' do?"

"I'm s'pose to carry water and ammunition to the soldiers when they're fighting. And then, if they get wounded, I'm s'pose to help get them back behind the lines. Oh, and Colonel Garis said sometimes he might want me to carry messages."

"I see. What's your name?"

"My friends call me Willie, sir. That's short for—"

Carter burst in. "My God . . . you're Wilhemina."

"Why, yes sir, that's right. Do I know you, sir?"

"Never mind. Willie, I want you to stay close by me when the fighting begins."

"But, sir—"

"No buts about it. I want to know where you are every minute."

"What's your name, sir?"

"Sam—Sam Jenkins."

"Sam Jenkins," repeated Willie, slowly and deliberately, as though committing it to memory.

Chapter Forty-Seven

Here They Come!

At the train depot Carter and Dieter, along with the rest of the Home Guard, spent a restless night.

Early the next morning they gathered outside in an open square to eat breakfast. Everyone jumped to their feet when they heard a shot, followed closely by a full volley.

"Where's that coming from?" someone yelled.

"Sounds like over on Magee Hill."

A second volley of shots rang out from another direction.

"That's from over by the bridge," said Dieter.

In the dim light they saw the flash of gunpowder, and heard the sound of fighting coming now from both locations. Within minutes, soldiers came running toward the depot, both from Magee Hill and from the bridge, the latter dripping wet from having forded the river in order to escape.

"Quick, men, inside!" shouted Colonel Berry. "Help get the wounded inside!"

Together, Willie and Carter grabbed one of the wounded men, and began to drag him into the depot. Dieter grabbed another. Bullets tore into the sides of the building.

"My God," shouted Dieter. "They're right here! The Rebs are shooting at us!"

Safely inside, everyone began returning fire through the windows at Morgan's troops, who continued their advance on the depot. Outside, other soldiers from the 168th did their best to hold off the larger Rebel force.

"Don't forget," Carter shouted to Willie over the noise of gunfire. "Stay close by me."

She nodded, and Carter saw the fear in her eyes. He knew the feeling. It was the same fear he experienced the first time he was in combat in Europe. Once again he felt that fear crawling up his spine.

He peeked out a window. What he saw brought back memories of the fighting in France. Men from both sides seemed to be in a jumble everywhere. It was difficult to distinguish friend from foe. Spotting a soldier carrying a Confederate flag, Carter lifted his rifle, took careful aim, and squeezed the trigger. He watched as the bullet ripped into the man's chest. He crumpled to his knees, still clutching the staff in his hands, the flag upright. Before Carter could react, another soldier ran by, grabbed the staff from the fallen man's hands, and lifted it high. A rebel yell erupted from his throat.

No more than ten feet from the window, two men came into view, grappling with one another. Then one of the men, a Johnny Reb, knocked the other man to the ground, and with a quick strike of his saber severed the fallen man's hand, causing the man's pistol to fly into the air. The Confederate raised his sword to plunge it into the other man's chest, but before he could do so, Carter got off a shot that caught him in the neck.

He staggered backwards a few feet, then fell onto the ground.

Without thinking, Carter dashed through the door to where the man lay and quickly wrapped a towel around the severed limb. Only then did he look at the man's face. It was Aloysius Quincy Montgomery. The man whom Al told him saved his grandfather was Carter, himself. And one day, this man's grandson would, in turn, save Carter's life.

Another man joined them and, together, they carried Al's grandfather inside and laid him against the back wall.

Dieter grabbed Carter by the sleeve. "Come on," he said.

"Where?"

"We're getting out of here." He pulled Carter to a window.

"Go!" he shouted.

"What about you?"

"I'm right behind you."

"Where's Willie?" asked Carter, looking around.

"I'm right here, sir."

As they crawled through the window, they saw men running along the railroad tracks toward Main Street. Carter couldn't tell if they were Union or Confederate.

"This way," said Dieter. He grabbed Carter's arm and they took off running north toward Pike Street as fast as they could, Willie some ten yards ahead of them. As Carter and Dieter turned the corner of the building, they pulled up short. Willie was backed up against a wall, a Confederate soldier's pistol aimed at her head. Carter rushed toward her, grabbed her and threw her to the ground. He heard the blast of the gun, and felt a searing pain, as though his left shoulder had exploded. Staggering, he got up, then fell again.

Before the soldier got off a second shot, Dieter put a minie ball right between his eyes. The soldier stood there for a moment, as though he didn't know what happened, then fell straight back on to the ground.

Dieter bent down to check Carter's shoulder. A crimson stain had begun to spread over his shirt. Dieter took his bandana and stuffed it under the shirt to stem the flow of blood. Then he picked up Carter's rifle, cradling it in one arm along with his own.

"Come on," he said, helping Carter to his feet, and placing his free arm around Carter's waist. Willie got on the other side and also put her arm around Carter's waist.

When they reached the courthouse, they found other Union soldiers, both from the 168th and the Home Guard, already gathered there. Willie put another bandage around Carter's shoulder.

"How bad is it?" asked Carter.

"You'll live," replied Dieter. "Looks like the bullet went clean through."

Carter felt the pain all the way down the side of his body. "Hurts like blue blazes."

"Sweet Jesus! Here they come!" someone cried out.

"Quick, up to the second floor!" shouted an officer. "We might be able to hold them off."

It soon became clear, though, that surrender was their only option. There were too many enemy troops.

As Carter started down the steps to the first floor, he stopped and turned. "Where's Willie?"

"I saw her with Edmund," said Dieter. "Come on, she'll be all right."

"I've got to go get her," said Carter.

"No," shouted Dieter, pulling him by his shirt. "She'll be okay. Edmund will watch out for her."

As they filed out onto the court house lawn, they were shocked by the sight that greeted them.

"Mother of God!" someone exclaimed.

Flames shot up from buildings all along Main and Pike Streets. Ash and the acrid smell of smoke permeated the air.

It appeared the whole town might burn to the ground. They were to learn later that Morgan ordered the structures set on fire in order to drive out the rest of the Union troops hiding in them. Altogether, thirty-seven structures, nearly half the town, were destroyed.

A Confederate officer rode up and spoke to one of his men.

"Corporal, I want you to move the prisoners out of town. Take them out to Millersburg Pike, and set up a camp there."

∞

By seven-thirty, less than four hours after the first shots were fired, Carter, along with the rest of the men he'd been with, found themselves in a temporary, hastily constructed campsite.

A half hour later, a stir went through the crowd.

"What is it?" asked one of the men.

"It's Morgan," said Dieter. "Morgan's here."

John Hunt Morgan cut an impressive figure sitting astride his big roan stallion, with his flowing mustache and goatee, and wearing his famous black, broad-brimmed hat with a long black ostrich plume that drooped down on one side, the other side pinned up with a rosette.

He sat studying his prisoners for a few moments before speaking.

"Gentlemen, I regret making you have to march even further, but we've set up another campsite three miles east of here, on the Claysville Pike. As I have only about a hundred men with me to guard you while we make this trip, and there are over 250 of you, I find it necessary to ask you to remove your shoes and boots, and hand them over to the sergeant here, who will transport them in the wagon. This is being done to ensure you will not try to escape. They will be returned to you when we reach the new campsite."

"Begging your pardon, sir," said one of the prisoners, "but that road is pretty rough. I know, 'cause I helped lay new rock on it not so long ago."

"I'm sorry," replied Morgan, "but I have no choice. I want you to form a line, and as you come by the wagon, hand your shoes to the sergeant. As I said, they'll be returned to you later."

Grumbling, they did as instructed, and one by one surrendered their shoes and boots.

"I don't like this," Dieter whispered. "I think they're going to take us out in the woods and shoot us. They want our shoes for themselves, and this way'll make it easier. They don't even have to bother to take them off our bodies."

"What should we do?"

"Nothing right now," said Dieter. "But if they start to march us off the pike into the woods, then we've got to fight back or run."

As they resumed their march, they heard gunfire coming from the northwest.

"Maybe we won't be prisoners long," said Dieter.

It took less than an hour to get to the new campsite, but it seemed much longer, as the sharp rocks that formed the road quickly bloodied their feet.

"You damn Johnny Reb," cried one of the men. "Give us back our shoes!"

"Shut up and sit down. And don't give us no trouble."

"What about our shoes?" asked Dieter.

"You'll get your damn shoes," growled the guard. He turned and barked out an order to two other guards, who climbed into the wagon and began to throw the shoes out onto the ground. When they finished, the guard in charge said, "Okay, come on up here ten at a time and find your shoes. And make it quick."

The first group of men began to sort through the pile, but because of the plethora of shoes to search through the process was taking too long for the guard's liking. "Take any pair of shoes," he said. "We ain't got all day."

Dieter, one of the first ten men, turned to the guard. "Why don't you relax? We're not going anywhere."

"Why don't you go to hell?" spat out the guard, and with one quick move brought the barrel of his rifle crashing down on Dieter's head.

Dieter stumbled backward, blood pouring from the wound over his ear. Carter jumped up and, with his good arm, caught him before he fell.

"You men get back with the others," yelled the guard, his face red with anger. "Y'all forget about those shoes for now. We'll see about you getting 'em later on."

Someone handed Carter a bandana and he tied it around Dieter's head. "Are you all right?"

Dieter's face was ashen, his teeth clenched in anger. "I'm okay. But first chance I get, that son of a bitch is a dead man."

"Listen," said one of the prisoners.

The sound of battle could still be heard. There was no way to know who was winning, or even which Union troops were involved. For the next several hours, the firing continued. Then, shortly after noon, the guns fell silent.

Chapter Forty-Eight

O'Doherty: One Last Time?

"Well, now, who do we got here?"

Carter sat cross-legged on the ground. At the sound of the voice, he looked up at the figure looming over him. The sun was at the man's back, and his features were hidden in shadow.

Carter felt the butt of a rifle as it cracked him alongside his head, knocking him over.

"I've waited a long time to meet up with you again," the man said.

Carter moved to one side, and now he saw the man's face: Kiernan O'Doherty!

O'Doherty rested the end of the gun barrel against Carter's nose. "I told you the next time I saw you I'd kill you. The only question is, am I going to do it slow and easy, or am I going to blow your fucking head off right now?"

Carter's heart raced as fear, mixed with anger, welled up in him like a bomb about to explode. "Go to hell," he said.

Before Carter could react, O'Doherty brought the rifle down again, this time smashing the barrel across Carter's injured shoulder. He screamed out in pain.

"Jenkins," said O'Doherty through clenched teeth. "Sam Jenkins. I ain't never going to forget you."

Out of the corner of his eye, Carter saw Dieter running toward them. Just as he reached them, two guards grabbed him and wrestled him to the ground.

"Don't think you want to get involved," grunted one guard. "Unless you want the same thing your buddy's gonna get."

O'Doherty glanced over at Dieter. "That's right, Yank."

Seeing his chance while O'Dohery was distracted, Carter reached up and grabbed the gun barrel, jerking it hard to one side and pulling it down, causing O'Doherty to lose his balance. As he fell to the ground, Carter rolled out of the way, then staggered to his feet. In a flash, O'Doherty jumped to his feet.

"You son of a bitch!" he cried. "I ain't even going to bother shooting you. I'm going to cut your fucking heart out!"

O'Doherty drew a knife from the sheath at his belt, the same knife, Carter figured, he used to kill Mornin.

They circled one another for a few seconds, then O'Doherty made a sudden lunge at Carter, who managed to sidestep him. As he did so, he brought his right arm down full across the back of O'Doherty's neck.

O'Doherty spun around, an expression of pure loathing on his face. Carter saw the blind rage in his eyes, and remembered what Mr. Clary said about him, that he was the most dangerous man he had ever known. And even though the person standing before him was still just a youth, Carter believed it.

O'Doherty circled again, more cautiously this time. He feinted a jab, and when Carter reacted, tried to strike again. But Carter saw what he was attempting and grabbed the wrist holding the knife. In one quick movement, Carter sent O'Doherty's legs out from under him, sending both of them sprawling in the dirt.

Everyone was watching and cheering, guards and prisoners alike, as the two men wrestled—O'Doherty doing his best to plunge his knife into Carter; Carter struggling hard to prevent that.

Suddenly Carter found the youth on top of him, the knife tip just inches from his neck. Carter's strength was fading fast from his shoulder wound, which had started to bleed again. With one last ounce of energy he twisted O'Doherty's wrist around so the blade now was pointed up toward O'Doherty. His hand on the boy's neck, Carter pushed him up—then let him go.

O'Doherty gasped as he came down hard onto the blade of the knife. A look of astonishment flashed across his eyes, and his jaw dropped open.

Carter pushed him off and had started to get up, when an explosion of pain wracked his head, and everything went black.

∞

When Carter came to, Dieter was holding his head, dabbing it gently with a wet rag.

"What happened?" asked Carter. His head throbbed.

"One of the other guards clubbed you," said Dieter. "Smacked you with his rifle."

Carter tried to rise up on one elbow, but fell back down.

"What about O'Doherty? Is he dead?"

"Don't know. They dragged him off, and left you with me. I'm not sure if he was still alive or not."

"I hope I killed the son of a bitch," muttered Carter, closing his eyes and drifting back into unconsciousness.

Chapter Forty-Nine

Paroled

When Carter came to again, Dieter was kneeling next to him, removing the bandage from his shoulder to check the wound. "How's the shoulder?" asked Dieter.

"Still hurts something fierce."

"And your head?"

"It hurts, too. How's *your* head?"

"I'll live," said Dieter. "It sounds like things have settled down over there by Keller's Bridge. I haven't heard any firing for hours. Maybe in a bit we'll be able to get a doctor to look at your shoulder."

"Look!" someone shouted.

Dieter and Carter both turned to see to where the soldier was pointing. Dieter got up, but Carter, still too woozy to stand, remained on the ground.

"Oh, shit," said Dieter.

"What?"

"More prisoners. Looks like Morgan whipped whatever Union troops those were out there. My God, there's hundreds of them," he added, as men continued to pour into the camp.

"Who you with?" Dieter asked one of the new men as he came by.

"The 171st Ohio. Who you with?"

"I'm with the Home Guard, but most of the men here are from the 168th Ohio. Some others, Morgan brought with him from Mt Sterling; I'm not sure what their regiment is. Where do you think they're going to take us?"

"They ain't taking us nowhere," answered the soldier. "They're going to parole us. Morgan ain't got enough men to handle everyone he's took prisoner. 'Sides, he's got to get his ass out of here 'fore Burbridge shows up."

"Burbridge?"

"General Burbridge. Hear tell he's got 3,000 men with him, and he ain't but a half day's march from here, maybe less. Ol' Morgan don't get going, and going fast, he's going to get his butt whipped."

"You reckon he'll parole all of us, too?"

"I reckon so. Unless he decides to shoot you." The man flashed Dieter a toothless grin. "Naw, he's going to parole you. Hell, he's an *officer* and a *gentleman,* ain't he? At least, that's what they say."

A Confederate officer rode by and swung his saber, rapping the talkative soldier in the head, sending him sprawling. "You'd best conserve your energy," he warned. "Tomorrow's going to be a long day for all of you."

"What do you mean?" asked Dieter.

"Shut up and go to sleep!" barked the officer.

Carter and Dieter spread their blankets out on the ground and lay down.

"What do you suppose he meant?" asked Carter.

"They're going to move us," answered Dieter. "Sure as shooting."

"But why, if they're going to parole us?"

"I don't know. Maybe they aren't going to parole us. Maybe Morgan wants to hold on to us as hostages, to use if Burbridge defeats him—to use for exchange. I don't know. I do know this, though. I'm not letting them take me to no

Southern prison to rot You and I'll take off before that happens."

"I'm not sure I can make it with this shoulder. I'm not sure I've got the strength to march, let alone run."

"Don't worry, I won't leave you. Whatever happens, we're in this together."

Carter closed his eyes and slipped into an uneasy sleep, one filled with visions of men fighting. Sometimes the soldiers wore uniforms from the Great War in which he had fought in 1917 and '18. Abruptly, the scene would change, and the men were the ones he'd seen that morning in the battle in town.

Suddenly, everything changed. He stood in a field, surrounded by thousands of gravestones. As he walked through the cemetery, he saw in the distance a large stone column, or monument. As he got closer, the column changed form, until it became a tree. Then Carter saw him. The rider on the horse! Once again, a rope, hanging from a tree limb, was cinched around the man's neck. Two other men, also on horseback, sat next to the rider. Carter kept walking, nearer and nearer, until the man was no more than five feet away from him. The rider looked up and stared directly at him, and Carter awoke with a start. The face on the man was his own!

"On your feet!"

Dieter, already standing, reached his hand down and helped Carter to his feet.

"Gentlemen!"

General Morgan sat ramrod straight in his saddle, still resplendent in his uniform in spite of having been engaged in almost constant battle for the past two days.

"Gentlemen, I regret the necessity of bringing you all this way, and under such adverse conditions. However, you are that much closer to Ohio. I am paroling all of you, so that you may return home. In order to do so, however, I must first ask you to take an oath not to take up arms again. Therefore, I ask each of you to raise your right hand."

"What kind of oath?" shouted one of the men.

"As I said," replied Morgan. "You will not take up arms again. In other words, for you the war is over."

For a few moments, the murmuring continued, then, one by one, the prisoners raised their hands. Dieter and Carter looked at one another. "What the hell," said Dieter. "If no Johnny Rebs come through the county again, I don't plan on any more fighting anyway. And you, I think with your shoulder, your fighting days are over, too."

They both raised their hands, along with all the other prisoners.

"Good," said Morgan. "Will you solemnly swear you will not take up arms again?"

"I swear," each of them answered.

"Sergeant, please see these men are released at once."

Dieter, Carter and the rest of the Home Guard watched as the men of the 168th and 171st regiments started out for the Union camp at Falmouth; and as Morgan and his men headed east, in the opposite direction, on their way back to Virginia. Then they turned, and headed back down the road they'd come on earlier that day.

They'd gone but a few miles when they met a detachment of General Burbridge's troops in hot pursuit of Morgan.

"Were you paroled?" asked the captain in charge of the detail.

"Yes, sir," replied one of the Home Guard.

"Where are the rest of the prisoners? Where's Morgan?"

"Sir, the 168th and 171st, they set out for Falmouth. General Morgan, he and his men, they rode out toward Kentontown. I reckon as how they're on their way back to Virginny. How'd it go back there, captain? Did you all give 'em a whuppin'?"

"We sure as sin did," said the captain, a big grin on his face. "Sent them Johnny Rebs to skedaddling every which way. Look, you fellers heading back to Cynthiana?"

"Yes, sir."

"This wagon I'm hauling along behind me is slowing me down. You all get in, and I'll have some of my men escort you back to town." He looked down at their feet, some shod only in socks, most of them bare and bloody. "Looks like you've walked enough today."

"Yes, sir!" they all answered enthusiastically as they clambered into the wagon.

"Sergeant," said the captain to a man mounted beside him. "Take two other men and escort these soldiers back to town. Then join up with General Burbridge. And inform the General we're still on Morgan's trail."

"Yes, sir. You, and you," said the sergeant. "You'll be accompanying us back to town. Corporal, let's get this wagon turned around."

As they rode along, one of the soldiers noticed Carter's shoulder. "Are you hurt bad?"

"I don't know for sure. My friend here says he thinks the bullet must have gone clean through."

"If I was you," said the private, "I'd have that looked at as soon as you get back home."

"I reckon you're right. I will."

"What unit you with, private?" asked Dieter.

"The Fortieth Kentucky."

"Fortieth Kentucky? Aren't there some men from Harrison County in that regiment?"

"Believe so. In fact, the corporal over there, the one on that big gray, I believe he's from around these parts."

Dieter and Carter looked at the soldier riding on the other side of the wagon. Carter thought he looked familiar. "What's his name?" asked Carter.

"Dunno," said the private. "I joined up with the regiment 'bout a week ago. I don't know everybody yet."

"Dieter, do you know him?" asked Carter.

"No, don't believe I do."

Carter looked at the man again, almost certain he'd seen him before. But where?

Dieter interrupted his thoughts. "Sam, I'm getting off in Oddville. I'll walk home from there. I think you should come with me, have my ma look at that shoulder."

Carter looked at his shoulder. The bleeding had stopped and, while it still ached, was not all that painful. But he was starting to get cold, and to shake. "No, I'm going on ahead. I'm anxious to get back to Helen, to let her know I'm all right. She'll take care of it when I get there."

"If you're sure," said Dieter. He took off his jacket and handed it to Carter. "Here, put this on. You're shivering something fierce. You cold?"

"Guess I am." By now, Carter's teeth were chattering. "Thanks. I'll get it back to you tomorrow."

Two other men got off at Oddville with Dieter, leaving fourteen still in the wagon. "I'll be by tomorrow to see how you're doing," said Dieter.

A few miles further along the wagon came to the road that would take Carter past his old home, and on to Helen's farm.

"Private, would you let me off here?"

The private pulled the horses to a stop.

As Carter started to climb down from the wagon his foot got caught up in the jacket of one of the other men. He tried to steady himself, but failed, tumbling onto the ground and landing on his bad shoulder. The pain was excruciating. He rolled over onto his back and grabbed the shoulder with his other hand. "Oh, Christ!"

The corporal was off his horse almost as soon as Carter hit the ground. Blood started to seep from Carter's wound.

"Quick," the corporal yelled to the driver. "Toss me down some toweling."

He caught the toweling and began to unbutton Carter's shirt. For an instant, his hands froze in midair. Carter looked to see what had spooked him. Apparently it was the medal—the man was staring at it. He looked at Carter, then finished wrapping the toweling around the wound.

"How far is your place from here?" asked the corporal.

"A mile or two."

"I'm going to go ahead and take this man home," the corporal said to the private. "You continue on to town, and drop these other men off anywhere they want. I'll catch up with the rest of the regiment by morning."

"Here, let me help you up," said the corporal, cupping his hands. "I'll walk. My horse doesn't need any more work tonight other than carrying you."

Carter placed his left foot into the corporal's hands and hoisted himself into the saddle with his good arm.

"I appreciate this," said Carter, relieved he wouldn't have to walk all the way to the farm. He felt better, but still faint. "This is a fine horse, a big horse. Must be—what? About sixteen hands?"

"More like seventeen," answered the corporal, taking the horse by the reins and starting off down the road.

They'd gone only a few hundred yards, out of sight of the wagon, when the corporal stopped and said, "I need you to get off for a minute."

Carter didn't understand, but he grabbed the saddle horn, and swung himself down off the horse. When he turned around, he found the long barrel of a revolver aimed at his head.

Chapter Fifty

A Prisoner Again

For a moment, Carter didn't comprehend what was happening.

"What . . . what are you doing?" he stammered.

"You and I are going to take a little walk, son," said the corporal, cocking his head toward the woods bordering the road. "Get moving."

"If you're planning on robbing me, you sure picked the wrong man," protested Carter. "I don't have anything on me worth stealing. Hell, I'm not even wearing shoes."

"Shut up and get moving," repeated the corporal.

As they walked into the woods, thoughts raced through Carter's head. Could he outrun the man? Should he try to wrestle the gun away from him? What the hell did he want?

Before he could come to any decision, the man ordered him to stop. "This is good, right here. Sit down there on that stump."

"What do you want?" asked Carter, again.

"What I want is simple. I want to know where you got that medal that's hanging around your neck."

"What? You want to know where I got this medal?"

"That's right, son. And I also want to know what happened to the other one."

"The other one?"

"Son, you're starting to try my patience. Now, first of all, where did you get the medal?" The corporal raised his gun and pointed it at Carter. "I want the answer *now*."

"I . . . I found it."

"You found it? And where did you find it?"

Carter was stumped. He couldn't tell him the truth. Who would believe it? And yet, if he didn't give some reasonable answer, this lunatic might just shoot him.

"Let me help you out, son," said the corporal. "I believe you found that medal on my brother's body after you killed him."

"What?" cried Carter. What the hell was he talking about?

"Look here." The corporal unbuttoned his shirt and spread the collars apart.

Carter stared in amazement at the two medals that hung around the man's neck. They were identical to the one he wore. "My brother wore two medals like these. You've got one of them on now. Since he wouldn't have taken those medals off if he were still alive, I have to assume he's dead. And since you've got one of the medals, I also have to assume you had something to do with his death. Now—you want to tell me the truth about how you come to be wearing one of my brother's medals?"

Carter thought for a few moments. Then: "Okay. I'll tell you the truth. But you won't believe me."

"Let me decide that."

For the next half hour, Carter explained how he came to have the medal: how he and Sara Jane had found it on the skeleton; how he received a second medal from Sara Jane's grandmother, Mary; and how he somehow had been transported back to 1863. When he finished, he looked at the corporal, who had shown no expression the whole time Carter spoke.

"See, I told you you wouldn't believe me."

"What happens to Mr. Lincoln?"

"What?"

"What happens to President Lincoln? How did he die? If you are from the future, you should know the answer."

"He was shot and killed at Ford's Theatre by John Wilkes Booth."

The corporal was quiet for a minute. Then he spoke. "Okay. I believe you."

"You do?" Now Carter truly was confused. He himself hardly believed the story he'd just told.

"You couldn't know what was going to happen next year unless you *are* from the future. What do you know about the skeleton you found the medal on?"

"Know about him?"

"That's right. You said you thought he was a Union soldier. You know anything more than that?"

"When we first found him," said Carter, "my father thought he might perhaps be his grandfather, my great-grandfather, because my father said his grandfather always wore two medals like the one the skeleton was wearing. But after a medical pathologist in Louisville determined the man was in his twenties or maybe his thirties when he died, we knew it couldn't be my great-grandfather, because he was in his fifties."

The corporal nodded. "Then it couldn't have been my brother, either, because he'd be a lot older than his thirties now. And if you're right about the uniform, it would have to have been someone from the war, and from around this time. What's your name, son?"

"Sam . . . Carter . . . Carter McGlone." Carter realized it was the first time he'd spoken his real name out loud since he'd arrived in this time period.

This time it was the corporal's turn to look puzzled. "What was your great-grandfather's name?" he asked.

"Owen. Owen McGlone."

The corporal threw his head back and roared with laughter. He lowered the pistol he had been pointing at Carter.

"What's so funny?" asked Carter.

"What's so funny," answered the corporal, still laughing, "is that *I'm* Owen McGlone. I'm your great-grandfather."

Chapter Fifty-One

Owen McGlone

Carter's mouth fell open. That's why he looked so familiar when Carter first saw him by the wagon! He looked exactly like Carter's great-uncle Rufus!

"My God!" was all Carter could get out.

"So," said Owen, still chuckling over this turn of events, "which one is your grandpa—Rufus, or Feargus?"

"Feargus," answered Carter, still not able to believe what he was hearing. "Feargus was—is—my grandfather."

"Not yet," said Owen. "You haven't even been born yet, son."

"I . . . I don't understand all of this," said Carter, still stunned by this new information.

Owen took a pipe from his knapsack, filled it with tobacco, and lit it. He took a deep puff and let the smoke curl out between his lips. "One of the few blessings about living now," he said. "We don't have tobacco where . . ." raising his eyebrows, ". . . when—I come from.

"Now, let's see if I can explain. My brother and I got here the same way you did—from the future. Except we came on purpose, on a mission. I can't tell you why we came, but that's not important now, anyway. The problem was that, right after we arrived, we were set upon by a band of renegade Indians. That was . . .," he hesitated, trying to remember, ". . . thirty-two years ago. I was twenty-five.

Nathan—that's my brother—was twenty-eight. So, like I said, right after we got here these redskins—I reckon there must have been eight or nine of them—came upon us. Nathan and I took off running. In the confusion, I ran one way, and he ran the other. That's the last I ever saw of him."

"Thirty-two years? You've been looking for your brother for thirty-two years?"

"Yep. I wasn't about to go home and try to explain why we hadn't come back together. Then I met a woman—your great-grandmother—and fell in love. We got married, had the boys, and here I still am."

"How do you know your brother didn't go back?"

"First of all, I know he wouldn't have gone without me, or without knowing what happened to me, like I wouldn't go without him. Now, you're wearing one of his medals. Which means he couldn't have gone. It also must mean he's dead because, like I said, he never would have taken the medals off if he were alive. I reckon whoever belonged to that skeleton you found must have killed him. By the way, where *is* the other medal?"

"I gave it to someone," said Carter, feeling rather sheepish.

"A woman?"

Carter explained about Helen, and how she turned out to be Sara Jane's grandmother, the one who gave him the second medal in the first place.

"Didn't you ever think about going back?" Owen asked.

"Oh, sure, when I first got here I did. But I wasn't certain what to do. I figured it must have something to do with the medals, because the last thing I remembered before leaving 1927 was Sara Jane fooling around with them. But I didn't know for sure how to do it."

"You screw the two together, like screwing a lid on a jar."

"I even thought about that. But then I wasn't sure if I'd go back to my own time, or some other time."

"I see."

"Because," Carter continued, "there I was in 1927, and all of a sudden I'm in 1863. Why 1863?"

"You travel through time by thinking of the date you want to go to," said Owen, tapping his head. "Then, while you have that date in your mind, you connect the medals and—*bingo!*—you're there. Where you are geographically doesn't change. You'll still be standing in the same spot when you move. But you move in time."

"Bingo?"

"Never mind. After your time, I reckon."

"But . . . why 1863? Why did I come to 1863? I wasn't thinking of any particular date when it happened."

"You must have been, or you wouldn't have moved. You'd still be in the same place, and the same time. Think about it. Besides this—Sara Jane . . .?"

"That's right, Sara Jane."

"Besides this Sara Jane doing something with the medals, what else do you recall?"

Carter concentrated, trying to remember. Then it came to him. "I know! The carving on the tree! I was looking at the carving on the tree. It said S.J. + H.J. 1863. That must have been it!"

"Must have been," said Owen. "When you ended up in 1863, was it the same month and date as in 1927?"

"Yes. Only a different day of the week, of course. How did you know?"

"If you were thinking just of the year—1863—that's all that would have changed, not the month or day of the month."

"And so to get back?"

"To get back, you think of the exact date you want to return to—the year, the month, the date—and put the medals together. Why, you thinking of going back?"

"I don't know." For the first time in a long time, Carter considered the possibility, now that he knew what to do. But what about Helen? "Could I take Helen with me?"

"'Fraid not," said Owen. "It's a 'one person' deal. Besides, do you think Helen could adapt to that new time? And, remember, her daughter and granddaughter would both be there, still alive, and older than she is. Or, not. If you take her to your time period, and she's carrying the baby, that baby wouldn't be born until then, which means Sara Jane and her mother might not even exist when you return. Gets pretty complicated, this time travel."

Carter knew he was right. If he returned to his own time, he'd have to go without Helen. He knew he couldn't do that.

"So, tell me," said Carter, "why couldn't you have gone back to the time before you and Nathan left on your journey, and changed the time you'd be arriving, since you knew you'd be encountering Indians?"

"Good question. The answer is it wouldn't have been possible, because then there would have been two of me there at the same time. But only one essence can exist in the same place at one time."

"Essence?"

"It's what you might call the soul. Although it's much more than that."

"I see." But Carter wasn't sure he did.

"Two *bodies* of the same person can be there simultaneously," Owen continued, "if one of them is dead. In other words, I could go forward to a point in time when my physical body has died, and the corpse—or the skeleton—is still there, but not the *essence*. I couldn't, however, go to a time where I was already living, since my essence would already be there. Does that make any sense to you?"

"Sort of. So it wouldn't be possible for me to go back to save Emmaline."

"Who's Emmaline?"

Carter told him about Emmaline and what happened to her.

"No, I'm afraid not," said Owen. "There's no way you can go back to that time, when you're already there."

"But someone could have come back in time from your era and looked for you, couldn't they?"

"They could have," acknowledged Owen. "Maybe even did. But it's a big country out here. And they wouldn't have computers or PPSs to make it easier for them to locate me."

"Computers? PPSs?"

"Never mind. Again, after your time."

"You asked me about President Lincoln," said Carter. "Since you know what's going to happen, couldn't you jump forward to that time and do something to prevent it."

"I could—if I wasn't already there. But that's not what I'm about. It's not my responsibility to try to change the past. Or, in this case, the future."

"Let me ask you this," said Carter. "What's the symbol inside the medal? The gold circle, or gold egg, whatever it is."

Owen laughed. "It's not a circle or an egg. Look."

He held up both of his medals, one behind the other, so

that what little light was left was visible through them. One medal displayed the symbol to the right, while the other clearly showed the symbol on the left.

"What do you see?"

Carter studied the medals for a few moments and then it came to him. Of course! The two tear drops together formed an infinity symbol!

"Infinity!"

"That's right—the infinity symbol. One of the descriptions and definitions of time which, of course, *is* infinite. When the two medals lock together and form the symbol, that's when the travel through time takes place."

"So, what now?"

"What now? Now I think maybe the time's come for me to go back. Mildred's—she was my wife—but you know that—Mildred's been dead these past six years, and the boys are old enough for sure to be on their own. In fact, they're around here someplace. They're riding with the 40th, like I am."

"But don't you want to stay and see how they turn out?"

"You tell me," said Owen, laughing. "You already know how they turn out. Were they good men? Did they lead good lives?"

Carter smiled. "They did. They both got married, had families. They were both good men."

"Then that's all I need to know. This war doesn't need me. You and I both know how it ends. Here." He handed Carter his revolver.

"What do you want me to do with this?"

"I won't need it where I'm going. We don't have—or need—guns there anymore. I'm leaving my horse, too. I'll miss her, but, like I said, it's a 'one person' trip. If you should run across my boys, give them the gun and the horse. But, if you don't, they're yours. Oh, and here." He took off his boots and handed them to Carter. "Looks like you could use these, too."

"One more question," said Carter, pulling the boots on. "Does anyone else know about this? About your . . . traveling through time?"

"No. The boys know nothing about it. I never even told Mildred. As I'm sure you must realize by now, how do you explain something like that? Who would believe you?"

Carter nodded. Who indeed?

"Carter, I'm glad I met up with you. And I'm thankful I finally got resolved—in my mind at least—that Nathan's dead. I can stop looking now. Looks like you got one of your questions answered, too."

"What's that?"

"Whatever happened to me."

They both laughed.

"I do have one last question for you," said Owen. "I thought I heard your friend back there call you 'Sam.' What was that all about?"

"When I first got here I thought some of my ancestors—like you, for instance—would be alive and living around here. It might have been hard to explain who I was with the name of McGlone. So, I took the name of my law partner back in Louisville, Sam Jenkins. Now, let me ask you something. I spent some time looking for the McGlone family around here, and never did find it. Where do you and your sons live?"

"Oh, we're from Bourbon County," answered Owen. "I never did live here in Harrison County."

"Then how did my grandfather Feargus come to live here? And Great-uncle Rufus and his family?"

"When the war started, both Feargus and Rufus were courting sisters who lived over the county line."

"Grandma Gracie and Great-aunt Goldie."

"That's right. So I reckon the boys must have married the girls after the war . . . ?"

". . . and moved here to this county." Carter finished the thought.

Owen stood and extended his hand. Carter rose and grasped it.

"Take care of yourself, Carter. Maybe we'll meet again sometime."

Then the idea hit Carter. While *he* couldn't go back to save Emmaline, Owen could. "One last th . . ."

But it was too late. Owen had already taken both medals in his hands, connected them—and was gone.

Carter stood for a moment, stunned. *This must have been how Sara Jane felt when I disappeared,* he thought. But at least he knew what happened to Owen.

Carter stuck the gun in his belt, mounted the horse, turned it back to the road, and once again headed for Helen's farm. His mind racing with what had just transpired, he was so deep in thought he didn't hear the two riders come up behind him.

Chapter Fifty-Two

The End?

"Stop right where you are, mister."

Carter pulled his horse up and looked around. Two men, both wearing Union uniforms, sat astride their horses facing him. One held a gun pointed at him.

"What do you want?" asked Carter.

"Get down off the horse," commanded the gunman.

"What?" Carter couldn't believe this was happening again. "Fellas, I don't have any money. I've just gotten back from Claysville, and I'm on my way home."

"I'm not saying it again," said the man. "Get down off the horse."

Cautiously, Carter dismounted. What was this all about?

The second man slowly circled Carter, studying the horse.

"Whadja do with our daddy?" he asked.

"What?" Carter was becoming more confused by the minute.

The man with the gun dismounted, and stood facing Carter. "We come riding up the road to meet up with our unit, and we run into a wagon heading to town with some parolees in it. The private tells us our daddy rode off this way taking a wounded soldier home. That would be you, I reckon. So we come riding this way looking for our daddy, and we find you riding his horse." Glancing down, he spotted the gun in Carter's belt, reached over, and pulled it out. "And this here's my daddy's gun," he said, lifting the barrel to his nose, and sniffing. "Been fired recently, too," he added.

"Your daddy—" Carter didn't get the next word out before the man struck him upside the head with the pistol. Carter staggered back against the horse, then sank to his knees. Pain seared through his head, and blood ran down the side of his face.

"You shot him, didn't you, you son of a bitch!" the man screamed.

"No, no, I . . ."

The man raised his gun to strike Carter again, but the other man spoke up. "That's enough, Rufus. You kill him, we won't find out what happened to Pa."

The second man dismounted, walked over to Carter, grabbed him by the hair, and jerked his head up.

"Mister, you're riding our daddy's horse, you've got his gun. Hell!" he exclaimed, looking down at Carter's feet. "You're even wearing his boots! You better talk fast, boy. Where is he?"

"Feargus," said Rufus, "let's get off the road. I know where we can go; nobody'll disturb us."

Feargus pulled Carter to his feet by the front of his shirt, and spun him around. "Put your hands behind you."

Carter did as the man directed, and felt the rope as it was twisted around his wrists, then tied off. The strain on his shoulder caused him to wince in pain. Before he could say anything else the man stuffed a rag into his mouth and secured it with a handkerchief.

"Now, get back up on the horse." Feargus helped him mount, then he and Rufus both mounted. Feargus took Carter's horse's reins in his hand. "Let's go."

Carter's head began to clear from the blow he'd taken, though the throbbing wouldn't go away. Feargus and Rufus. His grandfather and great-uncle! They had come looking for Owen and since he was riding his horse, and had his gun and boots, they thought he killed him!

When they finally stopped, Carter found himself in a familiar place: next to the old sycamore tree, the same tree where he carved Helen's initials along with his—Sam's; the same tree where Sara Jane and he found the skeleton and the medal.

Feargus reached over, untied the handkerchief, and removed the rag from Carter's mouth. "Now," he said, "I reckon you'd better start talking."

"You're Feargus and Rufus. And Owen McGlone is your father."

"So you *do* know what happened to him!" said Rufus.

Carter was stumped. Should he tell them the truth? Would they believe him? *It's worth a try*, he thought.

And so he told them everything that had happened, about his time travel, and about Owen's brother. But he didn't tell them he was Owen's great-grandson, Feargus's own grandson. Carter thought that would be more than they could swallow.

When he finished, neither of them spoke for a few minutes. Then Feargus said. "You don't expect us to believe that horse shit, do you?"

At first, Carter didn't reply. What could he say? He scarcely believed it himself. How could he expect these two to do so?

"I'm telling you the truth," he said, finally.

"Here's what I think," said Rufus. "I think you done shot and killed our pa, and stole his horse, and his gun, and his boots."

"But we don't know for sure," said Feargus.

"We know for sure he's got Pa's horse, and gun, and boots," replied Rufus. "So we know he done stole them, 'cause there's no way Pa would've given them to him, like this feller'd have us believe."

"I guess you're right," said Feargus. "So, what do we do now?"

"What you always do with horse thieves. Hang the son of a bitch. Then we go back and look for Pa's body."

Carter couldn't believe it! After everything he had gone through, was he destined to end his life here, hanged by his own grandfather? "Wait! It's all true! I swear it is!"

Rufus took a rope from his saddle horn, fashioned a noose, and slipped it around Carter's neck. He didn't notice the medal.

As Carter felt the noose tighten, he remembered Reverend Moundtree's sermon on First Corinthians, and the verse that had made such an impression on him: "For now we see through a glass, darkly. But then, face to face. Now, I know in part. But then shall I know, even as also I am known."

For the past year he had been seeing through that glass, darkly. Now, everything suddenly had become clear. He had found his great-grandfather and knew what happened to him; he'd discovered the secret of the medal; he knew the initials carved into the sycamore were his and Helen's—or, rather, Sam's and Helen's—and had been put there by his own hand. He thought of Helen, and the baby girl she was carrying: his daughter. Someday, he knew—he hoped—he would meet both of them again.

"You got anything else you wanta tell us, boy?" asked Feargus.

"I've told you the truth, but you won't believe me."

"Shit, no! How stupid do you think we are? Ain't nobody in their right mind gonna believe the load of crap you tried to feed us."

He didn't answer. There wasn't anything more to say. Nothing, at least, they would accept as the truth.

Once again his eyes were drawn to the tree, to the initials carved in its trunk:

S.J. + H.J.
1863

From the corner of his eye, Carter saw something—someone. A young boy, maybe twelve or thirteen years old, standing off a short distance, watching. He thought the boy looked familiar. Russell? No, but someone he'd seen before. Then it hit him!

It was he, himself. His dream! Except this time it was no dream—and he was seeing it from the other side.

He started to call out, but before the words escaped his lips he heard the *thwack* of something hitting the horse's rear end.

It was the last thing he heard.

Harrison County, Kentucky

1927

I opened my eyes to see Sara Jane sitting next to me in a rocking chair. Her eyes were closed and her head nodded as though she were trying to fend off sleep. I was in my bed in my old room at my parents' home.

"Sara Jane?"

Her head jerked up and her eyes flew open. "Carter? You're awake!" She reached over and took my hand.

"What happened?" I asked.

"You got knocked out cold. You been in a coma for two days."

"How? What happened?" I repeated.

"You remember you and me walking out to the old sycamore tree right after my Grandma Mary's funeral?"

I nodded.

"And you remember me giving you the medal she gave me to give you that was like the one you took off that skeleton?"

My hand went to the two medals resting on my chest. I picked them up. They were locked together. I unscrewed them and they came apart easily.

"Well, whilst you was studying the carving on the tree—you know those initials and the date—well, whilst you was doing that I moved those two medals around to your back. I was playing with them and I guess I screwed them together. Then you turned and jerked me and I fell against you, and you fell against the tree and knocked yourself out cold.

"I tried to bring you around, but I couldn't, so then I tried to unscrew the medals, but I couldn't do that neither. So then I run and got Malcolm, and him and his brother come and they picked you up and carried you here. Then Malcolm took off into town and fetched Doc Jackson and he come out and checked you out. Said you was pretty much okay, except you was in a coma. We was all scared to death, but he said wait, and you'd come out of it, probably in a day or two. And I guess he was right, 'cause here you are. You are feeling okay, ain't you?"

"Yes," I said. I looked at the glass of water on the nightstand. "Could you hand me that?" I asked.

I sat up in bed and Sara Jane handed me the glass. I took a long drink, then handed it back to her. She replaced it on the nightstand.

"Carter, I gotta show you something—something really strange. You remember I said Grandma Mary left me her locket? Here, take a look."

She handed me the heart-shaped locket. I held it up and looked at the photograph on the front. It was Helen!

"That's my Grandma Mary when she was young," said Sara Jane. "But look, here's what's really strange."

She took the locket back from me and pressed a small knob on one side. The lock sprung open.

"Look at this," she said, handing me the locket again.

Inside were two photographs. Glancing at the one on the left, I blinked my eyes.

It was Dieter Ruehmschuessel. Then I looked at the other photograph on the right.

It was the one Mr. Tillman had taken of Helen and me.

About the Author

Kenn Grimes' connection with Kentucky can be traced back to around 1800, when his great, great, great, great grandfather, Owen McGlone, moved his family from Virginia to what later became McGlone Creek in Carter County, Kentucky. Approximately a hundred years and four generations later, Kenn's grandmother, Ethel Weaver McGlone, left Kentucky to move to Ohio and marry Kenn's grandfather, George. The family settled in Springfield, where Kenn was born in 1938.

After two years of college followed by four years in the U.S. Navy and a series of jobs in banks, retail stores, and manufacturing, Kenn returned to school in 1972 to complete his education, graduating in 1973 with a Bachelor of Science Degree in Business from Wittenberg University. He continued his studies at Hamma School of Theology, from which he received his Master of Divinity Degree in 1976.

Kenn served several parishes from 1976 to 1984, and in that latter year reestablished the family line in Kentucky when he moved to Louisville to serve as the pastor of St. Mark Lutheran Church. Today, Kenn's two sons and their families still call Kentucky home, while he divides his time between there and Lower Northern Michigan, where he and his wife, Judy, also a minister, are retired but keep busy officiating weddings.

Besides Louisville, Kenn also served churches in Indiana, Missouri and Milton, Kentucky. From 1992 to 2000, while Judy served a church in Maui, Hawaii, Kenn owned and operated the largest wedding business on the island, during which time he personally officiated over 3,600 ceremonies. In 2000 the business, *Simply Married*, was recognized as the second fastest growing small business of any type in the whole state. Kenn sold the business later that year, retired and moved to Michigan, where Judy had taken a pastoral position in a Unity church.

Four of Kenn's passions in life are Scrabble, horse racing (betting, not riding), University of Louisville Athletics (particularly football and both men's and women's basketball), and hunting morel mushrooms in the spring (April in Kentucky, May in Michigan).

Kenn says two of his biggest regrets are that he didn't start writing seriously earlier in his life; and that he wasn't born in Kentucky.

The Other Side of Yesterday is Kenn's second published book.

The *Other Side of Yesterday* takes place during the years 1912, 1918-1919, 1923-1927, and 1863-64. But no story exists in a vacuum: other events were happening in the world, in Kentucky, and in Louisville during those time periods. Follow Kenn's weekly blog at http://kenngrimes.com as he takes a look at those events, some significant, others more mundane—but nonetheless interesting.

To contact Kenn Grimes email him at deerlakepress@aol.com. To see where Kenn will be appearing or to book him to speak see his website at http://Kenngrimes.com.

Also available from Kenn Grimes:

Camptown...one hundred and fifty years of stories from Camptown, Kentucky, published in 2005.

Available for sale on Amazon

Author Web site:
http://kenngrimes.com